MISERY PLAZA

J.J. ALO

SNE Horror LLC

Cover design by Richard Ljoenes Design LLC
https://richardljoenes.com

Edited by Nicole Arch
https://www.archeditorial.com/

Copyedited by Stephanie Scott
https://www.linkedin.com/in/stephanie-scott-802a7b101

This is a work of fiction. While certain characters and events may draw inspiration from real historical figures and occurrences, all personalities, and situations within this story are entirely fictionalized. Any resemblance to actual persons, living or dead, is purely coincidental.

Acknowledgements:
Will Timmreck, Beth Morris & Scott Cietanno, Justin Aleia, Frank Abel, Stephen Fortune, Dave Jensen, Dan & Beth Haynes, Matt Lariviere, Rick Vanaria, Nobu Haraguni, Marc Brainerd, Monique Albuja, Adam Sherburn, Phil Demiris, Kristen Zdrok, Stacie Seidman, Zach Shepard, Aaron Outama, Kerri Carbonneau, David Tyrie, Roger Miller, Niret Grobler

For Russell Miller

&

the many other incredibly generous donors (I had coerced, threatened and blackmailed) who saw this author's potential and "willingly" contributed to the production of this novel.

Thank you.

*(*waves* You'll soon receive an email regarding book III)*

From the award-winning author of
The Street Between the Pines

Author's Note

Missouri Plaza *is* real...

Well, of course it is.

In the same way that Jamestown is real to the people of Williamsburg, VA, or perhaps Constantinople still exists in the hearts of those in Istanbul (though that one may be a bit of a stretch). And, just like that, Missouri Plaza has transformed into... well, you'll see. Some of the characters and events you'll encounter are based on reality. Those familiar with *The Street Between the Pines* know I like to infuse my stories with a bit of history, shedding light on often forgotten details and weaving them into a tapestry of fantastical fiction... an alternate universe, if you will.

This is a *true* western (albeit a supernatural one). True, in the sense that it captures the dialect, the economic, political, and racial issues of the time period. I've left little to the imagination, and what you're about to read is the "true account" as it unfolds in this universe, the prelude to A Southern New England Horror.

I've taken great care to ensure the historical accuracy of the places and events, even though the story itself is entirely fictional. I did take some liberties with the timeline, so not everything is perfectly aligned with our reality (though it's close enough), as my stories likely belong to some strange, yet chilling parallel universe.

Enjoy your epic journey out west. Let me know if you happen to make it back.

*The Southern New England Horror series can all be enjoyed as stand-alone books. They can be binged in any order.

PROLOGUE

The pilot lurched forward in a violent, arcing spasm as the sharp object stabbed through its vulnerable chest. It had shed its protective gear prior to takeoff, and now, strapped under a shoulder harness, the Antiquarian found itself pinned to its seat. Its arms, fixed inside the cylindrical steering mechanism on either side of the helm, flexed and flared as it gaped down at the foreign weapon, then up at its surroundings.

Dark blood sprayed the control panel, leaving a streak across the crystalline navigation screen hanging from the ceiling of the cockpit. The spinning digits displayed beneath the splatter indicated that the craft had reached almost three hundred thousand feet. Close to departure. But the ship lurched forward, and the numbers on screen plummeted, the sheer thrust of the pilot's body sending the craft into a downward tailspin.

A creature encased in shiny silver material somersaulted over the helm with a sharp, clattering thud, rolling down the cockpit floor and sprawling across the wide, U-shaped windshield. The pilot blinked at its captive—the creature assumingly responsible for its assault. The WL-9768 native feebly struggled to his feet, gripping the near vertical floor for support, but fell backward as the cockpit rocked back and forth. The ship trembled in a merciless pirouette over the cerulean void of WL-9768's terrestrial sphere, hitting every blustery bump of the rough night sky as they accelerated into a turbulent nosedive.

Warm blood oozed over a curved pincer on the left side of the pilot's quivering mandible. The savory taste of seeping discharge promised that the hapless end neared.

Mission: incomplete.

The pilot braced itself, chest burning with each jostling twist and turn. It needed to land the ship safely, or at least as safely as it could, given the circumstances. With heavy arms, it pulled up and back on the steering mechanism, trying to slow and even the craft. Agony. The glowing landmass behind the oozing splatter rapidly increased, soaring closer and closer at a rough angle. The planet's surface lay just past fifty thousand feet now, and a break on the map indicating a body of water loomed too close for comfort.

The captive, gaining partial footing, slowly crawled the steep incline toward the helm, shakily making his way toward his captor. The pilot pulled its attention from the map, watching the creature from behind its ocular guards. The captive's malevolent stare burned through the visor of his shiny, sinister helmet.

The pilot shuddered. Now at ten thousand feet, it needed to land and proceed with activating the distress signal located under the control panel. But darkness threatened to overtake it, the blood still oozing steadily from its fading form.

Arms tired.

Steering heavy.

The creeping captive neared, gripping the empty seat in front of the helm for balance. The pilot's eyes held his hidden gaze, all three of its stomachs churning. Unable to reduce enough speed to land safely and avoid further savagery to its ship, it reluctantly opted for the last option.

The craft plunged into the water, slamming nose first into the side of the soft terrain. The impact wrenched the sharp object into the Antiquarian's flesh with a vengeance so searing, its vision swam. Something shiny thudded against the ceiling, then clattered back to the cockpit floor. Its captive. He lay unresponsive, possibly dead. Even with armor, the human specimen remained weak to heavy blows.

The pilot drew in quick, hollow breaths, unable to see clearly, waiting for the pain to subside enough for it to begin its work once again. Through the windshield, the craft sank under the blurry, dark current.

Forcing its weak arms to slide from the mechanism and unstrap the harness, the pilot slowly leaned forward, inch by trembling inch, the weapon's edge tearing up its internal organs. Its grisly mandible opened to squeal, though no sound came out.

Consciousness dwindling, the Antiquarian reached for the panel.

My father was a good man. A decent man, despite what you may have heard about him through folklore or read about him in your history books. That's not to say he wasn't an inherently flawed individual, as many of us can be described. I mean heck—back in those days, who wasn't? I would defy you to prove me otherwise. Now, don't get me wrong, he was no saint. Poles apart from one. I know this. A mere product of his egregious environment. And I'm certainly not going to stand here and begin to justify any of the things he did or those I happened to be privy to. Some of which stay with me to this very day. Things I couldn't explain at that time. Things beyond what you good folk would rightfully call rational comprehension. Now, I truly don't mean to harp on such things, but I would be completely remiss not to mention the impression he left on my brother and me. Especially me. There are some folks who can tell you their earliest memories at three, maybe four years old; even some as far back as a year—year and a half, if you can believe it. I am not one of those folks. Maybe it's something they refer to as repressed memory, but all I can tell you is that I don't remember much before I was nine years old. I can recall my mother's burial. I remember the Big Flood. I remember the first time I saw the broken soul that was Joseph Griffin, my father, cry. I will never forget the second time.

That's when we moved to Missouri Plaza.

Chapter I

Sullivan walked behind Eugene McCormac, about three feet back, pointing the filed down barrel of a sawed-off scattergun, waist height, at his lower back. Every few minutes he'd slow his pace a bit, enough to allow some slack between himself and his captive. Just in case McCormac decided to make a daring dash as they entered the heavily wooded area. Firing such a gun at close range meant spending the rest of the day picking Lord-knew-what from your clothing, all kinds of awful, and Sullivan knew better than most that a good clean change didn't come easy. And blood? Those pearly whites—one of only two pairs he owned—well, they'd be as good as horse shit.

Through the slits of tall, narrow trees, Sullivan caught a glimpse of the sun sinking down behind the silhouetted Pikes Peak range. Rays of golden light exploded from behind the jagged mountains, a partially hidden projection illuminating the distant northwest skyline, before the fresh spring growth completely obstructed his view.

They had walked quite a distance through the tranquil grove in silence, save for the irritating clink of McCormac's crooked boot spurs with every bowlegged step. Shrill calls from birds of prey circling high above the treetops punctuated the quiet, along with small woodland creatures rustling through the brush as they passed. Katydids, just beginning their evening song, resonated through the shaded proliferation. Their trilling slowly grew, encompassing the pair the farther they walked into the timberland.

McCormac's fingers—which had been behind his head, interlaced—separated, and his hands began to lower.

"Keep em up," Sullivan ordered, his voice rolling out low, deep, and slightly broken. He hadn't spoken since riding up on McCormac an hour earlier.

McCormac stopped. "I gotta itch."

The mosquitos, which trickled out only moments before, now flew out of the woodwork in droves. McCormac waved a hand around his head, paused, then began to turn around.

"Epp... eyes forward," Sullivan commanded with a slow wave of the gun. "Keep moving."

"What you planning on doing with me once we get to where we goin?" McCormac's hands rested at shoulder level, head tilted just enough for Sullivan to see the white of his right eye below the frayed brim of a black Stetson.

Sullivan had no idea. Well, some idea. He knew exactly what he wanted to do, what he should do. Whether that was going to happen, he just had to wait and see. He didn't like the situation this *chance encounter* with an old acquaintance now put him in.

He shook his head. *Everything is fine.* Fine as he supposed things could go, considering the circumstances.

The men trudged on. By this time, the sun had completely vanished behind the Front Range as the navy skies of civil twilight bled down from the upper atmosphere, nonchalantly blotting out the remains of the day. Sullivan hadn't brought a lantern, and if he progressed further, making his return could prove difficult. He was armed—heavily armed at that—but just the same, nobody wanted to stumble upon the business end of a grizzly bear in the dark.

"Stop," Sullivan uttered, following a moment later with "turn around."

They stood shrouded by the grove... as good of a place as any.

"When did you know?" McCormac said.

"Does it matter?"

"Just surprised is all. Been here a few weeks now. Neither one of us looking like the men we once was."

"How did you find me?"

"I-I didn't. Just dumb luck, I spose. It's a big country. We was bound to cross paths again at some point or another."

"Apparently not that big. I guess we were *destined* to do this dance, is what you're saying?"

"Huh?"

"I'm sposed to believe it was coincidence you stumbled upon Bennett's Mine?" Sullivan, gun in hand, slowly backed McCormac against a tree.

The other man held his arms out, hands crossed, as if to keep Sullivan at a distance.

Sullivan peeled back both hammers of the sawed-off.

2

"I-I swear I was just passin through," McCormac pleaded. "That's all! I-I-I was never gonna say nothin to nobody. Honest! I was plannin on leaving in a day or two, anyway, you-you know? I did what I came to do—now off to the next town, same-ol,' same-ol,' know what I mean?"

Sullivan stared down at him from under a weathered brown hat, motionless, eyes barely visible. Vacuous. The man's empty gaze bore into McCormac, and his heart stuttered. He'd never forgotten that look, despite the twenty years that passed since he'd last seen it.

"Besides, what would I stand to gain by sayin somethin? Ruh-ruh-right?" His filthy hands, still held out, began to quiver before his eyes. Whether his trembling stemmed from the chill in May evening air, or just fear poisoning his bloodstream, he couldn't say.

"You stand to gain everything," Sullivan said, sliding a leather sack down from the heavily worn shoulder of his long brown overcoat.

The bag hit the ground with such force, McCormac wondered—mostly feared—what it held.

Without another word, Sullivan pushed his coat aside, sliding his sawed-off into a handmade leather thigh sheath. A waist pistol sat holstered just above it. McCormac recognized its checkered walnut grip; its twin doubtless rested on Sullivan's opposite hip. His own Colt protruded from behind the buckle of Sullivan's gun belt, tucked away to the side of his groin.

Sullivan squatted and reached into the satchel, pulling out a length of twine. "Arms behind the tree."

The katydids' music, pervading the woodlands, amplified. McCormac's heart hammered against his sternum while Sullivan disappeared behind the old Cottonwood, binding his wrists to the trunk. The rigid bark and taut rope dug into his skin, and something warm hit his thigh and dripped down his quivering shins. He'd pissed himself.

The stench of ammonia filled the air as Sullivan reappeared from behind the tree. A short smirk brushed his bushy silver cheek. He'd smelled McCormac's fear, too. But any trace of a smile vanished as he reached for his ragged black gun belt, hung low on his narrow hips. Pulling McCormac's own silver Colt from behind the holster, he raised it a foot from the man's face, aiming for his forehead.

"Christ Almighty," McCormac squeaked out. His chest heaved with labored breath; the warm fog of his gasps visible before him in the chilly air.

"I used to think there were only two men in this world, Mac. Or whatever it is you call yourself these days," Sullivan said. "The hard truth of it all is there's only one. I'm convinced of that now. I truly am." Sullivan sucked in a breath and exhaled deeply, shaking his head. "It's plain as the Denver day is long. And at the end of it, we're all just chasing the same thing, whether we care to realize that, or not."

"Tuh-tuh-two-two men?"

"One that walks away. And one that doesn't."

Sullivan took a step back, twigs snapping under the Cuban heel of his black Wellingtons. "Now, who else you tell? You be straight with me; I'll make this nice and quick."

McCormac didn't need to consider the alternative: left here, defenseless, tied to tree in the Colorado woods at night. A fate worse than death.

The elements, even in May, would kill him—and that was assuming whatever *thing* lurking in the dark didn't find him first. Tales of men vanishing without a trace in the woods may have been something of campfire lore, but now, facing his current predicament, the thought unsettled him deeply.

He shuddered. "Oh-oh-okay, okay, okay... I-I sent cuh-correspondence buh-back home. Tha's it! Said I-I thought I might a seen't ya, but wasn't sure, ya-ya see."

3

Sullivan's heart sank in his chest. He'd figured McCormac would lie through gapped teeth, and he'd spend the night smacking him around to free himself of doubt. But even then, he didn't believe this fool would really have the audacity to cross him. Not so quickly, anyway.

To whom didn't make much difference. Sullivan knew the game. A thief or otherwise unsavory character would locate the whereabouts of an accomplice—usually the outcast of an old gang, long removed—and reach out to a friend or extended family member. The contact would tip off the local marshal, then cash in on the reward money and split the proceeds with the snitch. *Not a bad hustle.*

He sighed, wondering how much time he had left.

The occurrence of this ever-fleeting unit—the measure of a man's existence—had always seemed to elude Sullivan. To be honest, the man had never paid time's passage any mind. Not until Bessie. He was no stranger to death; he'd seen many lives taken. Taken many a life himself. But when his wife met her untimely demise two years earlier, he felt it. The Clock. Somehow his hourglass had turned, beginning his true countdown.

Sullivan had no illusion he wasn't a mortal man. And oh, he knew he'd crossed paths with the man in the black, tattered cloak. Brushed shoulders, even. He liked to think the pale rider trotted past in fear, its hooded head turning to glance back each time he passed by. But by now, he'd eluded death so many times, he had to wonder *when* karma would finally make his acquaintance.

"I—I'm ready," McCormac said.

And Sullivan could tell that he was. McCormac squeezed his eyes shut, bracing as if for a strike of the hand. His upper lip curled, revealing a sliver of checkered teeth—what remained intact, stained brown. With the creeping night unfolding around him in its ritual consummation, he waited in silence, ready to pay for his sins in eternity once he got to where they both knew he was heading.

Sullivan, struggling to see the barrel's end through the darkness, took an additional step back for safe measure. Pulling the hammer, he took aim best he could. His index finger grazed the polished steel trigger, feeling for the perfect position to pull, but eventually found himself, instead, slowly caressing it.

The enchanting tune of the katydids waned, fading into the melodic whirr of a chill breeze shifting down between the trees. Through the surrounding brush, the Cottonwood's fledgling leaves rustled. The woodlands spoke. And with the mellifluent sounds came intermittent, tiny flashes of amber light, which seemed to delicately drift about, encompassing the men. Just a handful at first, but as Sullivan glanced around, myriad flashes trailed curiously, a cluster sparkling as far as his aging eyes could see. The stellar forest erupted with light, the wind gently dispersing its itinerate constellation.

An odd, twinkling glow from inside the gun's barrel caught Sullivan's eye. He pulled the gun backward, turning it upon himself, and waited for the flash. The luminous filament of a tiny firefly flickered as it crept out of the tip, hovering in front of his face for a moment before extinguishing its curious light.

The deliberation ended.

Sullivan gently placed the hammer down. He emptied the six-cylinder chamber onto the cold earth and, by the barrel, tossed the pistol into the wooded void.

4

McCormac opened his eyes. Sullivan was gone.

"He-hey, where'd you go!? Duh-don't you leave me out here you sumbitch! You leave me out here, I'm a good as dead!" McCormac instinctually pulled away from the tree, the twine tearing into his wrists and drawing blood. "You get back here and finish the job, you no good yella coward! The whirlwind is comin for ya, just you wait! I swear to Christ, if I—"

Shrill howling in the distance shut him right up. A signaling of one coyote to another, the response to spotting a potential food source. He wasn't terribly concerned with coyotes, but what would follow—bear, cat—passing in the night.

Blood ran down his fingers.

5

In the distance, Sullivan heard a name being screamed. One he didn't immediately recognize, but one he once knew, decades ago, to be his. With the fireflies dissipating, he reached the edge of the woods, tied McCormac's horse to his own, and rode toward home.

The pale-yellow, nearly full moon still made its ascent, illuminating his pathway. The only source of light for miles through the woods and prairie. Not that he minded. Had he come across some stranger in passing, someone asking for directions, food, or water, he'd have to explain why he rode in the dark with an extra horse tied to his saddle. He could stumble into someone looking to rob him and steal his horses, or worse yet, someone hoping to recognize him. The thought nearly stole his breath. Though of course, as he knew from his recent outing, there were far worse things to be caught doing in the middle of the night.

Fortunately, Sullivan had planned for such contingencies well in advance, and he knew exactly where he was. Bennett's Silver Mine lay up ahead about a mile or so. His job there—as a manager, mind you—obliged him every six months to transport about one or two work horses that needed to be put down. He usually took them from the massive stable flanking the mine, not from dangerous criminals, but still, McCormac's nag certainly looked the part.

Sullivan gave the mare another appraising glance. *This girl is as tired as an old Bughouse whore. Shiiit. Probably stolen, too.*

Yet another thing for him to worry about. He shook his head and gave his horse a gentle nudge. Provided he remained on his own trail and stayed on the fringes of town, he would be fine.

Everything is fine.

Or everything *had* been fine until McCormac showed up in Bennett's Silver Mine not three weeks ago. At first, Sullivan thought him another drifter passing through, looking to make a quick buck. Such men comprised the primary challenge in the mining industry, particularly in Denver. Labor couldn't come cheaper. It also couldn't come more unreliable. Drifters tore through Bennett's like the cyclonic storm that buried Denver in snow about four weeks ago: materializing out of nowhere and capable of causing indiscriminate, cataclysmic destruction. They'd show up ragged, emaciated, and spitting a fake name, usually one Sullivan had heard so many times that he smelled their horseshit immediately.

He pulled a quirley cigarette from his inside pocket—one of his *special* recipes—and lit it with a thumbnail-struck match. *Something to help settle the nerves.* His gaze shifted towards the amber haze of gas-powered streetlamps, their faint flickering creating an ethereal ambiance over the town as he rolled past. The sounds of melodic tunes and laughter echoed through the air, emanating from a bustling saloon nearby where patrons were beginning their evening revelries. He couldn't shake the nagging thought that there might be an accomplice of McCormac's lurking in the shadows.

Not *all* drifters were a cause for worry, however. Many of these men kept their brows low, worked five to ten days, made some quick green, and went on their way. A few were even incredible finds—the kind that almost made him want to offer a higher wage, just to keep them on-hand.

A *Sun Dog,* as people called them—a bright spot, like the brilliant halo surrounding the sun on a gorgeous blue-bird day, high above a glistening blanket of unmarred snow. The kind of view you might be fortunate to catch if you rode over yonder through the Rocky's on a crisp February afternoon. Incredibly unique. Radiant. Few and far between.

McCormac, though, was neither cyclone nor Sun Dog. The man kept his head down, and the challenge of discerning "who's who" in a company of over thirty men—mostly drifters—left Sullivan focused on the more apparent troublemakers. But the day before last, on the transport wagon back to town from the secluded caverns where they worked, he had noticed McCormac in his peripherals, sitting across and four men down. Staring at him. Sullivan knew that look *all* too well. Quiet. Vigilant. Disconcerting. He could smell his own, and usually, his keen eye spotted such a man a hundred yards out. The fact he'd missed McCormac for so long disquieted him. Perhaps he was just getting old.

Home neared, signaled by the soothing trickle of Cherry Creek just beyond the outskirts of town. The low-hanging moon bathed the water's undulating surface in a shimmering saffron glow. His gaze lingered, captivated by the paradoxical nature of something both breathtaking and deadly.

He had four, maybe five days at the most to *make the decision.* The seasoned math told him the letter needed at least two days to reach Wichita, its most likely destination. After that, the marshal could either send a telegraph straight to Denver, alerting the authorities, or send his own squad, requiring another two to three days. Sullivan figured the latter more likely; different territories didn't much like the ubiquitous politics and the greasing of hands involved in using local authorities. *Everyone's got their dirty hand out.* Most marshals preferred to do things quietly. Covertly. Sullivan could only imagine the price on his head.

The whirlwind is coming.

His spontaneous decision to leave McCormac tied to a tree, without a bullet in his forehead, also worried him. Was he getting lazy, or just sloppy? He suspected neither. But he didn't have to pull the trigger to seal McCormac's fate. More than a decade had passed since he'd taken a life, long before the arrival of his firstborn. Hell, even before he got hitched. His eyes narrowed, lost in thought as he tightened his red paisley hanky to his throat and popped the worn coat collar. Fifteen years.

Christ. Where does the time go?

Sure, he'd flashed the blue steel many a time, mostly in an intimidation capacity... but since Bessie first entered his life, he had never been *this* close to pulling the trigger.

Still, he remained the fastest motherfucker on the draw. If nothing else, this he knew for a certainty.

He smirked. *Ain't no flies on* me.

CHAPTER 2

Sullivan stood over the gravesite at the far end of his property, which faced the Cherry Creek riverbank, and let the somber trickle of the stream put him in a sort of trance. Time stopped, the hourglass placed on its side, as he stared at the Roman-style headstone his wife's father had specifically chosen for her.

ELIZABETH SULLIVAN

1851 – 1882

LOVING WIFE & MOTHER

His father-in-law liked to say that the pretty blue-gray marker—made from King of Prussia Marble—was "quarried and imported from my boys down in Philadelphia." When the matter arose at business meetings and social gatherings, he uttered those words with the utmost pretension, despite the loss of his daughter. But the stone wasn't quite what Sullivan would have chosen after thirteen years of marriage, knowing Elizabeth far more intimately than her parents ever could, or did, *or would.*

"I'm sorry, Bessie, I am. I truly am sorry." He removed his hat, gripping it close to his chest. "I—I don't know how the hell we got here. Things just ain't been the same since you've gone. Been on the outs with your old man... hell, that ain't news to you, 'cept now he can't stand the sight of me." Not much of a change either, truth be told.

"But he never understood us, did he?" Sullivan shook his head, smiling wryly. "You know, the day we got married was one of the single best days I could recall ever having. You made an honest man out of this goddamn busted shell. Only person ever could. I couldn't fathom *love* or why anybody in their right mind would bother with such trivial things in an equally trivial world—hell, much less bring up young'uns. Something I could've never foreseen. And for that, I made you a promise. A vow. But I failed you, Bessie."

The words nearly caught in his throat, and he choked, struggling to force them out. "I failed to keep my word, and by God, I tried. I truly did, baby, I did. I didn't protect you to the end. I've been so... gone... since you left us, I couldn't care for the children like I said I would, like they deserve. And now, I can't even protect our land. I have to leave the home we built together. Leave you behind with it." Sullivan's eyes welled with unbridled tears. The drops spilled into the snare of his wiry beard, and he pulled out his red hanky, mopping back sunbaked cheeks. "I tried to consider an alternative, but I'm afraid this is the only rational decision, and it's solely for the sake of our two babies. Spose if things were different..."

A shrill laugh rang through the air behind him. Sullivan turned to see Clara running through the backyard, chickens scattering and clucking, while Isaac chased her at close distance. In the blink of an eye, his two children vanished around the front of the house, the laughter trailing off.

Sullivan paused a moment, listening. Inch by inch, he'd felt the give. Felt it for some time now. Inch by inch, his life slipped from his grasp. Though he couldn't tell if he kept releasing the slack, or if everything just pulled away, tearing through his weathered palms.

"Guess I was a goddamn fool to even fathom that this life was attainable," he whispered, turning back to Bessie. "To think we'd make it on in the years. The hell was I kidding? Joke was on me all along. To imagine we'd be sitting around the fireplace, reading to our grandchildren? But you know me, dear. I've never alluded to such things. Be a damn fool to do so. I tell ya, though, if by some act of God we *had* gotten there..."

He stared narrowly at the creek, almost through it, trying to envision that chimeric future. But he saw only the sun's golden white reflection, beaming off the water's trickling surface.

"If nothing else, at the very least, I thought... I *thought* I might end up here next to you one fine day."

2

With a crate hoisted in his arms, Sullivan used one foot to open the front door and step outside the house. Clara followed; hands full of clothing she had wrapped in a large bed sheet.

"Pa," Clara asked, "where did this..."

"Carriage," Sullivan interjected over his shoulder, still walking.

"*Carriage* come from?"

"We're borrowing this from Grandpa. And it's called a prairie schooner. Come on, curlicue."

"Oh. Well, won't he need it?"

"Not while he's away, he won't. Besides, Grandpa has plenty to spare." Sullivan unloaded his wooden crate full of household items onto the carriage, then took Clara's from her hands.

"Oh."

"I thought schooner meant ships, Pa?" Isaac called from the family room window, where he organized the unsorted odds and ends still remaining.

"It does, son. Spose the canvas cover may be the same material used on those ships."

Cargo filled most of the carriage already; Sullivan and his children had spent the previous day going through their belongings and deciding what would go and what would stay. Two days prior, he'd rummaged around the back alleys of downtown Denver for hours, scavenging up empty crates, barrels, and the like for packing. Three days prior, and after dark—much after dark—he had *borrowed* the carriage from his father-in-law's estate, a substantial piece of land on the outskirts of town. Wrought iron fortified his land, but such things never deterred Sullivan.

He placed the Winchester behind the front bench. An easy reach for the boy, if needed, though he doubted its necessity. His Colt scattergun and two sidearms should suffice. But hell, you just never knew. The world had changed in the fifteen years since he'd left it. He was sure of that much, at least. He turned to the narrow storage compartment under the bench. From a man-made pocket inside his coat, he pulled out a long, narrow blade—an old bayonet—one of a few relics from his past. It served little purpose during the war, yet it had since come in handy in a pinch. He rotated the oxidized piece of steel in his hands, giving it a once over before lifting the latch and tucking it away under the bench.

Isaac stumbled out of the house with his arms awkwardly wrapped around a heavy oak rocking chair.

Sullivan shot his boy a wary, warning look. "Careful, son. You don't want to hurt yourself. Or damage the wood. If you need help, let me know."

"I got it," Isaac said, unconvincingly. "Pa, how are we going to get all the furniture out and onto this carriage? It ain't big enough."

"We ain't taking it all. It's everything we packed in the living room, the food, kitchen stuff, your mother's rocking chair, and I'll show you what else. But just about everything else stays."

"What about our beds? We'll need beds, won't we?"

"No. Beds stay. There're beds there." But even as the words rolled off his tongue, Sullivan doubted them. *Maybe we'll roll up the mattresses; they're small enough.* Except, with so little room in the carriage to speak of, another part of him wondered whether he should take *anything*. Earlier in the week, he'd considered just saying "to hell with it" and setting the house ablaze. But arson would only raise suspicion, not to mention desecrating the land of Bessie's final resting place.

Clara came from the house with her hands full of more clothing. Sullivan recognized the items immediately: a couple of patterned dresses, all folded. All belonging to her mother.

Bracing himself, he summoned a stern but gentle tone. "Clara, darling, those ain't coming with us."

"Why?" Clara stopped in her tracks, squeezing the fabric to her chest as a look of horror scrunched her little face. "They're Ma's dresses, Pa!"

"We simply don't have the room."

"But we can't leave them here, Pa, we can't!"

Sullivan neared his daughter, catching sight of Isaac watching from the other side of the carriage. "Son, why don't you go on in and double check the house. Make sure you kids got everything you need that's yours. Especially Clara's room, please."

Isaac hesitated, but Sullivan stared until he moved toward the house.

He returned his focus to his daughter. "Clara, darling, listen to me. We cannot bring all your mother's belongings with us. We have limited space and can only take the essentials. These dresses—her clothing—will be safe here. Your grandpa owns this land. Ain't no one coming on it, especially anyone who knows better. This stuff will remain here, and when the time is right, your Pa will come back for it," he cajoled, praying Clara wouldn't see his lie—his intention of never returning. "Look, there's gonna be a lot of new changes we're gonna have to get used to. New town. New home. New name. Do you understand?"

"No, Pa, I don't!"

With the dresses in hand, Clara ran wailing back into the house. She almost knocked Isaac off balance on his way back down the stairs, his hands full of their belongings. Then she disappeared around the corner into her parent's bedroom.

Sullivan sighed, waited for his son to exit the front door, and slowly climbed the stairs leading to his bedroom. Clara had laid out a pile of dresses on the bed. He approached them, the hardwood floor creaking under his boots with every step.

A muffled shout rose from under the dresses. "Go away!"

"Claire..." Sullivan warned, continuing toward the bed.

"No! I won't go! I wanna live with Grandpa! At least he won't make me leave Ma!"

Something in Sullivan's heart gave a little. He stared down at the dresses, a confusing mixture of colors displayed. The two on top he recognized as Elizabeth's favorites, one specifically—the last one—gifted to her on her thirteenth birthday. She'd worn the beautiful yellow summer dress for her mid-July celebration, or so he was told. She was quite petite, but the fact she still fit in it at thirty-one always surprised him. The rest were mostly dinner dresses and similar styles. He guessed her father had purchased them, but he'd never asked. They were expensive, and that's all he knew.

Sullivan sat down gently at the edge of the four-post bed. "Clara..."

Snuffling arose from the dresses.

He gently placed his hand on the mound of fabric, caressing the trembling lump underneath. "Clara, darling."

He peeled away a layer of ruffled sage material, revealing rosy wet cheeks and matted, curly brown hair.

"I know this is hard to understand. This ain't something your pa ever wanted to do. Things just haven't been easy since your ma..." He glanced at her sprawled dresses, where Clara's little fingers still clutched the fabric, and fought the urge to break down again. "Since she's been gone. Work has just about dried up in these parts. I can find good, solid work where we're going. And we can start over there anew, baby. New *name*, new *house*, new *life*." He blotted her cheeks with his hanky. "It'll take a little time getting used to, I know, but this will all be worth doing. Trust your pa."

"What about Grandpa? Will we see him again!?"

God willing, we won't.

"Of course, you will."

"I miss Ma. Why—why, Pa, did God take her away from us?"

She had asked the same question in the past, but he hadn't an answer to give her then. And, as he thought on it, he still didn't. Not an answer she'd understand, at any rate, not for many years.

He sighed. "I don't know, Clara. Every one of us has a finite amount of time to be alive. To live. Be part of this world. Some just have more than some others, I suppose. And you can't beat the clock. Time always prevails."

"But I don't want to leave her, Pa. This is home. *She* is home. I don't want to leave home!"

"I know, darling. I know."

Slowly, Clara emerged from the fabric pool. Behind her crossed arms, she hugged a faded pamphlet to her chest, its papers compressed, worn, and wrinkled.

Sullivan stared at the word "PLAYBILL" stenciled across the top. "Where'd you find that?"

"In my nature book, when I was packing." She sat up, though her voice remained sullen. "It fell out. I forgot I had it."

Sullivan hadn't even suspected that Clara would keep such a memento of *Foggerty's Fairy*. He had never seen the stage production himself, but he certainly needed no reminders of the night Clara, her mother, and his mother-in-law had visited the theater. The night they'd lost Bessie.

"Come here." Sullivan leaned in and pulled her toward him. "She's not really here, remember? She's up there." He pointed to the ceiling, then to her chest. "She's in here. She will always be with you. You know that, right?"

"I'm scared."

"It's okay to be scared. That's as natural as daylight. But we don't have to be. The trick is to replace that fear with a little bit of faith—we like faith, right? Your Ma did. Funny thing is, faith and fear, they're essentially the same."

"They are?"

"Well, they are both a figment of your imagination, for sure. What you allow yourself to believe. You can think of fear like a weed, you know; it just grows and grows on its own, crops up out of nowhere, where you don't want it. Fear is like a plague of your mind. But faith, now, that's an intentional decision. You gotta plant that seed yourself. You can choose to have faith that everything's gonna be all right for us, that Ma will always be in your heart whether she's physically here or not. Now, you can let that fear weed flourish, or you can let it wither away and die. Replant faith over it, take a chance, and see what good can come of it."

Clara, head against her father's shoulder, pouted silently.

She'll get it. At least, he hoped. "Tell you what... pick out your favorite dress. You can bring one with you."

Clara came alive. She looked up at her pa, her green eyes wide and teary. "Can I?"

"Mm-hmm."

By noon, they had packed the carriage completely. Sullivan tied Bessie's beige horse, the mare with no name, and McCormac's poor nag to the front. Honestly, he worried that the old beast wouldn't survive the journey. Ever since he'd brought her home, the nag had left a trail of vile-smelling diarrhea wherever she stood. Possibly from old age, or perhaps stress induced. Either way, he sure related.

Isaac and Clara barreled out of the front door.

Despite himself, Sullivan smiled. "You kids got everything?"

A resounding "Yes, Pa" ensued.

"Now, you're sure?"

"Yes, Pa!"

"Absolutely sure we didn't leave anything behind?"

"We double and triple checked, Pa," Isaac said.

"All right, then. Climb aboard."

Isaac hesitated. "Pa, what's our new name gonna be?"

Sullivan hadn't given it much thought. He glanced around the property. Two clay vases, set on either side of the front door with fresh growth poking through the soil, caught his eye. "Potter."

"Potter," Isaac repeated, glancing back to the flowerpots. With a tentative smile, he scrambled up and sat in front.

Sullivan—Potter—picked up Clara, placing her on the seat before sitting down between his children.

She blinked up at him. "Pa, how long will we travel?"

"If we keep stops to a minimum and take brief rests, bout two days, I'd guess. You kids ready for an adventure?"

Both of his children grinned. "Yes, Pa!"

Chapter 3

"WELCOME TO NEW MEXICO, LAND OF ENCHANTMENT." Several small, old tree limbs held up the big orange sign, framed with dark wood. Potter squinted at the few splintered holes in the frame, likely from bullets. The shot-up sign didn't feel quite welcoming, let alone enchanting. Well, he guessed he'd have to wait and see.

The children had been in high spirits, despite Clara's meltdown days earlier. However, the young girl now sat wrapped in blankets, lost in the nature book she'd already read several times over. A gift from her grandpa. Isaac, bright-eyed and bushy-tailed as a youthful Denver squirrel, sat perched on the bench, eager and observant. Until today, his small world only revolved around home, Grandpa's, and eastern Denver.

Upon realizing the recent departure from Clara's usual cheerful disposition, Potter finally expressed his comfortable level of concern.

He gently nudged her. "How ya doing, kiddo?"

"I'm fine, Pa," she said, not looking up from the page.

"You must have memorized that book by now, I bet. You've been reading it for days."

"I'm basically an expert."

Potter smiled. He reached down placing a finger under her chin and gently lifted it so their eyes met. "Remember what I said. Faith over fear. Everything is going to be fine... your whole life. It's gonna be a long, long one. I promise. Okay?"

She nodded.

"Now, why don't you teach your old man something, then? You realize we're out right in the middle of nature, don't you?"

Isaac, sitting quietly to Clara's right, brushed away a fluttering bee.

Clara finally smiled. "Um... oh, did you know that honeybees have five eyes?"

"I did not."

"And the male bees are called drones... and the queen is capable of laying two thousand eggs a day!"

"That's incredible."

"Yes, and they communicate with each other through a process involving fare—fare—fare monies.

"Pheromones, my darling."

"What's that?"

"Uhm... it's just a chemical process." Unsure how to explain what he actually envisioned, he cut himself short, uneager for a follow up.

"Oh, and if the bees lose their stinger, they die."

"Fascinating."

Potter entertained listlessly, mind drifting as the energetic eight-year-old filled the hours with curious facts. After their day-and-a-half journey thus far, he suspected at least another half day of travel remained between them and their destination. Only his desire to steer clear of the main trails hindered their progress. Instead, they used longer, less traveled paths, relying on the help of a hand-drawn map he'd obtained from a friend in the black market years ago. But, since Lord-knew-who had charted their route, Potter predicted slower travel on account of poor map accuracy.

Something wet splattered on his nose. Potter glanced up at the light drizzle, gently falling from the overcast sky. Stormy weather would only delay things further, requiring him to stop and set up camp. But he needed to protect his children and his wife's mare, if nothing else.

Isaac and Clara laughed and sat forward on the bench, competing to see who could catch the most rain drops in their mouths. Who won was anyone's guess.

Their pa watched them, praying the storm would hold off. He knew all too well that once the rain began, you never knew what might follow.

2

A red bandanna shielded Potter's face from the windy morning's calcareous siltstone blowback. By his guess—and the sun's ascension—it was some time after nine. Thankfully, yesterday's storm had held off. In fact, in the last two hours, the temperature had increased comparably to the previous day. He'd immediately felt the change: drier, and much more arid. A blanket of warmth radiated from under his coat, moisture already developing under his pits as he unbuttoned his outer layer.

To be absolutely certain of their progress, he'd traveled straight through the night, guided by two lanterns hung between the horses. The young'uns, nestled in the back, gently stirred. Isaac snored softly. Now, exhausted, Potter fought the weight of his heavy, drooping eyelids. His body gently swayed while the reins let loose in his shallow grip. Every time Bessie's mare pulled, he'd snap back the reins and give his head a quick shake. Sleep was an impossibility. At least for now.

The open plains here offered no potential hiding places. Should a threat arise, they'd need to rely on the blue steel resting on either side of Potter's hips, along with the boom stick on his lap. But all worry aside, he had to admit the land was goddamn beautiful. Apart from the few otherwise scattered woodlands, nothing obstructed his view ahead for many miles. The sky met the earth harmoniously, as if he could see the end of world. Closing his eyes for a moment, he imagined that sailors voyaging the open sea shared a similar view, as did those simply standing on a whaling port dock, staring straight out. An infinite horizon.

He jerked in his seat, shaking his head to keep himself awake. He needed a quick jolt; one he knew to come from a cup of black coffee and a generous splash of moonshine. Good ol' bathtub bourbon. The same prescription would get him through most twelve-hour shifts in the mines. He'd finished the last tin of Arbuckles' Coffee around midnight, but every town, no matter how big or small, had a saloon. And every saloon served up some filthy concoction on the verge of poison, though most sane men would stay well clear.

At last, a building appeared on the horizon. He shook his head, the desert wind whipping through his hair, just to be certain it wasn't a mirage. Anything seemed possible at this point. Drawing closer, he identified what appeared to be a church, along with several other structures. He couldn't help but smile. *This must be the place.*

Stopping in town was the last thing Potter wanted to do, but he knew they'd depleted their rations. Bennett's house, wherever *that* was, was bound to be bare. Potter could have gone without eating; in fact, most days he did so, at least until supper time. But he knew the young'uns needed their breakfast. Besides, maybe someone could point them in the right direction. He reached back to wake the young'uns.

"Rise and shine... we're here, kiddos."

Potter nodded to himself, confirming his decision. *We'll be quick. In-and-out. In. And out.*

An archway marked the entrance to the little town, the words

"MISSOURI PLAZA"

stenciled across the top. As the prairie schooner passed beneath, a gust of wind kicked up a cloud of street dust, hazing their view of this mystical village. Potter clamped down on his Stetson with one hand before it blew clean off his shaggy head. The other gently pulled back on the reins, slowing the horses' pace. As the dust curtain somewhat settled and drew back, Missouri Plaza opened before them.

Small. Shit... *tiny.* Twelve buildings sat around them, mostly two-level, five on either side and two more at either end. The first endcap, a wooden church, stood at the entrance, slightly askew of the archway. The impressive round stained-glass window in the building's side captivated Potter. Shimmering fragments of vibrant blues, reds, and yellows reflected off the sun as it moved into view, coming together to create the apparition of the Virgin Mary. The endcap on the far side of town, also the only other structure made of wood, appeared to be a mill of sorts, tucked at the edge of a river, while a wooden waterwheel gently churned in the distance. A wide bridge spanned the entryway into the structure, linking its second level.

Much to his surprise, the street stretched a considerable width, somewhat superfluously. The eccentrically fashioned structures also stood extensively distanced from each other, creating the illusion of a larger settlement. Potter had stumbled by many a town in his travels from the northeast, journeying through much of the South and a good part of the Midwest. Few villages he'd encountered proved smaller than this one, and he'd seen no others constructed of mostly yellow mud bricks. Adobe brick, they called it. The citizens had built their facades in conjunction with wood clapboard lap siding, giving them a unique, albeit peculiar, presence. Although he found much of the architecture strange, especially for a man as well traveled as he, Potter only had eyes for one destination as he panned the structures. *That's some doxology works... tailor... general store, okay, okay... barber... barber attached? Hmph... post office... butcher... what do we have here... ooh, a bank, aaand it's next to the...* fucking marshal. *Ugh, great... luncheonette, food, good, good, but... I don't see it... where... where is it... where the f—*

A gentle whimper rose from the back. "I'm hungry, Pa."

Potter turned to his daughter, who innocently stared up at him with gorgeous green eyes. Same as her ma's.

Ugh, you got me, kid. Always do.

The strip bustled with a moderate amount of activity. Daily commerce, Potter assumed. Horses stood squarely tied to posts outside store fronts, some causally lapping water from long troughs while waiting for their riders to return. Several small carriages sat parked parallel on either side of the road. Potter intuitively tallied fourteen townspeople as he scanned the street, with sporadic arrivals on horseback coming from the bridge on the opposite end. *Always know your surroundings, partner.* The villagers wore casual dress, most men in slacks and white-collared shirts and a couple in woolen vests. None of them appeared to be grunt workers or businessmen, and from what Potter could tell, none carried a firearm. Quite surprising, though from experience, he knew to never judge a man by his wardrobe. The women—the three he saw—strolled along in long, floral-patterned dresses and bonnets. For a town which, as far as he knew, very few people had heard of, everything appeared rather mundane. The kind of innocent, small-town life he briefly recalled from bouncing around in the '60s, hiding in odd territories. Almost... quaint. Like no one here had an agenda at all.

Potter pulled the schooner alongside Miller's Luncheonette, a two-story, oblong, and uneven adobe-brick structure. The horses, just as exhausted as Potter, slammed their faces into a trough and drank heavily. After tying the reins to a post, he and the young'uns walked up the side of the porch, passing four empty two-top tables and crossing the wide-windowed store front. Dark, sheer curtains kept the inside a mystery, but the main entrance stood wide open, displaying a slender set of batwing doors. Potter pushed through them with a curious yet familiar air, the hinges squealing behind as they swung shut.

As expected, Miller's lacked much of a breakfast crowd. The store consisted of three occupied tables, one gentleman taking up each. Two, seemingly much older than Potter, hunched partially buried behind dated issues of the *Albuquerque Journal*. The third sat with his back to the door. An L-shaped counter hooked around the far-left corner, with ten empty stools curved in front. Behind it, a bartender clad in a puffed white shirt with garters wrapped around each arm stood polishing glassware without looking up, either unsuspecting or just oblivious. Presumably, Miller. Fifteen or so square tables and a row of booths on the right comprised the tight space. In the far back, a lonely Steinway Victorian grand piano rested to the side of a narrow stage. On either side, stairs led up to a hallway balcony on the second floor, likely ending in *private rooms*.

Potter guided Clara and Isaac to the far end of the counter to sit in the last three seats. The man sitting with his back to the door folded a corner of his paper in, giving a quick peek at the new patrons. Potter watched him in his peripherals.

"Folks like some menus," the gentleman behind the counter asked in a thick brogue as he placed his polished glass down and grabbed three pieces of paper.

Potter blinked. He'd met a few Scots in his day, but quite some time had passed since he'd last heard that accent.

He glanced back at the "BIG BREAKFAST" special, vaguely written on a chalkboard against the long mirror backdrop, and nodded toward it. "Three of those."

"Drink?" The Scot's *r*'s reverberated off his tongue.

"Coffee. Two milks if you got it. And a whiskey—strongest thing you got." He glanced back at the mirror. Except for the chalkboard and some stacked china, the area upfront, typically reserved for bottles, sat empty.

"Coffee 'n milk, aye. Whiskey, nae." The thin, almost gaunt man grabbed a kettle, cup, and saucer and sauntered down the counter. As he moved, his light auburn hair, parted down the center, caught the light. The color matched his long, wiry beard.

Potter watched him, guessing they were of a similar age. "There a saloon in town?"

"Nae, sir. We're a dry town 'ere."

Clara turned to give Isaac a screwy look. Potter couldn't believe his ears. "A dry—dry town, did you say?"

"Aye, sir." He long poured a steaming cup in front of Potter. It was oil thick. Black.

"And what exactly does that mean?"

"Well, all it means is we don' sell any alcohol on premise, or 'ere in town."

"You got beer?"

"Nae beer, sir."

"Swell."

"Sugar's still legal," the Scot said with a satirical half grin.

Potter nodded, and with a pair of tongs, the man dropped two brown cubes into the cup. A moment later, he produced two glasses of milk.

The newspaper shuffled and lowered. Potter, without moving his head, side-eyed his left. The unidentified man glanced at Potter, the star on his upper chest glinting in the light.

Of course—just my goddamn luck.

A dark, petite barmaid in black greeted the man with a steaming hot plate of steak and scrambled eggs. She placed it down gently with a hand towel and smiled.

"Much obliged, darlin," the man said, his hearty smile twitching his bushy mustache.

"You're welcome, marshal," she replied, with an accent and a sheepish smile.

Her blush only made her more striking. A leather headband secured her long hair, which draped elegantly past her buttocks, shiny and straight. Potter blinked. An Apache woman working at the café? This town sure piqued one's curiosity.

"You folks passin through?" The man behind the counter asked. "There's a town bout fifteen miles south o' 'ere. Gambling, liquor, ladies—the whole shebang."

"Just arriving. Actually, was hoping you can give me a sense of direction. My map only brought me so far, but I'm looking for the old Bennett property."

"You a Bennett, or a relative o'?"

"No. Friend of. Just passing through." He proceeded with reluctance. "Name's Potter."

"Potter, aye? You may 'ave already guessed. I'm Gus Miller. Proprietor o' this fine establishment." He spoke playfully, with a smile and a wave of an inviting arm.

"All right, *Gus.*"

"What you want to do is 'ead down past the mill, cross o'er the Pecos River bridge, an' follow the trail on the right bout a mile or so. Can't miss it... only thing out there. Large 'ouse on a clearing, not far from the river."

Potter, translating the brogue in his head, thanked the man. When the meal came, he and the children ate in silence as Miller and the barmaid, who he heard referred to as Sheyenne, tended to other tables and patrons.

When they finished the meal, Potter dug into his pocket and pulled out a handful of loose change. He fished a few coins from his palm, dropped them on the counter, and discreetly walked toward the exit. The marshal, still sitting behind his newspaper, glanced up as Potter walked past. He deliberately ignored the marshal, focusing on shuffling the young'uns out, which worked a treat until Miller caught sight of them.

"You folks 'ave a lovely mornin, now," the Scot called across the café.

Potter turned at the waist, just enough to glance at Miller behind the counter. Time froze. Sheyenne stopped mid-stride, tray in hand, to stare at him. Every seated patron followed suit, heads cocked. The marshal twisted, looking over his shoulder.

Miller's lips slightly parted, baring a smile with two gold teeth. "Welcome to Miss'rie."

Potter tipped his hat before walking out, the batwing doors creaking shut behind.

Clara scrunched her little nose as they headed toward the schooner. "*Misery?*"

"Mis-sor-ee, darling."

"That man talked funny, Pa."

"He ain't from round here."

"Then where?"

He shrugged, helping her and Isaac onto the bench before climbing up after. "Another world."

He pulled the schooner onto the main drag of the quaint, dusty village. The coffee would be enough to drive him to their destination. Already, the haze of two and half day's travel slowly dissipated, leaving him slightly more alert, or at least well fed. Still, he needed rest. All he wanted was to relinquish the reins of the packed carriage, but he knew the goddamned house would be bare. Assuming it still stood at all. Hell, *that* was a possibility he hadn't considered until now; but once they arrived, he was *not* leaving again without a proper night's rest. He couldn't, wouldn't, go back into town tonight. In fact, his plan hinged on keeping his public appearance scarce, sending Isaac to town whenever they needed things.

The schooner crawled past Miller's, stopping dead in front of T.S. Quinsberry Furniture & Undertaking. He yanked on the reins. Nothing.

Come on, girl, not now, not fuckin now...

She neighed and chuffed shrilly, shaking her golden mane in defiance. They were stuck—drawing unnecessary attention—and how in Christ would they get her moving again? Potter glanced around, face reddening. Studying the road, he spotted a massive pothole, previously invisible to his weary, traveling eyes. A dip that big would've surely shattered a wheel.

Potter, relieved, wiped his glistening forehead with his hanky and sat back down. A rustic squeaking noise caused him to glance at the under-taker's. Christ, what an odd shop. Two six-sided tapered coffins—emp-ty—with different wood finishes leaned against either side of the front door.

No one on display today, eh?

A mélange of dissimilar shaped blank headstones lined the perimeter alongside the building, stretching down the busy alley of scattered crates and barrels. A bearded man, mustacheless, sat on a rocker on the far side of the porch, awaiting his time to etch a stone with the yet-to-be-named deceased. He gently swayed to and fro in a black suit and top hat, sucking the end of a cob pipe. Potter could hear the porch creak under the chair's curved runners.

A water tower enclosed the back alley behind the luncheonette and undertaker's; it reminded Potter of a giant ale barrel.

If only.

About ten feet high, the tower sat atop an outhouse-sized room with a door, surrounded by a wooden lattice support structure. Next to it stood a small utility shed with a gabled roof. A twenty-foot conical tower, also composed of lattice, straddled the little building, leading to the steel windmill. It gently twisted in the breeze.

Potter glanced at his surroundings. Despite its deceivingly large layout, Main Street in this odd little village only provided the functional, bare minimum offerings expected of passersby. Though, of course, the town's unwarranted dry policy left much to be desired. He licked his lips, regretting that he'd neglected to bring at least one bottle of Laird's applejack brandy, and continued orienting himself.

Alongside the undertaker's stood the marshal's office, and beyond that, a small bank and an assay office, both of which seemed vacant. Peculiar. An assay usually indicated a mining town nearby, though who knew what precious metals southern New Mexico offered. Not that Potter had any interest in returning to mining, anyhow. Peering down the giant gaps in between storefronts, he noticed a small cemetery a hundred yards or so behind the assay office, near the river.

Across the street stood a butcher, and next door, a post office. A two-story one, at that. The Farmer's Alliance Store, Potter guessed, sold equipment and hardware. Across from Miller's sat Taylor's Tailor & Clothier, and next to that on his immediate left, Reynolds's Grocery and Buy & Sell: a wide, two-story structure combination of clapboard over yellow adobe brick. A barber's pole peeked through a layer of dust on the left corner of the store front, apparently a multipurpose, one-stop shop. Still, he hesitated to enter. As a new resident of this small town, he knew the importance of maintaining a low profile for as long as he could... but they'd already broken precedent at Miller's Luncheonette. At this point, he figured, what the hell.

Keep it simple. Bare essentials. Nothing more, nothing less. Perishables, bread, coffee—lots of coffee—fresh fruit... fruit, fruit. Clara eats fruit. What the hell's in season right now, strawberries? Need lard; need lard and eggs. Eggs are good, always the goddamn eggs, fuck. I need to find a guy to sell me some livestock. There was some scattered hens on the way in... ugh, don't interact with anyone. Don't engage the proprietor. In and out, in and out—but act natural, don't raise suspicion. Don't say anything more than you have to.

An overhead bell jingled as they entered. Clara ran inside first, and as she turned left toward the vacant checkout counter, Potter saw her eyes light up. He glanced toward the object of her excitement. Jars of candy surrounded the register—*candy!* Candy as far as her little emerald eyes could see: lemon drops, multicolored conversation hearts, packs of Black Jack chewing gum, Young & Smylie licorice sticks, jars of pyramid shaped candy corn, and decanters of green peppermint sticks.

"Peppermint sticks!" Clara galloped over to the counter, bouncing on the balls of her feet in a convulsive dance. "Pa, can I have a peppermint stick, please, please, please, please!?" She turned her head, Potter and Isaac barely through the door. "Please, Pa, pleeeaaase!?"

He winced. "Just one."

Just the bare minimum, partner. Once the coin starts rolling in, she can have all *the candy sticks.*

"Well, howdy, darlin," came a voice, magically appearing from behind the counter.

Clara and Potter turned to a woman bearing a ten-mile smile, the door behind her slightly ajar.

"What's your name," the jovial woman asked.

"I'm Clarissa. But everyone just calls me Clara."

"Well, now, ain't that just the prettiest name. Clara."

The woman, leaning over the counter in a blue, three-quarter sleeve dress with a ruffle-hemmed square neck, glanced at Potter. He turned quickly to Isaac, his heart skipping a momentary, unsettling beat. "Listen, son, let's be quick here. Need a few things is all for now. Get us a loaf, some tallow, and a sack of potatoes, will ya? Oh, and, uh, coffee beans. All right?"

Isaac nodded. Potter glanced around, eyes widening. This store offered just about anything one could want. Though a grocery first and foremost, the food selection appeared plenty picked over. Wicker bins with bread, fruit, and vegetables sat dispersed throughout. Nonperishable canned food items partially lined dusty aisle shelves. Interestingly, the store also held sections for minor hardware, home and farming tools, animal feed, seeds and grain, and... *artwork?* About a dozen or so canvas landscape paintings with price tags leaned against counter tops.

"That your daddy, young lady?" The woman whispered.

Clara nodded, face serious. "Yes, ma'am. He is."

Potter walked over, boot heels rattling across the floorboards. He tipped his hat.

"Hello."

"Welcome, stranger. I'm Eleanor. Eleanor Reynolds." She peered down at Clara. "Round here, people just call me Nora."

"Potter."

"Potter. That a first or a last name, Potter?" Nora spoke with a high-pitched twang, phrases quickly paced and a tad nasal.

Potter found himself strangely captivated. He hadn't heard such an accent in decades, and he had a pretty good idea from whereabouts she hailed. Southern Texas if he had to guess. Among all the regions in the West, he found Texan folk to be the most welcoming, always ready to lend a helping hand.

Realizing he had inadvertently hesitated, he hurried to answer, as if snapping awake from a trance. "Bill. Bill Potter."

"Pleasure to meet you, Mr. Bill Potter. You and your lovely family just passin through, I presume?" She smiled, pulling on one of her loose blonde curls. Most she wore pulled tightly back, though a few cascaded down her neck, framing her tan face.

"Uhh..." He began to flounder, unsure what to say. He wrestled to provide anything but the truth, then vaguely blurted, "Well, we're heading to the old Bennett property across the river." He blinked.

Ugh, you horse's ass.

"Oh... how lovely. Nice piece of land, that is. Wasn't sure if anybody would ever take up residence there or do anything with it again. Been so long."

Clara's head whipped up from the candy. "That's my great uncle's land!"

Isaac appeared with a basket of food items he placed on the counter.

"Ehhh, how much for the, uh, items?" Potter, ignoring his daughter's interjection, dug deep in his trousers and pulled a handful of silver.

"We'll just call it a buck, even. How'd that be?"

He fished through a bunch of coins, picking through odd change. A twenty-cent piece, several two-cent pieces, a few liberty-head nickels, some three-cent silver pennies. He counted them out and stacked them on the counter, slightly embarrassed, though confident his poker face withheld any sign of his emotions.

Nora broke the slightly awkward silence. "Mr. Bennett was a very quiet man. Didn't know him too well. Rarely came into town, and when he did, he sorta just kept to himself."

"My uncle in-law. Didn't know him very well." *At all, actually.*

Nora looked down at a ring on Potter's finger as he cleared the coins from his palm. Then she glanced out the side window to the unoccupied carriage.

"Saw much of his chauffeur, though," she continued. "At least twice a week, he'd come in, buy the usual items. Always appreciative of the business. Lemrich was his name. When John passed, Lemrich showed up to the funeral. Never in all my days have I ever seen a man so torn up over his employer passin. Then he was gone. Just never saw him again."

"That picture is so beautiful!" Clara pointed to a painting on the wall behind Nora.

The gorgeous landscape captured a sunset, with blended colors of yellow and orange, behind a slightly silhouetted Missouri Plaza. The artist appeared to have stood near the mill, the church off center-right, the cross tipped cupola contrasting inside the tangerine half sun.

"You like it?"

"Very much so!"

"Noticed your store is full of them," Potter said. "You sell art?"

"On occasion. If I'm lucky. Sell all sorts of interestin things people bring in on consignment. Not much of an audience for art here in town. Sometimes I get a passerby stoppin through who'll pick one up. Tough business, though. Thankfully, people still need to *eat*," she added, playfully.

"I bet. Well, we must be on our way." Potter cracked a momentary smile, picked up the basket. He paused, glancing at the shelf behind Nora, then turned to his children. "You two meet me outside. I'll be right out."

As the children left, Nora turned to look behind. "Somethin else catch your eye, Mr. Potter?"

"As a matter of fact..."

Potter exited the store moments later with a small package tucked under his right arm. Clara and Isaac eagerly awaited him on the street.

"She was real pretty, wasn't she, Pa?" Clara asked her father as they crossed the schooner.

Huh... she was, wasn't she? He shook his head, lifting Clara with an exaggerated grunt. "Not as pretty as you, my darling. Though someone's getting heavy!" He put her down gently in the schooner, climbed aboard, and handed her the package he'd tucked under his arm.

"For me!?" She slowly untied the bow, clearly savoring the experience of separating twine from sheet. Then she unfolded each side, finally pulling back the top to reveal her prize. She immediately saw the horse logo in the center and exploded with excitement.

"It's a horse book!?" she gaped, studying the cover design, turning it over, and tracing the mildly frayed fabric edges with her tiny fingers.

Potter cracked a smile. He knew this small token wouldn't make up for two years of neglect; but maybe, he hoped, it provided a decent start. "I want to make sure you keep on your reading. I'm not sure what to expect here as far as schooling."

"I love it, Pa! I can't wait to read it! But as soon as I finish *The Book of Nature.* Did you know arth—arth-roo-pods' eyes only allow them to see moving objects?"

"I did not, my smart young lady. I'll keep that in mind if locusts start falling from the sky."

Clara smiled with wide, green lips, the peppermint stick dangling from her mouth as the schooner started down the center of Main Street.

3

As the wagon pulled away, two men watched the new arrivals from their individual porches. Postmaster Van Smith, returning to the office from duty, tied his steed to the post and glanced back at the schooner crossing the bridge. He turned to his steps, catching a glimpse of Charon, the butcher, in his usual attire—a blood-streaked white apron, dried and rust colored—next door, standing on his porch and staring out toward the river.

CHAPTER 4

The narrow trail, almost indiscernible with overgrowth, snaked them through a scattered grove of woodlands before opening suddenly into a small clearing. Potter sat staring at three other trailheads across the field, wondering where they led. Where to go from here?

"You can't miss it," Miller had said.

Right.

He eyed one, hoping it would lead them to salvation. Well, he guessed they'd find out soon enough.

As the schooner pushed forward, faint shouts and whistling erupted in the distance. Heavy galloping echoed. He hesitated.

To the northwest, at the beginning of a mystery trail, a man emerged—a colored man—on foot, running. Three men on horseback followed close behind, gaining on him.

Potter jerked the reins to the right, steering the schooner in the opposite direction. He had the chosen trail within his grasp. He just needed to distance his family from the inevitable aftermath.

The company across the clearing—although small—remained quite a distance away. Gun shots rang out as two riders fired pistols heedlessly into the air. The sound startled Clara, and she twitched in the seat. The hollering increased, mostly unintelligible sounds, a sort of celebratory tone—one Potter knew all too well. Nothing good came of noises like that.

Hugging the perimeter of the woodlands, he continued toward their intended trail in the impossible hope of not being noticed.

2

Discovering he approached an open clearing, Coffey hooked a left toward the other trail, still running at full sprint. Panting, he chanced a look over his shoulder.

"Where you think you runnin off to, coon?" Grant yelled, his blonde hair protruding from under a hat. "Must be stupid, thinkin you goin outrun a horse!" He snickered.

Stringer laughed. "You tell em, Grant! Go get that boy!"

He fired off a few more rounds, this time toward Coffey. They struck the ground near the edge of the woods, sending up whiffs of dirt five feet from him. He barely managed to judder out of the way as he ran, still tracking his pursuers' progress from the corner of his eye.

"Damn, he's a quick sumbitch, ain't he?" Warren laughed, trailing several paces behind the other two. He pulled some rolled tobacco from inside a long gray coat—which flurried in the breeze alongside his nag—and popped it in his mouth.

"You can't hide from us, Coffey!" Grant sneered, gaining.

Coffey refocused on the path before him, only to realize he now headed inadvertently for the clearing. Breathless, panting, he slackened his pace, his glistening head in a whirl, attempting to gain a sense of direction, and, in that moment, his legs buckled, driving him forward, causing him to somersault over the prairie's terrain. A swift and forceful boot to the back knocked out any remaining breath. Unbelievably, he recuperated immediately, teetering towards the only clear pathway from the men who were withdrawing, pivoting their steeds.

Playtime was over.

"Watch this, brothers." Stinger pulled a lasso from his horse's side and sent it twirling high above, intentionally giving his tired victim a generous head start. The horse neighed as he yanked back on the reins, the beast kicking up its front legs before firing down the clearing.

The woodlands lay in sight. Coffey, grunting, gasping, sprinted for their borders with everything he had. Once he made it in, *if* he made it in, he had a fighting chance of evading capture. Even a skilled rider struggled to make their way through the thick brush on horseback, let alone at high speeds. Flying bullets concerned him more, but with the heavy pines, he'd find hiding spots aplenty. His legs wobbled like jelly; he hadn't used them in such a capacity in years. He'd almost forgotten the shock of accompanying dread and panic, what he knew to be the *collywobbles*.

So close. He could taste freedom like salty sweat in his mouth.

Five yards from possible salvation, Coffey fell backward, crashing down on his tailbone. The cool breeze whisked through his wiry hair as his hat twisted off to parts unknown. He twitched violently, struggling to break the jarring fall but unable to do so with his arms now wrenched to his body. With barely enough time to catch the wind stolen from his lungs upon impact, his body jerked away from the woods, dragged back along the rough-hewn earth.

He'd been lassoed.

3

"Pa! Pa, what are they doing to that poor man!?" Clara, horrified, clung to the horse book pressed against her chest, pointing with her other hand.

The horses pulled at a faster pace. Potter gave the reins a good snap.

"Quiet, Clara," Isaac returned in a high whisper.

"You don't pay that any mind, Claire, you hear me? I want you kids in the back. Now."

Isaac did exactly as Potter said, climbing over the seat into the schooner's bed.

Clara didn't budge. "But, Pa, they're hurting him! You must do something!"

"Darling, listen to me. We don't have an idea what that is over there. We don't know who those men are or why they're after that man. Do you understand what I'm saying?"

"No—no, Pa! Look what they're doing!"

"Claire, if we draw attention to ourselves, they could very well come after us and hurt *us,* too. Please tell me you understand that."

Clara began to flounce around in her seat, flailing for some way to help, before staring up at her father in unfathomed desperation. A look of horror and agonizing futility filled her welling eyes, as if she watched a loved one in grave danger without any power to save them. The realization struck him like a bullet, tearing through his callous exterior. *This* wasn't her first time witnessing violence or—if he didn't intervene—death. A subject he cared not to think of.

He glanced behind his daughter to Isaac, peering out with raised brows. In their otherwise sheltered lives, neither one had born witness to such intentional, such *human* violence. He'd be lying if he said he was surprised it had taken this long.

Potter climbed down the schooner and untied McCormac's nag. Bessie's mare neighed loudly and snuffled, shaking its silky mane. He checked his pistols, unsnapping the holster safeties. The sawed-off cracked open, exposing two cartridges of buckshot.

He looked back. "You two stay in the carriage."

He watched as Clara jumped in the back, where Isaac found the rifle and grabbed it. The two sat peering through the canvas opening as he turned away.

He knew two things. Today his young'uns' innocence would forever be askew. No getting around that. And no matter how much he'd resist; he would break his promise to Bessie yet again. No negotiation worked with these kinds of men. Regardless of his newfound penitence, he remained impotent to disavow a violent life.

4

Coffey, on his back, quivered.

"Go on Stringer. Go on an tie'im up," Warren said. "We gonna have ourselves a proper execution."

Stringer, lasso in hand, hopped down from his horse, which finally stopped at the edge of the woodlands after dragging their victim completely across the clearing. "Sumbitch, you c'mere! Teach you to take things, ain't yours."

"Please! Please! I-I didn't take *nothin*!" Despite being restrained, Coffey held his forearms up, his hands raised in futile defense.

"You can shut that filthy, lyin nigger mouth of yours, Coffey, before I shove my goddamn boot in it." Grant climbed off his stallion, so heavyset that the horse almost buckled as he dismounted.

"You think we's fuckin stupid? I'm sure that ol' codger sent you up here to spy on us—steal our livestock, did he?" Warren accused, calm and collective from his horse. He kept his pistol aimed at Coffey.

Coffey dug his heels in the dirt, kicking backwards, crawling, as Grant approached.

"I bet he did, Warren. That don't surprise me much." Grant pulled two pistols. "Ain't that right?"

"I-I swear, I swear I was ju-jus passin through. Was jus givin the boy a-a once over. He looked to be jus wanderin an-an-and-uh—"

Stinger yanked the lasso to the side, flipping Coffey mid-sentence, burying his face in the dirt.

"Christ, just shut that boy up." Warren, enervated, puffed an exhausting sigh, tipped his gray hat up, and dabbed at grimy brow sweat with a tattered brown handkerchief.

Grant's denim knee dug into Coffey's middle back. His spine cracked, sending a fury of warm prickling up his back and neck. His grueling whimper hung in the air while the fleshy, crushing weight of Grant bound his wrists with the lasso slack, tearing into his skin. A moment later the large man stood, roughly yanking the rope—and Coffey—upright. Coffey's knees buckled, gravity disappearing. Through glassy eyes, he watched Warren's lasso land in Stringer's arms, who holstered his pistol and flung the rope over a low oak branch. Grant awkwardly jerked the braided loop over Coffey's high hair, fitting it snuggly around his neck.

"Christ, boy, that head of hair is somethin else," Grant mused, smiling.

"Almost wish we had time to cut it. You'd like that, boy—make a good display outside Quinsberry's, I bet. Match that nice suit Boss Man is sure to dress his favorite slave in." Warren smirked.

"Oh, I'd say they a little closer than *that*. You tuck'im in bed, smooch'im goodnight?" Stinger crowed.

His cackle, reminiscent of a tortured bird, aroused the group. Grant guffawed, and Warren's shit-eating grin stretched a bit further.

"Stop! Please, please, don't do this, I-I beg you—"

The lasso tightened. Muffled, strained sounds of prayer, unintelligible, flooded from Coffey's glossy lips. Sweat flooded down his furrowed brow. He squeezed his eyes shut from the burning, salty drip. The cackling continued, from who didn't make any difference. His terror left no room for curiosity, or even anger. He only thought, between words of contrition, that he had foreseen this event long ago, in his youth. The inherent repercussion of living in the south as a black man. Yet, to his incredulity, his dreaded fate had not arrived for much longer than he'd ever expected. He'd lived a long life in an equivocal world where men like him didn't survive.

It wasn't all bad.

His throat clenched in anticipation. Awaiting his last moments, he closed his eyes.

A rugged voice split the mounting dissention. "Pardon me, fellers..."

5

Potter stood twenty feet away, his horse another fifty feet behind.

The three men turned to him. The one they'd called Warren yanked his reins, twisting around his grunting stallion and his pistol. He seemed to be the oldest, the one in charge of the group.

Potter glanced down at himself. He looked old enough to be their father, dressed in a shabby long coat and hat. Not much of a threat.

Still, he held up his hands quickly, only partially raised. "Ain't looking for trouble." And he wasn't. He knew this encounter could be it. The end. Here. Today. He stood in close range of three men with—*slightly*—more firepower. "Just wanna know what this man here has done to warrant such abuse?"

The one named Grant turned his pistols on him while the other brother, Stringer, stood still, holding the rope taut.

Warren, mouth full of tobacco, discharged a greenish brown geyser from his puffed lower lip, aiming it toward the stranger. "That here ain't none your goddamn concern, mister. I suggest you turn round and go bout your business."

Potter didn't move, didn't speak. He stood tall—taller than the common man.

The boys waited too, not intimidated in the least.

After a few tense seconds of silence, Warren added, "You understandin me, stranger?" Tobacco spittle quivered and dripped from his chin stubble.

"'Fraid I can't do that."

"An why's that?" Warren flashed a crooked smile of gold teeth to his two cronies, who turned to one another, sharing the same sentiment.

"You see, you're on private property, here."

"Private property?" Stringer shot a bemused look to his brothers. "The hell you say. This here, this old Bennett land. Ain't nothin but abandoned, long ago."

"*I'm* the new landowner. There ain't gonna be an execution on it. Not today. Not tomorrow. Not any other time." Potter stood motionless, staring at Warren. "Now, I'm gonna ask you to unhand this man. Cut him loose and get off my land."

"Unhand him!? This no-good, thievin nigger ain't goin nowhere but with us," Grant grumbled.

"I don't want no trouble. Please. Just go." Potter kept his tone stern, still directed at Warren. He would bargain no further, his offer plenty sufficient.

6

Coffey, managing to pull his eyelids open, could barely see the stranger. Burning sweat stung his gaze, and Grant's wide body blocked his view. The rope, tightening every time Stringer intentionally or unintentionally gave a tug, partially constricted his breathing, obstructing his speech to the point he stopped audibly praying. Still, he now had one last chance. He needed to say something.

He struggled like hell to force air into his lungs, and, with a slow, long breath, he spit out, "I—I didn't steal nothin, mister." He paused a moment, waiting for his triggered gag reflex to subside. Saliva hung from his quivering lip. Then, through clenched teeth, he added, "Ya-got-to-be-lieve me—please—please!"

"Shut the fuck up!" Grant yelled.

Stringer yanked on the rope, and the noose dug into Coffey's esophagus. He sucked in his last whimpering breath, the ground pulling from beneath his feet as his stomach churned in somersaults. *This is it.*

Everything went black.

7

The second Grant's head instinctually turned to view the hanging, Potter pulled both diamond-gripped pistols from their worn holsters. They slid out with crackerjack speed. With precision. Grant only needed a second—a second before he realized he'd turned his head on the stranger in the long coat.

Potter squeezed off two rounds. Gray smoke discharged from each barrel.

Grant, no slouch himself, had kept his guns pointing at the stranger. He fired at roughly the same time; however, Potter moved laterally between each subsequent shot, dodging Grant's immediate return by mere inches. His first two rounds plunged into the blue plaid of Grant's bulging chest; he stumbled backward with a quick, strained yelp before tumbling. Only a grainy thud and two puffs of smoke rising from oozing fissures remained.

Stringer, waylaid and fumbling, reached for his gun, desperately attempting to grasp both the rope and weapon. In order to help his brother, he'd have to let go. In an act of dithering, dumb brilliance, he jumped up and straddled the rope, wrapping his feet and left hand around the lasso while he pulled his pistol with his right. His weight, similar to his captive's, allowed both men to hang evenly from the limb, with the man they'd called Coffey writhing at the other end of the noose. Stringer popped off at Potter while swaying from the rope, minimally avoiding return fire as Potter continued to sidestep and shoot.

Unbeknownst to the brothers, however, Potter had them at a grave disadvantage. His pistols held more ammunition than theirs. Then *anybody's*, for that matter. About thirty percent more.

After mere seconds, Stringer's six shooter emptied. As a look of anguish flashed across his furrowed face, Potter stopped, aimed his left gun, and struck him between the eyes.

The convulsing Coffey, wrenched by gravity, crashed to the dirt, wheezing and coughing. With a bit of force, he slid a hand from the poorly tied restraints, struggling to stick his fingers between the noose and his throat.

Seeing the poor man still lived, Potter sidestepped into the woodlands, taking cover behind a thick oak trunk as gunshots ricocheted through the air. Panting, he pushed his head back and closed his eyes, his heart jabbering in his chest. The smoking pistols, held against either side of his head, warmed his cheeks.

<h1 style="text-align:center">8</h1>

Warren twisted back and forth in his saddle, blood racing in his ears, firing his pistol until empty. *Damn it.* He glanced over to Stringer, slumping backwards against the tree. Blood thinly trickled between his open eyes and down the bridge of his crooked nose. His younger brother lay lifeless, mere feet away.

Something moved in the corner of his eye. Coffey, having staggered to his feet, bolted into the woodlands.

Warren whirled around, kicked his heel spur into the side of his old stallion, and tore after the stranger and Coffey. Pulling the spare—his prized Colt Peacemaker—he fired recklessly into the brush. "You killed my brothers, you goddamn sumbitch! I'm a *kill* both a yous!"

The stranger, hiding somewhere in the forest, nearly struck him with each round from his return fire. One bullet tore through his wafting coattails. The gunfire only ceased as Warren encroached on the grove, wakeful, scanning the backdrop of tall yellow pine and quaking aspen trees under a parasol of fresh, golden foliage.

Silence.

Afraid he'd gone too far, Warren slowed to a halt, perched, on high alert. He just needed a sound. Any sound.

A direction to aim his fire.

9

Coffey, quivering, stood against the notched white bark of an aspen. With a quick snap of the head, he spotted Warren skulking far ahead. Across the grove, he also saw the stranger, propped and peering from behind his tree. Warren stood too far for the man in the overcoat to get a clean shot off, and he clearly didn't plan to give up his position. The silence between gun shots, albeit deafening for all parties, did very little to secure positions. Any noise, regardless how subtle, immediately diminished, silenced by one of Warren's projectiles slicing through the thicket.

Just beyond Warren's line of sight, Coffey slowly made his break, tiptoeing through the brush, taking brief but scanty cover behind each narrow tree. Currently, he knew two things to be true. One: no matter how quietly and safely he maneuvered in his feeble attempt to escape the woodlands, Warren was likely to see—and, if by some damn miracle, he missed him today, he'd only await him in future shadows. Two: he remained defenseless and alone, having yet to face the unknown person in the lengthy coat, still lurking in these woods. What this stranger wanted was anyone's guess. Sooner or later, Coffey knew he would need to make a stand.

Inadvertently, however, his stand came far sooner than he'd expected. As Coffey turned, attempting to clear the woods, he came face to face with a majestic mule deer. A buck, no less. He stopped abruptly, slack mouthed, hands slightly raised. The deer, ten feet away, stared blankly back, his reflection paling in its large, obsidian eyes. The imposing creature dwarfed Coffey, its antlers splendidly long and gnarled. Encompassing. Would it attack? Holler? Jet off into the brush?

Gently turning his head, Coffey saw Warren, back turned in the distance, slightly veiled by sparse proliferation. A clear view to freedom waited just past the golden buck, still staring as it stood in his path. The literal horns of dilemma. Maybe, just maybe, Warren stood too far to hear.

Ain't no chance.

Slowly, he took a step backward, his foot landing on a rock half the size of his fist and nearly tripping him up. He stumbled, quickly regaining his balance as the cold sweat dripped from his face. Fortunately, Warren, still pacing, didn't notice. Stooping, Coffey grabbed the stone, wound his arm back, and whipped it in the direction from which he originally entered the woods. The rock flew quite a distance before clanking off a thick fir, sending squirrels scurrying through the brush. Warren whirled, firing several rounds. The stranger, twenty yards from impact, simultaneously turned and gave up his position. Warren, seeing that brown Stetson, sent his stallion galloping toward the man, firing several rounds.

The buck scampered off, leaving Coffey with a straight shot to freedom... *so to speak*. He began to run, then stopped. The consequences of his uncertain future loomed.

If not for the stranger in the long coat, he'd already be dead.

10

Bullets discharged chipped bark from either side of the Ponderosa pine with force, one sliver slicing Potter's cheek bone. He ducked and ran to another tree ten yards back, plugging back with both revolvers until he heard the disheartening snaps of an empty chamber—two empty chambers, at that.

"You can't hide, stranger!" Warren slowed, pacing toward him about a hundred feet out. He'd either forgotten about Coffey in favor of pursuing Potter or decided the other man would eventually get *his*. Either way, he popped off yet another round in Potter's direction, hitting the tree directly behind his head.

Potter, breathing heavily, holstered his pistols and pulled out the sawed-off. *This is it.* Only two shots left now—two *real* shots, in the essence of time—and, by his count, Warren neared empty himself.

Warren inched closer; his presence betrayed by the rustling crescendo of the horse's hooves. His impending doom hung heavy in the air; Potter could almost taste it.

"Ahh!" Warren yelped.

He raised his hand to the back of his bleeding head; a rock tumbled to the ground.

Turning, he caught sight of Coffey, standing off in the distance. "Goddamn you, Coffey! You's a dead ni—"

Potter turned to Warren, sawed-off raised, hammers back.

CLICK! CLICK!

Potter, wide eyed, looked down in disbelief, then back to his target. *Fucking gun jammed!*

Warren, mid-insult, turned to Potter's shoddy shotgun and smiled with two gold fronts. He had him.

The man slowly raised his Peacemaker and pulled back the hammer with a greasy thumb, taking all the time in the world. A figurative spit to the face, one last *fuck you* before death.

Well, Potter saw things just a little differently. With crackerjack speed, he pulled his left revolver and, with his thumb, flipped a little lever on the end of the hammer, which allowed the pin to strike the lower barrel. The *secret* barrel. A wary smile flashed across Warren's dirty face. Within a tenth of a second, he knew what lay in store for him.

Time's up.

The buckshot hit him square in the face, knocking him backward off his horse, which scampered out of the way. The shot didn't kill him, though. Not yet. He lay twisted over uneven ground in the thicket, gently convulsing, face cocked and twitching and staring off into Lord-knew-where. Eight or so small holes peppered his cheek and forehead. A dark, fleshy notch remained where the left eye once lived; it oozed gore while the right eye filled with red. His breathing labored; his chest slowly heaved. Potter stood over him, staring. Warren glared back—*another* look Potter had seen before. Anger. Fear. Desperation.

The other two were so quick, Potter hadn't had a chance to think, much less feel, anything. But this sight pierced through him. To take a man's life was one thing. To watch him leave this plane of existence was quite another. A sour taste flooded the back of his throat. With the other revolver in a trembling hand, he sent his final round, the last of the buckshot, into Warren's head.

His pistol lay nearby. The Peacemaker. The irony was not lost on Potter as he picked it up, examining its features. A silver Colt bearing an intricate foliate scrollwork engraved along the barrel and cylinder, finished with a carved ivory hand grip. Quite beautiful. Tainted. But beautiful. He wondered where this piece of gutter trash picked up such an item. He tossed the besmirched gun onto Warren's corpse.

A stick snapped in the distance.

Potter jerked up his head to see the man they'd called Coffey, still quite a distance away, staring at the unmoving Warren. Potter waved the gun in his hand—a gentle *come hither*. Coffey, hands up, cautiously but quickly tramped over.

"Relax." Potter holstered his pistol. "I ain't gonna hurt ya."

Coffey stared at Potter from twenty feet out. "I-I ain't got nothing—I don't want no trouble now, mister!"

"I said, I ain't gonna hurt ya."

"Wuh-Whatcha want, then, m-mister?"

"Don't want anything."

Coffey lowered his shaky hands to shoulder level. "Why-why'd ya help mm-me out, then?"

"Why'd those men say you stole from them?"

"I-I don't know."

"Look, I just shot three men to death. Ain't something I planned to do this morning when I woke up." He shrugged, supposing that no one *really* planned for such things. "*That*, I don't take too lightly. And if I'm to make some sort of sense of it, I need to know why these men are dead."

"Jus... Jus some bad blood is all, ya know."

"I can sort a guess that. Who were these men?" Potter shuddered, turning away from Warren's vacuous stare, and both men began to walk.

"Them's the Criley brothers. Family lives there, over yonder." Coffey nodded behind.

He spoke with a gentle, almost laggardly cadence, as if to avoid the likelihood of repeating himself. Possibly something developed from past trauma, Potter figured.

"They say I-I stole a horse," Coffey continued. "I ain't stole nothin! I ain't never stole nothin in my life, 'cept maybe some food from a garden ain't mine, but them was desperate times, see. But that horse, I jus came cross it. Found it wanderin bout, ya know, as ya sometimes do round these woods. Jus was givin it a look over when them boys rode up on me. Reckon it must've wandered off their farm or something. Well, that be bout it. Then you rode up."

Potter glanced Coffey over. Certainly not a spring chicken. A vertical scar, barely visible, notched his black cheek, stretching from his eye to curve around his awkward, wary smile. He looked about as weathered as the disheveled clothing he stood in. His woolen pants, flannel, and vest bore more holes than fabric, dirt covered his spurred boots, and a threadbare bandana draped from his red, rawhide neck. Typical ranch-hand attire—except he lacked one essential thing. Well, *two*.

Potter stared at his hips. "You don't carry any weapons?"

"No, sir. Well... got a knife in my pocket. Bout it."

"Why?"

Coffey smacked the dirt from his thighs and sleeves. "Never much needed one, I reckon. Don't wander off the beaten path too much, if ya know what I mean. Usually not alone when I do, neither."

Potter cocked his head. *How odd.* Then again, based on his observations upon arriving, not many people here carried weapons. "What's this you were saying bout 'bad blood?'"

"Crileys worked for my boss. Got into some bad stuff, put my boss in a bad way. Got kicked off the ranch. Prolly still angry bout it. I tell ya, them boys is as crooked as a dog's hind leg. Good riddance, I say."

"Why didn't you just let it be? Doesn't seem a smart thing for a man such as yourself to be doing in these parts." Potter stepped out of the woods and into the field, glancing to the bodies of Stringer and Grant. Some shock still clung to him, and he required physical evidence of the gunfight to confirm its reality. He wondered, not for the first time, how he remained standing.

"I work with horses, mister. Over at the Jinglebob Ranch."

"*Jinglebob Ranch?*" Potter, pulling a one-inch sliver of wood from his cheek, winced. He looked the chip over, then tossed it.

"Yes, sir, that be John Chisum's place." His head twisted, nodding in another direction. "There, over yonder."

"Huh. Work with horses, you say?"

Potter raised a brow, casting a second look at his companion. He judged him to be similar to himself in height and age, though his wild, wiry hair made his long, lanky frame seem much taller. Abundant white strands streaked the man's dark mane. Save for trimmed mutton chops, also streaked white, he kept his face clean shaven. Potter found himself surprisingly impressed. They were in the South—the deep South—and although Lincoln emancipated colored folk two decades ago, now, a well-groomed, employed man of color was, well, not something Potter saw every day.

"Why, yes, sir. Best in the county, I might say." Coffey cracked a crooked smile.

At least the man seemed more relaxed. He still had all his teeth, too, at least from what Potter could see. Also not very common on older gentlemen, especially men of color, those formally deemed *property*.

"That's a fine lookin animal ya got there yourself, if I may say so," Coffey said, nodding at Potter's horse. "She got a name?"

"She doesn't," Potter admitted.

"Oh, come on now. A fine creature like that's gotta be called somethin!"

"She was my wife's. She never bothered to name her steeds."

"Oh... well, anyway, I do a number a jobs for Mr. Chisum. You a-a rancher, mister? The way ya handle a gun, I'd a taken ya for the law, or bounty hunter—somethin."

Potter smiled. "No. No law. As far as ranching, well, I know my way round."

"Well, I don't reckon to know your story, mister, but Mr. Chisum is always lookin for good help. Loyal help, ya know what I'm sayin?"

Potter had some idea. Apparently, this Chisum character was the *Big Bug* in town. And Coffey, well, he appeared a nice enough individual. Maybe even an honest man—if such a thing existed. Potter had yet to meet a feller in this lifetime who wasn't a bunko artist, coffee boiler, chiseler, crook, or outright murderer.

He ran a hand through his sweaty, dirtied hair. He'd arrived in Missouri Plaza with no prospects, hoping for a stroke of good luck. After taking one look at the town, though, he knew his prospects were Jack and shit... and as for Jack, that sonofabitch already had a foot out the door. *Bartending* was certainly out of the question.

"Well..." Potter glanced at the light blue sky above the clearing. "I'd be much obliged by that." He turned to Coffey. "Name's Potter. Bill Potter."

"Coffey."

Potter shot him a wry smile as they shook hands.

"Ya, I know. Was given that name, long ago. Kinda just stuck, if ya know what I mean." Coffey grinned again, the expression like a snug-fitting suit.

A signature smile, Potter figured, nodding. "I believe I do."

"Potter, ya say? Did I hear ya own the Bennett property?" Coffey panned the clearing with incredulity. "This all *your* land?"

"Have no idea, to be honest." Potter followed Coffey's eyes, sharing his wonderment.

Coffey laughed. "Well, I bes be on my way, Mr. Potter. Don't ya worry bout this here mess, I'm-a get it cleaned up. Must leave no trace behind. Don't need no marshal snoopin round Chisum's place." Coffey picked up his hat, dusted it off, and placed it over his head. He began to walk off, then stopped and turned back. "Don't forget to swing by... the *man* awaits. Can't thank ya enough for whatcha done."

"Thank my daughter." Potter peered over to see Clara and Isaac standing on the spring-loaded seat, looking at their pa and the man he rescued from imminent demise. "Truth be told, if it were any other day, friend, I'd-a just turned the other way."

Chapter 5

"Will you teach me to shoot a rifle, Pa," Isaac asked, breaking the awkward silence in the schooner, which had followed them since leaving Coffey back at the clearing. He was holding the rifle butt down with the barrel propped against his shoulder.

Potter realized he hadn't addressed the violent incident with his young'uns, still shocked and largely silent on the bench. The thought hadn't even crossed his mind until now. He knew what they must be asking themselves. Who *was* that man they saw back there? No man at all, though it wore their father's cloak. No, this thing had crawled out from the murky depths of obscurity. The unfettered Beast. Repatriated, it unleashed its fury. The only consolation he found—though not much—was that the Beast stopped an innocent man from hanging.

Potter squeezed the reins, knuckles white, to stop his hands from shaking—the image of Warren's obliterated face lingering. His blood pressure rose. "A rifle ain't a toy to be trifled with, Isaac. It's a dangerous tool. You just saw what one of these can do to a man. You think that's an easy thing?"

"What, Pa?"

"Killing a man. You thinking that's an easy thing to do? To take the life of another person. To remove them from existence. That's akin to taking everything they were in this world. Everything they left behind. Pals, family... loved ones. There just ain't no reconciling something like that—try as you might to forget it, ignore it, sweep it away. A piece of their soul now belongs to you, whether you want that or not."

"Well, I—I just want to do what *you* do, Pa. You know, to protect us from the Bad People."

The Bad People.

This sentiment should have made Potter feel better, maybe even put a smile on his hardened face. Instead, his heart only sank further. *If the damn boy only knew.*

Isaac stared up at him, his young eyes solemn. "I'll be real carful, Pa. Honest."

Potter considered his boy, already growing so close to a man. If violence intended to follow them, he figured Isaac should know how to defend himself.

Potter nodded. "Spose I could show you a thing or two."

The woodlands thinned out. By the trail's end, another mile or so ahead, the trees completely dissipated into a stretch of infinite flat land that stopped, if it stopped at all, at a mirage of mountains eons away. Potter, with subtle awe, stared out at the shimmering horizon between the vast green ocean of grass and the bluish white hue of saw-tooth peaks, slicing into crisp, clear, azure skies. A gorgeous view. Not quite as pretty as Colorado, he supposed, but it'd do just fine.

"Are we here, Pa?" Isaac marveled. He followed his father's gaze.

"I believe we're home."

The property itself comprised the substantial, secluded clearing, flanked by the Pecos River. The fast waters wrapped around the meadow, starting from one end of the woodlands and vanishing seamlessly into the other. No bridges crossed the Pecos. The trail they rode upon offered the only way on or off the Bennett property.

Potter knew little of John Bennett—an old Confederate recluse he'd never met—except that the man hadn't acquired his brother's affluence. Happily, however, the house proved considerably larger than Potter had expected, albeit significantly smaller than his previous residence. The early American saltbox colonial, at least a hundred years old, actually reminded him of neighborhood homes growing up in rural New England—ones he happened to know a thing or two about from learning the family business, now three decades removed.

The building's architecture resembled early English medieval style, featuring a long and sloping rear roof, massive hand-hewn doors with thick hobnail studs, and small diamond pane windows, four on each side. All indubitably out of place in these parts. The two-level rectangular structure, in classic dog-shit brown, slightly narrowed at the rear and extended outward. A kitchen, Potter figured. A small, attached barn sat opposite.

The house stood center in the not-so-clear clearing, slightly obscured in tall, slumping patches of erratic Bermuda grass that had grown wild and uncut for who knew how long. Mowing down the unruly turf would likely take an entire day, in addition to providing Potter's first exhausting expense: a scythe.

He sighed, adding the task to his mental to-do list as he surveyed the rest of the yard.

A low three-foot irregular stone wall squared off the front of the house about a hundred feet from the porch, the entrance obscurely marked by a decorative set of faded gray batwing doors. The charming touch of an entrance appeared suspended in midair, accented with large iron nails and a pair of oxidized horseshoes. Most likely as old as the house itself, the doors splintered at the edges, showing signs of advanced deterioration.

Feeling the warmth of the rising New Mexican sun, Potter removed his coat. Isaac removed his coat as well. Underneath, he wore comparable attire to his father: brown trousers, a white Henley shirt, and red suspenders. His resemblance didn't stop there, however. They shared the same big hazel-green eyes, the same shoulder length, shaggy brown hair. Even the same big front teeth, with the same gaping space between them. His son only lacked his bushy, silver-streaked beard, which Potter had worn since long before his marriage to Bessie. Beyond that, Isaac had inherited most of Potter's aesthetic features. An uncanny, miniature Potter. As father sided-eyed son, admiring his winsome boy, he prayed to God that's *all* Isaac inherited of his Pa.

The schooner reached the floating batwing doors, coming in from the right side. Not a snowball's chance in hell they could clear it. On the far-left side of the property, the stone wall had either collapsed or had been systematically deconstructed, most likely for a carriage to enter. As they rode up on it, Potter noticed two horses protruding from the backside of the house.

Isaac pointed ahead. "Pa, there's someone here!"

"Looks that way, son." Heart sinking, Potter considered who possibly awaited them. Were marshals already here? With two empty pistols and a jammed shotgun, he relied solely on the old Winchester .22 rifle. Might do just fine... if they were held up by rabbits. Though, if Potter's niggling suspicion proved correct, he wouldn't need any weapons at all. Just a hell of a lot of patience.

Entering the property, Potter scanned the two chocolate stallions harnessed to a small red stagecoach, almost as elegant as the Seward trunk and luggage piled on top and secured by rope. He glowered. Unfortunately, even *shittier* news appeared as they drew closer. Just beyond the house, off to the left, stood a narrow, boxlike structure, a crescent moon carved into the front door—a door which swung open. A stocky, white-haired gentleman stepped forth, buttoning his gray wool vest under a matching suit and hat wrapped around a brown corduroy jacket.

"It's Grandpa!" Clara stood and shouted, holding her brother's shoulder for support.

"Pa," the boy asked, "did you know Grandpa would be here?"

Potter shook his head. He didn't suspect a thing, not until a few moments prior, but he damn well should have.

"What is *that*, Pa?" Clara pointed at the wooden box from which Grandpa emerged.

"*That*, my darling, is an outhouse."

"What's an out-house?"

"Well, I will tell you, it's *not* for hide and seek."

"It's for having a shit!" Isaac laughed.

"Isaac." Potter kept his voice stern, though in truth he *was* amused by his son's comment.

The shock and horror on Clara's face surpassed that of the gunfight. "Ewwww!"

Potter shared Clara's disappointment, but he'd also suspected as much. "Lotta changes, kids." He looked at Isaac. "Your first lesson on your journey into manhood is one I've lived by my whole life: be prepared, son. Be prepared."

As the schooner came to a halt, Clara climbed down and ran straight into Grandpa's wide-open arms. "Grandpa! Grandpa!"

He bent down and scooped her up, the crow's feet prominent in each eye. "Hiya, sweetheart! How's my beautiful little lady?" He kissed her cheek and smiled, his thin, white beard stretching his tan, aging face.

She giggled, rubbing her cheek against his scratchy beard. "Are you staying here with us?" Though she spoke with enthusiasm, a slight inflection of uncertainty arose by the time she finished her question. A moroseness, as if she already suspected the answer.

Morgan pulled back to look her in the eyes. "No, darling. Unfortunately, not. I'll be staying the night, then heading out, bright and early in the morning. Most likely before you and your brother wake. Long trip ahead."

"Aww, but we just got here." She pouted.

"I know, Clarissa, I know." With a strained groan, he put her down.

Isaac made his way over. "Hi, Grandpa."

Morgan acknowledged him with a jovial nod. "Isaac, dear boy! I must say, you two are sprouting up like dandelions. Soon your heads will turn yellow. My Lord, your grandpa can't even recall the last time he's seen you. What's it been—a month?" He smiled; a full mouth of gray teeth glistened.

"A month!?" Clara gaped, flabbergasted. She didn't have much concept of time, but she knew a month wasn't long, and Grandpa's last visit had passed much longer. Seasons longer.

"Two months?"

"Six months, Grandpa," Isaac corrected, less enthused.

"That's preposterous." He scratched his beard, playfully pensive. "Guess we'll just have to make up for lost time tonight. How does that sound? I want to hear all about your trip. It must've been quite an adventure, none of you having *ever* left home before."

"Morgan." Potter, finally making his way over, acknowledged his father-in-law with a nod. To the young'uns, he added, "Why don't you kids go on in and take a look around."

"Race you!" Clara said, immediately taking off towards the front door. Isaac followed close behind, leaving her to lead.

"Where's your driver?" Potter knew Morgan would never travel alone, much less *drive* his own carriage.

"Out, retrieving tonight's dinner."

If he'd retrieved dinner a little closer to the firefight, he'd possibly *be* dinner. Potter cringed—fuck, where did this thought even creep up from? *No. No, thank you.* A grim vision, a soufflé of savagery, crept into the forefront of his mind. He spurned the memory posthaste, bore it down and buried it away. He fervently desired to never again experience such desperation, knowing the chilling consequences that sort of a meal left for a man.

He forced a sneer instead of a shudder. "How primitive. Wasn't aware you still knew how to hunt and gather. I apologize for bringing you down to my level."

"Let's cut the horseshit, Sullivan. I received a telegram from my staff that one of our schooners rode off the property with a man behind the reins. One with your description."

Potter kept his mouth shut. He hadn't expected Morgan so soon, but he'd known one of the man's servants would eventually send word from the Denver Western Union to Tucson, where a note must've been delivered post haste to his, uh, cattle farm. Though *winter estate* certainly fit better. Potter had been aware of Morgan's new Arizona "business," where he'd been escaping the brutal Colorado winters the last two years.

But he never believed Bennett, Silver Baron of twenty-four years, knew a good goddamn thing about herding cattle.

Morgan fixed him with knowing glare. "Why didn't you write me you were leaving? You pack up my grandchildren on me and you just take off?"

"Ah, hell, cuz there wasn't time." Potter removed his hat and wiped his glistening brow with his hanky. "That's all, Morgan. There ain't no conspiracy here to disappear with *your grandchildren*. Christ. Can you even remember the last time you saw them?"

"I did not travel all the way here, days out of my way, to argue with you, Edward."

"Then to what do we owe this visit?"

"How long you think you can hide for? You think whoever they are won't be keen on eventually checking my brother's old estate? I mean, hell, I know it's way out here in the middle of nowhere, but people know who *I* am. Won't be too hard to put the pieces together."

"Guess time will tell."

"Sullivan—"

"The name's Potter. *We* are the Potters, so if you're going to refer to us—"

"Potters..." Morgan shook his head. "I decided to head back to Denver—early—on account of *you*, of course. Figured I'd stop here and see my grandchildren. Make sure they made it safely."

"They're with their father."

"I know exactly who they're with. I won't lay claim to presume otherwise. You know, I curse the day *my* Elizabeth met the likes of you. Could never, *never* understand what she ever saw in a man of your stature. A man twenty years her senior, for Christ's sake. What's more is I can't believe *I* allowed it, just based on age alone. God only knows what I've come to learn since. But by then, I was too late to stop you, Sullivan—Potter, whatever horseshit fabrication you go by these days. And believe me, I know your *real* name. I couldn't keep you from stealing my baby girl, just like you've done with everything else in your no good, rotten existence.

Can't even call it a *life*. Out of all the things, the only commodity worth *anything*, you fucking *stole* my only daughter away."

"I never put a gun to her head, Morgan. Ain't never forced myself upon her. She knew exactly who I was. Even gave her the chance to reconsider, though I still wonder like hell if I would've let her. Glad I never had to make that decision. Bessie was the love of my life."

"As she was *mine!* And now she's gone. Her *and* her mother. I lost both women in my life. Only reason *you're* alive is those two kids in there. Bad enough they'll grow up without their mother." He shook his head. "In this miserable life, all men bear a debt. Some more than others, I reckon. Now, I don't know what kind of shit you've gotten yourself into, ending up here, but this here's the deal." Morgan inched closer, a seething grin on his rugged face. "There's a post in town. You make sure those kids write me—bi-weekly—so I know they're safe. I miss one letter, and I won't hesitate to send the full weight of the United States Calvary straight up your ass. Now, I'll be down this way on my way back to Tucson—early, again, mind you—end of summer."

Potter glanced over and noticed Isaac standing behind a filthy window, then quickly looked off behind Morgan towards the mountain range in the distance, a tentative mirage. He squinted at the sun, feeling the tackiness of dried blood under his eye. At this point, he'd just as soon shoot Morgan and dump him in the river. Hell, he was already on a roll, but murdering Grandpa might prove difficult to explain to the young'uns, and he supposed he'd more than reached his quota for today. His father-in-law had him right by the balls.

Sighing, he nodded and glanced back to the window. Isaac was gone. Potter doubted the boy had heard anything, or at least, he sure hoped as much.

Morgan smirked. "Now... let's go in and make nice, while I'm with the only family I have left."

Without another word, Potter walked to the door, opened it, and waved Morgan inside with a bit of *yes, your highness*.

Clara called, faintly, from somewhere down the hall. "Paaaa! Where do I make pee!?"

2

Joseph Griffin nearly tripped over his feet lurching sideways to avoid gunfire.

Union soldiers scattered, taking cover behind spread out trees to avoid gunfire from the large, Georgian colonial's second-floor window. The decorative wagon wheel, marking the pillared, Greek-revival structure as the Frohrmann homestead, dinged and clattered under stray bullets.

The ragtag group of eight troops, filthy and emaciated, returned fire from behind the bulky trunks of four southern live oak trees framing the front of the estate—two on either side, and two more ahead of those, just on the outskirts. The men worked in a disciplined, two-by-two formation. One group tore gunpowder packets, dumping and stuffing Minie ball rounds down the barrels of their Springfield rifles, while another group strategically took aim. The unit hammered back in near unison, but the house's high foundation, above a steep set of stairs, put them at a slight disadvantage. Not to mention the veiled, silken drapery of luscious Spanish moss, which shielded the men but also, consequently, obstructed their view of the intended target.

The August sun blistered down, even though the morning had barely broken. The soldiers sweated profusely in the heat, weakened by famine, insomnia, and newfound delirium. Every few minutes or so, another man's forage cap came off, and his sleeve wiped his wet brow and pushed back some greasy hair before restoring his uniform.

Griffin, panting, unraveled a low-hanging grayish bushel of foliage, using the oak's scaly moss leaves to blot his beading forehead before the grimy liquid reached his wary eyes. His rifle sat beside him, empty, though the gravelly pops and inaudibly shouted commands of his unit continued to resonate through him, earsplitting. Back against the tree, he leaned, staring into vast fields of cotton.

What the fuck am I doing, what the fuck am I doing, what the fuck am I doing, what the fuck am I doing, what the fuck am I doing, what the fuck am I doing—

Too late. It was all too late. Turning back meant death.

Visions. Over and over.

The man. The man in the grocery store—*defending his store*—pulled a revolver, firing. Griffin shot him in the face with his rifle. The soldiers pilfered: loose register change, the proprietor's jewelry and watch, and the few canned food items on display. The proprietor, still alive, gurgled faintly, struggling to breathe as the men hastily exited the store.

Cotton blew in the gentle breeze. A breeze that failed to reach the stupefied Griffin.

He wouldn't listen, he wouldn't listen, I told him, I told him to put it down, I told him, he wouldn't fucking listen...

The sign. *Welcome to Fredericksburg.* The little piece of wood swung, creaking in his brain. The men had stumbled into a quaint Virginian village somewhere, near the Potomac River.

More inaudible shouting sounded in the distance, punctuated with extended gunfire.

Griffin turned. A comrade shouted at him. Pointing. His face looked screwy. Blurred. His brother in arms. *Familiar.* So familiar. But where was he pointing? Griffin turned to another fellow solider, yelling, up close in his face.

"Come on—let's go, Joe!" He yanked the frayed shoulder of his sack coat, pulling him along.

The two ducked and scurried toward the side of the mansion as their unit sprayed the façade with cover fire. Griffin couldn't keep a straight pair of legs; like jelly, they gave way. He slid through a patch of dirt, taking a digger. His comrade, a faceless man, stopped and extended his free hand. Griffin, grabbing it, was quickly yanked from the dusty earth. A bullet struck a patch of dirt nearby as he attempted to regain any feeling in his legs.

His comrade turned and heedlessly fired back, before turning to Griffin. *"Come on—"*

The front of his skull cracked open like a hatching eggshell, the warm, viscous matter inside spurting into Griffin's shocked face. Blood and brain matter bits beaded down with his perspiration. He didn't know what was worse: his eyes stinging with gore or the fact his open mouth could taste this dead man. Salty and coppery. The world slowed down as the soldier, now truly faceless, gently hit the ground. Griffin's ears, already ringing from the muzzle blasts, amplified. He could hear all of his internal organs, working, churning; his lungs cumbrously pulled in air and shoved it out. Everything circulating a rapidly thumping heart somewhere within.

All other sounds dampened to echoes, the depths of his internal cacophony pervading.

His comrade's rifle was suddenly in his hands, though he couldn't recall picking it up. Nor did he know how he ended up alongside the house, or why needed to get in. *Find an entrance.* Windows. Windows everywhere. The foundation windows, easiest to reach—all shut. Locked. He could smash them with the butt of the gun. Easy in, but it might alert the residents of his impending arrival. Maybe not. Too much gunfire... stairs! Long, elegant steps. He found himself on them, pacing up each one deliberately. They seemed to go on forever. Finally, he stepped onto an empty bright white back deck with matching bright white French doors. They pushed open with ease.

He couldn't believe it. He was in the main part of the house—a large, white vestibule with an imperial staircase, branching, leading in opposing directions at the top. Echoes of faint gunfire reverberated as if he'd systematically moved away from the firefight, though he knew he'd done the opposite. Rather, his heartbeat, thumping in his ears, drowned out most of the noise. He crept slowly, body floating of its own accord through this empty, wide space.

Movement hit his peripherals. Oh shit. A man holding a long rifle stood near, and Griffin jumped, twisting away and jerking his rifle at the unknown assailant. Simultaneously, the other man followed suit, both men turning and both pulling their trigger. Griffin's hammer struck an empty chamber. The sound of his heart jabbering flooded his ears at full volume. He dropped the rifle and quickly fumbled for his sidearm, still stuck in its holster, before freezing.

The assailant, in a torn navy jacket and faded blue slacks, froze too. He stared at the ragged soldier of war, *him*, a hollow reflection in a long wall mirror. His squalid face peered back, a young man obscured by blood spatter.

The sound of gunfire amplified over his thumping chest. He found himself skipping up the right set of stairs—skipping—though progressing at a sloth's pace, gently sinking into each carpeted step like quicksand. Finally, halfway up, Griffin paused on the ample half landing before proceeding with caution to the second level. The capacious, white gallery walkway before him led to the roof deck over the front entrance. On either side stood two bedrooms. Griffin, clearing the first one, stopped.

A sound—whimpering. Quiet, but unmistakable.

He turned, drawn to a set of louvered doors. A closet. He stared curiously at these white bifold doors and, for an instant, noticed the faintest flutter. His body coasted across the room. A kid's room, maybe. He noted stuffed animals and a small, four-post bed as he crossed. Slowly, he found his hands grasping both knobs before yanking them open.

A yelp and shudder came from three women huddled on the floor against the wall. He studied the dark-haired woman, flanked by two girls—teens, possibly—with her arms locked around them in a firm embrace. Their bodied twitched, shaking with the terror engraved on their faces. The mother peered up at Griffin with desperate deep blues, owl eyed, her grip tightening over her cowering daughters as they burrowed into the crook of her armpit.

The window shattered. Griffin flinched, twisting, gun raised high in defense. A stray bullet had struck a bedpost. With tentative relief, he turned back to the Frohrmann girls. Mom still crouched, glaring at him—head against the wall—except those pretty blues had faded to a cloudy white. Sooty skin bounded her empty, sunken gaze, face pallid, mouth agape. The girls draped across her lap, all dead. Dead for some time.

His rifle fell, clanking on the hardwood floor. He reached down.

Mom's head lulled forward. "Miss me, Joe?"

Griffin gasped and stumbled backward, though managing to remain on his feet.

The woman rose grimly, with the lethargic grace of a marionette dangling from its strings. The bodies of her girls fell to the floor like rag dolls.

Griffin backed away from the closet.

Her head cocked to the side of her tattered negligee, mouth twisting into a deranged grin. "I'll be waitin on the other side for you, darlin. It's the least I can do for all you done for me."

Griffin, still in motion, backed himself out of the bedroom door. It slammed shut in his face. *Time to go.* He turned for the stairs and found himself in another bedroom. The one opposite of the roof deck, he presumed. Identical. Toys. Four-post bed. His body eddied, panning the enclosed space. No way out. And *not* alone. Two individuals—a man and boy, both in red suspenders—sat on their knees, strategically positioned at the front wall, discharging weapons from two distinct windows. Panic set in. Just a matter of—

The boy turned to Griffin with his rifle. He couldn't have been older than ten, eleven.

Fuck.

The boy gasped. *"Pa!"*

His voice sounded muffled, all muffled. Cotton stuffed both of Griffin's canals as the relentless clamor of his heart seized his ears, the sound reminiscent of field drums played by frightened cavalry drummer boys. Beating, thumping, pervading.

"Don't do it, kid." Despite the clatter of gunfire, his words echoed.

Please don't.

The old man turned, swinging his rifle. Griffin, without thought, pulled his sidearm—a blue LeMat diamond-gripped pistol—and popped off two quick rounds, blowing holes into the old man's stocky chest and sending him crashing against the window frame. His lifeless body slid down to the seat of his pants, a crimson trail streaking behind.

The boy screamed.

"Put down the gun, kid," Griffin commanded.

"You killed my pa, you filthy, stinkin bastard!" The boy ran to his father and shook him. "Pa! Get up, Pa! Please! You need to help me, Pa!"

The old man's head lulled in the boy's arms; blood streamed thinly from the corner of his bristly mouth, eyes rolling in his head. Gaze narrowing, Griffin slowly stepped forth with a heavy foot. Loud. Reverberating. His heart—the drummer boy pounding away. The man's face. Utterly familiar. His dark hair, long and shaggy, his scraggly beard streaked silver. Eyes wide open, hazel-green, void of life.

The troops stormed the bedroom, rifles hoisted.

"What we got here, Joe? Hey! Hey, man!" Voices echoed, bodies shoving.

Griffin, at a loss, glanced over. The soldier—he *knew* him. His face, young, mustached, but *young*... Christ, it was... it was Eugene McCormac!

The young boy yelled something about killing his pa. Everything muffled. Two soldiers pulled the boy off and away, kicking and screaming. Griffin now saw the dead man's face clearly, the scar on the left cheekbone, the red suspenders. *It can't be...*

The man was *him*.

The soldiers pushed the boy against the wall, rifles up in formation. Griffin turned.

The boy, *Isaac,* looked him in his eyes. "Pa, you can't let them take us! Don't let them—"

"NO! WAIT!" Griffin reached for Isaac.

Too far, too far away. The soldiers opened fire, executing his boy at close range. With the muzzle blasts still reverberating, Griffin stared at the blood-spattered wall, then turned for the absent exit.

The graying corpse of Mrs. Frohrmann awaited him, her black mouth slack but her frosted eyes locked on his. She reached for his throat.

3

A wretched yelp heaved from Potter's dry throat as he shot up from bed, drenched in a cold sweat, drooling and panting like a rabid animal. His shaking hand slammed the bedside table, feverishly feeling for a revolver. He couldn't tell where the hell he was, and, most terrifying of all—*when* he was. He jumped out of bed, spinning, scanning his dark surroundings. Could he be dead? Was this some strange, time-fixed purgatory? He couldn't see much, save for the faint glow of a mostly melted candle on the dresser top across the room. He grabbed the metal candlestick and waved it around.

After thirty seconds, he finally flashed the flickering candlelight across a Bennett family portrait looming on the wall. A youthful John and Morgan stood with both parents; a sight almost as terrifying as his nightmare. He sighed and shook his head. He was *home*. The unfamiliar and antiquated environment had made his first night a little more bewildering and unsettling, that's all. He must have passed out the moment his head hit the pillow, neglecting to put out the candle before succumbing to his prolonged fatigue.

His guns, still holstered—*and empty*—sat nestled securely in his gun belt, hanging from a coat hook in the corner near the door. Potter, hands still quivering, reached for the cure for all that which ails: his suede satchel.

By the waning candlelight glow, he roamed the hallway, pacing back and forth. The cold hardwood, pressed flat against his bare feet, grounded him. He stopped in front of the first bedroom door and opened it. Morgan lay fast asleep, with his driver on the floor at the foot of the bed. Immersed in blankets, his father-in-law snored with such ruckus that Potter had no idea how the driver slept through it. He closed the door before the noise could wake the young'uns. They, too, he found fast asleep, adorably sharing a bed in the last room across the hallway as he peeked in the cracked door. *This is all new for them as well.* He hoped they slept tightly. Things were sure to be different, now that they'd taken the ultimate detour from Easy Street. The young were resilient, though. And, if nothing else, at least they had each other.

As he pulled the door shut, a white ruffled sleeve swayed by the edge of the doorjamb. Pushing it back before it caught, he stopped, immediately recognizing the fabric as a dress—*the* dress, to be exact. One he hadn't seen since his wedding night. He wondered why, out of all the gorgeous styles, this was the one Clara chose: Bessie's sprigged lace white satin dress, imported from England by Morgan. They'd exchanged nuptials at home, next to Cherry Creek, on a breezy August evening under the old oak. Her current resting place.

He brushed the silky material over his palm.

Oh, his Bessie. A charmed goddess if he ever saw one. She differed from the high-born ladies he'd grown up around in New England and had come to expect from reading Shakespeare as a young man. Though, if he had to choose a comparison, her razor-sharp wit most reminded him of Portia from *The Merchant of Venice*. As an iconoclast frustrated with the high walls of societal gender limitations, Bessie had disavowed affluence and married a criminal. Still, sometimes, he couldn't help but wonder whether mere defiance formed the foundation of their union.

Potter lit a dusty glass lantern and stepped onto the porch. He removed a suede pouch from his inside coat pocket and pulled out a gunpowder paper cartridge, something he possessed in abundance. Fine Colorado tobacco filled the other half of the suede pouch, minced and ready to use. He dug through it for the miniature brown glass vial lying at the bottom, its liquid contents sealed with a dropper. He sprinkled some shake into the paper cartridge.

Just a few drops.

He moistened the shake with the opium before rolling it tight between his fingertips, licking the seal. With the tip of his thumbnail, he struck a match; the sulfur sizzled, awakening the amber flame which ignited the paper cone tip. Potter pulled the sweet smoke deep into his lungs, then exhaled into the void.

A guilty pleasure. *Like walking on air.*

By the end of the quirley cigarette, Potter grew plenty relaxed. Comfortably numb, as they say. Smoking significantly elevated his sense of wellbeing, perhaps even to the point of happiness. The twilight sky yawned open around him, incredibly clear. He stepped off the porch to admire the mostly barren view, which stretched to the far end of the cosmos. The waning full moon descended methodically over the valley. Myriad stars lighted the vast New Mexican skies; every so often, he'd catch one that seemed to flicker. The view reminded him much of the spectacular display of fireflies back in the Denver woodlands, drifting in the windfall. The ones whose brilliant appearance helped lead him out and away from temptation.

He shook his head at himself. He must be suffering some residual effect from the shit he just smoked.

Dawn would arrive in an hour, or so Potter figured. Futile to sleep at this point. He rolled another quirley and camped himself in Bessie's rocker, now situated on the porch, enjoying the satisfying chill in the night air. Soon, the tobacco took root, evening him out. Potter, who had fallen asleep fully dressed, sat quite comfortably, gently rocking in the creaking chair and enjoying the tranquility of his new rural life. His instinct suggested this placid state wouldn't last long, however. Even in the middle of nowhere, you were never alone. Not really.

And as sure as the dawn, Potter watched as someone stumbled onto his property from the woodlands. This person—a man, he presumed, though he couldn't quite tell yet—traipsed through the high grass, slightly crouched, arms wrapped around his body. And there was something else. Something peculiar he couldn't quite put his finger on until the stranger, headed toward him, got about halfway in. The man, yes, a man, he could now see, wore no shirt. In fact, he lacked any clothing at all, by the looks of him, though tough to tell for sure in this early, dim light.

Potter, in his euphoric state, considered the Winchester but decided against it. He couldn't seem to peel himself from the rocker, and, if his instincts were correct, he had nothing to worry about anyway. Sure enough, when the stranger broke through the vegetation, limping to the porch, he received quite a surprise from Potter, still sitting in the chair. The man, stark naked, shuddered but didn't speak, stopping short and raising his hands defensively. His wafer frame quivered in the brisk morning air. The look of shock on his filthy sallow face, barely visible behind long, curly blonde locks, suggested to Potter that this morning wasn't his first time here.

An awkward silence followed as Potter pinched the cherry from the quirley, wondering if he'd over indulged. He'd done so from time to time, and he usually suffered unfavorable outcomes as a result. He'd hoped not, but this encounter was just too goddamn strange. He considered the Winchester once again.

"Don't want no trouble, partner," the young man said, his Texan drawl heavy.

Potter returned a stoic glance. Blood comprised the majority of the filth on this man, mostly dried on his face and mouth. The side of his upper thigh bled too, punctured somehow. Yet the filth and blood strangely paled behind the man's striking blue gaze. Potter had never seen eyes quite like his. Rare, like Indicolite—a gemstone he'd been most fortunate to encounter in cave digging.

"This here your land, I reckon." The man's chin slightly pointed back toward it.

Potter nodded. The man's wounded appearance struck him as strange—not to mention his nude façade—although he refrained from inquiring. Didn't much care. Encountering something so unexpected, however, disquieted him.

"Well, just damn me to hell if I didn't see that comin." The man's mouth opened, flashing a beaming grin of perfect pearly whites.

Potter would be damned if these teeth weren't the best set of porcelain choppers he'd seen—the 1884 poster boy for dental hygiene. A smile like that didn't come cheaply.

He blinked. "Come again?"

"Been passin through here couple times a year. Stay a night or two, usually, then on my merry way." The man glanced around. "Just figured this place was abandoned, or at least forgotten about, out here. Secluded, at the edge of nowhere." He leaned in, extending his hand. "Name's Haynes. Julian D. Haynes, Esquire. Though I suppose I just go by Danny."

Lawyer money. Now it all made sense. Potter held back a groan. *Swell. A naked, injured lawyer on my land. Not a great start, partner.*

Without volunteering his name, Potter leaned forward, taking the man's hand. "Well, Danny, mind telling me what you're doing out here—*at the edge of nowhere*—stark naked, that is?"

"Couldn't say. Last I recall, had myself bout half a bottle of Renz's blackberry brandy, then woke up in a field without my clothes. Wouldn't ya just know it? I, uh... tend to black out. Quite frequently, actually." Danny's smile diminished; he brushed greasy yellow locks away from his face, cautiously observing Potter in the rocker. "Could I, uh, borrow a pair of trousers, mister—maybe trouble you for a ride to town?"

"Guess you're in luck." Once this man found his trousers, Potter figured, perhaps he'd return with a bit of a reward for his kind service. "I'm headed out shortly. Ain't headed to town, but I'll take you as far as the trail leads."

Potter fetched the strange, injured man a pair of old trousers and kept his word, bringing Danny to the small clearing, leaving him by the trail which led to town.

CHAPTER 6

Potter paused on the covered porch of the two-and-a-half story Greek Revival-style Victorian, then knocked.

With a surprised but delighted smile, Coffey answered the door. "Well, if it ain't Mr. Bill Potter." In a black blazer, slacks, and bowtie, he appeared almost unrecognizably sharp and clean shaved—likely tending to his morning chauffeur duties.

Potter, wondering if the man of the house foot the bill for his grooming or if Coffey did it himself, grinned. "Hiya, Coffey. You clean up real nice."

"Almost didn't recognize ya there in that fancy get up," Coffey teased. "How goes it?"

"Hell, I might've said the same." Potter took off his hat. Beneath his long, shabby coat stood a raffish man in a charcoal blazer, woolen waistcoat, and pair of matching slacks. He'd break out the suit maybe twice a year for a wedding, holiday, or, more commonly, funeral, though he hadn't worn the outfit in two years. "Was hoping now might be a fine time to meet with Mr. Chisum."

Coffey waved a hand at the building around him. "Like I says, I do many an odd job for the boss round here. Though, this mornin, it'd be a more standard job. Makin coffee, layin out the boss's suit, whippin up a mean breakfast for the boys, ya know"—Coffey nodded to the side—"out at the ranch, yonder."

Potter glanced over the side of the porch to a long, single level ranch. Several cowboys, mainly of Mexican descent, walked the long porch, going about their business. The house and ranch sat nestled in a vast and impressive estate, seemingly isolated from civilization. A large cow-shed stood behind, filled with livestock wandering through open doors. Rectangular oak fencing flanked the cowshed and contained a few meandering horses. Much of the grass around the immediate property had eroded away to a fine clay, which seem to just sit in the air and leave the yard dusty. But beyond that—green pastures for days.

Coffey took a step back, gesturing behind him. "Won't ya come in?"

Potter nodded, following him inside and down a narrow hallway to the opposite end of the house, into a wide parlor room. A salt-and-pepper haired gentleman sat behind a walnut desk in the back center of the space, quill in hand, jotting on paper. The sun shone through a large window behind, slightly silhouetting the gentleman and making him difficult to see. The pervasive scratch of the quill hung heavy in the air as they stood awkwardly, waiting in near silence.

Potter glanced around the impressive room, or office, rather. A leather couch with two matching armchairs, the centerpieces, sat squarely around a rectangular coffee table over a red Oriental rug. A wide credenza accented the paisley wall to the left side of the man's desk, the top holding crystalware. The glasses and long neck decanters filled with caramel colored liquid snared Potter's eye. Alcohol, most like. The right side of the office housed a stone fireplace with a rectangular mirror above the mantle, conveniently situated between two entranceways leading to an adjacent room. The left side showcased a towering library of shelved hardcover works next to a seven-foot-high grandfather clock. A grand piano over a smaller Oriental rug gleamed a high shine in the front right corner, the bench pushed out and awaiting its meister. *Oh, it's been years.*

Finally, the man put his quill down and stood, revealing his brown pinstriped three piece. He sauntered over to the credenza and pulled the glass bulb off the decanter with an audible *clink*. With his middle fingers and thumb, he plucked two short glasses from a shelf above.

"Come, have a seat." The man's voice reverberated in the space, deep and proper.

Potter walked over, meeting him in front of the coffee table before glancing back to Coffey. He flashed a seasoned, you're-in-good-hands smile and exited, closing the door behind him.

Potter dwarfed Chisum in size, but that hardly surprised him; he stood six-foot-four and generally towered over most people. The stocky man made up for any lack in height with an excess of girth, however. He possessed broad shoulders, and his petticoat looked like it needed to be let out a few inches, the top two buttons clinging to his belly for dear mercy. Well fed, by Potter's estimate.

The men sat, with Chisum on the couch. Next to him, nestled against the corner armrest, lay a large, fluffy white cat. Potter wondered how he'd only just noticed the feline.

"Oh, that's just Sandy. Don't mind her. Her central preoccupation is sleepin, killin vermin, and harassin my ranchers." Chisum chuckled and poured a drink into one glass. "Would you like one?"

"Uhhh." Potter looked over at the grandfather clock to the left of the desk: seven a.m. But he didn't want to seem rude. "Please."

"The name's Chisum. But you already know that." He sat and pulled a stogie from his inner right blazer pocket, biting the tip and spitting it into a crystal ashtray. Then he struck two matches, lighting the end. "And you are William Potter."

Tobacco smoke permeated above, filling Potter's nostrils.

He inhaled the sweet scent. "Bill, yes."

Silence.

"From Denver," Potter added.

"Bill Potter. From Denver." Chisum stared at Potter through a thin haze of smoke.

"Yes, sir." Potter slowly turned the rocks glass, swirling the reddish-brown liquid in his palm.

"Coffey mentioned you helped him out yesterday," Chisum drawled. "Just wanted to begin by thankin you. As you must have already gathered, he is an indispensable part of my organization. Would have been a painful blow to hear of him passin. Especially at the hands of *those animals*." He puffed the cigar. "And for that, I am grateful and in your debt."

Potter didn't speak. Just nodded, sipped his drink. The sweet burn of brandy coated his throat.

"I wasn't expectin you so soon, however."

"I once read, 'tardiness can often rob us of opportunity and can prevent the dispatching of our forces,' so to speak."

Chisum smiled. "Machiavelli. And I agree. Time waits for no man. A smart man knows to strike that horseshoe iron while it's still hot."

Sandy woke, likely irritated by the cigar smoke, and jumped down, though not before elongating in a slow, deep stretch with a twitch and chasmic yawn.

"Noticed the book on your shelf there. Used to own a copy myself." Potter rarely quoted philosophy—never, actually—but he felt the need to distinguish himself from "those animals." And first impressions were essential.

"Gotta bunch there, as you can see. Love to read. Lord knows I don't get a lot of time to do so these days. Shakespeare's my favorite. Don't spose you're too familiar?"

"I'm quite partial to Hamlet."

Chisum offered a crooked smile. "Well, mister, I can assure you, you won't find anythin *rotten* here."

Potter, though amused by the reference, didn't return the grin.

"I was the county clerk in Lamar County, Texas, for a short time, mind, before buildin this empire you see before you. A menial job, but not without its benefits. Early on, I learned you could buy steer at six dollars a head, and if you had an open range to graze, you were years ahead of any viable competition. Hell, the only expense was buildin a headquarters for operations. And drovers—dirt cheap labor." Chisum leisurely sat back against the couch, splayed one arm along the top, and crossed his legs. With the cigar pinched between his teeth, he massaged his thick mustache. "What kind of work did you do in Denver?"

"Worked in the silver mines for a bit."

"Mm-hmm. Tough business up there these days. Egregious business, at that." Chisum pulled on the cigar. "Mineral minin is not what it used to be. Especially silver. Heh. Five years ago, it wasn't worth the dog shit on the bottom of my heel. Even today, gold is drivin out whatever value is left, am I right?"

Potter tipped his head in a slow nod.

"The world's in a great depression, my new friend, despite the recent *turnaround* of things. Inflation is through the roof, banks, overextended with investments in the failin railway business, are goin bankrupt. Government fraud on top of all that. Country-wide panic as people pull out all their earnins. Only safe place to keep your money is buried away in your basement floor." With a sardonic grin, Chisum ashed the cigar and wiped the charred remnants along the ashtray's edge.

"I would agree, sir."

"Please, call me John." He sipped the caramel-colored liquor and cleared his throat. "Where were you before Denver?"

"I'm from back east."

"Bill Potter, from back east... I hear you're on the old Bennett property. I knew John Bennett. Strange man. I know his brother, Morgan, too. Prominent business man. Could never have met two different men cut from the same cloth."

Potter nodded, sipped his drink. The alcohol—likely brandy, from the taste—lit up all his dormant nerves.

"What brings you to the middle of nowhere, Potter?"

"Looking for a fresh start, is all."

"No one intentionally arrives in Missouri Plaza"—which Chisum pronounced *Mi-zzer-ah Plaza*—"and stays, Potter. Lincoln, maybe. Santa Fe, I'd understand. This place ain't even on a map. You familiar with the Seventh Day Adventist Church?"

Before Potter could shake his head, Chisum continued.

"They're an interestin bunch. An odd group of Protestants *preachin* bout the Second Coming, and the biblical *Day of Atonement,* an all that, which apparently was supposed to happen forty years ago and obviously didn't. They don't cuss, don't eat red meat, and if you can believe it, don't *drink*. As I'm sure you've realized after stoppin into town, we're a dry county." Chisum smiled and raised his glass. "I'll drink to that."

Potter followed suit, taking another sip.

"I'm told they migrated here, oh, ten years ago or so from Missouri. Built a few storefronts in town. The church, obviously, though back then it was bout the size out of an outhouse. Used to practice their strange *religion* underground, probably to avoid persecution—who the hell knows what they were doing down there. Then one by one they just..." Chisum clapped his hands. "*Poof!* Vanished. They're a migratory bunch, so who knows?

"Don't know if you've been acquainted with the postmaster yet; Vance Smith's his name. His father's a big shot lawyer upstate. The two of them and his friend—a Chinaman, Aaron Wilburn, who runs the mill—showed up here bout five years back, same time the Protestants sort of *took off*. They began buildin this town up, expanded the church and such. Though it hasn't been without its problems, of course."

"Problems?"

"We've had riffraff come through over the years, and we've had to deal with them. Bandits, cattle thieves and the like, which is somethin we'll discuss. Armed robbers. Our pretty little grocer's been held up. Miller's as well. Not often, but it does happen. Likely why Protestants began the dry town, and why we've sustained it." Chisum held up his glass. "No booze, no violent crimes. That's mainly it. I understand you have two young'uns?"

Potter nodded. "My son Isaac, and my youngest, Clara."

"Well, I don't believe it's much cause for concern, but I should at least mention a few kids seemed to have gone missing over the years."

He narrowed his eyes. "Missing... how?"

"No one knows. The marshal, Dave Mathers, investigated it, but didn't come up with much. Figured maybe they'd either run off or drowned in the Pecos. It does happen, unfortunately. Parents don't seem to pursue it beyond that, and sadly end up packin and leavin. Likely afraid of being discovered by someone they don't want to. This town is a bit of a cultural melting pot, if you will. A peculiar group of individuals you'll undoubtedly meet, though I honestly wouldn't be surprised to learn they all had fabricated names. How anyone is drawn here, well, your guess is as good as mine."

Potter shrugged. *Maybe they all had the map.*

Chisum glanced out the side window next to the liquor credenza. "It's got its benefits, too. I employ, at this ranch alone, twenty or so men at any given time, and at any given time, there's roughly five to ten that stay here at the South Spring Ranch. Some Mexican, mostly all just drifters, passing through."

Potter smirked. He sure related to that.

"My men, you can probably guess, come from colorful backgrounds. Found a safe haven here, I spose much like the residents who drifted into Missouri Plaza. I don't ask questions, and they don't tell me no lies. They're good workers, my men, and with two hundred miles of herdin up and down the Pecos to the South Spring River here on my land, they're free of worry. And, to be honest, I prefer them to your average John Joe passerby. They're not bad people, just mostly dealt a shit hand. I can only presume you have an idea of whom I speak. No... no, the *real* monsters, they exist elsewhere."

"And where's that?"

"You remember the Union Pacific Railway scandal?"

Potter shook his head.

"Just a group of debauched men tryin to attain what, I can only imagine, they'd consider the *American Dream*. What lengths they'd go to achieve it, too. Not quite the desperate men *you* might've seen: faces wrapped in bandanas, stickin up a stagecoach or robbin banks. No. These licentious men, they wear suits. They're in every capital in every state. They sit in offices, creatin policy." Chisum sighed. "You probably wouldn't believe it by lookin at me, but I've dealt with rival gangs, gunslingers, and the like in the cattle wars down here. Dirty business, it can be. But by God, the type of money stolen by the common thief pales to the tens of millions profited by this railway scheme and the politicians involved—congressmen, senators, even President Grant. Hell, he probably used the money in his reelection campaign."

"Huh. That just may be the wildest thing I ever heard."

"Ain't it? Profitin mainly from the exorbitant construction costs. One of these men, the president or vice president of the Union Pacific, I can't recall which—Passerini, was his name—was an Italian businessman from New York City. He and his partner also owned a fake bank purchased from an old Pennsylvania reserve, which the railway *contracted,* so to speak, with the government for—*listen to this*—one-hundred million dollars to fund the project. Then this bank sold these government men, who they also bribed, astronomical stock at astronomically low costs, *not market value*, from its fraudulent profits. The government men then sold the stock off to investors. What it really came down to was just simple accountin and billin fraud."

"Incredible."

"It's somethin, ain't it? Another reason I work for myself. At least *these* animals I can trust, and they sure have brought quite a profit."

"Cattle business seems quite lucrative."

"Twenty years ago, I wouldn't have agreed more. The ranchers all fought in the war, save for me; I supplied Confederate soldiers with steer, and at top dollar, mind you. Comin out of the war, the stray cattle had multiplied five-fold with no one to pick up the reins in the economically crippled South."

Chisum took a drink. "I've seen severe drought the last couple of years, which is concernin. Lost a few hundred steers. The open range will soon have an expiration, I fear. Last year I barbed much of my land to keep cattle from wanderin away from the river, what with labor dwindlin. Cowboys are hangin up their chaps and runnin off to the gold mines to *get rich*. Others are enterin labor unions with the equivocal promise of security and fewer workin man hours. Mechanization steals the jobs of trade craftsmen in factories. Hell, not two months ago, a German feller I met in a Fort Worth saloon on business told me of a carriage back home driven by engines, if you can believe that. The goddamn horse may be obsolete come turn of the century." Chisum snickered. "The world is quickly changin, Potter. Not much room left in it for men like you and me. I guess time just makes fools of us all."

That much, Potter believed. He gave the man an appraising look. *John Chisum... certainly not what I'd expected.* In his experience, all businessmen were the same: pompous, monopolists, robber barons. Chisum didn't appear any different in those regards, reminding him a bit of his father-in-law. The man surely loved to hear himself speak. Though Chisum, at his core, also seemed inherently different. A working man, one who built something from nothing. But that didn't come without a price. He had a feeling Chisum had no problem getting his hands dirty, and he respected that.

"Other than all that," Chisum continued, "I lose ten to twenty steers a year due to poachers. Disease. Wild animals. Hell, late last night, the boys found one torn asunder out in the pasture. Too dark to see the assailant precisely, but they fired at some giant sumbitchin bear or somethin attackin it. Disappeared in the dark."

Chisum placed his drink on the table, leaning forward in his seat. "But I do digress... you seem a very smart individual, Potter. Whatever brought you from those silver mines and down to here, *nowhere*, I haven't the slightest, nor do I give a good goddamn. With that said, whatever you're runnin from, do me the favor: don't bring it my way."

Potter gave a slight nod and took another drink.

Chisum leaned back again. "Coffey says you were once a rancher?"

"I have experience. Been some time, but I'm no slouch. Pick things up real fast. I can show you, if you need."

A hearty chortle rose from within Chisum, the cigar firm between his teeth. "I'm sure you'll do just fine. Be here at sunrise tomorrow."

Potter threw back his drink. "You referred to this as the South Springs Ranch. Coffey calls it the Jinglebob Ranch. Why's that?"

Chisum smiled as both men stood. "I can assure you—you'll see."

Chapter 7

At sunup, Clara woke next to her brother, out cold and dead to the world. She considered waking him, then hesitated, worried he'd be grouchy and annoyed. She didn't need that this morning. Instead, she crawled over Isaac's snoring corpse and checked the two bedrooms, which turned up empty, though a savory aroma tantalized her nostrils.

She ran downstairs to find Grandpa cooking up breakfast on the stovetop. His driver, a similarly ancient man in a black suit, sat at a rectangular table in the dining room, reading a newspaper and sipping coffee.

She beamed. "Grandpa! You're still here!?"

"Why good morning, Clarissa, my darling." Scrambled eggs sizzled in tallow as he whisked them around with a wooden spoon, the venison frying up on the cast iron pan behind. "Sleep well, did we?"

"Okay, I guess, but not really."

New *old* bed, new *old* house, some sort of unperceived anxiety she didn't quite understand. She couldn't fathom living in a place with *no goddamn plumbing,* as Pa so succinctly put it. Things would be different now. Harder. She thought of Ma. Her absence struck her oddly, in a way she hadn't endured in several months. She thought she'd finally gained the strength to move on, although two years sometimes felt like yesterday. But in an unfamiliar house, with no memories beyond those of yesterday, Ma felt truly gone. And Clara, more than ever, needed her.

Faith over fear... that's what Pa says.

She slid gently onto the bench, her back against the table, facing Grandpa.

"I know. First time away from home," Grandpa said. "Strange surroundings can sometimes do that. Not to worry, you'll get used to the place soon enough. I can assure you of that. And I have something that may help with the stress of new home jitters."

"Where's Pa?"

"I believe he has gone off to meet a potential employer. Should be home soon, I presume."

Isaac, pounding down the steps, appeared moments later, rubbing sleepy eyes. His wild hair twisted to one side where he'd slept, comatose. "That smells incredible, Grandpa."

"That it does, Isaac. That it does, indeed!" Grandpa's tan face bunched in wrinkles; his white beard curved with an inviting grin. "Why don't you go fetch us a pail of water while I'm finishing up here."

"Uhh, okay. Isaac trailed off with an enormous yawn, then glanced around in confusion. "Where's the well at?"

"There isn't one, I am sorry to say." Grandpa's grin withered slightly as he focused on flipping sizzling venison chops. "You'll have to head on down to the river and fill up."

Isaac blinked. "Really?"

"Inconvenient, I know. My brother lived the last years of his life here, *off the reservation*, so to speak. No water closet or open pluming."

Isaac, mouth ajar, just stared at his sister. She shrugged.

After breakfast, Grandpa took Clara, still in her nightgown, alongside the house.

"Close your eyes, darling," he instructed her. "And no peeking!"

She stood in brisk anticipation, hands over her eyes. A quick peek through finger slits revealed that Grandpa remained gone, likely in the small barn in the back of the house. Shivers from the morning air whisked up her back.

After an eternity, a rustling preceded multiple footfalls in her direction, announcing Grandpa's return. She snapped her eyes shut. When she finally opened them again, she gaped, heart soaring.

Grandpa stood in front of her with a black stallion!

He grinned at her. "His name is Blanco, Clarissa."

"He's so beautiful!"

"He was your great uncle's horse. Was staying at my Arizona ranch for a while, and finally I have the pleasure of bringing him back to his home. Now, he's all yours." Grandpa patted Blanco's silky mane, his forehead wrinkled over white, bushy brows. "You be careful with this one. He's quite the escape artist. Gotta knack for untying his straps. You think you can take care of him?"

With a resounding "YES," Clara gave her grandpa a great big hug. "My *own* black beauty! You said his name is…"

"Blanco. It's a Spanish word. Means *white*."

She glanced up curiously at Grandpa. "But he's…"

"Yup, I know. My brother was an interesting man. Your guess is as good as mine."

"I never knew him," she said with a twinge of remorse. A vision of Ma flashed to the forefront of her mind.

"No. People regarded him as unusual. Bizarre." Her grandfather stiffened. "He was *reserved*. Preferred to keep to himself mostly, especially in his later years, after the Rebellion War. Yet, his ability to verbally express his eccentricities was quite profound." He smiled gently, as if recalling a particular memory. "Deep down, he was a gentle soul. I think you would've liked him."

Clara, not quite understanding what her grandpa meant, glanced down at her feet. "He died, right?"

"He did."

She hesitated. "How, Grandpa?"

Now it was his turn to pause. "Eh… it was of his own accord."

"Why?"

"Oh, I don't know. He was not a well man, I presume." He gave Blanco a pensive glance, continuing to stroke his mane.

Blanco neighed.

"No, why do we die?"

"I'm afraid I don't have a good answer for that. It's just a part of living, I guess. Everyone's time is different."

The Pecos suddenly interjected with a gurgle. Clara glanced over at the trickle of the garrulous river, having unwittingly disregarded its presence. She shuddered, staring somberly at the water.

"Why did it have to be *their* time, Grandpa? Why wasn't it mine?"

"Oh darling, you mustn't think in such dour terms. What happened was nothing more than an unfortunate event beyond anyone's control. An act of Go—uh, a reckless force of nature."

The crawl of flowing water eclipsed the other sounds of the living, breathing countryside. Clara felt it amplify around her, the property cordoned off by the unyielding "reckless force of nature."

"Are they in heaven? Is that where we go? Pa says so."

"Many people believe that, yes. Others believe we come back again, but as other people. Some say the end is just that. The End. That's why you, Clarissa, have to make the most of each given day you have here in this world. Live yourself a good and decent life. Never can tell what's waiting on the other side."

"Where do *you* spose Mama and Grandma are?"

"They're watching over you, sweetheart. Wherever they are. I believe there's a force out there, perhaps some higher state of consciousness guiding us all. And *that's* why you're here."

A brief smile touched the corners of her mouth. She didn't quite understand his words, nor did she know if she felt any better, but she trusted Grandpa knew what he was talking about.

The patter of trotting hooves nearing suppressed the chatty river, drawing Clara's attention to the road.

She bounced up and down. "Pa's home!"

He dismounted the horse in front of the house. Faint clucking sounded somewhere, but Clara ignored the sound, too consumed by charging up to him.

"Look, Pa," she yelled. "Grandpa gave me my own horse!"

He scooped her up in his arms. "That was very kind of him, now, wasn't it?"

Clara nodded, trying to glance over his shoulder at the faint noise.

"Why don't you bring your new friend into the barn, hon," he said, putting her down.

"Come on, Blanco!" Blanco neighed as she took him by the reins, leading him away, though she swore she could hear a chicken. Listening, she could also just about hear Pa and Grandpa's exchange. She stopped near the barn, looking back.

A canvas sack, draped over Bessie's mare, twitched and clucked. Clara's eyes lit up.

Grandpa looked on over, then back to Pa. "My son-in-law. A true *bird of passage.*" A smirk swept his face.

"Thought you'd be on your way by now."

"Leaving now, as a matter of fact." Grandpa checked his pocket watch.

"Buying the young'uns love and affection, I see."

"I don't want them to forget who they can turn to, if need be. You take care of my grandchildren, you hear? And I'll be expecting those letters in about two to three weeks."

"Ya'll have a safe trip home now," Pa said, then entered the side kitchen door of the house.

Clara walked into the barn, frowning. Since the death of Ma and Grandma, Pa and Grandpa were always fighting—and even prior to those sad days, she'd sensed tension between them. Pa hated when she and Isaac argued, but Grandpa was family too. One of the few loved ones she had left. Why didn't he and Pa try to get along? She didn't understand the conflict of their grownup world, but, looking around the unfamiliar barn, she suddenly realized such fighting came with a terrible price.

Exile.

Although she knew Grandpa would pass through on his way back to Tucson come fall, eons away, her eyes welled with the sudden realization she may never see him again. Natural disasters, shootouts... the dangers lurking in her once safe world became increasingly apparent. She ran from the barn to where he stood by his stagecoach and threw her small arms around him.

"Promise you'll return." She peered up, glassy-eyed.

"Now, now, darling." He bent down to her level. "You've nothing to worry about. I'll write you and Isaac as I receive your letters. Okay?"

She nodded.

"If there's an urgent need, the Western Union in town can reach me much sooner, but I believe you're going to be just fine. See you in a few short months." He kissed her on the cheek and stepped into the stagecoach, his driver closing the door behind.

She watched it vanish into the woodlands, her skin prickling at the thought of losing everyone she ever cared for.

2

The following morning, the young'uns woke shortly after their pa set out for the Jinglebob Ranch. He'd left a cauldron hanging in the kitchen's beehive brick oven fireplace with leftover game from the evening before, stewing over a small, smoldering fire. A loaf of potato bread sat warming in the brick cubby alongside it. Basically, they had everything they'd need until his return. They figured he must've been up *real* early. He'd explicitly instructed them the night before to stay inside, only leaving to use the outhouse and gather water, and he'd tasked Isaac to keep the rifle on him at all times, be vigilant of the property, and, above all else, let no one in. The charge made her brother nervous, never having fired a gun before.

Do not leave this house, Pa had said.

Well, Clara figured, there was plenty to explore *inside.*

Having slept slightly better than the previous evening, she skipped down the steps, habitually looking to begin daily chores so she could get on with playing. But other than helping prepare breakfast with Isaac, she had utterly no idea what to do in this foreign space. No duster, broom, or mop and bucket. No carpet to sweep with the Bissell. No livestock needing attending, with her ma's mare gone with Pa, save for Blanco and that *other* horse with no name Pa brought home last week. Not exactly a tabula rasa—still plenty to do—but perhaps best left for another day. For both siblings, perfectly ignorant of their whereabouts in this uncharted world as well as in this unknown dwelling, exploration came first and foremost. At the very least, it would help occupy her dwelling mind of this unwavering loneliness, if only for a short time.

The saltbox's interior had an unconventional layout, especially compared to their old colonial—something they'd already heard Pa comment about. *A strange house, commensurate with a strange man.* Whatever that meant. Instead of a massive central chimney, accessible from all living quarters and accentuating this style home, a small hearth and a set of winder stairs sat in the center of the building, leading to the second floor. To the left of the ascending stairs lay a door to the basement, though such stairs usually descended from a back corner. Her father had chuckled wryly when he pointed out the lack of chimney space. *Southern living* must *require little heat!*

The stairs and fireplace were accessible from the massive living room, which comprised the front half of the house and stood in complete disarray. Great Uncle Bennett's furniture rested throughout, untouched for some time and covered in white sheets. Clara discerned the silhouettes of a long couch, tufted parlor chairs, wooden chairs, and a coffee table. Amongst the sheeted items, the Potters' family affects, partially unpacked and scattered about, trailed into the "dining room." The long, narrow space connected the living room to the kitchen like an afterthought; only a long table and six chairs furnished the small room.

Opposite the dining room—across the house—lived a bijou parlor, Bennett's study. Quaint. The only kept space in the Salt Box, perhaps where Great Uncle Bennett's precious time had been spent. Not much to see: a small desk with a two partially melted candles on either side, a clean ashtray, and a lonely pen and inkwell. Behind sat a comfy velvet armchair draped with a folded quilt alongside a bookshelf with a few frayed hardcovers, mostly reference. The earthy scent of must tickled Clara's nostrils.

In the back, slightly offset from the main housing quarters, stood the open galley kitchen with its beehive brick oven built into the central wall. A casual and unimpressive long table with bench seats composed a small breakfast area. Not quite cozy, though she figured they'd cloth it soon enough. And, oddly hidden behind the kitchen, sat the water closet. One with no water. A cast iron tub. And a decorative toilet.

Decorative. Toilet.

?

A long hallway connected the house from the mostly useless *faux* bathroom, through the kitchen, and down to the living room. Evidently, Uncle Bennett, a *Great Minimalist* according to Pa, lived his remaining days in practical obscurity.

The mysterious, six-foot tall object in the living room fascinated Clara most, positioned kitty corner between the front right and side windows. She gawked up at the towering white sheet, picturing a grandiose bookcase filled with enlightening tomes she'd spend her days in Missouri sinking her teeth into... oh, if only. But unlikely. Maybe the cloth hid a wardrobe filled with lavish dresses like Ma's, dresses she'd long to grow into. A bit too narrow, but a girl could dream. She pulled the sheet, and a smile touched the corners of her mouth.

A great grandfather clock.

Not quite what she'd hoped, but she loved it just the same, staring up at its large, tranquil face. A pretty auburn, likely hand-crafted from rich mahogany, much like their furniture back in Denver. She liked that word: *mahogany*. The thin hands, undisturbed, rested peacefully at four thirty-five. Time standing still. She would not have this. As Pa said, time *always* prevails. A small key extended from the door lock, and with a gentle twist, she opened the glass door with a click. At the bottom, she found a long brass key propped against the back wall. Standing on the coffee table, she carefully slid it into each of the three holes in the elegant, roman-numeral dial and cranked. The cogs behind the face sprung to life, and with a *clink*, the minute hand struck four thirty-six.

Clara did not know the actual time, but that didn't matter. She had oodles.

She attempted to unpack. The playbill for Foggerty's Fairy, found atop the items in the first crate, saddened her. She'd held on to it as a precious reminder of the last time she'd seen her ma and grandma alive; and now it just served as a wistful trinket of the life she'd left behind.

That fateful night still plagued her. Her face flushed with overwhelming discomfort when the theater's patrons turned to witness the horrific display of Mama's outburst and Grandma's disappointed eyes at her refusal to be quiet and attentive during the lackluster performance. She could have died from embarrassment. Oh, she'll teach them. When the curtain dropped, she fled for the exit, only to be met by that rain falling in sheets, transforming the road into a quagmire. She stopped on the porch as Mama and Grandma rushed ahead, boarding the stagecoach, begging her to follow. Despite Mama's pleas, she stubbornly refused.

The gas-powered streetlamps suddenly extinguished. Just darkness. Then, moments later, it happened. Quickly. Like a tidal wave, the flood torrents barreled in. Mama and Grandma vanished. Instantly. Before she could scream, a man yanked her inside, the splintering wood and groaning sounds of the deck's collapse echoing in her ears just as the structure gave way.

Clara dropped the playbill. She'd unpack another day.

3

A quarter inch of dust had adorned all surfaces upon their entry two days earlier, and with the utilization of the kitchen and bedroom spaces aside, most rooms remained buried in the stuff. Clara and Isaac considered the option of dusting, cleaning, and unpacking, which Pa would have expected, but they just didn't have the proper tools. Pa had yet to pick them up at Reynolds's. Now, with him busy at the ranch, they would likely need to wait some time for cleaning supplies. Not to mention the gorgeous bluebird day beckoning from outside. Even if they *could* clean, Clara figured, surely an afternoon of sunshine, games, and outdoor exploration would be the most efficient use of their time. If nothing else, Big Brother's close company would be a source of comfort and reassurance.

She and Isaac shuffled through their standard repertoire of charades, checkers, hide 'n seek, and cat's cradle—an easy improvisation, using string from packing boxes. The charades took on a fresh perspective with the new surroundings, a guessing game of acting out different objects in each room. The excitement waned quickly, though, as most items already belonged to them, and Isaac had reached mastery status. The checkers, a gift to Isaac from Grandpa on his sixth birthday—now missing pieces, replaced over time with torn doll parts and shiny yard stones—grew competitive, as Clara excelled at puzzles increasingly with age. They sat, Indian style, on the porch floor, the warm sun shining down upon them. Isaac, annoyed at losing several games in a row, stood up, plopped down in the rocking chair, and folded his arms, pouting. Clara, always a good sport, offered conciliation in the form of hide and seek, which he obliged on the condition that he hide first.

Clara immediately found him in the small loft inside the barn, the neighing Blanco giving him away. She gave the stallion a pat. *Clever horses!* She resolved to be less predictable than her brother. Indeed, she knew exactly where she wanted to hide: the basement. The space remained some of the only undiscovered territory thus far, though she figured she'd find a suitable spot within the allotted ten seconds.

The basement, dark and dingy, offered an array of possibilities as Clara crossed the frigid threshold. She barreled down the winding stairs and jumped from the last step to the dirt floor, a plume of dust rising and causing her to sneeze. Goose pimples crawled her skin, which she tried rubbing away, inducing more chills. Only sparse lighting filtered through the window, hindering her ability to see, but she found the space much like the living room: white sheets veiling bulky objects, haphazardly placed.

From somewhere upstairs, a loud "ready or not, here I come!" resonated down. Clara panicked. She ran from object to object, lifting the sheets and unveiling furniture piece by piece, searching for a proper hiding place. She found armoires, dressers, buffet hutches, even a tack piano, all left in disrepair—but nothing that fit her needs. Finally, just as she heard footfalls on the steps, she revealed the perfect spot: an oak sideboard buffet along the wall. She crawled into one of three cabinets, pulling the sheet back over her but leaving the door ajar.

"I know you're down here!" Isaac, starting from the opposite end of the basement, began pulling sheets away from each object. He coughed as ancient dust billowed.

Clara could just about make him out through the chiffon fabric. She smiled as he neared, getting ready. Just as he turned to the sideboard, Clara exploded from the cabinet.

"AH-HA," she shrieked, arms flared high. The sheet pulled from the buffet, wrapping her into a ghostly figure.

"AHHH!" Isaac stumbled back, arms raised defensively.

Clara giggled, pointing at her terrified, fuming brother.

"Damn you, Clarissa, you goddamming scared me!" He balled his fists by his side. "I'm gonna *kill* you!"

Clara, without hesitation, made a blind beeline for the stairs, Isaac two steps behind. She pulled off the sheet, but as she crossed the center of the basement, her foot snagged on a small object protruding from the ground, sending her tumbling down with a shrill scream.

"Ha-ha, that's what you get!" Isaac stood over her, taking the last laugh.

"Shut up." Clara, with scraped knees and a dirty dress, glowered at Isaac, pouting as she picked herself up and kicked the dumb object that tripped her.

It moved ever so slightly. *Huh.* With the toe of her shoe, she gave it a few more jabs.

"What is it?" Isaac nudged the thing with his toe, revealing a gray material. "Metal?"

The two exchanged curious glances. Without a moment to spare, they fell to their knees, digging erratically with eager fingers. What had begun as a day of the mundane chores and games had just become the most exciting event of the year. Pulling back the cold earth revealed a small chain link. More links lay attached, brown with oxidization, which Isaac pulled from the thick ground until taut.

"What do you spose it's attached to," Clara asked, brushing her hand over the cold steel.

"Dunno," Isaac whispered, then looked at his sister. "We should find out."

Pulling the chain didn't budge the other end from the ground, try as they might—and they did. Finally, Clara ran upstairs, returning with a couple of large metal spoons from an unpacked box of kitchen items.

"Absolutely brilliant," Isaac said, ruffling her hair.

The two dug down a few inches rather quickly, only to be hindered by an impenetrable mass. Clearing away some dirt, they discovered a flat object, likely wooden. The chain protruded from a narrow hook nailed down at the edge. How far the wood stretched, well, that was the imposing question.

Isaac knocked on the tightly cleared space, then looked to his sister with wide eyes. "Hollow."

The siblings dug and dug, filling pails and redistributing the contents to the backyard. While they worked, their imaginations ran wild with ideas of what may lie beneath. Clara hoped for treasure and riches; Isaac suspected an ancient catacomb. By the time they'd finished, they'd dug themselves a six-inch hole in the basement, clearing the edges of an eight-by-five space in the damp ground. Isaac and Clara alike marveled at their accomplishment, standing head to toe in filth. Finally, a game they'd agreed upon, both coming up victorious.

They'd unearthed a plywood doorway, damp and in the early stages of deterioration. It sat snuggly inside a wooden two-by-four frame.

The moment she'd diligently worked toward all afternoon had arrived. Clara bounced almost unperceivably in place. She needed to find out what lay inside, but part of her didn't want to know. Knowing meant a possible dark cloud blotting out a sunny day with Big Brother. Fear crept in; the opportunity for further disaffection loomed, unaware what secrets this new place held.

Isaac confidently yanked the chain, but the door proved quite heavy and awkward.

"Come give a hand!"

Clara hesitated, then grabbed hold of the chain, deciding to let faith guide her. Even with both siblings pulling together, the plywood only lifted an inch or two. They needed something to prop open the door. Clara ran over to the sideboard buffet where she had hidden, grabbing a piece of unused shelving lying at the base of the cabinet. She barely squeezed the wood under as Isaac pulled the chain, but once they got their fingers into the crack, they managed to slide the door open, albeit haphazardly and with some effort.

Cold air rose from the dark cavern, chilling Clara. The base, visible through the dark, lay about six feet or so down, by Isaac's estimate. Barely discernible objects sat below: the lids of several barrels and two massive, sturdy wooden crates. Someone had painted an image resembling a flag on top of one of the crates, obscured mostly by dust and difficult to recognize. She had never seen a flag like it before. Steps at the edge of the cavern led below, but Isaac jumped down instead.

Clara gasped. "Isaac, don't!"

Isaac landed, staggering, in a foot-high network of cobwebs, which he interrupted further with each step regaining his balance. "I'm fine, stay up there," he called, wiping away web lacing.

Clara watched as he walked around quickly, examining the box crates, giving a swift tug on the top of each. Nailed shut, to their dismay. Next, he tried lifting a barrel, leaking black dust from a hole in the side onto his shirt.

A door slammed upstairs. Clara and Isaac jumped, her brother dropping the barrel.

4

"Kids?" Potter, holding two dead rabbits by their hinds, placed his rifle on a wall rack next to the door and glanced around for his young'uns.

Moments later, they charged up the steps. "Pa! Pa! Pa!"

Isaac finally strung a sentence together. "Pa! We—we found something in the—the basement! You must come and look!"

Potter stared at his children. Something else to worry about, the last thing he needed. He had inspected the basement the first night and saw nothing concerning, save for maybe Clara discovering a piano. Now his imagination ran wild with what they could have found in John Bennett's secluded, domicile basement.

Three minutes later, he found himself standing, bewildered, above the gaping hole in the ground, ambivalent of how to proceed in handling the situation. In his experience, no one buried something without reason. Maybe they'd stumbled upon something dangerous. Then the rousing notion of treasure smoothed his furrowed brow. How could he be upset? After all, he *did* tell them *not* to leave the house. He stifled a smile, trying not to salivate at the fresh anticipation of what waited down there.

"Son, get me the lantern." Potter pushed the top board completely out of the way, then stepped down the rickety ladder and waited for Isaac to return with light. "And a hammer!"

Isaac appeared in the stairwell. "Which one, Pa?"

"Claw hammer. It's in one of the boxes."

Isaac returned and lowered the items into his father's hands. Potter waved the lantern over the flagged crate, gently brushing away dirt with his palm under the soft amber glow. A faded blue cross with thirteen stars revealed itself under the remaining smeared film, obscuring the equally faded red box which contained it.

Isaac bent over the hole, owl eyed and eager. "What is that, Pa?"

"That's a flag, Isaac... Confederate flag." Potter, inspecting the crate, turned to view the other items.

Isaac recoiled. He must've learned a bit about the Rebellion War in his Denver schooling, albeit briefly, but now he encountered the subject up close and personal for the first time. Potter saw the weight of the flag's meaning manifesting in his son with dread and incredulity.

Yup, your great uncle's a Rebel, kid. The irony wasn't completely lost on Potter. *If only you knew who your old man really is.*

Potter placed the lantern down on the powder keg, slid the curved edge of the hammer into the groove under the lid on each side, and pulled, loosening the restraints. Using the heel of his hand, he forced up the cover, releasing it. A stale odor of must and metal surfaced from inside the crate as Potter waved the lantern overhead. He swiftly exhaled through his nostrils in a disappointed sigh. Though far from the riches he and his children hoped for, the crate's dusty contents didn't surprise him.

Rifles. Tarpley Carbine rifles, to be exact. *The Confederate kind.* An entire arsenal of them sat alongside small boxes of pre-made fifty caliber paper cartridge rounds. Potter picked one up and turned it over in his hands, finding "1863" engraved underneath. *Tarpley*—the man who invented the breechloading carbine. He'd heard of these rare and troublesome single-shot firearms. Now, with disbelief, he stood over twenty or more, all piled on a bundle of wilted straw. Next to them lay a handful of... Ketchum grenades?! The funny things looked like little torpedoes with their large tail fin sticking from the back, a monstrous version of an arrow feather.

"Wowww," Isaac called from above.

Potter concurred.

He pried open the second crate. Another rotten smell emanated from within, this one slightly more sulfuric. The absence of substantial monetary or geological value left him disheartened. Nevertheless, his pulse skyrocketed upon realizing what lay before him. He lifted a long, thin cardboard cylinder, dry and soft to the touch, wiping away the surface dust to reveal one word: "EXPLOSIVE."

Isaac, again, called down. "Pa, what's that?"

By the dangling wick, Potter placed the device down, nestled once again with the rest. "Dynamite, son."

Potter had only come across dynamite in the mines in recent years, and his experience and utilization of it remained minimal at best. Though he'd certainly inspected wiring jobs and supervised plenty of detonations, clearing fresh tunnels in Bennett's mines. The low man on the totem pole usually handled explosives and anything deemed dangerous, and knowledgeable volunteers constantly worked with the element. Where had his uncle-in-law had gotten hands on some, much less an entire cache, he had no idea. He knew with certainty that it received limited use during the war, practically nonexistent.

His mind jumped to the dynamite's potential value, considering the options for where to sell it. *Nowhere. You're in hiding, fool.* Old habits died hard, he supposed.

Isaac gaped down at him. "You think is still works, Pa?"

Potter, curious himself, turned the stick over in his hands. "It's very old."

Intermittent squeaking sounded from behind. Potter held out the lantern, casting dim light on a brown field mouse. It stood on hind legs, staring back at him before turning and scurrying off. Its echoing squeaks and chirps trailed away into the void. Potter squinted after it. *Maybe there's more to this mysterious cache.*

Holding the lantern aloft, he stepped forth behind the little feller and discovered another space, slightly more complex than he had imagined. Two-by-fours of wood stood built into the walls, the makings of a framework for a seemingly incomplete project. The path then narrowed to a four-foot crawl space.

Potter called up to the young'uns over his shoulder. "Wait here!"

Already crouching, he soon found himself kneeling in the damp, soft clay. Dancing shadows from the swaying lantern reflected over the plywood walls and ceiling. He crawled over the cold ground, his insatiable brain already leaping straight back to riches. *Well, Christ, what else is there? Gotta be a good explanation for all this.*

The trail went for some distance, and his heartbeat spiked, the dirt walls and trelliswork of cobwebs closing in around him as he clawed away the tacky fibers. He wondered where that mouse went, and if there were others. Perhaps a colony. Or rats.

He froze. Eerie memories of crawling through dark, muddy, rat-filled trenches fluttered from his subconscious like the flame of his depleting oil lantern: fading in and out, difficult to discern one image from another. Nipping. Biting. Squeaking. He'd camped underground for a dog's age, waiting for safe passage from the bodies and the acrid smell of decaying flesh. An escape from Virginia's heinous subterranean internment.

Something squeaked, scuttling in the distance.

Potter shuddered, unsure which noises sounded now and which echoed from twenty-two years past. *Turn back, turn back, turn back...* But twisting around in such confines seemed physically impossible. He panted, stifled.

Noticing he still wore his coat, he slid off the extra garment and unbuttoned his flannel as well. Cool. Sort of. He closed his eyes and took several deep breaths, exhaling completely, then pressed forward.

The light extinguished.

With a deep groan, and keeping one hand on either side of the wall, Potter felt his way around the curved tunnel, only bumping his head a few times, until he eventually came to a dead end. He reached around; the plywood returned to cold clay once again. No riches. And thankfully, no rat colony. And... no ceiling? Infinite space stretched above his head, along with a twinge of cool air. Something solid pressed against one side: a ladder of wooden planks. Gently standing, Potter reached up and touched something solid but pliable. He pushed, and it rattled without budging. Feeling around, he found the door above him had been latched shut, held with piano wire from within. After disentangling everything, he lifted the door with the force of his upper back. The brisk—fresh—dusk air swept his face as he pushed open the door, along with an inch of meadow.

Forget riches. He couldn't have been happier to see the nearby batwing doors, the front of Bennett's house, and the fading light of day.

5

Potter walked in the front door and entered the kitchen. His son and daughter fired up the stairs and through the door with bewildered expressions.

"Listen to me..." Potter grabbed a rabbit by the legs and slammed it down on the kitchen counter, its body flumping. With an eight-inch butcher knife, he split the hide from tail to throat, leaning the animal over to drain and into the sink. "I don't want either of you playing in that hole in the ground, you hear me?" Both gave a resounding "Yes, Pa," though Clara scrunched her nose at the sight of the spilling blood staining the white porcelain.

"I'm serious. Stay away from it. Everything inside is dangerous."

"What is it all," Isaac asked.

"Don't know, son. Your mother's uncle was a general who fought in the Rebellion War. Fought for the Confederates." He shook the carcass of its remaining blood drips, then placed it on its back. His blade split the sternum, making a hollow crunching sound like a dog chewing on bone. "Must've stockpiled supplies. Dug this... hidden escape route."

"For what, Pa," Clara asked, still recoiling in visible disgust.

She had been privy to the gutting and cleaning ritual of house chickens over the years, Ma's chore, though she'd never watched. Having the ranch-to-dinner-table experience of her father hunting, killing, cleaning, and cooking the pretty wild animals dwelling in their backyard must have been relatively shocking for her.

"Hard to say." Potter reached into the carcass, scooping out the internal organs and viscera. They splashed into the sink with a wet plop. He wiped his filthy hands on a rag, then went right to work, carefully cutting and removing the bladder. "Fear. Safety."

"Was Uncle John a bad man?"

A fair question. Short answer: *yes.*

"I didn't really know him," Potter said after a brief pause.

A doleful look crossed Isaac's round face. "But he was a Confederate, right?"

"That don't make him a bad person necessarily, Isaac. The one thing I need you to know bout that war is most people who served either side, if not all of them, didn't have much choice in the matter. It's just what you did," Potter explained, oversimplifying for the sake of ending the conversation.

Grandpa Morgan was one thing; Potter had no interest in disparaging another blood relative of his son's and leaving him with a needless unease over a man he'd never know. Though Potter understood what fighting for the deplorable South meant. Fighting at all, even. North. South. Didn't matter. Warring put your soul at hazard.

Every man makes a choice, he thought. *Then the whirlwind begins.*

He wished to stay honest with his son, which meant complete defection. *His* truth had no relevance here. "The man lived a bit of an unconventional life. It was just his way, is all." With a firm grip, he peeled off the tacky hide, tearing the membrane between skin and meat. "All right, let's get supper going. Claire, peel some potatoes, please. Isaac, run out to the well. We're going to need more water for the stew pot."

"Uhh... about that, Pa. Didn't Grandpa tell ya? There ain't no well. Been getting water from the river."

"Huh." Wiping his slimy red hands on a towel, Potter realized he'd been too busy to even notice. "Well, ain't that just swell. We're gonna have to do something about that, now, won't we." Under his breath, he added, "Whenever it is I get paid."

Chapter 8

Tynan Dunkin sat at the far edge of an oblong center bar. The vivacious Bughouse Saloon thrummed with life. A crescendo of harmonics playfully belted from dueling Tack pianos, offset on either side of a long, narrow stage straight back against the wall. Only the sporadic amble of patrons veiled his view of the instruments. Men jovially entered and exited the stairs on either side, leading up to a labyrinth of hallways and interconnected themed rooms—spaces *mostly* reserved for explicit business. The kind of business the Bughouse was known for, the kind that allured and beguiled Louisiana patrons from far and wide. The kind that made Tynan cringe. On stage, four ladies in light blue corsets and petticoats held matching parasols, putting on a sprightly, provocative performance of burlesque for imbibing spectators at short, round top tables.

Though only early evening, the house bumped with crowds. Men from all walks shacked up in the Bughouse: cowboys, miners, tradesmen, hunters, lumberjacks, lawmen, men of business. *Men of pleasure.*

And men like Tynan, in search of their quarry, knew of one place where the trail always ended...

Oklahoma City.

An unceasing, dynamic throng of cultural diversity inhabited the American capitalism, all under one roof. Transactional relationships left and right. To walk in the door invited the abandoning of one's morals to a new economy of frivolous luxury and impulsive desire, utterly depraved and lawless. When the good city folk finished a week's work, they took their hard-earned wages and invested in the pleasurable commodities the Bughouse offered. And the Bughouse specialized in a little something for everybody.

Fully occupied gaming tables lined the perimeter of this honky-tonk carnival, offering a variety of opportunities to test one's wits and skill. The more popular choices included craps, roulette, faro, Spanish monte, and, of course, poker. The clink of clay chips resounded, shuffled between fingers and stacked on tables, so loud that the noise rivaled the rattle of roulette wheels. Both sounds resonated below a haze of billowing cigar smoke, pooling high above. The soft amber glow of gaslight from crystal chandeliers, barely visible, flickered like stars fighting through the fog of an overcast night sky.

Then there were the women of the house—the girls of virtue—the *real* attraction. The *Ladies in White,* they'd come to be known inside, though some misogynists outside referred to them as *Soiled Doves*. Sauntering about with flirtatious laughter and persuasive winks, these Man Charmers leisurely gestured in doorways and hung out second floor parlor windows, waving silk handkerchiefs, the banner of suggestive bliss, at passersby.

Tynan noticed all from the long mirror behind the bar's hazel-stained liquor bottles. He stared at his own reflection through round lightly tinted specs while he sipped a short glass of golden ale. Stoic. Vigilant. A perfect vantage point. His bottom lip, full of tobacco, quivered as he moved the shredded leaf along his gumline, working in the product; anything to get the sour taste of the Bughouse from his mouth. This particular spot symbolized the immorality plaguing the world. He believed the thin floorboards beneath his boots concealed the gates of Hell.

It was dark magic...

Behind his left shoulder, he watched several rounds of faro played on a short, square table, the dealer's profile exposed. Four men in three-piece suits and oval derby hats shared a round of laughs, collecting their winnings and placing their next chip wagers on the board of spaded cards. However, they would not have the last laugh. Not this round. Unbeknownst to the patrons, the dealer slyly edged the top card in the card box opposite of its intended path and quickly glanced down before applying some pressure and sliding *two together,* to appear as one, from the proper end: the *dealer* card (the card they think they're getting; the high card) followed by the *player* card (the card underneath they're actually getting; the low card). The euphoric chatter diminished.

Dealer wins.

A prism... in the damn card box. Clever son of a bitch.

This dark magic required colorful magicians. And the Bughouse served as this circus's Big Top.

Just beyond the bar, off to the far left at a round top in front of the stage show, a Lady in White sat sideways on a businessman's lap. She massaged the chest inside his double-breasted jacket with one hand, the other wrapped around his neck as she whispered in his ear, kissing with crimson lips. His two pals, thoroughly engrossed in the show, turned back to exchange hearty smiles and garish remarks.

A scantily clad bar maid in black arrived with full shot glasses. With a quick sleight of her massaging hand, the Lady in White lifted a watch from the man's vest pocket and quickly passed the prize to her left hand, still draped over his shoulder. The men cheered to good times while the Lady, accepting a drink with her right hand, used her left to slide the watch by the chain into an artificial pocket of the barmaid's long, lacy undergarment. The barmaid turned away, on to other patrons, as the Lady in White spilled her own brown libation down her man's gullet.

No matter what one purchased—an hour of lust, a bottle of bathtub bourbon, or an ante-in of five-card stud—everything at the Bughouse came at a price. The patrons mostly left gratified, and the house always won. Just a series of commercial transactions, the erotica of commerce.

Tynan finished his drink, wiped his mouth on a fresh spittoon towel hanging from the edge of the bar, and habitually twisted up the ends of his bushy brown mustache with the leather tips of a black glove. The compulsion soothed him as, from the corner of his eye, he watched two men approach.

"Well, well, well, looky here, Ellis. If it ain't the infamous Tynan Dunkin!" Murphy came up on Tynan's right, firmly patting his shoulder.

Instant irritation.

Ellis crossed behind to his left. "So it is, so it is."

The two unsolicited men flanked Tynan, a bit rough around the edges. They wore leisurely dress: flannel button downs, woolen slacks, long jackets, Stetson hats. A bath wouldn't have killed them. Tynan's nose crinkled, taking in the odious scent.

Murphy's rotund belly poked his side as he leaned in. "To what does Oklahoma City owe the honor of your arrival?"

Tynan sighed. "Murphy. Ellis. Can I offer you a drink?" He put a hand up, though unenthusiastic. "Barkeep, let me set these gentlemen up."

The barman, pouring whiskey shots for two men nearby, nodded. "What, uh, what'll it be, boys? Perhaps somethin from the trough?" Tynan's words flowed with an aristocratic air, inflected with a splash of southern drawl. Deep and tranquil.

Murphy glowered. "A funny guy, you is."

"We don't want anythin from you, Dunkin. We know you're here for Plummer, and so are we. Well, I got some shit news for ya. We was here first, so you can just fuck on off from wherever it is you came. You and your dirty goddamn horse." Ellis, a tall crony with long blonde hair, slid back his black, three-quarter length coat, exposing the two silver Colts in his holster.

Tynan seethed. *Intimidation tactics. Oh, I like this game... mm-hmm. I like it, I like it.*

"Now Ellis, what'd his pretty little white horse ever do to you?" Murphy flashed a big, shit-eating grin of crooked teeth.

"What is that you ridin, anyway—a yoonie-corn?" Ellis scoffed and giggled, making an invisible horn protrude from his forehead with his fingers.

Tynan's face glowed burgundy. He dropped some shiny silver change on the bar and stood, straightening his violet ascot.

"Now hold on, Dunkin, let us by *your* drink!" Murphy turned to the barman. "Three Whiskeys! And make it snappy, our friend here is on *high* order of business!" He chuckled.

"I don't drink that fiery piss," Tynan snapped, scowling.

He reached into the pocket of his gray vest, under a matching blazer, and pulled a gold watch. Depressing the crown, he snapped open the front lid. The Roman numerals on the white face indicated twenty-three after eight. Time to go. He snapped it shut and tipped his black top hat, looking both Murphy and Ellis in their presumptuous eyes before turning. Their gazes burned his back all the way to the batwing doors.

2

"That man right there is slicker than deer guts on a doorknob. I don't trust him, not one iota, I don't. And what's with the specs?" Ellis shook his head in contempt.

"I hear he's got *sensitive eyes*," Murphy mocked. "Hell if I know. Maybe the light bothers him."

Ellis smirked, head still shaking as he looked up and around at the dimly lit space. "Sensitive eyes, huh. Everything bout that man seems *sensitive*. Especially them silly clothes. The hell he think he is?" After a moment of silence, he glanced at Murphy. "Time is it?"

"Hell, I don't know. Half past eight?"

"Where in Christ is she?"

The men stood at the bar, drinking. The dark brown fuel not only burned, but instantly dried out their mouths, leaving frenzied tongues to massage the fleshy inner walls for moisture.

They downed another round.

A sizable woman, tall, broad shouldered, and built like a brick shit-house, shuffled down from the second floor. The madam of the house, Big Kitty Rodgers, descended the stairs with deliberate steps, marked unmistakably by her size and infamous black raven's bonnet. The hat featured an enchanting, bird-adorned trim—its wing feathers fanned upward to add another three inches to her daunting stature—with a streak of red silk crepe tied around, holding the contraption in place. Her painted, pouty lips stretched into a hearty grin.

The Queen of the Oklahoma underworld crossed the stage, moseying through rows of tables and greeting patrons with either a ginger wave of a black glove, a blow of a kiss, or a warm touch on the shoulder. A Victorian ball gown of black silk draped her rotund bodice with an asymmetrical overskirt of powdered cinnamon that glimmered depending on how the light hit it, shifting and twisting with every turn.

As Kitty approached the bar, her grin twisted to a grimace at the sight of Murphy and Ellis. Her demeanor only soured the closer she came, until she stood right in front of them. She looked over to the barkeep and, without asking, was presented with a hardy glass of liquid fire.

She threw back the drink, not even wincing, and spoke with a voice both heavy and assertive. "Been waitin on you boys now for bout a spell."

Murphy shrugged. "We was held up a bit. Ain't never been here before. Couldn't find the damn place."

"This *place* is the only spot in all the OK even a blind man could point you in the direction of. Who's the *flaneur?*"

"The what?"

"The peacockish gent you was talkin to at the bar. Quiet. Aloof. Starin at himself in the mirror for the last hour or so? You understand, even when I'm not in the room, I see *everythin* in my palace."

"That ain't nobody. An old acquaintance, is all." Ellis cocked his partner a quick glance.

"I wouldn't worry bout him," Murphy added.

"Well, then, let's hurry this up, boys. I can't be standin here all evenin—everybody's gotta wanderin eye, if you know what I mean."

"Where is he," Ellis demanded.

A lengthy pause followed.

Kitty put a hand on her voluptuous hip, leaned into the opposite leg, and sighed in annoyance. "You boys wanna keep wastin time here?"

"Pay her," Ellis huffed.

Murphy pulled some folded bills from his trousers and held them up.

Kitty snatched the money from his grasp, gave the dollars a quick once over with a twist of the wrist, and slid her earnings behind the ruffled black ribbon trim accents of her bodice beside her bulging, pale bosom. "Third floor. Right hallway. Last door on the left. The Conquistador Room."

"Christ..." Murphy shook his head at the Bughouse's eccentric operations. "What's he doin?"

She shrugged. "Last I knew? Bath."

3

Murphy kicked open the door of the Conquistador Room, tearing the knob's lock plate from its strike pad and shattering the front jamb with his boot heel. He exploded in, pistol raised.

Much to his immediate delight, he found Plummer sitting in a porcelain tub on the far-right side of a partially veiled room. He sat, placidly soaking with his bald head and back to Murphy, reading a newspaper. Almost as if he'd expected them. This unforeseen apathy disquieted Murphy. His gaze flicked to the man's handgun, lying an arm's length away on a nearby side table.

"Don't you move, Plummer!" He inched his way in with swift glances left and right.

Mahogany furniture filled the space. A round table, chairs, a four-drawer dresser, and two small buffet hutches lined the perimeter, at least from what he could see behind the sheer white curtains dividing the room. Etagere shelving and bookcases stood indiscriminately shoved between, muddled with bizarre objects and trinkets: porcelain Spanish figurines, vases, decanters, fine decorative china. On one shelf, a shiny helmet, fit with an arching plume of red ostrich feathers, sat next to a model ship with three tall canvas masts. A small centered table, clothed, held a silver tray with silver teapots, goblets, and fruit. Murphy shook his head with incredulity, mouth ajar at a six-foot *decorative* medieval ax hanging at a forty-five-degree angle on a wall. *Fucking specialty room.*

Plummer slowly turned his head to Murphy, exposing blonde mutton chops connected to a grinning mustache and crow's feet eyes. "Who that be!?"

"Don't ya goddamn move—hands where I can see em!"

Plummer dropped the paper, his arms at ninety degrees, resting on the tub's edge. Curtains on either side of him gently billowed from the cool breeze of a nearby open window. "How'd ya find me?"

"Don't concern you. Now, you're gonna stand up, slowly, and step out the tub." Murphy inched his way into the room, gun pointed steadily at the man in the tub. "Any quick movements, Plummer, and I won't hesitate to put a bullet in that head of yours. Believe you, me."

"Now don't do nothin stupid, ya hear? I'm a gettin." Plummer, using the edge of the tub, pushed himself up, water cascading off his thin, bare body. He stepped out, slowly grabbed a towel from a coat hook, and began drying off, eyes locked on Murphy's.

Murphy stared back. Fuck, tried to. Decorative *skulls* resting on the windowsill drew his gaze. Still, he noticed a slight twitch in Plummer's eye, one that almost seemed to glance up and over his shoulder.

Oh fuck!

Murphy turned to a furious halberd crashing down at him. Recoiling, he leaned backward, legs twisting and causing him to stumble. With fierce momentum, the curved blade arced past his torso by inches. As it hammered down, splitting the floorboard, the long shaft collided with his raised arms and knocked the gun from his grip.

A wrathful Lady in White stood above him, bending over the jammed ax in a sheer nightgown and struggling to dislodge the weapon from the floor. Fire filled her wide, screaming eyes, and she belted out a shrill wail. With the rage of a charging steer, she yanked the halberd out with such force, the curved blade on its backside fired up and stuck in the ceiling.

Something wet and warm hit Murphy in his face. He flinched, struggling to regain his footing. When he opened his left eye, a viscous, translucent string clung from his eyelashes, partially obstructing his vision.

Saliva. And likely tuberculosis riddled.

"You filthy, goddamn harlot!" Murphy palmed the bitch's face.

The blow launched her backward, tumbling her into the small table and spilling its silver contents to the floor.

Murphy turned to Plummer, who, clothes in hand, fired two shots before ducking out the window. Murphy—stunned—pulled his second pistol and returned fire, only hitting the frame.

Plummer was gone.

Murphy picked up his other gun and darted to the window. Pulling in a deep breath to regain his confidence, he slowly inched his head out. Plummer, who had managed to make it to the alley's first-floor fire escape landing, leered up while strenuously pulling trousers over a wet body. Both men fired simultaneously, with Plummer jetting down the remaining stairs, pulling on his button-down shirt, and fixing his suspenders while Murphy ducked back inside.

4

Plummer's boots and jacket remained upstairs, but he would have to contend with that another time. Instead, he ran barefoot down the dim alley, glancing back for his assailant in the window. He held a slight advantage; the sun had set, and the skies deepened to a darker shade of blue. Not quite night, but difficult to hit a moving target, nevertheless.

As he turned to face the alley for a clean break, a tall stack of wooden crates fell from under the dark shadows of the adjacent building's fire escape. His foot stuck in a rung, tripping him up as he tried to clear the debris with a jump. Plummer, refusing to drop his Colt, fell face first into the hard dirt, smashing his nose and splitting the bridge.

From the dark, a tall, blonde man appeared. He drew two guns as Plummer rolled to his back, pulling his gun, still in his hand. Blood gushed from his swelling nostril. After a brief standoff, Plummer heard the other man plodding down the fire escape and knew he'd lost. He dropped the gun.

"Wise choice, scum," the blond taunted. "Get up. Slowly, now. Let's go."

Ha-ha! You got'im!" The rounder man galloped over from the stairs. "You are a worth one pretty penny, shit heel."

The silvery snap of pistol hammers cocked behind the men. Their heads turned deliberately, glancing over their shoulders before turning completely to face whatever adversary loomed.

An exquisitely clad man appeared from the darkness, materializing from tenebrous dust and shadows with two leather-glove wrapped Colts in hand, one pointing at each standing man. Plummer stared at the apparition, unnerved—wondering whether friend or foe lay behind those inscrutable, tinted specs.

5

"You boys shouldn't have," Tynan obliged. "But I do appreciate the effort. On behalf of the Wichita County sheriff's office, I want to personally thank you for your services. I'll take it from here."

Murphy groaned. "Oh, what the fuck is this?"

"He's ours, Dunkin!" Ellis seethed. "We found him fair and square! There's a goddamn code of ethics out here. A man like you oughta know that."

"What in holy horseshit is goin on," Plummer spewed from the ground, holding his shirt against his oozing nose.

"Shut up," Murphy snapped.

"Code?" Tynan said, baffled. "Oh—oh, yes, right. The code. Right, right... well, I might recall one particular code. One governed code, you know, back in the days of the Rebellion, commissioned by a man named Lieber. One we swore an oath to abide. One restricting all wanton violence, stealin, pillagin, torture... rape. And the vilest of all acts, in my humble opinion: desertion."

Murphy and Ellis exchanged nonplussed glances. Behind Tynan, the gas lamp alongside the saloon slowly shimmered on, casting a dull amber limelight over the men.

"No? That ain't the *ethical code* you mean." Tynan smirked. "Didn't know there was such honor amongst common gutter trash. You may think nobody remembers, and you may be right. Sportin a different name, different look. Don't matter none. I know. You two belong at the end of a rope next to Plummer. In all actuality, by law, you ain't even United States citizens no more, I reckon. I ought a let him go"—he gestured to Plummer—"and just take you both in instead."

"That's—that's a swell idea," Plummer squawked, muffled under his shirt. Blood drenched the fabric, though his nosebleed began to wane.

"Shut up," Tynan said.

"You dirty four-flushin bastard. If you think you're leavin this god-damn alley, you got another thing comin," Murphy said. His guns, and Ellis', still angled at Plummer.

A moment of strained silence fell. Plummer, owl-eyed, glared up at all three men. Tynan, hidden behind his tinted specs, could sense his fear.

"I think I gotta fair way to settle this, boys. How bout we play a little game?" Tynan slowly holstered one Colt and, with his free hand, removed his top hat. "Wichita Rules. It's real easy, so pay close attention. Now, I'm goin toss this here hat in the air. When it hits the ground, we draw. Savvy?"

The other two men exchanged awkward, tentative glances before holstering their pistols and backing up and away, forming a triangle around Plummer. Tynan holstered his Colt.

The hat, a moment later, shot straight up into the air. Murphy's and Ellis's gazes followed it, but only for a moment. Just as Tynan, and they, had suspected. Regardless, it gave Tynan the edge he needed. That split second. And Tynan knew better than most that every second counted.

The three men drew their weapons with infectious speed, followed by a quick smattering of gun fire.

6

Golden muzzle blasts flashed over Plummer's head as he braced for cover with one arm, feeling for his gun under a crate with the other. As two bodies fell around him, he brushed over his pistol, grabbing it and quickly rolling on his back. He didn't know, nor care, who was still standing. This was his moment, the final reckoning. He'd die before returning to jail.

A hat landed on his belly. Much to his chagrin, the last man standing loomed before him: the spectacled stranger. Before he could squeeze off a round, two fingers ripped clean from his knuckles with a single *pop* from the other man's gun. Plummer's gun fell from a shredded hand, leaving a nickel-sized hole between where his index and middle fingers once were.

He squealed in agony—screaming like a stuck pig—staring at the shallow, blood-spurting void. "AHHH, CHRIST! MY HAND! MY FUCKIN HAND! YOU BLEW OFF MY FINGERS, YOU NO GOOD GODDAMN SODOMITE!"

The damned stranger just crouched calmly over the fresh corpses, rummaging through pockets. Writhing on the ground, Plummer dimly noted him pull a folded wanted poster with a hand drawn picture of Plummer from a coat. Another held chewing tobacco and two speed loaders, which he removed and placed in his own pocket. Finally, he stopped, retrieving the object he sought.

"Wrap it in this." The man in spectacles threw a white handkerchief at Plummer, the fabric landing beside the hat on his blood-soaked stomach. "It's goin be a good while before anyone can flash a peek at that."

"Namby-pamby sumbitch," Plummer eked out, barely able to speak through the pain and anger.

"Mmm. You got some mouth on *you*." The man squatted, lowered his specs, and looked Plummer in the eye. "You don't shut it, I'm gonna fill it with somethin you ain't gonna like very much. Savvy?" He replaced his hat and smirked.

Plummer winced. "Christ!"

CHAPTER 9

Dead cattle.

The familiar stench pierced Potter's nostrils long before he rode up on it. Nauseating, to say the least. The scorching sun hung high above, its rays intensifying the scent in the air. Potter shed his overcoat, draping it across the horse's shoulders—one of Chisum's work steeds. He patted the trickle of salty sweat on his brow with a hanky before lowering it to covering his nose. The end of the week loomed. Pay day. Finally. All he had to do was get through it.

Chisum had him plenty busy with daily chores, and the exhaustion in his body was a constant reminder of the labor he had forgotten. Every step of the process, from the painstaking plowing and planting of grass seed in the pasture to the backbreaking harvesting of hay bales, was carried out by hand. Repairing downed posts and mending barbed wire tears along the fence line proved an endless and monotonous chore. He'd spent much of the morning riding the line, inspecting for breaches about five miles southwest of the property. Tedious work, but simple. He preferred it to herding, however—the least desirable of his tasks. Long drives on horseback delivering cattle to Lincoln and Fort Sumner caused his back to throb. It still ached from the previous evening, when he had returned from an overnight stay delivering product to Lincoln. Six dismal hours there, and six back.

To his dismay, Chisum recruited him specifically to carry on as a professional safeguard during the delivery process, making herding his primary function. A gun for hire, so to speak. Mutilated cattle and random stickups had become a major problem for the boss. Dead cows appeared about once a month, with virtually no evidence of an assailant, though Chisum spouted conspiracies about a single group behind it all. Potter figured some residual paranoia from the Lincoln County War still lingered in the man's mind.

The cow he stumbled upon had been dead for at least a week, judging by its severely decomposed state. Torn asunder. Black with rot. He struggled to envision the nature of the intruder. Black bear? Cougar? Apache Indians sending a message, perhaps. Not uncommon in these parts. Between the lurking cattle thieves and the mysterious entities responsible for their demise, he had to remain vigilant. Thus far, he'd managed to avoid the jarring sound of his rifle firing at another human target.

Warren's cold, dead eye staring up at him flashed through his mind.

He dismounted, walked past the carcass, and inspected the fence post, wafting away a swarm of black flies. Two poles leaned in at a forty-five-degree angle. The wire bowed slightly, as if it had gotten caught on something and pulled. A pale-yellow, threadlike substance wrapped one of the barbs. He unraveled the silky material and rubbed it between his finger and thumb.

Fur.

2

"Mr. Potter." Nora nodded, a curious smile flashing across her radiant face as she entered from the open door behind the counter. "Didn't expect you back so soon."

Potter, holding two shovels, a scythe, and a pickax, simpered awkwardly, trying to think of something to say. All he could muster was "Didn't expect to have a project so soon." He regretted the words immediately.

"Not surprised. This whole town seems to be a constant work in progress."

Potter struggled not to stare by avoiding direct eye contact. He had already seen too much. Nora captivated the eye in a baby blue paisley dress, this one off-the-shoulder and short sleeved. Her skin shone a shade darker than during his previous encounter, just a week ago. Potter's own face, feeling the effects of the sun's strength since arriving in town, wore a constant sunbaked scarlet; he'd soon have to get used to it, as the summer season was only beginning. Nora's complexion, however, looked sun-kissed and stunning.

His cheeks, already red, darkened slightly. "Uhh, how much do I owe ya?"

"That'll be five dollars. You know, you probably could've gotten these new over at the Farmer's Alliance for a few pennies more, I reckon."

"Oh... uh, yeah, I spose you're right." He hadn't even considered buying new specialty tools. "I, uh, usually prefer to buy second-hand when I can. Already broken in. They just get beat up anyway, don't they?" Potter confidently pulled five silver pieces from his pocket, stacking them on the counter. He could clearly afford new. Right now, however, he just needed a good save. "Uh, also, I need a bag of flour. The young'uns, they love potato bread."

"Always a pleasure."

Potter grinned awkwardly. The expression felt unnatural, making him self-conscious once again. He found himself staring at her bosom—now uncertain for how long, though certainly she'd noticed—and glanced off to her side, where the landscape painting hung on the wall. "How much for the painting?"

Nora, surprised, looked behind, then back to Potter. "The painting?"

Potter fumbled for his next words, foolishly unsure of himself yet eager to be supportive and offer some business. "Uhh, for Clara. She loves that depiction of the town."

"My favorite, too. The girl's got good taste. That, for Clara, is on the house."

Challenge, met.

"Oh, I—I couldn't possibly."

"Consider it a welcome gift." Nora turned to the painting, unhooking it from the wall.

"Well, what about the painter? Won't he be upset?"

"We're a community of barterers here, Mr. Potter. I'm sure it'll just work itself out."

"Well, thank you, Ms. Nora. That is mighty kind of you."

"Just as long as you come to service tomorrow."

"Service?"

"After all, it is Sunday. Minister Healy's sermons are usually interestin, to say the least. Thought provokin, I might add. A real passionate man."

"I think I can arrange that." Potter, realizing he wore an unprecedented layer of filth on his skin, blanched. The more he thought about it, the stench of his body odor could likely clear a church. He wondered if Nora had noticed, hoping against hope she hadn't. "Uhhh, know a place a man can get a bath round here?"

"Right next door. Through that door behind me, as a matter of fact." Potter blinked, not understanding.

"That's my place, too. As well as the place upstairs. Where I live."

"Oh." He gaped at her, dumbfounded. *Right... the barber pole.*

"Might I suggest a shave as well, Mr. Potter?"

He looked down, realizing his fingers had habitually begun stroking his silver chin hair. "Bill, please, call me Bill. And no. Thanks." For the past two decades, the scruff had been hiding his old face, distancing him from the image in the last Wanted poster he had stumbled across.

Waving farewell to Nora, he stepped out of Reynolds's Buy & Sell to find his two young'uns playfully chasing each other around the schooner, stirring up dust.

He smiled and placed the tools in the back, followed by the painting, wrapped in a white sheet. "Kids got your letters for Grandpa?"

He was early, very early. Intentionally so. He had no idea what this postal service was like, how often they traveled, and how long it would take a letter to reach Denver. Now Denver ran a crackerjack operation with their team of postmen: daily delivery, same time, without cessation. Like clockwork. However, Denver had a population of over three thousand. And this sure as shit wasn't Denver. He couldn't be late, and he wasn't taking any chances.

The young'uns responded with a resounding "Yes, Pa."

"Well, all right. Let's go."

Clara pointed at the large, thin, square object her father had placed in the back. "What's that?"

"A gift from Ms. Nora."

Clara gasped. "What is it!?"

"You'll just have to wait and see."

Potter walked guiltily past the Alliance, wishing he'd bought new tools. He liked *new*. On the other side of the building, two doors down from Nora's general store, the Potters entered the narrow, two-story post office. Isaac, in front, opened the door for an elderly couple exiting, carrying luggage. Two men in another room, behind the long counter and through an open doorway, chatted animatedly—bickered, if Potter had to guess. One sorted through a basket of mail while the man to his left ate a piece of fruit, what looked to be a peach. Potter could just about make them out in the dim space as they entered.

"Look, Aaron," the tall man sorting mail continued, "my father is goin to be here next week. He's arrivin with the head of the land office, to evaluate everythin we been doin here. Everythin!" He brushed dirty blonde bangs back from his eyes. "You know how long we been waitin on this shit?"

"I'm completely aware," the Asian man said. Next to the blonde man, he looked noticeably shorter.

"Five sonovabitchin years, pal. That's how goddamn long it was since we filed that paperwork. We did what we was supposed to be doin. Held up our end of things."

Potter glanced around, waiting. The vestibule looked mostly bare, its only offering an aluminum sign for *Western Union & Telegraph*, nailed to the side wall. *How bout that?* Beyond, on the wall behind the counter, two dozen or so cubbies hung with resident's names stenciled under each. Potter raised a brow, pleasantly surprised by the efficiency of such an insignificant operation in such an insignificant town.

"I know, I know. I am only asking, are we rushing things? The mill is not producing like it used to. Deliveries have dwindled, Van, and we do not even have a financial windfall."

"Look, we didn't spend the last six months tunnelin out that abandoned *hole* under the church for nothin." The man lowered his voice. "We need to have everythin in place for when this charter passes and my father takes over. Mr. Chisum gave us his word he'd be backin this little *operation* of ours."

The Asian man sighed. "But even *he* does not know what we are doing."

"The less Mr. Chisum knows, the better, I say. By the end of summer, we'll get in a truckload of our first haul."

"I am just worried is all. There is a lot to go wrong here if your father catches wind of this or, God forbid, if the minister happens to stumble upon—"

"Don't be so yellow, my friend. That kooky old drunk can't see five feet in front of his own eyes." The blonde man giggled. "Prob'ly be our biggest customer!"

Confused by what he thought he heard, Potter cautiously returned to the door, opened it, and slammed it shut, pretending they had just arrived. Being a fresh face, he preferred to stay inconspicuous.

The men stopped speaking, followed by a brief silence. Both entered the room.

"Mr. Potter," the blonde said in a surprised voice.

Potter blinked, surprised himself. He narrowed his gaze. "Do we know each other?"

You never can tell.

"Small town." The man, nonplussed, continued sifting through letters, sliding them in little cubbies as he spoke. "Tiny town, actually. News of travel *travels* fast. Plus, I'm the postmaster round here. It's my business to know the who's who. Name's Vance. Vance Smith. Just go by Van, though." He extended a free hand, and Potter shook it.

Firm grip.

The man to Van's left spoke. "Hi, Aaron Wilburn. I run the mill in town." Wilburn initiated a handshake, but abruptly withdrew to wipe away the peach juice dribbling down his chin. "Sorry." He smiled awkwardly.

More accents. Both different. Smith had a strong midwestern dialect, while Wilburn, for a Chinaman, spoke damn near perfect English—much easier to discern, especially compared to Smith.

Chisum's words rang in Potter's ears: *This town's a bit of a cultural melting pot, if you will, a peculiar group of individuals you'll undoubtedly meet.*

Potter gaped, struggling to believe these two were the men who essentially ran this small town. Both appeared young, younger than Potter by leaps and bounds. If he had to guess, at least twenty years his junior. Shy enough to avoid enlistment, that's for sure. Wilburn need never hold Van, missing a limb or riddled with bullet holes, as he bled out in his arms. He'd never dole out platitudes of comfort to his friend's pallid face, watching the curtains slowly close in those horror-stricken eyes—those windows—before his soul dissipates. Oh, what a time to be young. These men, no, *boys,* carried an unperceived innocence they'd never comprehend, much less appreciate. He winced ever so slightly at the thought. Perhaps Aaron and Van formed the generation Chisum had referenced as the "ones to carry things on."

Potter shook his head at himself, regaining his composure. "This here's my son, Isaac, and his sister, Clara." He gestured to the two, standing on either side of him with stoic expressions. "Was surprised to see a mill, of all things."

"Yes, sir. This here is the pinnacle of modernization," Aaron said facetiously, opening his arms as if to encompass the entire town.

"Oh... what's that?"

"Textiles."

"Textiles?"

Aaron turned to the young'uns. "That would be sheep's wool." He looked back at Potter. "Did you expect me to say opium joint?"

Potter smiled thinly.

"That's okay." Aaron grinned; his thin mustache bunched under wide nostrils. "Most do. My folks run one in Omaha. Grew up around that poison. Seen enough good people lose their way, lose *everything,* because of it. Seen a lifetime's worth." Aaron glanced morosely at the ground.

"Yeah." Potter understood. What was more, he too knew the euphoric dangers of such a potion. Was he a slave to opium? No, not by his own admission. Maybe more of a seasoned retainer. *Modestly* loyal.

"Anyway, a sheep farm is about fifty miles west of here in the forest highlands, over by the Capitan range. We are closest, so all the pelts end up here, of course. Great business. Keeps us plenty busy."

"Smart hustle."

"Sure beats doping up rich city folk."

"Me and Aaron moved here from Omaha a few years after the first settlers arrived," Van interjected. "They came here bout fifteen years ago from Missouri, hence the name. But we built half the structures here in town. Wasn't much here at all, completely underdeveloped. A church, a few barterin huts is all, really. We saw immediate opportunity, ain't that right?" He nudged Aaron.

"Right on the money. Church is the oldest building. Was nowhere half the size you see it today, mind you. We expanded it. Previous settlers had dug out a makeshift basement for worship or something, we guess, but we straightened the space out for Minister Healy." Wilburn puffed up his chest. "Had that stained-glass window you see there imported straight from Rome."

"Rome, you say?"

"Well, Van's father helped facilitate that project."

"He did indeed. My father, fortunately, has many connections. In fact, he arranged my openin of this here U.S. Postal Service. Once that was in place, we could finally call Missouri Plaza a real town. Got a sleepin quarters upstairs for travelin guests. In all honesty, we don't get much of that, though. Miller's also boards travelers and does a better business, probably cause he's got the restaurant below. But it's there if need be. Truth be told, I actually stay in one of them rooms myself. You on the old Bennett farm, I hear."

Potter nodded.

"My old man's been tryin to snatch up that land for years. His stubborn brother won't sell, though. Tryin to expand this town, ya know. Ya must know Morgan Bennett?"

"Not really, no. His associates agreed to rent out the land to me."

"Huh. How bout that?" Van's tone came out dry.

If Potter hadn't observed the haughty undertone before, and he most certainly did, Van's blatant disbelief smacked the taste from his mouth. He stood silent, a cool glare his only response. The air, staling, hung among them for a moment.

Aaron, cringing under the quiet's stifling weight, broke the tension. "Hey, uh, you looking for some work, Mr. Potter? I might have a need at the mill. At least until we start building. Then, of course, we will have plenty of work, if you are handy with carpentry."

"Then, my friend, we will have to import the help!" Smith interjected. "Plenty of cheap labor just south of here. And I tell you, it's certainly gonna take a village."

"Call me, Bill. And no. Thank you."

"How bout you, little feller? I can teach *you* to run a factory. How would that be? Invaluable life skills await a young man such as yourself."

Isaac, wide eyed with eager interest, turned to his father. "Can I, Pa?"

Potter took a moment to answer, unsure what to make of either feller in the post office. He hadn't much experience with Chinamen, outside an Opium joint, but from what he knew, Oriental culture prioritized hard work, ancestral traditions, and strong family values. Wilburn certainly *seemed* friendly enough. Could Potter trust him with something as important as Isaac's safety? *I mean, hell—not like I trust people, anyhow.* He loathed the idea of making their presence in the village known so hastily, but he didn't know how much longer he could honestly hold out.

The hourglass drains.

Potter sighed. "Maybe a day or two a week. Someone still needs to be home to look after your sister."

Isaac's eyes lit up.

"Before I forget." Potter reached for the young'uns' letters, handing them over to Van.

"Need anythin, don't ever hesitate to ask, ya hear." Van offered a squirrely smile. "Welcome to our little town."

Potter tipped his hat. *Thanks.*

Once the schooner pulled away, Clara, sitting next to her pa, looked up at him with an inquisitive expression. "Pa, *everybody* here talks funny."

He laughed. "I noticed, darling. But you know what?"

Clara shook her head.

"All these people, they probably think *we* talk funny. Bet ya didn't take that into consideration, did ya?"

She shook her head again.

"As a matter of fact, your pa also used to talk funny at one time. A long, long time ago."

"Quit teasing, Pa!"

A tight smile touched the corners of Potter's mouth while he stared out into the open valley beyond the mill, remembering his family's Tudor manor in southeast Connecticut—a lifetime ago—as the schooner crossed the bridge.

4

"Now grip it. Tightly, son." Potter stood behind Isaac and peered over his shoulder, ensuring everything aligned properly. "You got it?"

"Yes, Pa."

"Keep the butt in the crook of your armpit. And close your left eye."

"Okay."

Potter glanced up. Dawn glowed around them. Following a night of vicious rain, splotchy gray painted the morning skies. Fair conditions, apart from the breeze; the late spring air bore a slight chill which would, hopefully, dissipate from the soon-to-be-rising valley sun. The patchy grass, heavily saturated from a midnight storm, sponged under their boots.

Across the yard, fifty yards or so, an old barrel stood with a two-by-four propped across. Potter had lined six empty bean cans atop. He wondered if he and the boy stood far enough back, but since his son had never fired a weapon, he at least needed to establish a baseline. With any luck, the exercise wouldn't take too long. Training Isaac wasn't exactly the first order of business, but they'd been here a week now—too long—and the boy's eagerness only grew.

A yawn struggled to escape Potter's mouth. So much for all the Arbuckles' he'd drunk this morning. The fulmination of cracking thunderclaps had jolted him awake hours earlier, causing him to toss and turn, numbly, to no avail. His aging body, exhausted and achy, wanted to shut down, but his mind stayed on. Drifting. How many sleepless nights until he felt safe? Dead men tell no tales, assuming McCormac's corpse stood propped against a tree. But this feeling of borrowed time lingered. Without sleep, the futility of the day's forthcoming, undeniably toilsome activities loomed monumental. And letting down a man like John Chisum was not in the cards. Not here, not now, anyway.

Really, only one choice remained to him.

Potter, stifling any self-critique about justifying a precarious habit, had rolled himself a *special* quirley. Then he'd stepped out onto the deck, following it around to where it wrapped the side of the house. Leaning on the railing, rain misting his cheeks, he'd smoked and watched nature's light show. Jagged silver flashes, in rapid succession, haphazardly lit the valley's infinite landscape while the Capitan Mountains flickered ominously in the distance. Molten firebolts discharged from the heavens, splitting the earth and dissolving on impact. For a moment, and only a moment, he'd stood in the midst of a battlefield.

Potter shook his head and stepped to his right, his Cuban heel sinking into sludgy clay, and lined up his sight with his son's. "With your right eye, look straight down the barrel. Line up the notch in the site with your target."

"I got it," Isaac whined, fidgeting.

"Okay, okay." Potter backed up. "Take a deep breath... hold it."

His son's chest puffed, held.

"When you're ready, squeeze the trigger."

Isaac, without hesitation, fired, the recoil jolting him.

Miss.

Just as Potter expected. "That's okay, that's okay, son. We're gonna try it again."

Isaac pulled back on the finger lever, snapping another round into the chamber. His father gave him the *go*. He fired another two shots, one completely missing, the other hitting the barrel, before sighing in frustration.

"Steady, Isaac," Potter instructed. "Just breathe. This time, try to look *through* your target. Just beyond."

Isaac inhaled deeply, loaded another round, and took aim. The wind picked up, gently blowing his bangs into his eyes. His opportunity would come, Potter knew. His son just needed a little patience. The second the wind diminished—moments later—he fired. The can tumbled back off the barrel. His mouth gaped, and he looked at his pa wide-eyed, ecstatic.

"Good. Good, son. Let's hit a few more, then it's time to grab a shovel." Potter sighed, back already aching. "We got some digging to do."

The clouds broke by mid-morning, the sun sneaking its way through to warm the early June skies. Forty yards from the property, the boys stood six feet deep in an oblong hole, mounds of moist dirt scattered about. The digging, for the most part, proved easy; they quickly worked through the damp dirt. However, they also worked up quite a sweat. Not much of a day for rest and relaxation.

Potter, already down to his undershirt—sleeves removed—held up his slacks with damp red suspenders. He wiped his brow and took a drink of water from a pail, ladling some into his mouth before offering a sip to the boy.

Looking up, he saw Clara feeding the hens outside the barn, Blanco standing not far behind her. Delight beamed from her little sun-kissed face. She'd fallen in love with that old nag. The sight brought ease to Potter's otherwise callous old soul.

"How much further, Pa?" Isaac panted.

"I don't know. We should've seen a sign by now. The dirt seems to keep getting drier the further we dig."

They remained quite a distance from the riverbank. One-hundred-fifty yards or so, if Potter had to guess. Still plenty close, however. He just couldn't understand the problem.

The sun slowly crept beyond the clouds, drawing Potter's attention. His internal sundial remained a bit off in this new territory, but he had a feeling they were now running late. The well would have to wait.

He cleared his throat. "Let's finish this later. Time to get ready."

<h1 style="text-align:center">5</h1>

Potter, in the same suit he wore in his meeting with Chisum, kneeled down to tie the yellow pinafore around Clara's handmade dress, light green with a ruffled yoke top. A tad small, Potter thought. Bessie had originally designed it—and many like it—a couple sizes over, intending for Clara to get plenty of use over time. After a recent growth spurt, that time had finally passed; she'd just about grown out of it. Isaac, sitting on the bottom step of the staircase, wore his Sunday best: brown knickerbockers and a matching blazer, similarly made by Ma. Bessie had always been quite savvy with a needle and thread.

"Pa, why are we going to church," Clara asked.

"You two used to go with your mother, don't you recall?"

"But we stopped when she went to heaven."

"Church ain't never given me the proper guidance, darling." With his hand, Potter swept her curly bangs back from her curious eyes. "But it was wrong of me to prevent you two from making the decision to go, based on your own experience. Didn't realize you enjoyed it all that much."

"Are you going with us?"

"Of course I am."

As the words left his mouth, he remembered attending church meant making a public appearance. But the other town residents probably kept their heads low too, minding their own business. At least, according to Chisum. Better to test the waters now, before they settled in. Besides, he needed to get an idea of who all lived around here.

Potter stood, brushing off his own Sunday best. *You just never know when you might need a favor.*

6

The left side of the French double doors gently pulled open, creaking with a sharp reverberance over the quiet congregation. Daylight spilled down the center aisle as the Potters *tried* to enter quietly. A few heads peered back, disinterested, though the golden light through the open door shone directly on one seething gentleman, turning in his seat to glare back at them. Potter immediately noticed the slightly older man's prominent, *and bad*, salt-and-pepper comb-over.

The minister, Healy, Potter presumed, stood front and center, behind a podium. His voice, piercing and emphatic, carried from his short and portly frame all the way back to the last pew. "Brothers and sisters, if someone is caught in a sin, you who are spiritual should restore them gently. But watch yourself, or you also may be tempted. Carry each other's burdens, and in this way, you will fulfill the law of Christ. If anyone thinks they are something when they are nothing, they deceive themselves. Each one should test his own actions. Then they can take pride in themselves, without comparing themselves to somebody else, for each one should carry their own load. Anyone who receives instruction in the Word must share all good things with their instructor..."

The Potters had arrived much later than expected.

Potter removed his hat and glanced around a mostly full church, hoping to see a specific familiar face. A difficult task, from behind the seated congregation. The nave, much smaller than he'd expected based on the impressive outside construction, comprised twelve well-spaced pews, six on either side. Still, he guessed most of the community sat in attendance.

To his immediate delight, a hand raised in the last pew on the far left, behind the seething comb-over man. Nora smiled with an inviting wave. As she pushed over, allowing them to slide in, Potter noticed her mostly empty pew and wondered if she'd intentionally sat alone, anticipating his tentative arrival.

Nora leaned in and whispered, "Morning, Bill. Didn't think you'd make it."

"Do not be deceived," Healy shouted. "God *cannot* be mocked. A man reaps what he sows. The one who sows to please his sinful nature, from that nature, will reap destruction; the one who sows to please the Spirit, from the Spirit will reap eternal life."

Heat rose to his cheeks. "My apologies, Ma'am. We seem to have lost track of the time."

"Sounds like a real quandary. Perhaps a new timepiece may rectify the situation," she said, curtly.

Time...

Potter sensed he displeased her with his tardiness, though her smile didn't falter. Neither did his blush. "Don't believe in em, ma'am."

"Please, call me Nora. We're plenty acquainted now."

"Let us not become weary in doing good," Healy continued, "for at the proper time we will reap a harvest if we do not give up. Therefore, as we have opportunity, let us do good to all people, especially to those who belong to the family of believers."

"Pa, the whole town's here," Clara whispered, loudly enough for the couple in front to turn back and cast wrathful glances. She slunk, horrified, in her seat.

Isaac pointed to the middle of the right pew. "There's Mr. Wilburn and Mr. Smith!"

"SHHHH!" The comb-over man hissed over his shoulder, spittle discharging from a pursed lip. Scarlet-faced, he glared once again at Potter and his children, pausing this time to take a long, explicit look at Clara and Isaac. The uncomely woman next to him, also with salt-and-pepper hair, glared back nastily with the same contemptuous expression.

Potter's eyes narrowed. An uncomfortable warmth, almost burning, radiated under his skin.

"Excuse *us*... please! No need to be rude," Nora fired back a stern whisper, pointing her finger forward in rotation. The universal sign to turn-around-and-mind-your-own-fucking-business.

The man scowled at her before averting his eyes and turning forward, shaking his purple head. The wife scoffed, appalled.

Nora leaned into Potter and muttered, "Don't you mind them, Bill. That's just Charon and Lamiya Dotterweich. Bunch of unfriendly old kooks."

Potter's brows raised, awestricken by the fiery Nora Reynolds—a side he had not anticipated.

Healy rambled on, oblivious to the minor disturbance in his congregation. "Those who want to make a good impression outwardly are trying to compel you to be purified spiritually. The only reason they do this is to avoid being persecuted for the cross of Christ. Not even those who are purified obey the law, yet they want you to be purified that they may boast about your flesh. May I never boast except in the cross of our Lord Jesus Christ, through which the world has been crucified to me, and I to the world. Neither purification nor impurification means anything; what counts is a new creation. Peace and mercy to all who follow this rule, even to the Israel of God. Finally, let no one cause me trouble, for I bear on my body the marks of Jesus."

Hours must have passed since stepping into the church. Now, recalling another reason he didn't attend Sunday service, Potter wished he had a timepiece, if, for nothing else, to see how long they listened to Healy drone on. With brow crinkled upon his glossy face, the man animatedly waved his arms behind his post, his long green and yellow ecclesiastical robe glittering in the light. A bejeweled miter sat atop his head, embroidered with a six-winged seraph. Bishop's attire, Potter immediately recognized. Something about the man struck him as odd... something about his vehemence Potter just couldn't place.

"The grace of our Lord Jesus Christ be with your spirit, brothers and sisters," he finally finished.

The congregation's resounding "amen" echoed through the rafters.

Thick beads of sweat trickled from under Healy's miter, which he audaciously dabbed with a white handkerchief.

The congregation filtered out in order at the service's end, starting with the front pew. Charon Dotterweich guided his wife down the pew with a gentleman's open arms, as if she didn't have the willpower to find the way herself. Rounding the corner down the aisle toward the exit, he shot another scowling glance at the Potters, which Nora, and Clara, clearly caught.

"Did you enjoy the service, Clara," Nora asked, pointedly ignoring the Dotterweichs.

Clara scrunched her face. "I think so. I don't understand the minister's talk, though."

"It's okay, sweetheart. I agree, Minister Healy can be a bit much. The sermon was about Paul the apostle, who gave his life for the good of his people once he realized he did everythin he could here on this earth. He says those who've done bad will have the same bad inflicted upon them, and those who've done good will be graciously rewarded. And, most importantly, you must hinder your fellow brother and sister from fallin towards the dark." She turned to Potter. "That bout what you got out of it, Bill?"

Potter only smirked. They stood waiting their turn to exit, then walked out into the aisle, Potter stepping aside to let Nora out.

"Thank you, Bill. You are quite the gentleman." Nora headed to the open French doors, then paused, turning back. "Please forgive me for rushin away. I must go on ahead and open the store. This time of day is prime for business, with the post-service foot traffic and all. Thank you for indulgin me today."

"Our pleasure, Nora."

Nora, exiting the church, bustled down the dusty walkway... but not before turning and stealing one last glance. Potter gazed back at her as he and the young'uns stepped through the French doors, Isaac and Clara skipping out.

Sweet, sweet freedom. Though he found himself missing Nora's floral essence, a bouquet of scents reminiscent of lavender.

7

Charon and Lamiya Dotterweich promptly returned to their two-story adobe brick farmhouse, just beyond the woodlands on a three-hundred-acre open prairie. Though "promptly" somewhat overstated their speed. Buckley, clad in his usual black suit and top hat, moved the carriage forward at a dreadful snail's pace. Charon knew better than to heckle his silver-haired driver, however. The ancient one-eyed Irish Yankee tended toward crankiness.

Charon remained plenty miffed himself, red in the face as he reflected on that tacky troglodyte of a man and his unruly offspring. Who enters the house of God *after* the start of service?

The wrath of God is revealed from heaven against all ungodliness and unrighteousness of men.

Romans 1:18 reminded him of today's sermon. Quite delightful, and appropriate. The minister touched upon such topics too rarely, though, and Healy had been a bit gregarious in his sermon deliverance. Not the *best* administer of the Lord's word, Healy... but these days, proper practice in southeast New Mexico seemed scarce.

Charon sighed. *The world's an imperfect place; no hiding that.* If only the minister spent more time on Zephaniah 1:15. Now *that* was the verse Charon most feared.

Buckley, jowls sagging like a basset hound as he mustered a frowning smile, finally let them out at the front door before parking the rig alongside the barn.

Charon exited the coach and reached for his better half. With a gentle grasp of his hand, Lamiya elegantly made her way down onto the iron step, one foot entangled within the long chemise beneath her dress.

"Careful, my dear, careful now," he warned, gently lifting the dress to help her descend and ending with a soft kiss on her gloved hand.

She blushed, bearing a sheepish grin.

The Dotterweichs, devout Christo-pagans of the highest order—though just devout *Christians,* as far as the nosey God-fearing community needed to know—met in church, fell in love in church, and subsequently, and obviously, married in church. They'd spent the entire sanctity of their union spreading *God's Work,* as they called their benevolent practice, to cities in need, across many denominations, all over God's green earth. Anything to avert the possibility of Zephaniah 1:15, The Day of Wrath, from coming to fruition.

Lamiya's careful and slow descent, a reminder of their age, worried him that this mission could prove to be their last. Sure, Charon felt great, but he'd be lying if he said he hadn't, too, felt the slow deteriorating effects of Father Time. Regardless, in retrospect, he saw *The Work* as a monumental achievement, the culmination of years of tireless effort.

Upon its establishment in 1876, they relocated from the nascent town of Wichita Falls, Texas, to Missouri Plaza. Prior to that was Jonesboro, Arkansas, and before that, Chattanooga, Tennessee, right along the Trail of Tears—a period in the Southeast when Charon worked under Andrew Jackson, *vanishing Indians,* as the ethnic cleansing work had been coined. Truly, the best of both worlds. Charon, paid handsomely, traveled with his government contract while he and Lamiya spread benevolence, *a religious cleansing,* in the infancy of each previously unfamiliar territory. They never stayed anywhere longer than two to four years. The incorporation of a township meant The Work was finished. Time to move on.

But they knew The Work could never be finished. Not really. Not when sinful townships demanding a proper cleansing were establishing across this incredible Land of Liberty. The Trail of Tears may have dried up with the Jackson Campaign concluding; Charon aged out of government work at roughly the same time. However, God's Work... horns a plenty. And they didn't need to travel too far to find it. Eight years ago, just three hundred and fifty short miles away, they stumbled upon a newly budding settlement.

Missouri Plaza.

Now, this newfound, albeit peculiar, community was in dire need of purification. And this purification had an expiration. There were rules, simple rules to decontaminating the inherent sins and secrets fabricated and weaved into a settlement. Only this time, initially unbeknownst to Charon and Lamiya, the work took much longer than before. Years, even. They supposed this was okay. Even though their soaring spirits had endured the toils of time, their aging bodies had not. Travel proved difficult. Besides, the Dotterweichs quite enjoyed settling into their new abode in the middle of nowhere, New Mexico.

Lamiya walked inside ahead of Charon, who paused to admire the old farmhouse. At one time, it had flourished with livestock: horses, cows, chickens, pigs, sheep. The place had previously belonged to the McDermotts, an elderly couple from Odessa. The retired farmers had built this home with their bare hands in the 1830s, raised nine children, and fostered and maintained said livestock.

8

Buckley saw their dairy cow—their only cow—grazing by the small creek, far from the property, by the edge of the woodlands. She must have escaped from the fenced pen behind the barn, the wood suffering severe dry rot from age. He readjusted his eye patch, just to be absolutely certain his eye didn't deceive him. As usual, it didn't. He huffed and ambled his way out to bring her back in. After securing the cow and giving a good slap on her hind, sending her in motion, he stopped and glanced at the poorly constructed grave markers. Two busted pieces of wood comprised each one, tied together to form a cross. Eight of them haphazardly lined the perimeter.

Buckley crossed himself and lit a cigarette.

9

Charon walked through the front door and hung his hat, placing his jacket on a corner rack alongside it. Then he turned and peered up at the large crucifix above the door. Blessing himself, he walked back out. Time to prepare an early lunch.

Save for the remnants of decaying straw and dried, decomposed dung scattered over cracked clay, the barn which once housed horses now lay mostly barren. *Mostly.* A barrel containing a sectioned side of Chisum's beef awaited him. He stuck his hand into the brining solution and pulled out the hind, placing it on the small table beside. As he picked up the cleaver from its place on the wall, he could already imagine the satisfying sound it would make as it sliced into the salted flesh.

He smiled. Upon their arrival in town, he'd known the best course of action from experience: immerse himself into the community and set up shop. No better way to do so than providing a necessary service. Of course, he wasn't classically trained, so to speak. But oh, he had oodles of experience in the abattoir arts—mostly with those savage and wayward Redskins—and wouldn't you just know it? Such shop had yet to be established in the plaza. *God's Will.* Charon was sure of it.

Charon the Butcher opened for business in spring of 1876.

With precision, he sliced the hind into half inch strips, his fingers coated in the cold, slick blood. He instinctively reached for a nearby towel to wipe them off when a crucifix hanging on the wall grabbed his attention. One of many. He turned to glance around at the crosses. At least thirty or so covered the walls, nailed helter-skelter. He followed their winding path with fond memory toward the back, stopping halfway to admire the set of old shackles, desolately hanging from oxidized chains bolted to metal wall plates. Gently, he lifted one, turning it over in his hand; he did the same with the set next to it. Then he continued to the end, overlooking a long table horizontally situated alongside the back wall. Chains and shackles rested in each corner. His hand brushed over the dusted, splintered wood, over reddish-brown stains engrained on the top board.

Having his shop in earshot of the postmaster, Charon was privy to some good news. Exciting news: the conclusion of their work in Missouri Plaza. Soon this town would be official in the law's eyes, with Smith likely appointed first mayor. And, on top of that, new blood had arrived. Fresh, young blood. The cleansing was almost complete... though the threat of Zephaniah 1:15 still loomed over the town. *The day of wrath; the day of distress and anguish; the day of trouble and ruin; the day of darkness and gloom; the day of clouds and blackness.*

But one needn't worry...

He kneeled in front of the altar and crossed himself in front of a large crucifix on the wall above. From underneath, he pulled a skull from his tzompantli of eight, one for each year in Missouri Plaza—not counting the McDermotts'. All children.

Charon knew the cautionary tale of Abraham being tested by God to sacrifice his own son; he figured that was why so many people today frowned upon human sacrifice. But what about the Old Testament—more specifically, the Book of Amos, or the Book of Leviticus? The New Testament's Acts of the Apostles? The mention of ancient deity Moloch particularly sparked Charon's curiosity. "Passing children through the fire," Moloch called it: a sacrifice of purification. Charon's discovery of a similar Incan ritual, through his studies at Oxford as a boy, had made its appearance along the Trail of Tears. And the results proved undeniable.

He caressed the small skull, softly wiping away dust and admiring its chiseled features. His hand brushed over the mandible, the grin. A loose tooth fell from the upper front palate, and he smiled too. A seed. A seed that would ensure continued growth and prosperity. As he returned the skull to its home, two hands firmly squeezed and rubbed his upper back on either side of his neck.

He placed a hand on Lamiya's. "It's time again, my lady. It's time for rejuvenation."

"Yes, dear."

"We must prepare for *Capacocha*. We must prepare for the strawberry moon." He offered her a thin smile. "To restore cosmological order, to satisfy the Almighty, I must once again ferry over these innocent souls."

CHAPTER 10

Ida Horton poked her graying head in the doorway of McKinney's disheveled office. The racket coming from the holding cells down the hall, along the rear of the corridor, etched her weathered face with bewilderment. The sheriff didn't seem bothered, though. The stale scent of coffee lingered in the heavily stagnant air of the windowless room where he sat, parked behind a busy desk, meticulously filling out paperwork in the overcrowded shoebox of a space. She watched, waiting an eternity for him to notice her.

Lately, this chaos was their life. Boxes of case files, mostly old records, flanked his desk, stacked from floor to ceiling, while every day McKinney painfully yet skillfully maneuvered around them while dealing with the other soon-to-be-filed paperwork. A task, it seemed, he'd never be free from. A sea of folders, papers, and an overflowing ashtray engulfed his desk; a shiny red apple sat forlorn in the far corner. His rotund body could be partially to blame for the lack of adequate mobility, though the fact he could do much of his job from his seat always impressed Ida. The lifestyle suited him just fine.

Ida knocked on the door frame. "Tolbert?"

"Yeup," McKinney replied, not looking up from writing. His tongue peeked out from the side of mouth.

"You're about to have some company."

"Heh?"

Ida sighed. She spoke in a nasally, soft voice, which she knew he found invariably frustrating, moreover with a full house. The noise from the jail increased, a riotous echo spreading up the corridor.

"Company!" Ida declared over the racket. "Yuh-you're marshal's walking in." She pushed her large, sliding specs back up the bridge of her nose.

"Christ, Ida, can we get someone to shut these delinquents up!? I-I can't even hear myself think for God's sake. Where the hell is Gobson?"

"Just returning from lunch," she said with mock relief.

Deputy Gobson appeared, ducking under the frame—his blocky body barely fit through the doorway—and holding a thick sandwich. "*Share-wiff,*" the bear of a man said, particles falling from his mouth as he gnashed his food.

"I need you to shut those men up in there!" McKinney, hilariously shorter, peered up into Gobson's doe eyes.

Gobson stopped chewing and gawked down the corridor, finally noticing the noise. "How?"

McKinney stopped writing and slammed his fists on the desk. "Shit, Gobson, I don't know... use that good sense of yours. Maybe try the usual—a pail of trough water in the face oughta do it."

2

Tynan entered the Wichita County Sheriff's office, holding Plummer by the back of his grimy neck, his hands shackled behind. Blood soaked the dirty bandage on his captive's injured, poorly treated limb. Tynan had found a Covington physician to apply sutures on day one into their three-day travel north, more than enough kindness, before letting nature take its course.

Gobson, standing in the doorway of McKinney's office, turned to the slamming of the front door. "Well, goddamn!"

"McKinney here?" Tynan spoke sharply, walking Plummer to Gobson. He already knew the answer.

"Why yes, sir, he is."

"Is that Dunkin?" McKinney shouted from the back, trying to squeeze himself from the restraints of his work area.

Gobson smiled, taking Plummer by the arm. "This man give you any trouble, sir?"

"Oh, I don't know." Tynan turned to Plummer. "What do you say, Plummer? How's that trigger finger?"

Plummer spit at Tynan, hitting his ascot; he shimmied from Gobson's grasp, kicking his legs up toward Tynan's face. Tynan backed away as Gobson dropped his lunch to grab Plummer, locking him—with little effort—in a bear hug.

Plummer continued to kick and thrust with all his weight. "Piss on you, Mary, you filthy sumbitch! You pray to Christ I never run into you again, shiny shit-heel!"

"All right, come on," Gobson said through gritted teeth. "Let's go!"

Plummer looked up at Gobson. "Lips on my ass, you!"

"And he calls *me* Mary." Tynan dabbed the dirtied ascot with its matching pocket square.

"Okay." Gobson dragged him backwards, past McKinney's office, toward the jail. "You made me drop my sandwich."

"Hey! Hey!" Plummer shouted back at Tynan through the doorway, still in aggravated transit. "You—you tell em how many innocent men you shot to git me!?"

McKinney appeared, completely filling the doorframe of the front room. "You found him! Christ, that was quick." He beamed. "Come in, have a seat."

Tynan, deadpan, sat with his legs crossed in the chair in front of the desk, carefully removing his tinted specs and using the pocket square to polish each lens.

McKinney squeezed his wide backside into his screaming seat. "What's that he's spewing about 'innocent men,' now?"

"Got into an altercation with an Edward Murphy and a Frank Ellis. Evidently, they *also* got word of the bounty." Tynan glared up at McKinney. "Now, how do you spose that is?"

"Wasn't by me," McKinney said defensively.

"Mm-hmm." Tynan held his specs up, inspecting them in the gas-powered wall lamp.

"Those names, uh... sound familiar. How do I know em?"

"Maybe it's because they're fuckin outlaws, Tolbert. They obviously weren't usin their real identities. Hell, they don't even look the same—barely recognized them, myself. Sure smelled the same, though. Trash." Tynan popped a piece of rolled leaf into his mouth.

"Christ." McKinney shook his head.

"I don't know what kind of horseshit show you runnin here."

The banter from the jail cells increased two-fold.

"Sorry, Tynan, as you can see—*and hear*—this place is absolute goddamn chaos."

"Yeah, what *is* all that?" Tynan turned his head and glanced over his shoulder.

"It's a real monkey farm over here, I tell ya. Those cages you're hearing have been full every day the last two weeks. Crime is up. People seem to be losing their minds over something. And we're short staffed! Lost a good man just the other day, and hell, some days I'm lucky to pick my head off this desk here. Buried in bullshit seven days a week. We just can't keep up the comings and goings of men who volunteer themselves to lend a helpful hand. So, I apologize if someone slipped one past me. This city is in a plague, and I honestly can't tell if things is getting better or worse."

Tynan put a gloved hand up. "All right, all right."

"I don't know if there's any papers on them. Was it at least a righteous shoot?"

"A righteous shoot?" Tynan scoffed. "They're war deserters. Guilty of every war crime imaginable." He spit hotly into a pail on the floor, unsure of its intended purpose—likely a wastebasket—but not giving enough of a shit to ask. "I knew them from before. Truth be told, I thought they were dead till I saw them in Oklahoma City."

"Christ." McKinney continued to shake his head.

"They're lucky that's all they got. The story around the campfire on those two..." Tynan *huffed*. Moot point. He pulled his watch, snapping it open. "Got my money?"

"Two grand?"

"Two grand."

McKinney leaned back, glancing through the open doorway, and called, "Ida!"

She appeared instantly in the door frame, as if she'd been present in the room the whole time. "Yes, Tolbert?"

McKinney jumped. "Christ, you scared me, woman! Quit listening in on my conversations."

She rolled her eyes. "My apologies."

"Bring this man his money, will ya?"

Ida nodded and stepped out.

"Ooh, speaking of which, you might like this." McKinney swiveled in his chair to face a tall credenza alongside his desk against the wall. Rummaging through an open drawer cluttered with only wanted posters, he pulled one and placed it over scattered file folders across the desk. "Got word the other day that Joseph Griffin was spotted in Denver. Wouldn't you just believe it!?"

Tynan leaned over to see the picture, hand drawn, of a clean-cut young man. The name struck a chord. "Griffin?"

"Yeah. His crew robbed the Kansas Pacific, not once, but twice in '63 and '64. Left a whole slew of bodies behind. Law *and* civilian."

"Huh." Recognition hit Tynan, shifting his demeanor from impassive to bewildered. He'd read the name in the paper before, as he did many a wanted man, but quite some time had passed since he'd seen Griffin's. "We were actually from the same neighborhood. Southeast Connecticut."

"You know him?"

"Not really. Enlisted together. Served in the same company. Older gentleman. Older than me, anyhow. Presumed him dead or imprisoned, like most of them men."

"He's very much alive. Got two kids. Boy and girl."

Tynan waved his hands in protest. "Wait, how do you know any of this? The way things are runnin here these days, sounds like a buncha hearsay horseshit. A wild goose chase, if you ask me."

"Well, first we got a tip from an older lady, fifties, I'd say. Came on in and said she thought she recognized him while 'passing through.' Couple days later, we found her *late* husband—old outlaw named Mc-Cormac—in the middle of the Denver woods. Couple hunters stumbled upon him tied to a tree, half frozen and delirious. They brought him to the Denver sheriff, who identified him through old papers."

"I thought you said *late* husband?"

"Oh, yeah, he's been presumed dead for years." McKinney chuckled. "Sonovabitch was a Cowtown Marauder!"

Tynan's eyes narrowed inquisitively.

"Griffin's old gang."

"No shit."

"No shit. Just arrived this morning. Locked up in the back with the other animals. Unfortunately, he ain't talking, but that don't matter much."

"So, where's Griffin?"

"Skipped town, I would guess. Only thing we got from McCormac was that he worked in the mines out there. We've had correspondence with the mine's owner, a man named Bennett, but that turned up nothing, other than he was going by the name Sullivan. No residency. No nothing. I know it's not much to go on, but if you want to pursue, the bounty is ten grand dead. Twenty-five, alive."

Tynan's eyes lit up. He spit in the pail, catching the dribble with a leather finger.

"This is an egregiously violent individual who's eluded capture on many occasions. And he's likely aware he's been discovered and will be looking over his shoulder. Why he left this sorry sack of shit alive is beyond me. At any rate, with that said, I'll send you along with two of my marshals."

"I don't need any of *your* men."

"It wasn't a request. This sonovabitch will *not* disappear again. If you want the bounty, this is the deal."

"Why not send your own men alone? Why ask me?"

"You're the best tracker I know, and I want this done quickly. Before he vanishes. Two men is all I can spare right now, all things considered. I think three of yous can bring him down."

Tynan stood up and once again checked his watch.

"And we want him alive. Got it?"

"Loud and clear, sheriff." He flashed a sly grin. "On second thought... bring me McCormac."

McKinney blinked, clearly disquieted by the expression on Tynan's typically deadpan face. "I already told you, he ain't talking."

Tynan snapped his watch shut. "Persuading conversation from another man is my specialty, wouldn't you say?"

3

Deputy Gobson, by the arm, firmly placed a ragged McCormac in the chair Tynan had previously occupied. Then he plodded off to stand to the side, picking doughy bread from crooked teeth with a pick.

Tynan, now sitting comfortably in McKinney's chair, removed his hat, exposing his long, fringed hair. The dark tresses parted down the middle, draped over tightly cropped sides. He leaned back, plucked the apple from the desk, and gently turned it over in his leathered palm. A shiny red delicious apple.

McKinney stood stoically in his open doorway, his rotundness completely blocking the entrance.

The room fell silent.

McCormac, apparently just as sullied as the day he was found, reeked something God awful. He glanced between the three men, bewildered. One could almost hear the ticking of the clock on the far wall. He scratched his head with cuffed wrists, the rattle of his chains breaking the stale, noxious silence.

Tynan needed a few moments—McCormac's face, older, much more haggard—but he soon recognized this scum. His blood boiled, radiating under his clothing and across his face. He turned to McKinney. "Leave us."

McKinney nodded sideways toward the open door at Gobson. They exited.

Tynan stared impassively through tinted lenses, waiting for McCormac to speak first.

McCormac, still seated, picked his nose and wiped the wet snot on his jacket sleeve. The ticking sound of the second hand on the wall clock hammered in the silence. Music to Tynan's ears. He needn't wait long, either.

McCormac finally broke. "You gonna eat that apple, mister?"

"Ohhh, that depends," Tynan said slyly.

"On?"

"On what it is you can tell me about the man who tied you to a tree and left you for dead." Tynan waved the apple under his nose teasingly, then took an ample snap into its crisp, juicy flesh. He chewed, mouth open with slow deliberation.

McCormac didn't respond. He eyed the apple.

"You look like you could use a hot meal." The words stuck in his throat, but Tynan forced them out with a hard gulp. "I can arrange that."

Though he loathed the presence of such scum, and he sure as hell didn't advocate bribery under usual circumstances, Tynan recognized the uniqueness of this situation. A waiting game. Soon, the entire country would know of this bounty, and convoys of hunters spanning from specialists to novices would flock to find Griffin. Everyone looking to cash in, including the savages. The worst of the worst.

Tynan would not let such a free-for-all happen now, not with this little ace up his sleeve. Griffin was *his*.

"A hot meal, huh?" McCormac flouted. "They gonna hang me by the neck or worse, an you wanna offer me a free lunch?"

"There ain't no free lunches. At least, that's what my father once told me. No... but what I can offer is a deal of sorts. One where you at least live and maybe don't rot in a cage the rest of your days." Tynan placed the bitten apple in the middle of the desk.

McCormac, interest piqued, gazed longingly at the apple. "What, uh, is it I gotta do?"

Tynan removed his specs and leaned forward. "Tell me *everything* you know about Joseph Griffin."

CHAPTER 11

"Welcome to the exciting world of textiles, Isaac!" Mr. Wilburn held the front doors of the mill open, a huge, squinting grin painted across his narrow face.

Isaac smiled, Mr. Wilburn's elation easing some of the knots tied in his stomach during the transit on his father's old nag. After all, today was a proud day for him: his first as a working man. Like Pa.

He stepped into a spacious, open room. Loud. Six large metal contraptions lined the front perimeter, each operated by six women sitting on stools. A deep whirring, the clicking and clanking of moving pieces, resonated through the hollow space, requiring them to raise their voices to speak above it.

Isaac took it all in, eyes wide. "Wow."

Mr. Wilburn smiled. "Let me give you the ten-penny tour!"

"I—I don't have any money, Mr. Wilburn."

His boss laughed, leading Isaac around in a semicircle. "Well, looks like you are in the right place, then. Along the wall, as you can see, we have spinning and weaving machines."

"Machines?"

"Yes. These giant, clunky pieces of metal. They separate the bushels of clean wool, which the workers over here feed into it." Mr. Wilburn pointed to the side of the machine.

Isaac watched the soft material "feed" the contraption as an elder, about his grandmother's age, pressed on a lower paddle with her foot. On the opposite end, thin strands fired out, spooling around narrow wooden rods. He'd never seen such an intricate process.

"And," Mr. Wilburn continued, "with the power of *dark sorcery* inside this machine, the wool *magically* turns to twine."

Isaac's mouth fell open, then snapped shut. He shot a suspicious glance at Mr. Wilburn.

The man just smiled wider. "Want to see your workstation!?"

Isaac nodded eagerly, and the two walked down the winding stairs to the first level, which stood below the bridge on a squat piece of land along the riverbank. The wheel on this side slowly churned, its paddles scooping water loudly enough to be heard through the thin walls.

"How are you and your family settling in—been about two weeks now?"

"Good. Pa's working for Mr. Chisum. I spend most of the time looking after Clara while he's away. Been working a lot, myself! Pa showed me how to shoot a rifle, so I hunt now. And we've been digging up the backyard trying to hit water from the river for our well. It's tiring, I tell ya."

"See, you're already on your way. Hard work pays off. Trust me."

They reached the first floor, and Isaac immediately noticed the absence of windows. Dim. Very dim. Warm as well. A few steam-powered lanterns hung from the walls, casting a sparse, flickering illumination. Barrels and crates, some filled with fabric waste and others empty, cluttered the area, all placed in a disorderly manner. Spools of twine, in various drab colors and sizes, lined the lattice of metal shelving high against the wall. The wooden floor, unrecognizable with dinge, lay shrouded in fabric pieces and woolen dust balls, which shifted about as the two walked along the only clear path to the back. Isaac raised his brow, highly doubting whether anyone had ever swept or cleaned the place.

Mr. Wilburn pointed to the narrow hallway to the right of the stairs, which led to a door. "That—is where I live. It's not much, but it's home."

Piles of pelts rested in one corner; another corner held a large crate with the bottom cut out. Raw sheep's wool filled the container, filthy, some stained red. Next to the crate, and immediately snaring Isaac's eye, stood a giant monstrosity, the likes of which Isaac had never seen. Several rows of tightly wound cylindrical blades comprised the façade of the machine, aligned in rows and rows like honed teeth.

"This is the carding machine," Mr. Wilburn explained.

"Carding?" Isaac gulped, analyzing every belt, every wheel, every blade.

"Textile separator is all it is. You see, this machine processes the wool before we clean it and it reaches the upstairs. It filters out all the dirt, blood, and gunk from the material. Stretches it out some, too. *Your* job is to feed the wool into the separator, slowly, mind you, and make sure it doesn't jam up! Sounds much more complicated than it is. Think you can handle that?"

Isaac nodded tentatively, unable to avert his eyes.

"Used to be my job, but we are getting quite busy. I can't keep up with running this mill and all the projects me and Van will soon be involved in."

Mr. Wilburn pulled a ripcord, and the carding machine came to life with a vociferous squeal, the noise soon dissolving into a deep, uninterrupted grumble.

A bead of sweat trickled down Isaac's brow.

2

Isaac, exhausted, ended his first day of manly work, his clothing drenched from hours of feeding the carding machine. The lack of ventilation didn't help, either. He couldn't wait to go home. He smiled as he climbed the stairs toward Mr. Wilburn's office, already imagining the proud look on Pa's face.

Eerie quiet hung heavy in the mill as he reached an empty factory floor. The women, too, had ended their day and departed.

Mr. Wilburn's office, a long rectangular room, loomed high in the back center of the mill floor, enclosed by four-foot pony walls with beams—empty frames where one would usually find a window—leading to the ceiling. Two desks faced each other, both covered in paperwork, and Mr. Wilburn sat at the one facing the doorway. The chaos in the basement closely mirrored the office; small crates filled with random sized twine spools mingled with dismantled carding machine guts, pieces scattered helter-skelter.

Mr. Wilburn looked up with an awkward smile. "Don't mind the mess. Been working on fixing this machine for a time now." He stared with disgust at the bulk of parts in the corner. "Come, have a seat."

"Who shares the office with you?"

"No one, yet. In time, when we expand, that space will hopefully be occupied by my future right-hand man." Mr. Wilburn nodded at the empty desk. "This is big business, Isaac. As you can see, there are six machines out there. In five years, I would like to double that number. That is my dream."

Isaac, impressed, gazed serenely at the mill floor from his seat. He could almost rejoice in Mr. Wilburn's vision. Certainly, the mill held plenty of room for these *machines*.

"What is yours?" Mr. Wilburn asked.

Isaac blinked, the novel question catching him off guard. No one had ever bothered to inquire about his thoughts on anything before. "I—I—uh, I just don't know, Mr. Wilburn."

"It's okay to not know. I didn't. I only knew what I did *not* want. And when you know *that*, the rest tends to come."

Isaac wondered what exactly Mr. Wilburn meant. But he liked the ring of the words, and he certainly needed a place to start. At the very least, he knew he enjoyed a man's work far more than his usual chores.

After thanking Mr. Wilburn, Isaac jovially stepped from the front door onto the bridge, squinting as the blinding light penetrated his shocked pupils. Like the sun, gratification beamed from his narrow face. He had just completed his first full day of proper work. Grown up work. *So, this is what it's like to earn your keep.* An indescribable feeling washed over him, a euphoric emulsion of accomplishment and purpose. He turned his hands over, staring at the filth and fingernail grime. Callouses covered the middle part of his thumbs, palms too, from sweeping and mopping the basement floor.

Today, he was a man.

The orange sun's brilliant melancholy descent behind the Capitan Mountains marked the end of a gorgeous day. Hopefully, the first of many. Time to head home. He walked across to the Missouri Plaza side and untied Blanco from a long post which secured, he guessed, several employees' steeds. As he mounted and turned to cross the bridge, recollection of this morning's errand dawned on him. Pa had given him some silver before he left the house, requesting he stop at the butcher's shop for two pounds of tenderloin—the first time that the family would purchase meat in Missouri Plaza, as opposed to hunting it.

Lately, game proved scarce. Since acquiring the Bennett house, he and Pa had shot every expendable woodland creature on the property. Squirrel and jackrabbit didn't quite fill the belly, and until Pa ingratiated himself with Mr. Chisum, they'd be "up in Dick's meadow." Whatever that meant. Pa said funny things when tired, and ever since he started working for Mr. Chisum, he came home too tired to hunt or even to move, croaking about his "old body." Before bed, Isaac would find Pa sitting on the porch rocker, smoking one of those cigarette things he rolled and no doubt thought Isaac wasn't aware of.

Isaac entered the empty butcher shop. A long counter separated the front of the wide, horizontal room from the partially walled-off back, from which the proprietor emerged. His crimson hands, wet with fresh blood, mopped a heavily stained towel between his fingers, smearing the crimson around more than removing it. His apron, which must have appeared at one time white, had tanned and yellowed from either poor cleaning or heavy use. Maybe both. An age of dried blood blotched the fabric. But the rest paled in comparison to his horrible face.

Isaac stared, wide eyed. It was that mean old man from church!

The butcher pushed back the thinning bangs over his crown and attempted an awkward smile, more like a snarl. "You need something, son?"

Isaac tensed up, unable to process a thought. His skin flashed ice cold, and gooseflesh crawled up the back of his neck. He wanted to turn and leave, but something rooted his feet to the hardwood floor. Unable to avert his eyes from the red rag turning in the man's hands, he managed to sputter, "Uhhh... umm—"

"Speak up, boy," the man snapped. "You gotta tongue now, don't ya?"

"Yeh-yeh-yeh-yes—yes, sir. May-may I have two pounds uh-uh-of tenderloin, please, suh-sir?" Isaac wiped his forehead, which misted with perspiration.

The butcher paused briefly, gazing intently at Isaac with penetrating eyes before withdrawing to the chamber beyond the partition. The impulse to flee resurged, but the man returned moments later. He held a long, jagged, fatty cut of raw beef, which looked to Isaac like a mallet sculpted in flesh.

The butcher slammed the whole tenderloin down on the counter. "What's your name, son?" he said evenly.

Isaac, a foot away, recoiled. "Uh, Isaac, sir."

"You can call me Charon. No need to be all proper, though I do appreciate the respect. You and your family just move to town, I see?" He pulled a sharp, narrow blade from a knife sheath attached to his trousers and held it up. The metal gleamed in the golden light piercing through the side window.

"Yes, suh... Charon."

"Your father and sister, I saw. No mother?"

"Sh-she died. When we lived in Denver."

"Denver, you say. Now, that's quite a distance to travel to move to our little town. Must be tough getting along without a mother, I imagine." Charon trimmed away strips of fat and connective tissue with ease, tossing them to the side. "Can always depend on the power of God by your side, however. I saw yous in Church. Yous a religious family?"

Isaac watched with fascination as Charon sliced off the thin, fatty chain from one side, then flipped the meat, slicing away the silver skin and muscle. Aside from Pa dicing up a few rabbits, foxes, and other small woodland creatures, Isaac had never seen the barbaric mutilation of preparing meat—though, as he'd come to realize in recent weeks, such brutality merely served as a means for survival for most men. The art of catching, cleaning, and cooking meat felt like a rite of passage.

"Well, it's been the first time for a couple years for me and my sister. Our Ma used to bring us. But then we stopped going when she passed." Isaac glanced at the floor, slightly ashamed but not completely understanding why.

"You know it's a sin—a violation of your baptismal oath—to miss your weekly responsibility to assemble with your community. To be present for the Passion of our Christ, Lord, and Savior," Charon said, pointing the gritty blade at Isaac while wiping his tacky meat hand down the apron side.

Isaac, swallowing dryly as he peered at the knife, shook his head.

Charon began slicing two-inch medallions from the tenderloin strip. "Oh, yes. Your community, especially. They're there to support and guide you from straying from the narrow path that can only lead to eternal life. You recall your denomination?"

"Uhhh..." Isaac, nervous he didn't have an answer, stared off behind Charon.

"Best guess is you're Protestant. Makes the most sense, up in Colorado. Are you Methodist, like Minister Healy's church? Baptist? Presbyterian? Please, please to holy God"—Charon glanced up at the ceiling—"don't tell me you're Mormon." The blade, yet again, inched closer to the boy's face.

"I—don't really know. I know—I know I'm Christian."

Charon beamed brightly. He jabbed the tip of the knife into the countertop. "Well, we can at least thank Jesus for that, now, can't we?" He placed the medallions on one side of the cast iron scale; the cylindrical counterweight raised at the opposite end. The meat weighed in over two pounds, closer to three.

Charon began wrapping the pieces in brown paper. "I, myself, am Roman Catholic. However, beggars certainly can't be choosers, so the wife and I have converted to the mission's faith. We do, however, have a rousing suspicion our minister has come from Catholicism. His sermons, the way he carries himself. Been in many Protestant churches; I know the Lord's Prayer has been extended. They sure don't pray to the Saints during service. Mass usually ends with Benediction too. Not here, though.

"Your father a religious man? From first glance, I'm guessing no."

Isaac shrugged, unsure. "I spose not. He never went to church with us before last week."

Even though he never asked, Ma would often mention that Pa was either too exhausted or overwhelmed from his long shifts in the mine. Pa rarely mentioned God, which piqued Isaac's imagination about his beliefs.

"I knew it. Had him pegged for an atheist, soon as I saw his face. That's okay. What you need, son, is to receive the sacrament of confirmation. You won't get that here—Methodists stop at Baptism. Only then will you be fully received in the house of God, you hear? Lord knows how long you'll be kicking around this town. You want to get married someday, don't you?"

Isaac nodded.

"Speak up, son!"

Isaac twitched, jumping out of his skin. "Yes, Charon."

"All right then. Now, my brother, he's a traveling priest. Comes two, maybe three times a year to visit. And I tell you, you are in luck, son! He's gonna be arriving in town, end of the month. If you want, I can arrange a Confirmation service for you." Charon handed him the meat package. "I think that would be in your best interest, don't you?"

"Yes," Isaac said eagerly, nodding. "Uh, how much do I owe you?" He pulled loose change from his pocket, pushing it around with a thumb.

"Fifty-five cents, that'd be... however, for *you,* it's on the house."

"Huh?" Isaac glanced up, eyes wide. Surely, he'd heard wrong.

"You keep your pa's money, now. Buy yourself some new clothes. Supper's on me. Just as long as you meet my brother, Father Henry, at the end of the month. We'll get you properly confirmed, so you can live a long, holy life with the rest of us, among the *righteous*. At the end of it, you'll get right into those pearly gates where our Almighty Savior waits. That sound good to you?"

"Yes," Isaac said quickly, not totally convinced but knowing what Charon wanted to hear.

"All right then." Charon glanced toward the door. "You go on now."

Isaac hurried toward the exit. Confirmation did sound good, in theory. But coming from this daunting man's mouth? Some internal instinct immediately clicked, an inherent alarm sensing something... off. He reached for the door—

"One last thing."

Isaac froze at the entrance, slowly turning in the direction of Charon's chilling voice.

"Probably best not to tell your old man, at least not until after. He may not approve, or at least quite understand, your wanting to be in the House of God." Charon grinned, his full, gray teeth eerily reminiscent of the carding machine. "Wouldn't you agree, son?"

Isaac tentatively nodded his head and walked out.

Something about Charon struck him as odd, but as he rode the nag back home, he couldn't place what. Catholicism sounded interesting. Eternal salvation, even better. Free beef? Truly *amazing*. Though, for some reason, he doubted Pa would like the idea of him returning after discovering who ran the shop. Best not stress about that now, though. Too many things on the plate already. Hell, would Isaac even *have* time for a Confirmation? A working man earned his keep, and he took his responsibilities at the mill seriously. Not to mention his new promotion to primitive hunter/gatherer, in addition to his previous position as a full-time child rearing professional. After all, someone had to keep an eye on Clara. Isaac trotted proudly into the woodlands.

Eternal salvation might have to wait.

Chapter 12

"Come. It's time."

"Time?" Potter, exhausted from the day's work, gave Coffey a perplexed glance as he slipped out of his chaps on the ranch porch. His spine cracked as he leaned forward, his hips tightening and shooting warm pain down his left thigh. The long ride, after an even longer day under the blazing sun, left him sore and wearied to the bone. "Time for what?"

"Ya wanna know why we's the Jinglebob ranch, don'tcha?" Coffey teased.

Potter, despite a mild curiosity, at this point wanted nothing more than to slip out and head home.

Coffey evidently sensed his reluctance. "Come on. It be quick, I promise ya."

The duo entered the enclosed cowshed at the back of the ranch—a spacious area, currently occupied by recently arrived cattle. Potter had noticed them slowly pouring in over the last week, though he'd wondered why no one yet acclimated them to the herd.

"This here's our soon to be Jinglebob Cattle," Coffey explained, gesturing to the animals. "Our job, for the next week. Bill, we's gonna be brandin this here cattle with Chisum's *special* mark."

"What's that?"

"Watch."

Coffey pulled a six-inch blade from his back pocket and walked up to the first steer. Taking the floppy left ear and pulling it taut, he stuck the blade into the flesh at the root of the ear and, in one swift motion, sliced upward, splitting the ear into two separate segments. The cow bellowed hard, snorting and grunting.

The two men backed away.

For a moment, Potter wondered how much pain the animal felt. He didn't know much about cow ranching, but he doubted the necessity of splitting the ear to mark one's territory. Nevertheless, he found the endeavor interesting. "So, why's it called a 'Jinglebob?'"

Coffey smiled. "Ohhh, ya see, at one time or another some of the fellas used to wear these little metal trinkets on the spurs of their boots, that jingled when they walked. They called them jinglebobs. Boss liked it so much he decided to use the same name for his unique brandin."

That sounded about right, Potter thought, considering the capricious personality of his employer. He watched Coffey, who seemed capable of any job, work with an impressive and skillful touch. His loyalty to the ranch was matched only by his exceptional work ethic. It struck Potter that he hadn't asked yet.

He sighed, scratching the back of his grimy neck. "Hey, Coffey, can I ask you a favor?"

"Mm-hmm. Been waitin for this." Coffey ran the blade through another ear.

The cow bellowed.

"Me and the boy have been digging out a well in the backyard. Thing is, it's just two of us, and we're not making much headway. Don't know why, either." Potter scratched his head. "The boy, strong as he is, tires quickly, and, well, hell, I ain't no spring chicken either. Could sure use another hand out there."

"A well, eh?"

"Yeah, for whatever reason, there ain't one on the property. I can pay ya a few bucks for your time. That ain't no problem for me."

And it wasn't. Chisum paid handsomely for a day's work. Not mine money, but more than enough. Potter shoved a pre-rolled quirley between his lips.

"I owe ya a debt for my life, Bill. It be the least I can do for ya."

"You don't owe me anything, Coffey." Potter struck a match and lit the quirley, sucking back deeply on the tip and exhaling. Smoke remnants feathered from his nostrils. "Of all the reasons I ever had to pull the steel, yours has given me my only solace."

This made Coffey smile. He nodded in appreciation. "I'll jus go clear it with the Big Man, first. Should be no problem, though."

The men walked out of the shed, Coffey toward the main house, Potter to Bessie's mare, still tied to a post outside the ranch. Behind his horse, off the side of the cowshed, several ranch-hands surrounded a large, gated pen. Elija, Hiram, and Salvador leaned against the outside, whistling and hollering, while Emiliano and Gustine stood inside. The black stallion loomed just past them. Massive. Striking in both size and beauty. A majestic creature, wild and stunning.

The beast, neighing and snorting, edged itself into the corner of the pen, trying to avoid the unrelenting ranch hands. So far, it had successfully run one man, Emiliano, ragged in circles; though, in an oblong space, the horse possessed limited means of escape. Emiliano slowly and gently inched his way forward, a lasso draped between his two hands. Unbeknownst to the beast, the other hand, Gustine, stealthily climbed the gate's middle rung behind it, gripping a stock saddle. The beast beheld its captor, pacing each step for creeping step, the sunlight shimmering across its silky broad shoulders.

Emiliano locked eyes with the beast, now nearing pen's edge, and began twirling the lasso side to side.

The stallion neighed, rearing.

Potter slowed his pace, turning his head to see what he knew would come next.

Gustine leaned in, hands stretched forward to hover a saddle over the stallion's back. Emiliano's lasso loop enlarged—in direct proportion to his shit-eating grin—the faster he butterflied, zigzagging elaborately side to side and rolling behind his back before he finally raised it above his head. A bit garish, Potter thought.

The stallion's nostrils flared as it drove its front hoof into the ground with a snort, pawing back dirt with vicious strokes. Its head thrashed back and forth, heaving its shaggy, long mane. Emiliano, ten feet from the beast, launched the rope. It landed swiftly around its neck, Emiliano quickly pulling taut. The stallion resisted, yanking back on the rope and thrusting violently. Emiliano fell to a knee, holding tight to his side. Gustine, now over the struggling beast, dropped the saddle on its back.

"I got'im! I got'im! Get on!" Emiliano called through gritted teeth, holding on for dear life.

Gustine jumped on top, gripping the beast's neck to keep from sliding off, while two other hands jumped over the railing into the pen to quickly batten down the saddle. The task proved an impossibility. Emiliano's grip slipped, the rope tearing through callused hands as the horse thrashed. Finally, he let go, and the beast shot up, kicking out its front legs. The other men turned for the closest railing.

NEEEIIIGGGGHHHH!

Gustine fired off the saddle, somersaulting over the edge of the pen and slamming face first on the dirt. The stallion bolted toward Emiliano, who turned and ran for the pen's edge, fifteen feet away. Without a second to spare, he escaped the horse's trampling hooves and flipped himself over the gate, landing on his back, while the other men standing alongside had a good, hearty laugh.

Potter smiled, kept walking. He'd almost reached Bessie's mare when a voice stopped him dead in his tracks.

"Where is the new guy? You know, Mr. Silent." Emiliano shouted, smacking his chaps and dusting himself off. "Get his ass here! See what *he* can do!"

Approaching Bessie's horse, Potter flipped up the collar of his jacket and pulled his hat low. Not the friendliest bunch, the ranch hands. In fact, Potter got nothing but cold shoulders and frosty stares the first week, with the second diverging only with the addition of brief and brusque observational remarks regarding the task at hand. Thankfully, Coffey, at least half of the time, had been there to talk to. But Potter understood the animosity. New man. Strange man. No one is to be trusted, not until they've proven themselves. Of course, staying strangers suited Potter just fine… and if his critical change in clothing sufficed long enough for him to escape notice and return home, so much the better.

"There he is!" Elija shouted, pointing. A marijuana cigarette hung from his lips. He mumbled something inaudible to the other men, then yelled, "You can sure herd in some cattle, but can *you* tame the beast!?"

Ugghh… ain't this just swell.

"Yeah, we hear you's got a special way with horses, gringo!" Salvador taunted.

Coffey, on the porch at Chisum's rear screened door, stopped short of stepping into the kitchen.

"Let's see what you got, New Guy," Hiram chimed in.

Potter continued to untie the reins. "Sorry fellers. Not today."

"What chicken-shit. Ya know, I'm tired of Boss bringin in these no-good pasture strays. Ain't none ever been worth the steer shit on my heels."

Potter stopped. He turned with the thousand-yard stare down, blood pressure soaring. What does one do? Challenging these men—men he had to see on the daily—wasn't much of an option. Neither was walking away. Certainly not. It would happen again tomorrow and the day after that. Can't shoot them either. Though, a man's got to have principals. Can't just drop every man that cracks wise. Else, you'd be no different from common gutter trash.

Potter glanced over to where Coffey watched. Sandy, sitting next to Coffey, watched too, dust clinging to her shaggy, waxen coat.

He dropped the reins, faced the leering men, and headed straight toward Hiram, standing confidently by his horse with a smirk. As Potter neared, though, Hiram backed against his steed, hand cautiously hovering over his sidearm. Potter, without stop or hesitation, swiftly reached toward his throat. He seized the rope slumped around the horse's saddle horn, just above the ranch hand's neck, and continued straight past Hiram, who stepped from his path as Potter entered the pen.

The stallion snorted and shook its head, dragging its front leg with a penetrating gaze. This boy was worked up. Potter, with utter caution, inched his way forward, rope in hand; his eyes locked with the distressed creature. It hoofed its way left, right, looking for a way around the advancing man. The lasso, still draped over its shoulders, dragged behind.

Potter stepped forth, beginning the gentle swing of the rope in his hands. The stallion's meticulous retreat ended abruptly, cut short when its hindquarters met the gate. A wind picked up; dust emanated from the sandy loam, circulating through the pen. A fine mist obstructed Potter's view of his grunting opponent. He waited for his moment, dancing the lasso full swing above his head. And, as the dust settled, the anxious creature, cornered, got an eye full of its tall aggressor. Instantly, it reared up on hind legs, kicking forth its front hooves.

NEEEIIIIGGGGHHH!

The rope wrapped around the front legs, and, as it landed, Potter pulled taut and held tight. In a fruitless endeavor to evade, the horse managed to entwine itself, promptly collapsing onto both front knees.

The ranch-hands exchanged bewildered glances, Gustine gaping in surprise.

Potter approached the scared animal, and, with a gentle hand, began stroking its silky, long mane. He whispered into the stallion's ear, acutely aware of the other men leaning in to listen without any possibility of making out the tune. The same one Bessie would sing to ease her stubborn mare, ironically titled, "All the Pretty Little Horses." A moment later, the horse lay down fully, almost serene. Elija cautiously entered the pen, and Potter turned and handed over the reins. A look of shock still hung on Elija's sun-drenched face as he began tightening the saddle.

"Here." Elija handed over his green cigarette. "Good for the nerves."

Potter gave it a quick, narrow look. "No, thanks. Got my own recipe."

Coffey, still grinning in the doorway, shook his head and finally entered. Potter walked out of the pen, brooding, his face vexed as he tipped his hat to the men before turning toward the ranch.

He grinned. *Ain't no flies on me.*

2

The woodlands abruptly broke, revealing the concealed—and recently sickled—enclosure as Potter and Coffey arrived at the Bennett house.

Coffey whistled. "Color me impressed, Bill. This here is some range ya got. I can see why everyone wants a piece."

"Father in-law owns it," Potter explained. "He had it built for his brother sometime after the war. Lent him the money to do so. Why here, you may ask. I couldn't rightfully tell ya. The man could have had it made had he gone into business with his brother."

"No well, eh?"

The men dismounted and walked to the backyard.

"Nope. Had to cut the grass down to be absolutely certain. It's crazy." Potter pointed out a distance beyond the house. "Evidently, Bennett used to fetch his water from the Pecos there."

Coffey looked over. "Sweet heavenly Jesus."

"Yup. My sentiment exactly. John Bennett was a peculiar feller. You see, me and the boy started one just beyond the outhouse." Potter pointed again. "But it turned up shit. Got some shovels in the barn. Figured we'll start fifty yards or so up from that one."

The men unmounted, and the young'uns exploded from the front door, Clara in the lead.

Potter scooped her up in his tired arms. "Kids, you remember Mr. Coffey, don't ya?"

They both nodded, exchanging perplexed glances. Their pa hadn't brought anyone to their homestead since Ma's funeral.

"*Mr. Coffey.* That sounds funny, Pa." Clara smiled.

"Well now, young lady, it sure does. But you can jus call me Coffey. Most of my friends do. I believe an overdue thank you is in order."

"For what, mist—er, uh-um, Coffey?" Her face twisted with bemusement.

Coffey beamed a mouth full of teeth followed by an if-the-poor-girl-only-knew laugh. "Ya got ya self a special little girl, Bill."

"Don't I know it."

3

Two hours into the dig, with sweat soaking through his Henley, Potter could no longer bare the strength of the blazing orange ball finally making its methodical descent through the sky. He peeled off his shirt, fixed his suspenders on wet shoulders, and drank a ladle of river water from a wooden pail. Coffey himself had stripped to an open button down, exposing his frail, dark frame. Depending how the sun hit, Potter glimpsed marks across his chest. Long, vague outlines of deep scaring. Many, many outlines.

By mid-evening, the men managed to dig themselves a wide, eight-foot hole. Impressive, considering they had just put in a twelve-hour day at Chisum's ranch. They delegated to Isaac the task of ceaselessly pouring dirt by the pailful into the schooner. Upon his last return, Potter sent his son inside for his suede pouch and to check on Clara. He then offered water to Coffey, who delightfully dropped the shovel to take a well-earned break.

Potter squatted and scooped up a handful of dry soil, thumbing the silky mixture of clay and calcium carbonate around in his palm. "I—I just can't reconcile this, Coffey. My goddamn head is spinning."

"What's that?" Coffey took down another ladleful, water dribbling down his chin onto his shiny chest.

"Why in the Christ haven't we struck water, yet, huh?" Potter stood, frustrated. "We've been at this all evening. Such a waste of goddamn time." He chucked the dirt against the pit wall.

"Maybe we go down another few yards or so? Ya know, for proper measure."

Potter shook his head and stared into the pit around them with an appreciative smile. "If not for you... I would've called it quits three feet ago." He stood and stretched, arching his crackling spine, and stretched his long arms with a gentle rock side to side.

"You was in the war?"

Potter blinked. "Huh?"

"Them marks on ya. Scars, looks like."

Potter peered down upon himself. The right shoulder bore a tre-foil-shaped depression, about the size of a quarter. Five inches over, another marred his upper chest. "Yeah..." Potter plunged the spade back into the dirt, twisting, hoping for water. "Infantry. Potomac Army. Virginia." He tossed dirt into a pail. "Fought in Bull Run. You heard of it?"

"Yes, sir." Now it was Coffey's turn to blink. "Heard it was the most violent battle in the whole war."

"Couldn't say if it was or wasn't. Sure can't imagine anything else being much worse."

"You's a lucky man, Bill. That where ya got them scars?"

The sound of the whistle nearly deafened him.

He blinked, shaking his head. He paced a long stretch of the racing Kansas Pacific cabin, guns in hand. Men and women—passengers—stood terrified, arms raised against the windows, shielding the armed men inside. Outside, men on horseback raced alongside, somehow keeping pace with the train. Marshals, bounty hunters.

Clad in long dark coats, hats, and cloth to veil their faces, the Cowtown Marauders, so dubbed by Sedwick County officials, fired out open windows between the human shields. And as the train gained momentum, what began with a meticulous modicum of return fire became scattered. Almost ubiquitous. Lead projectiles in rapid-fire succession struck every part of the train, shattering windows, tearing into cabins. One stray shot a shield, a woman, through the head. The bullet exited her skull, along with brain matter, and struck Potter, followed by a second as he toppled backward over a table.

Potter gripped the side of the pit, the grit of dirt under his nails centering him in the present moment. After all these years, he still questioned the casualty, the collateral damage, as it were, and the real motives of those *law*men in pursuit. They'd known the risk involved, and they'd decided what they'd sacrifice, *who* they'd sacrifice, to put him and his gang down.

"Most of em," Potter offered finally.

"I served in the sixth U.S. Artillery Color Regiment. One of many, I 'spose." Coffey, with the spade, chiseled away at the hard sediment. "You heard of a Fort Pillow? Tennessee?"

"Yeah."

"Day a reckonin." He shook his head. "I was for sure it was. We was held up inside there, six hundred men or so, I reckon. There was this general—General Forrest, his name—he was the leader of this Ku-Klux-Klan, ya know. Jus bout the epitome of pure evil, I say. Him and his men surrounded us up on the high grounds there. We was at a grave disadvantage. The fort, surrounded by hills, down by the river there, stood no chance. Slowly but surely, they picked us off like sheep, one by one. The fight lasted for hours. Hours, I tell ya. A butchery, it was, till we finally jus surrendered the fort.

"We figured, by then, we'd be taken as prisoners, sumtin. But they had sumtin else in mind, I guess. They came in guns ablaze.

"In the end, they took bout a hundred or so of us. The rest, mostly colored types, they slaughtered. Up close. Quite personally. All I could do was watch and wait for the good Lord to pass his judgement on each one of us. Felt like the longest day of my life, that." Coffey stopped digging. "They tied us together like cattle, single file. Carted the herd of us off. I can't begin to tell ya the sight to be seen outside that fort. Bodies strewn about. Piles of the dead as far as the wary eye can see, Bill. Some, still alive, moanin, wailin, twitchin. Left to the buzzards." Coffey shook his head.

"They walked us along the Mississippi. The waters stained red for miles. I tell ya, I ain't never seen such horror in all my days."

Potter stared off. "It changes you, don't it? That kind of violence."

Isaac returned and lowered the pouch down.

Potter reached for it. "Son, you can call it quits here. Actually, why don't you test those new shooting skills of yours and fetch us something for supper."

His eyes lit up. "Well, what should I shoot, Pa?"

"Hmm... well, I've had a hankering for mountain lion for some time now, boy." He smiled at Coffey. "What do ya think?"

Coffey grinned. "Mmm-mmm, mountain lion sound mighty tasty, if ya ask me."

"Bring us the largest beast you can find."

Isaac, ecstatic, ran off, and Potter pulled his papers and tobacco shake. Pre-torn. Shredded. He quick-rolled a quirley, offering it to Coffey.

He shook his head. "No, sir."

"A group of us broke away from *our* unit." Potter struck a match with a thumb and lit up. Leaning against the clay tomb wall, he inhaled the sweet smoke. "Have no illusions, we never intended to return. Not after Bull Run. Well, I guess it was still during. The mayhem, it never ceased to end. So we hid underground in the collapsed trenches for two days, waiting out the fighting. Survived on our hard tack, or what remained of it. The smell of decay above in the scorching sun eventually became unbearable, so we made our move. For days, we walked those empty woods. Days.

"Eventually, we ended up in the mountains. Hid out there a couple months, I guess. Hell, could have been years, for all we knew. No concept of time, up there. We were famished, emaciated. Had to conserve ammunition for safety reasons, so hunting was difficult. We ate what little plant life the mountain offered. Berries, plants, fungus. Risky, but at that point, death would have been better. Hunger played hell with our heads.

"Shit got real strange, I tell ya. Began to see things, hear things. Things that weren't there, you know? Idle chatter. Laughing, eerie like. Deep in those woods. Cackling. It'd just echo through the grove, day, night, didn't matter. We walked the perimeter daily, and I tell ya: not another man for miles. But the noises never stopped. We'd hear knocking behind our campsite in the middle of the night, like someone banging a rock against a tree. Strange shit. Twigs broke behind us while we pissed or squatted in a hole, but there'd be no one there. Paranoia plagued the group. At some point, I don't know when, some of us began to have visions. See men from the brigade wandering those woods. Ones that had been killed, Coffey. Rotted faces of dead men, just standing in the distance. Casting spiteful glares. Others would just be passing through. As if we weren't even there. The men, terrified beyond all rational comprehension, thought we'd found the trapped souls of the dead stuck up in those mountains. A sort of perdition, I spose." Potter shook his head. "Now, I don't know about all that. You think battle is bad... a man can go crazy out in that wilderness, believe you me.

"I kept seeing this morose flag boy, uh... Henry. Henry, his name was. Fifteen or so. Good kid. Got real chummy with him in the camps. Began to look after him a bit. You know, they had all these kids out there on the frontline, raising flags and shit, for God knows what reason. Anyway, he was with us a long time... till Bull Run. Took a bayonet in the neck. I dragged him into the trench. Tried to stop the bleeding, and he just stared up at me with these scared eyes. Desperate, merciful eyes. Begging me not to let him die. But there was nothing I could do. He lay there suffering till he finally bled out.

"Now he lingered in those woods, watching me with resentment. Like he thought his life and death *my* responsibility, and I failed to protect him. Spose he was right... but that was the final straw. In some bleak effort to stay alive, stay out of our own heads, we left the mountains.

"We walked a few more days. Couldn't believe how quiet things were. In our ignorance, we thought maybe the war was over." Potter smirked. "In time, we stumbled across a small town. Fredericksburg, I believe. Almost deserted. I would guess most of its village had been enlisted.

"We headed for the general store. The only place of business here. Older man and woman, probably bout my age today, well, they took one sight at us coming around the corner, and the old man, he came out and pulled a gun, told us we ain't welcome. Though I'll never forget the look of fear on him and his wife's face." Potter snubbed the butt, then lit a pre-rolled *special* quirley. "Well, we cut them right down where they stood. Didn't even hesitate to reason. Looted the store for the limited food, supplies, the money and jewelry they had on them, you name it."

Coffey, leaning against the pit wall, just watched intently.

"Apparently, that theft wasn't enough. Heading out, we came up on a big, beautiful house. Looked much like a—a plantation or something, though we didn't see any laborers. The men decided that was it; they wanted what they had, and they were gonna get it. They knew we could hide out there, survive months or longer. And I assure you, we did just that." Potter took another long drag. "Inside... inside was a family. Tried to defend it, best they could. Father and young boy fired upon us, but we got the best of em. Just about ran out of bullets trying, though, and they managed to kill two of us in the process.

"I was first inside. Happened to find the wife and her two daughters hiding in this room, a hidden room, inside..." He paused, trying to remember. The location always varied in his nightmare. "Inside the kitchen pantry, I spose. I heard the low whimpering, found the door. They were terrified, huddled together on the floor. One of the fellers saw them and ran back to the others. I could hear them hollering, all excited like. The wife, she stared up at me. I tell ya, Coffey, just like that boy Henry. Those same merciful eyes. She knew what was to come, I reckon. So did I. Did the only thing I could think and pulled my sidearm. Problem was, I only had two bullets left." He paused a moment, fighting the cold lump in his throat, fidgeting with the quirley in his fingertips. "Freed them daughters, though, from a fate worse than hell. That's about the hardest thing I've ever done. Well... almost, I spose." Potter pulled in the opiate infused shake vapor, exhaling a feathery plume through his nostrils.

"Wish I could tell you all our prayers were answered. Far from it. We didn't find much. Some dry goods. Couple cows in the pasture—we needed at least one alive. A hen house, is all. But we knew that sure wasn't enough. Not to get through winter. Found plenty of salt in the house, though. Came in handy for what was to come." Potter revulsed, chills crawling up his wet spine. "It was savage, Coffey. Fucking savage, I tell ya. We survived on that for... shit. Too goddamn long."

"Wuh—what happened to the wife?"

Potter studied the incredulous look on Coffey's face. Not a surprising reaction, but grounding nonetheless. He didn't want to overburden this poor man, especially since he'd come to like him. Even respect him. But now that he'd started sharing, he couldn't stop. The story flowed like water in the dry air.

"Can't tell you for a certainty what happened to the wife." He glanced to the ground, unable to meet Coffey's eyes. "I can assure you, nothing good. We kept her alive. I know that. I know... I know that. Then, one morning, found her dead. Hanging there from the corner of a four-post bed in—in one of the kid's rooms. Sheet tied around her neck. Couldn't say how it happened. Self-inflicted, I imagine. No clothes on. Sh-she was all banged up. That was it. I skinned out after that, just before sunrise. Slowly made my way out west.

"I never touched that poor woman, Coffey, but I think about her sometimes. Dream about her, even. Wished to God I had done something about it." Potter flicked the butt of the quirley. "War does a horrible thing to men. Changes em overnight. Turns boys into men, and men into monsters. No one comes back the same. But I guess you know that."

He glanced up.

Coffey, pensive, held the shovel handle in both hands, the spade wedged in the ground. He looked directly into Potter's eyes. "Certainly, changed *my* view of this world. I say it made me more appreciate the few things I got."

"I spose."

"Can't change what's done, Bill. You'd be dead alongside that woman if ya had. Ain't no sense dwellin. Ain't no sense in that at all. Never did any man any good, ya hear? You got a lovely family. A home. You alive, right?"

Potter nodded.

"Well, shit, you alive, *ain'tcha*!?"

Potter grinned thinly. "Yeah."

"Can't ask for anythin more."

The men finished by sundown, having dug themselves a ten-foot hole which required fetching a ladder. Isaac eventually returned, albeit without mountain lion. Potter was okay with what he did have, though. They enjoyed raccoon, pit roasted to perfection, with a bottle of brandy brought by Coffey from Chisum's private collection.

As they finished eating around the fire, Coffey pulled an old banjo from a threadbare case he said he'd won in a poker game some years back. He began strumming a peppy tune with a varying rhythm. The melody jumped and changed on the dime, as if he made it up on the spot. And he pretty much did, Potter figured, staring in wonderment at the mystery musician. *This man, always full of surprises.*

Coffey's right foot stomped, and Potter's hands, as if they had a mind of their own, began to clap in a rhythmic beat. Isaac and Clara stood from their blanket and followed suit, clapping and laughing. The two began to twist and jump, encircling the burning pit in some crazed ritual rain dance—the one thing they'd yet to see upon arriving in town.

Watching them, Potter couldn't help but smile. "Be careful now, you two don't get too close to those flames!"

"We're professionals, Pa!" Isaac quipped before tripping over his own feet, tumbling into the shadows. Clara cackled.

When the brown bottles emptied and the young'uns passed out on their blankets under a half-moon lighted sky, Potter lay back against a log, arms folded behind his head, and stared bleary-eyed at the starry cosmos, fading away in a drunken haze of ragtime. Eventually, even Coffey, leaning against his own log, relinquished the banjo and tipped his hat down below his brow for a nap. He'd be needed back at the Jinglebob Ranch; he'd depart bright and early, before dawn. The bonfire, down to a dull smolder of orange and red embers, soon threatened full abandonment, close to extinguishing the night's remaining light as Potter closed his eyes.

After a long day's work, sleep came swift, deep, and sound.

4

Potter slumped against the wall of the six-foot pit, at his wit's end. Four days of digging holes, each day's another fifty yards out from the previous, and still, nothing. He didn't know if he had it in him to try again. The sweltering heat scorched his skin, even with the sun setting overhead, and the schooner towered with sediment and rock. He and Coffey still needed to return all that sediment to the earth once they finally struck gold. Or water.

He spat at the dusty ground, picked up his shovel, and resumed digging. *Just the strangest thing.*

Neither Potter nor Coffey could figure out why the holes kept turning up dry. The goddamn Pecos was *right there*. Potter could toss a stone and hit the surface from the bank of the pit. No point to digging a well any farther out. He stared at the dirt around him, almost too tired to think. His joints ached; his fingers burned with callouses and blisters. His lower back throbbed, but hell, a man twenty years his junior would struggle with this level of labor. He supposed his aging, fifty-four-year-old body held up better than most.

Coffey, lifting his spade to toss another shovel full, paused, staring at the mound of dirt.

Potter stopped digging, mostly to catch his breath. "Whatcha got?"

Some strange anomaly poked through the dust. Small. Brown. Cylindrical. Frayed at the edges, almost charred.

Coffey lifted it from the dirt, rolling it between his fingers, analyzing it. He waved it under his nose, taking a whiff as his eyes filled with wonder. "Tobacco!?"

He tossed the item over to Potter, who also inspected it before taking a whiff.

"Looks like the butt of an old cigar... strange." Potter disregarded the relic stogie, tossing it over his head. With his handkerchief, he wiped his saturated brow.

"You sure there is water in these here parts, Bill? We been at this almost a week, I say." Coffey, still out of breath himself, dropped his shovel.

He pulled a pocket watch from his trousers. "Boss got a special dinner meetin tonight with some business type men. Need to cut out soon and make my way on back, if ya don't mind. Hate to leave ya here, though."

Potter glanced around the sultry pit. "It's gotta be here, Coffey! It's goddamn gotta be!"

Frustrated, he grabbed the pickax, swinging it over his head and drilling it into the hard clay. Coffey backed himself to the wall, too close for comfort. With everything left in him, Potter plunged into the earth again. Then again. Grunting. A fine dust plumed upward, coating his wet skin as he hacked away, choking on the mist.

Coffey wafted the grit from his face. "Come on, Bill. You gonna hurt ya self, now. Stop that!"

Potter, huffing, grunted and stuck the pick one last time. A profound *thud* echoed through the space, accompanied by a resonating tremor surging up the handle. The reverberation pulsed through Potter's arms, forcing his release. He slipped back, falling to the seat of his pants.

With an open hand, Coffey rushed toward Potter. "Ya all right, Bill?"

"That... was strange." He stared, dumbfounded, at the handle.

"Whatcha got there? You hit a rock, something?"

"I—I don't know." Potter pulled the pickax and dug down with his hands a few inches, scooping away the damp dirt.

Something solid met his fingers. He cleared away several inches, exposing a flat surface—high sheen, charcoal color. Like gunmetal. The more he brushed away, the more it shined. Pristine. And, oddly enough, no ax mark.

Coffey gaped. "That a cannon buried down here!?"

The men took their spades and cleared away as much of the pit floor as they could. Coffey kept checking his watch, now running late, though his face shone with curiosity.

Potter shot him a bemused, interested smile. But, as they continued working, his expression shifted to owl eyes and a full-on gape.

"Coffey..." Potter stared down at their mystery object, which dwarfed the hole in which they stood. "This ain't no cannon."

5

Isaac rode up on the old nag, returning from work as his pa and Mr. Coffey climbed out from the pit.

"Hiya, Pa. Hiya, Mr. Coffey." Isaac dismounted. "How's the well coming along?"

Mr. Coffey shot his pa a wry, crooked smile. "Mighty uneventful till jus now, I'd say. How's the nag treatin ya?"

"Awful." Isaac grimaced. "Horse keeps stopping and shitting up all over the place. Ain't never seen a horse do that before!"

Pa tried, and failed, to stifle a grin. "From now on, you take Blanco. Son, grab a shovel, will ya?"

That was the last thing Isaac wanted to hear. Exhaustion weighed heavily on every bone in his body. Still, he'd risk hurting worse if he upset his father.

Without question, Isaac picked up Coffey's shovel and peered into the hole. Something shiny peeked back from the surface.

Isaac squinted. "What is it, Pa?"

"Not sure. We're going to dig it out, whatever it is."

Isaac fought the urge to roll his eyes. He didn't care if the hole held the lost city of Atlantis—a story his ma used to tell him. He needed water and a change of clothing. Plus, someone would need to tend to dinner, since clearly Pa had been digging all afternoon.

Since arriving in Missouri Plaza, Isaac had embraced the additional responsibilities entrusted to him. People now relied on him. And he knew, both to his delight and chagrin, that a man earns his keep.

Mr. Coffey, reluctant to leave, glanced back at the pit. "I wish I could stay, Bill, but I reckon I must be gettin back to the ranch. The boss awaits."

"That's all right," Pa assured him. "Appreciate the help, Coffey. Look, I don't know what we're looking at here, but let's keep this just between us till we figure out what we've got, yes?"

"Ya got my word."

CHAPTER 13

Potter and Isaac widened the diameter by five feet over the next two hours, only stopping for water breaks and a quick dinner of baked beans and bread. The sun sank on its final descent behind the Capitan Mountains, leaving them with a mere half hour of dwindling light, but Potter remained mesmerized by the enigmatic object beneath his feet. The solid surface below stretched on, seemingly infinite. With the help of a broom—a recent purchase from Reynolds'—Isaac swept away the dirt while Potter, guided by a lantern overhead, wandered the perimeter, his imagination unleashed. *Could it—nooo. Could it* really *be a ship, a goddamn ironclad, run aground right here in my own backyard!?* They stood on the flat top deck, plated in some alloy. Steel, most likely. *You old sonovabitch, John. I knew you'd been up to some shady shit out here... but the USS Merrimack!?*

According to legends, the scuttled Union battleship, salvaged and converted to serve the Confederacy, vanished after engaging in a face-off with its Union counterpart, the Monitor, in the historic Hampton Road battle. Rumors suggested the Confederates deliberately destroyed the ship to keep the Union from reclaiming it. Certainly, the Merrimack's presence in the yard shed some light on his uncle-in-law's secretive post-war lifestyle. The buried arsenal cache suddenly made some sort of sense.

Potter got down on his knees with a lantern to inspect the ship's immaculate surface. Preserved—well preserved. *This should be oxidized to all hell.* He noticed something else unusual, too: a glimmering, iridescent shimmer. For a moment, he thought his eyes played tricks as the light oscillated back and forth. *Colors.* Depending on how the light hit the metallic surface, and his angle of sight, the material produced a spectrum of radiant, microscopic color. A fine glitter, much like a diamond, though it ranged from dark to light.

However, the surface proved less than perfect. Upon further inspection, Potter discovered an area of slight discoloration. It still exhibited its natural iridescence, albeit camouflaged by a dusky sheen. Almost singed. He noticed a thin, slightly indented line running down the surface, which trailed off under the ground. Sliding a fingernail into the crevice, he considered whether he could slip a wedge into the space. Unearthing an accessible spot might take days, or even weeks, though he harbored some reluctance about revealing it at all.

The consideration of saying *fuck it*, and just filling the hole in right now, crossed his confused mind. But the curiosity would eat at him. He knew it. Despite everything, his outlaw mindset prevailed, whirling with speculation about the potential value tucked away inside. With this imagined treasure, they could abandon the Bennett house and disappear south to Mexico. Or Rio. He'd met a feller from Rio's seaside who'd described the beauty of its captivating clear water.

With newfound determination, Potter retrieved his tools from an unpacked box inside and got to work hammering a pick into the metal wedge along the groove. The surface, though solid, had a measure of perplexing pliability. He had never seen or touched anything quite like it before. Once the space widened a centimeter or so, which didn't take long, Potter slid in the pickax. Gently, he pulled back, reversed it, and pulled again. The slight inward folding of one side confirmed his intuition: he had made a breakthrough. He tugged with all his might, careful not to break the ax, but the stubborn seal wouldn't budge. Using his Cuban heel, he stomped the surface with one foot. Then, utilizing his two feet, he eventually found himself springing up and down. Gasping for air, rapidly losing his breath, he could sense the metal shifting, albeit slightly, beneath his feet. Stuck.

Isaac, holding a lantern, watched from above. "Careful, Pa! Careful!"

"You ain't gotta worry about me, son." Potter grunted out in frustration, leaning forward, hands on his thighs. "This goddamn thing won't bud—"

FLOOOOOM!

A seal burst, and the hatch yielded under his weight as he plummeted, releasing a surge of musty air. Potter dropped ten or so feet, bouncing off the soles of his boots, tumbling down on his side. The pickax clinked along the solid floor nearby.

"PA!!" Isaac's scream rang down in an echo, hollow between the walls.

Eyes closed and heart racing, Potter rolled over. "Holy horse shit."

His eyes fluttered open, fixating on the latch overhead. The last remnants of daylight streamed through the opening; particles of dust gleamed, floating through the dusky stream. He sat upright, sweeping his gaze through the obscure space. His hands met the floor, cold to the touch, veiled in dust and cobwebs. Visible wisps escaped his mouth as he finally began to breathe in the stale, cool air.

Isaac ducked his head in from above. "Pa, you okay!?"

"Yeah." Potter stood, dusting his trousers and sleeves. "Lower that lamp down, will ya."

Isaac did as his pa bade.

Potter reached up and grasped the bottom, taking the light from his son. "Listen, I'm going to need you to get the ladder from the barn. Should be just about long enough to reach the bottom. Do not come down here. It's not safe, you got it?"

Isaac nodded, turned, and ran for the barn.

The corridor in which Potter found himself pressed in narrowly, maybe fifteen feet wide by his estimate, with dust coating every surface in a fine, gray ash. He held out the lantern. The flickering light danced against the walls, projecting the same glittering metallic shine as the exterior surface. He brushed his fingers across the cold metal, leaving an imprint in the dust. Stepping into an ironclad for the first time, he couldn't shake a mystifying feeling of unease. Almost foreboding.

Potter advanced incrementally down the corridor. Darkness permeated the air, though not as totally as he expected. Along either wall, every ten feet or so, little squares emanated a soft, pale glow from high above. Twenty-five yards up, one light illuminated a structural change on his left. A recession in the wall, no... an open doorway.

The lantern gently unveiled the space around him as he entered. The room, though wider than the corridor, wasn't much larger by comparison. About the size of his new living room space, he reckoned. Empty, too.

Well, almost.

At first, he only noticed the small square panel, about the size of his hand, hanging twelve inches from the side of the door frame, attached by a bundle of metal threading feeding into the wall. But as he swung the lantern, the light exposed a small mass protruding from the right-side floor, hard to discern below an age of settled grit. He squinted, holding the light higher. Half of the mass extended up the wall, and the second half lay across the floor, splitting into a matching pair, parallel, two feet away. Legs, stretched out. He walked over, inspecting the person sitting back against the wall.

Potter wasn't shocked, nor surprised. In fact, he had almost expected a body. Just one of many things you'd find in a buried warship... though the figure's attire, difficult to make out through the grime, bore no resemblance to any uniform he'd seen before, Union or Confederate. A shimmer from the obscured torso reflected Potter's light. He blinked. From head to toe, this man sat encased in dull metal.

Potter bent next to the body, inspecting the concealed oval head. The horizontal arm of a gold cross covered the slits for eyes; the base of the cross lay down the center. Battle armor, Potter figured. Armor for a war he knew nothing about, likely from a land he knew nothing of. With a curious touch, he shifted the face piece, pushing gently until the hinge loosened from its rusted restraints. The visor slid up. Behind the mask, the warrior's skull rested, missing every tooth except a few made of gold. A necklace of similar material draped his notched metal torso, and, at its end, a round pendant glimmered. *The reflective object.* Potter held it in his hand. The center contained a red cross in a design unlike any he'd seen, with words in an unfamiliar language written around the perimeter.

Another glimmer caught his eye, this time on the far side of the room. Something lay behind a clear wall, perhaps glass, though veiled in dusting. Potter straightened and walked to the edge of the room. With a brush of his sleeve, he wiped away the grime and held the lamp to his freshly unobstructed view. His mouth fell ajar. Though shadows still dimmed the case, the gleam in his eyes lit the scene right up.

Gold, silver, precious metals. All the metals Potter could think of, actually. Gemstones, mostly unrefined, some of which he recognized. He stepped back and waved the lamp. Rows of shelves encased this wall, all lined with exquisite trinkets unlike anything he'd ever seen.

Vessels comprised much of the displayed collection. Pots, pitchers, chalices, vases, and urns, most brass or bronze, some cloisonné with colored glass and floral patterns, all with carvings of figures and strange animals. Others, maybe marble or ceramic statuettes, boasted figures of phoenixes, dragons, and serpents. Some appeared gold or silver, and some carved jade and ivory. What the vessels contained, Potter hadn't the slightest, nor did he care. He salivated.

Brooches and necklaces took the shape of winged scarabs, dragonflies, butterflies—insects—many encrusted with stones of emeralds, rubies, diamonds, and sapphires. A bronze bell the size of a wagon wheel, with intricate double dragon hooks on either side, sat alone on a shelf; below that, a much smaller hourglass rested inside a double rotating frame of circular alloy. The glass lay angled, a modicum of sand, untouched, stuck in the upper hemisphere. Time trapped in a bottle.

And weapons. So many weapons. Strange ones: thin, three-pronged daggers; long, curve-edged swords; and small, star-shaped metals, sharply edged. Wooden antiquities: batons, bows, arrows, spears, and shields. Bronze shields, with tiny lines etched into them. Characters. A language, perhaps. And black sheathing, or what appeared to be protective layering. Spiked sheathing: vests and chest plates; shoulder, arm, and hand plates; thigh and calf dressings.

"Wow" was all Potter could muster. A kid in a candy shop.

The artifacts originated from eras and civilizations unknown to him, all long past, but Potter guessed the value far exceeded the sum of any-thing he'd ever had his hands on before, stolen or earned. However, much to his dismay, he found no gold coins or bullion. In his experiences, anyone so foolhardy as to pawn such "treasure" was liable to be robbed and killed long before unloading it. *Still...*

Beyond the wall of unattainable riches and the dead warrior, the room appeared barren. With one last, long look, Potter continued down the mysterious corridor, passing sealed-off doorways. At least, he guessed the recessions were doors. None seemed hinged, and they lacked knobs or handles. Just dusted windows. Upon reaching the end, a vertical split wall appeared with a narrow aperture. Film-coated windows adorned either side of the opening.

Potter slid his hands in the cold crack, pulling and pushing with all his might. After inadvertently sweeping away floor dirt with his boots over the course of several attempts, he discovered that this door stood set inside a grooved floor, opening with a sliding mechanism. Though he failed just the same in his effort to pull the double doors apart.

The pickax.

He returned with the tool, wedged its blunt tip inside the crack, and drew back on the handle horizontally. The door moved ever so slightly. Grunting through gritted teeth, Potter yanked again and again, giving the effort his all. Inch by inch, the door trudged, squealing along the dry track. He squeezed his body into the narrow opening, forcing the door along another inch or two until he slipped through.

Potter took a moment to regain his breath, wiping the cold perspi-ration away from his head with a dirty sleeve. This room, wider, busier, offered much more than the previous by virtue of tangible objects. Spell-binding gadgets filled the space, their surfaces aglow from the small wall squares now lining the center of the ceiling.

Semi-clear flat panels, rectangular and three to four feet wide from corner to corner, lined the rear wall, some of which hung above some sort of console protruding out by a foot.

Potter panned the lamp over one station. The panels contained maybe switches or buttons, not embossed, but strangely flush with the dusty surface. He dragged his fingers across, clearing away film. Smooth. Swirls of strange writing, like a foreign language—chicken scratch—scrawled out under each. This room must be the control center of this vessel, though Potter questioned how anyone, even the U.S. government, had access to such an advanced system.

Technology sprang to mind—a word he'd read about as a young man in his father's quarterly Harvard journals. Indeed, these ironclads were the pinnacle of *technology* during the war. Potter shuddered. Though he lacked the firsthand experience to ascertain the prevailing norms of such ships, something about the space sent chills up his spine.

He stepped forward along the central path, about the width of a doorway. The floor gradually declined under his Wellingtons as his lamp panned structures akin to armchairs. Six, he counted, three on either side, each one sloping in front of the other. Slightly wider than any chairs he'd seen. Taller, even. Strangely different. Thin seating. Thin backing. Unupholstered. Deconstructed, yet all attached by a thin framework. And no... no *legs*? Potter looked up. Tubing extended down from the ceiling, connecting each seatback. A flat panel accompanied the front of each seat, smaller but otherwise similar to the ones in the rear, also hanging from the ceiling by a thin cabling.

Upon reaching the far wall, approximately twenty feet away, Potter cleared the film using his palm, running it across several feet. All glass. The entire front of the control room, all glass. He contemplated the possibility of touching the ceiling, questioning whether it, too, comprised glass. Impossible, surely. But he knew one thing for certain: he'd reached the end of the journey. Nowhere further to go, and, he suddenly recalled, he'd left Isaac up in the pit some time ago. Potter didn't want to worry the boy, and he certainly didn't want him down here looking for his pa in the dark. Hastily turning back, he raised the lantern to make his ascent—

He gasped, stopping short. Someone, or some*thing,* sat in the far-right chair, slumped slightly forward. *Just a dead man...* but big, bigger than any man he'd ever met. The swaying lantern glow danced around the corpse, exposing blackish skin: wrinkled and weathered like old leather, almost completely decayed around the skeletal remains. Its head, oval, almost heart-shaped, draped forward. The empty, fist-sized sockets along the upper edge gaped at him. Its unclothed arms—longer than any man's, bony and serrated along the edge of its forearms—sat folded neatly at the elbow crook. A hand was missing on one side. The other, still intact, ended in three phalanges, sharp to the tip. Potter bent slightly, lowering the lamp. Its legs, also longer than any man's, inverted at the knee like a bird or a dog to drape alongside the seat its strangely humanoid body rested on.

Straightening himself up, Potter caught a silvery gleam reflecting from within the center of the slumped being. He paused, then reached out slowly. The arm flesh, cold and rubbery, nearly made him recoil, but his curiosity overpowered his reluctance. He pushed the withered limb aside for a better look.

A long blade protruded through the center of the strange torso, a black stain smeared across the edge. Potter walked behind the chair, finding its narrow hilt extending from the back. Gently, he placed the lantern on the floor, wrapped his hands around the handle, and pulled. The weapon's weight, heavy as a boulder, jerked him forward unexpectedly. He almost dropped the sword, barely managing to remain upright as he released the deceased from its entombed restraint.

Panting, he held the ancient blade above, twisting it in his hands to admire the remarkable craftsmanship. Steel arms curved toward the blade, and the lightly bronzed handle and cross-guard, finely engraved, brandished winged horses and yellow medallions on either side. The handle's bottom knob had the same cross as the deceased metal-man's pendant, its sharply edged blade etched in the same language.

As if this discovery wasn't fascinating enough, something else struck his gluttonous eye. A soft, white glow faintly pulsed in front of the deceased, just below the hanging panel. It emanated from inside a console—the only such device before all the six chairs, likely the control panel. Flush buttons covered its surface.

Potter placed the sword down, figuring its value paled in comparison to whatever he stood poised to unveil.

The control box, about three feet high, sat at a long arm's length from the deceased. The gleam emanated through the thin slit of the front panel. With some jostling, Potter figured out how to slide the compartment door off and removed it.

A black box sat inside. A large globe lived at its center, the glow pulsing under a thin dusting. The sphere reminded Potter of a crystal ball, one which once had supposedly shown his future from the wrinkled hand of an old gypsy in some bayou brothel parlor room. With his hanky, he wiped the ball in a circular motion, though its contents appeared just as the surface did: clouded at best. And the noise. A soft, pulsing noise, almost inaudible. The orb, whatever it was, enchanted him. He gripped either end with his large palms and yanked at the device, which loosened with each sharp pull. With one last tug, it released, sending Potter onto the seat of his pants.

Something tugged slightly at his shoulder—a bony, three-fingered hand gripped him. He turned to see the empty sockets of the dead, leaning over, staring at him. The creature's jaw dropped, exposing a mouth of shiny, gray teeth, sharp and serrated.

Potter squirmed back. "AHHHAHH!"

The being slumped off the seat and onto him, engulfing him in its soft, sponge-like corpse. He struggled to roll from under the heavy carcass, hyperventilating, barely managing to push off the creature and slide himself out. Within seconds of his escape, he scrambled up and sprinted toward the door. Phantom fingers gripped his shoulder again and again, and he shuddered, slowing to take one last look behind him. The glow now engulfed the space, pulsing in, pulsing out. He backed through the tight opening and turned to a dark figure, grabbing his arm.

A shrill whimper squeezed from his mouth. He swung the lantern over.

A pale moon of a face stared up at him, wide eyed. "Pa!"

"Christ, Isaac!" He pulled in several deep breaths, his pounding heart radiating from his torso through the eardrums. "What the hell are you doing in here? Didn't I tell you, stay up top there, huh?"

"I got scared, Pa. What is it—what is it in there?"

"Never you mind that. You hear me, boy? Come on."

Clara stood waiting outside the hole as her father and brother climbed out of the latch and out of the dirt tomb. "What are you two doing? What's that down there?"

Her brother bounded toward her. "You should a seen it, Clara—"

"Isaac! That's enough. Listen, the two of you, right now." Potter bent down, grabbing the young'uns by the arms, practically squeezing them together. "You *do not* go into that hole. Ever. Do—you—understand?"

They nodded.

"NO. No." Potter quickly mocked their head nod. "I need to hear you say it. I need a 'yes, Pa,' you got it? Tell me you understand!"

"Yes, Pa," Isaac and Clara said in unison, looking at one another fearfully.

"Good. We don't tell anyone about what we found here, you hear?"

They nodded again. Potter sighed and slumped his head.

"What-what did we find here, Pa," Isaac asked carefully.

Potter turned, looking back toward the pit. "I don't know, son."

2

Potter tossed and turned. Strange metal garb from a foreign land. Unquestionably not associated with the Confederacy. And that *thing*, that creature at the helm. Not human. Not a goddamn chance. Not to mention those artifacts. The *treasure*, so to speak. But, for some reason, the glowing box intrigued him most. That white light had an energy, one that had pulsed through him when he placed his hands upon it.

Unable to sleep, Potter rose from bed, cracked the young'un's door, and peaked inside. His children appeared fast asleep. Isaac certainly was; his snoring could be heard from town. Clara slept on her side, facing the opposite wall. Quiet. Always quiet. Gently, he closed the door. The hinge creaked loudly, and he cringed, listening.

Clara rolled over. Then, silence.

Potter waited, frozen, for several tense moments. Finally, satisfied Clara still slept, he released the doorknob with a silent sigh.

With two lanterns, he set out for the pit, grabbing the pickax and climbing down into the dank corridor for the artifact room. He stood one lamp in the center of the floor, sparsely illuminating the room, while he sat the other before the clear wall, lighting his way as he wound back the pickax and laid it into the sheer surface. The ax recoiled on impact, the reverberation rattling up Potter's arms as he stumbled backward. Not a dent or a scratch in the wall, as if he'd struck stone. His mouth gaped. The strange material, certainly not glass, offered no entry point.

Potter turned to view the room, now in clear view. The metal man watched mockingly from behind as his eyes fully adjusted to the dark. Two other doors stood in corners of the room, both sealed. A square, tri-pronged panel sat adjacent to each, in proximity to where a knob or handle would typically protrude. Potter played around, feeling the recessed plate, but for the life of him, he couldn't figure out the mechanism. He clenched his fists. Though he fortunately had no *actual* interest in the treasure trove, his inability to get to it provoked his desire, primarily fueled by spite.

Fuck it.

The treasure trove wasn't what he came down for, anyway. He paused at the metal warrior, taking the necklace, and turned toward his true destination.

Entering the control room, he walked to the glowing panel, slowly maneuvering around the bizarre carcass. Just the sight of it sent him shuddering once more, chills rippling down his spine and shattering every nerve. If only he'd smoked that quirley beforehand. For a moment, he considered the heavy, cumbersome sword. Fascinating, but he had no use for it. The glow in his peripherals beckoned.

The misty white globe remained where he'd left it, pulsing in and out. He stared, wide eyed, his intrigued face reflecting in its white light. What would he find under his clouded future?

Tell me my fortune.

The device proved heavy, much heavier than the sword. He swung it over a shoulder anyway and hauled it up the ladder, out of the pit, and straight into the shed. Panting, he opened a small tool closet and placed the orb down, covering it with straw. With his heart still racing, he backed away. The milky glow poured through the slits of the door and walls. Mesmerizing.

With a shaky hand, he pulled a special quirley from a shirt pocket.

Just a couple drags. Just a couple.

3

"AHHHH—AHHHH—AH, AH!" Potter sat bolt upright, wheezing, gasping for air, spinning his head from side to side.

No Frohrmanns.

He sat alone in a room, in a bed. His bed, he thought—*hoped*—glancing at his surroundings.

Alone...

The nightmare had returned, just as horrifying as before, and he woke up in a panic, the memories of twenty years ago flooding back. A cold sweat dripped from his furrowed brow, his bed sheets thoroughly soaked through. For a moment, Potter wondered if he'd pissed himself. He had no recollection of falling asleep, much less returning inside from his late-night treasure hunt. Though mostly dark in the room, he could see the early light of dawn from his window, the night sky just about evaporated. Five, maybe five thirty in the morning, if he had to guess.

He struggled to regain control of his breathing, trembling as he reached for the side table drawer and the suede pouch. He needed the pouch—

The floorboard creaked.

Potter froze and glanced toward the door. A shift in the void. A figure. Someone standing in the corner. A hat brim moved into the dim lighting of the dawn. Potter reached for his guns on the bedside table, but, again, they weren't there.

From the shadows stepped a man in a long, dark coat, caked in dirt. Debris shook from his body with each spur clinking step. He looked at Potter, baring a hard, grisly grin, ear to ear. Potter noticed something else peculiar: a missing eye with tiny, black holes surrounding it. And the mouth—torn at the cheeks, the lips and flesh all gnawed away to brown, checkered teeth with two gold fronts. As he neared, the light fell on his pale green face, the edges heavily moldered.

This man was clearly dead.

Potter squeezed his eyes closed, vigorously shaking his head. He counted slowly to three, and with much reluctance, loosened the tension. Peeking through blurred eyelashes, he felt his heart stop. The corpse was still there. Walking. Nearing.

This was no dream.

Potter recoiled, backing himself against the headboard, grabbing the sheets for a futile sense of support. The man removed his Stetson. The crown of his head, like a cracked egg, split open vertically in a jagged line, dark, decaying brain matter protruding from the wound.

Fuck me, Lord, and all that is unholy... that's... that's... that's...

Warren. The glint of gold teeth and the ornate ivory grip of the Colt Peacemaker, intricately engraved and nestled in his decaying hand, betrayed him.

Potter pulled the covers over his head and squeezed his eyes shut. "No, no, no, no, no, no, no, no, no! No fucking way! You're dead—I shot you—I shot you dead!"

The sheets flew off.

Warren stood bedside. Potter cowered, arms up over his head, convulsing. The corpse leaned forward with a slow gait, and Potter, paralyzed, unintentionally locked onto his frosted, vacuous stare. Maggots, imbedded inside the vacant socket, released. A foul, viscous fluid oozed from the scalp wound down his forehead; it drizzled, spilling maggots onto Potter's raised arms and face.

With startling desperation, he slapped away the squirming larva, wincing and moaning emphatically.

"There is many a slip twixt the cup and the lip, Joe," Warren said in a gargled, broken voice. Monotonal. Inhuman. He stared desolately through Potter, subdued, as if devoid of his soul. "Rid yourself of that box."

Potter broke free from its stony gaze and clenched his lids shut. In the fetal position, he lay quivering, waiting for the nightmare to end.

The voice, seemingly further away, spoke again. "You were right. There *is* only one type of man in this shit world…"

Potter opened his eyes.

"You are looking at him." Warren, now at the door, turned to exit. Potter watched him dissipate into the void.

He checked his arms, his bedsheets. No blood. No maggots. Oddly, all clean.

That goddamn opium. He really overdid it this time. *No more!*

Potter, regaining his faculties, took the mini glass vial, hurried downstairs, and, from the porch, launched it into the arid morning air. It arced through the sky, soaring, just barely, all the way to the pit. It bounced down, disappearing into the darkness.

No chance of sleeping. No. Not yet.

Potter found his pistols still holstered, hanging from a coat hook. The cylinders remained empty, untouched for weeks—since the showdown in the woodlands. To his relief, the pistols had actually fired when needed. Almost a year had passed since he'd fired them prior to that day, and he did so only for general target practice. The guns were heavy, cumbersome, and impractical at best. Obsolete. But they were, at one time, his prized possession. The deadliest weapon of the Rebellion War: the LeMat revolver.

Potter's infantry had inadvertently thwarted a Confederate shipment of the pistols coming in from the Potomac River. Shrewdly, the gray coats had managed to sneak the guns past the Union naval blockade with a duplicitous shipment proof from the United Kingdom. *Oh how clever, Johnny Reb.* But the guns didn't go very far, waylaid on their southbound journey during the war's bloodiest battle. Out of three-thousand pieces of blue steel set to arrive in the South, five hundred had made their way into the hands of Union soldiers.

Potter brought his pistols downstairs and plopped down on the kitchen bench. The Confederates had contracted a Frenchman by the name LeMat to create the unique weapon. The cylinder held *nine* rounds. No revolver prior to or yet since had held such capacity. And that wasn't even the most intriguing aspect of the gun. No. It was the *second* barrel, the twenty-gauge short barrel shotgun. But, apart from their unwieldy and excessive weight, these guns possessed a fundamental problem: their use of a muzzle loading, cap-lock bullet system. Potter had no cap-locks. Primitive. He sat with nothing but a pack of old paper cartridges—same ones he'd been using to roll quirleys—a container of gunpowder, and a box of .40 caliber lead balls.

Creating a thin paste with candle wax and beef tallow, he thoroughly greased each cylinder chamber. He didn't tend to the pistols frequently, but with their age, limited use, and recent tendency of jamming, he needed them in prime condition. Each chamber held a paper cartridge, each filled with twenty grains of gunpowder. A bullet capped each gunpowder-filled cartridge. The muzzle loader, a thin rod connected barrel-side, compacted each cartridge into each cylinder. The wildly inefficient work took several minutes for each chamber.

Last, using a small sheet of paper and the width of a cigar to mold, Potter rolled a cartridge large enough for each revolvers' shotgun barrel, which he filled with grapeshot, or small caliber rounds. Many, many rounds.

Finishing his work, Potter fleetingly wondered if such tedious, unruly weapons just wasted his time. But something about the pistols gave him an unparalleled confidence, a sense of empowerment. Some psychological advantage over his opponent. He smiled. Few dared to stand in his haughty and destructive path, and those who had, well, they'd tasted the end of his cold blue barrel. Excluding Confederate men, these two revolvers harbored the unfortunate souls of thirty-six men. Or thirty-nine, considering the recent encounter in the clearing.

Potter cringed, pushing the pistols across the table. He'd thought quite enough of Warren for one night.

Chapter 14

Tynan dismounted. He stood, tobacco wedged in his cheek, staring up through dark lenses at the vacant Sullivan homestead. Behind, his insipid new entourage—Claude and Grover, appointed especially by McKinney—followed suit.

The former home looked serene. A few scattered hens in front skipped away as the men stepped forth. Beyond the bird's clucking, he heard nothing but the mellow trickle of the riverbank echoing from beyond the house.

Not an easy find, for sure. No road existed that led here, just somewhere off the beaten path a few miles from town, behind Cherry Creek. The men spent quite some time working off directions from a drunken local questioned in a downtown saloon, a former employee of Bennett's Mines. The acquired information yielded a general but tenuous sense of direction. Apparently, this man had stumbled across Griffin and brought him home after Griffin put down his injured horse. However, the man was unable to verify whether Griffin had a wife or children, as he saw none present upon his arrival.

Tynan hadn't expected an easy undertaking, considering who McKinney'd tasked him to find, but the roadblocks loomed abundant. The man at the Land Office, Daly, his name was, proved absolutely hopeless. He had no records of property owned by a Griffin or a Sullivan, and in fact, much of the city's land and municipal records had perished in the Big Flood of '82. Daly seemed inordinately overwhelmed in just discussing the matter and the interminable real estate battles he'd adjudicated ever since.

Bennett's Mines, a venture fraught with potential, proved equally futile. Tynan could smell a morsel of horseshit and tell you the color, sex, and animal breed if he had to. Nothing got past him. But he'd never met such a tight-lipped group of miners. Not a single one offered a piece of viable information regarding Griffin's—*Sullivan's*—family. In fact, everybody had the same response, the same cold, bewildered disposition. Their shared, almost compulsory, reticence gave Tynan the sense they'd been forewarned. *But what in Christ are they protecting?*

Finally, he and McKinney's cronies did a thorough sweep through the house. Their findings proved meager: stripped beds, a sparse collection of utensils in a kitchen drawer, and sheer curtains hanging from every window. They did, however, stumble upon a wardrobe in the master bedroom that contained a plethora of dresses and ballgowns. Exquisite pieces: some of silk fabrics, others lavish, velvet materials with decorative brocade patterns and damask. Tynan had seen such styles working past cases, usually in prestigious estates, but even the uninitiated eye could recognize the expense and elegance of such fashions. The wealth needed to own just one, much less an entire wardrobe.

Tynan stood, laying out each garment on the bed for further study. Griffin, or someone else, cared deeply for this woman.

Tynan licked his leather fingertips, twisting the edges of his furled mustache. Settling down was never in the cards for him. Heh, settling down... no, not an option. Could never be. Not in several lifetimes. A man could be killed, strung up, even, just alluding to that sort of thing. He swallowed the thought down, stifling it. *Work is life.*

"These some mighty pretty dresses, ain't they, Dunkin?" Claude, walking up behind Tynan, smirked.

Tynan, not in a gaming mood, turned to the door. "Let's go."

They walked behind the house, where Grover had just exited the barn.

"Ain't nothin here." Grover sighed, disappointed, though his typical demeanor was invariably that of disappointment: vitriolic and morose, looking like someone had shit in his morning Granula.

Tynan gazed the backyard. "Nothin?"

"Well, just some tools, is all. But nothin of any use to us."

He stared toward the creek. "Tools, you say?"

"That's what I said, ain't it?"

Tynan shoved a fresh roll of tobacco in his mouth. A moment later, he walked into the barn. *Nothin of any use to us, my ass.* If he had to endure unwanted "help," he would have preferred the company of associates with at least *some* field experience. He never asked his companions' age, or for anything that wasn't pertinent to the job at hand, but he saw it. They wore their youth on their faces, in their speech, their attitude. Tynan, always spot on, figured late twenties; but even without his uncanny knack for reading people, he saw right through their bullshit like an empty bottle of Jack Daniels.

Not that Tynan was an old soul. At forty-one, he'd already spent two decades in the field; after ten years as a deputy in Wichita, he'd hung up the uniform to work for himself. He never cared much for the smoked-filled room of backdoor politics or the coerced, *potential* corruption that came along with the job as a lawman. Not to mention, he hated Wichita. But he'd paid his dues, the check long mailed. His *marshals,* on the other hand...

Useless as ever, Claude and Grover stood around outside the barn, audibly bitchin while Tynan worked.

"Nothin, huh? Well, that don't sound much like a surprise." Claude grunted, conjuring up some throat mucus, and spit on the ground.

"What y'all find," Grover asked with disinterest.

"Ain't shit here but a bunch of dresses." With that, Claude lowered his voice, though not as much as he might have thought. "Had I waited a minute longer, I'd-a said he was bout to put one on."

Tynan scowled at the wall in his marshals' direction. Intimidating boys, sure. Broad shouldered. Rugged. Fearless. Admirable traits, all wasted on them. Grover and Claude's palpable absence of ambition accompanied an immaturity that bordered on infantile. Simply stated, they lacked gumption. Gumption was a precondition for the job. To Tynan, it was something innate, hardly developed.

A man didn't have to be a genius to be successful, though. Just focused. Bounty hunting demanded an unwavering commitment to one's purpose. Finding outlaws necessitated the use of geographical and personal resources, networks, only gained with time; success required an unyielding tenacity to finish the game. Not to mention, handiness with the steel. You needed willingness to die to even do this job in the first place, a fact which surely deterred most common folk. And the men in *this* field, often remnants of the old war, proved anything but common. The job attracted rugged survivors. Seasoned men. The initiated. Because you needed to be detached to do this work. Removed from the outside—physically, emotionally, mentally—and shrouded in solitude.

Outside the barn, Claude hooted and hollered with laughter. Even the morose Grover snickered.

Tynan just searched the barn in silence. Though he would have loved nothing more than to share his extensive knowledge and expertise—a refinement of skills, decades cultivated—with his two subordinates, he wished not to waste time with the uninitiated.

He doubted they would live to see thirty.

2

Holding two shovels from the barn, Tynan walked past his marshals, heading toward the creek. They followed.

"We ain't found diddly squat here, Dunkin. What's your next big, bright idea?" Claude spit again, then turned, grinning at Grover.

Tynan dropped the shovels by the old oak tree, in front of the headstone labeled *Elizabeth*. "Dig."

"Dig?" Grover, scratching his bushy, dark beard, peered at Claude.

"That's what I said. Ain't it?" Tynan removed his specs, staring with contemptuous gray eyes.

"You really ain't expectin us to—"

"Well, I didn't bring you here on holiday. Or to question my instruction."

"Hey, we don't work for you, shit-heel." Grover stepped toward Tynan.

Casually, Tynan opened his coat, exposing his holstered pistols. "If there's a problem, you can go back to Wichita. Air your grievance with McKinney." He spat tobacco juice at Grover's feet. From his vest pocket, he pulled the gold watch, flicking it open before giving it a long glance. "Better pick up that shovel. Sun'll be up sky high real soon."

For the next hour, Claude and Grover dug and dug deep. They'd expected to find the pine box two, maybe three feet down, but to their dismay, it was not. Nor was it four feet or five feet down. Tynan watched over, perched on a low, thick oak branch, feeling only the slightest hint of guilt at dirtying his marshal's three-piece. He wondered, recalling Daly's claims of the devastating Big Flood, if disaster precaution explained the unfathomable depth of the casket.

Another hour into the excavation, their shovels finally struck something. Both men, now down to their undershirts and suspenders, dropped the shovels and climbed from the hole, exasperated and dripping sweat. Grover, covered in dirt, rolled onto his back in the grass, splayed out for much needed rest and cool air.

With the spade, Claude pried the lid off the casket. Though adhered by sludge and time, the seal broke after a few minutes of labor. The lid opened.

Elizabeth's remains lay wrapped in a sheer, white fabric. Claude, straddling the casket, unfolded the sheet to reveal her body, heavily decomposed. Wrinkled, dark brown skin, exsiccated, clung to the bones like worn leather. Her hands, completely exposed bone, rested, neatly folded, over her sternum. Her mouth retained a complete set of teeth, and long, dark hair flowed from her head.

Even in death, Elizabeth appeared to be a woman of elegance. She lay clad in a black lace and satin dress with an A-line scoop neck, similar to the styles of those in her wardrobe but much more tattered—likely due to chemical reactions from body decomposition. Victorian gold intaglio earrings lay at the base on either side of her head, her ears long deteriorated. Two of her phalanges bore rings, both gold, one of which held a diamond. Draped from her neck, just above folded hands, sat a heart-shaped locket, also gold; it rested on her breastbone.

"Get on up outta there," Tynan commanded.

Claude paused, still straddled, glancing at the body before climbing from the grave. Tynan removed his coat and hung it over the oak branch, then squatted and jumped down, landing on the side edges of the casket. The locket, doubtless pristine as the day it was buried, glimmered in the sunlight. Tynan squatted over her torso and placed the locket in his right hand. Heavier than expected. Solid. With his thumbnail, he pried the jewelry open. Portraits of two children fit snuggly inside. A boy and girl. Now straddling the box, he examined the remains.

Something looked off, but a few moments passed before he finally considered the neatly ruffled sheet lining. Odd, to wrap a body in such a veil. Like royalty. As one who'd been privy to many a burial, he'd never seen a pine box prepared with such care and elegance.

He felt along the inner edges between the body and casket, searching for embroidery. People from a certain social class, mostly upper, plastered their surname on their fine linens, bedding, towels, and sometimes even clothing. Maybe the rich feared the help stealing their belongings, or maybe they just enjoyed flaunting wealth and class. Either way, Tynan hated the arrogance of the affluent. His fingertips traced over an unusual stitching... a name sewn into the sheet.

The embroidery read *Bennett.*

Tynan climbed out. "Let's go."

"Where to," Grover asked.

"Land office."

"Again!?"

Tynan stopped and glared.

Grover gulped, finally realizing his place. "Uh—what do you want we should do—"

"Close it. Cover it. Quickly."

3

Claude jumped back down as Tynan walked out of sight. With haste, he slid the rings from the woman's bony fingers, scooped the earrings from the base, and shoved everything in his pockets. The locket, shining brightly, beckoned. He placed his hands around the chain—

Click-snap.

Above his head, a pistol hammer yanked back. Claude froze, slowly glancing up.

4

"*Leave* it." Tynan stood at the head of the plot, his Colt pointed down at Claude's head. "Show some goddamn respect."

Claude, frozen, just stared back.

"We savvy?"

Claude sneered. "Whatever you say, boss."

Tynan watched as Claude returned the items and closed the casket lid. Now, bounty hunting required an infallible conviction that your actions were morally, ethically, and inherently correct. And although Tynan subscribed to these beliefs, his code of ethics differed—*just slightly*—from his peers. Depending on the severity of the crime, he'd choose to skip the middleman, so to speak. The politics, the headache, the bullshit. He'd rain down his own form of justice, as with Murphy and Ellis.

He spat, wiping his mouth with a leather index finger. He couldn't wait to get his hands on Griffin.

Chapter 15

Potter opened the toolshed door. The device, still under the hay, pulsed its ominous glow.

Isaac had woken him up, worried that his pa hadn't gotten out of bed. Potter never slept past the young'uns, but he hadn't dozed off again until just before sunrise, when the easing effects of the opium dosage finally mitigated enough for him to cease contemplating Warren's unwelcome visit. At least McCormac hadn't crept into his thoughts and dreams yet. Perhaps he'd survived... a troubling possibility.

Potter needed a new contingency plan, preparation to drop everything and go at a moment's notice, if need be. Missouri Plaza may have been the salvation he'd been longing for, but something in his gut warned they'd never be safe here.

His head pounded, triggering the daze of withdrawal symptoms. An unavoidable repercussion of overindulgence.

Sighing, Potter swept off the hay and picked up the device, taking a moment to look it over in the mid-morning light. Interesting... not a perfect rectangle. Intricate patchworks of vertical lines appeared *carved* into it. Other lines, much smaller, sprawled out, scrawled over a bronze-colored metallic geometric surface on the edge of either side. Chicken scratch—the same language he'd seen written on the console. He shifted the device in his hands, inspecting its finely carved intricacies. Small indentations, grooves, marked the edges of the strange box surrounding the globe.

"What's that, Pa?"

Potter, startled, turned to see his daughter in the outside doorway, long pigtails draped over each shoulder. Her round, wide-eyed face brimmed with curiosity.

He couldn't deny that he possessed something, so he headed towards her. "It's nothing, Clara. Why don't you go run back inside?" He exited the barn toward the schooner.

"Did you get that from the buried warship?"

He nearly tripped over his own shoes. "Who said anything about a buried warship?"

"Who else!?" Clara, walking side-by-side, stared up at her pa matter-of-factly.

"Your brother and I are going to have a long talk about discretion."

"What is *de*-creshing?"

"Never mind, hon."

"But did you!?"

"I did. And I'm giving it away."

"To who?"

"*To whom.*"

"To whom!?"

Potter dropped the device in the back of the wagon. "Well, you are just full of questions this morning, aren't ya?"

He turned, scooping her up, and kissed her cheek. He held her—*boy, was she getting heavy*—gazing into her pretty eyes. For a moment, he saw Bessie. She looked more and more like her mother every day.

The reminder pained him, but he only smiled. "You know, with your quest for answers, you could run for town marshal!"

"Can I touch it?"

"Absolutely not. We don't know what this thing is."

"Who does?"

"Maybe Mr. Wilburn." He put his daughter down and climbed onto the schooner bench. "I'm headed to the mill, so you be a good girl and do your chores. I'll be back this afternoon. Oh, before I forget, you and your brother make sure you have your letters for Grandpa."

"Yes, Pa."

As he set out for town, he reconsidered his own words. He loathed the risk involved with introducing fresh eyes to this strange contraption, but if the law crept up at his doorstep, he'd rather not hightail it out of town empty-handed. The idea of obtaining the jewels behind the wall grew increasingly enticing. Something deep inside called to him, whispering, no—*beckoning*—to probe into the box. Perhaps it held the answer.

Clutched tight against his chest, the globe pulsed.

2

When Potter arrived, the noise of the busy mill accosted him. A bright whirring thrummed with an intermittent rattling of moving parts. Loud. Incredibly loud. Six women sat at six spooling machines, twine firing through back and forth at different angles, all collecting along the sides around wooden handles. He found Aaron at a desk tinkering with a massive piece of mechanical material, likely a spooling part.

Potter gave the open door three curious raps with his back knuckles.

"Mr. Potter—uh, Bill!" Aaron stood.

"Aaron." Potter nodded. "I apologize for the unannounced visit."

"No apologies needed. I welcome the distraction. What can I do you for?"

"I was hoping you could take a look at something." Potter, attempting to sound casual, instead found the words dripping ominously. Leading Aaron outside to the bridge, he pulled back the sheet in the schooner's bed.

Aaron's eyes lit up. "Why, what do we have here," he asked, speaking directly to the device.

"I haven't an idea."

"Where did you find this?"

"Just sort of stumbled up on it." Noting Aaron's brow furrow slightly, as if he intended to probe further, Potter added, "You seem a man who's gotta way with mechanicals and what not. Thought maybe you can take a look at it. Would appreciate your opinion." He didn't voice the other reason why Aaron was the most well suited to inspect this object: as an Asian immigrant in the unmerciful white man's West, he seemed most likely keep his trap shut.

"This... this is very curious. Would be honored to give it a look. Let's get it to my office."

Potter slid the device out, lifting it up over his shoulder and following Aaron back inside.

Aaron pulled the piece of spooling machine off his desk, tossing it to the side, and scooped loose papers and such into a pile thrown into a crate on the floor. Potter placed the device gently on the cleared surface. Aaron, with a piece of damp cloth dipped into his glass of drinking water, gently wiped down the box's face. Using a short, thin metal rod—some broken piece of spooling equipment lying around—he prodded the cloth into each nook and cranny, wiping out the residual dirt and cob-webbing. Potter, impressed by Aaron's meticulous handling, stood aside and watched. Last, he carefully polished the globe, clearly hoping, along with Potter, that the fog lived on the surface. To their disappointment, the interior remained clouded, the glow, faint.

"Incredible!" Aaron stood back. "This contraption is very curious, indeed. You say you just stumbled upon it?"

"Yeah." Potter glanced back and forth from Aaron to the device, evading the question. "What do you spose it does?" *What's it* worth, *Aaron. Don't toy with me.*

"Couldn't be certain."

"Saw this writing on the side here." Potter pointed to the chicken scratch. "Is this Chinese or Japanese or something? Maybe this came from Asia?"

Aaron snickered. "Is that why you brought this to me?"

Potter, face reddening, floundered. "Uhhh, I don't... just, you know, curious is all. Umm..."

"It's okay, Bill, it's okay." Aaron smiled. "I can see how you might have thought that. To be honest, I have seen nothing like it before. Although, if, uh, if I had to guess, I would have to say, maybe an engine of sorts. Was this all you found?"

His mind flashed to those rotting remains falling atop him, the sharp fingernails grazing his shoulder. He gulped. "Just about. You think it's worth anything?"

Aaron stared, unhearing, at the orb.

"Aaron?"

"Huh?" He looked up at Potter. "Oh, uh, that's hard to say without knowing what this thing does."

"How bout this." From his inner coat pocket, Potter revealed the chain and cross. "This gotta be worth something. Cocksure, it does."

3

Aaron held the necklace in his hand with a gentle up and down motion, giving a feel for its weight. Heavy. He shrugged. "Sure, this could be. Though, without knowing the type of alloy, it's also hard to say. Just from looking at the cross, you might want to check with Minister Healy."

He turned immediately back to the strange device. The fog almost danced in its pulsing light. *Beautiful.*

"Healy, huh," Potter said, interrupting his inspection. He didn't seem too happy about Aaron's suggestion, either.

Aaron gulped, hurrying to explain. "I know, he is kind of a lot. Interesting feller, though."

"How's that?"

"Wasn't always clergy. Well, he was, I suppose, part of the ministry back east before he came here. Teacher, I believe."

"Teacher to clergy? How peculiar. First *I've* heard of such a thing."

Aaron flushed, realizing how much he'd revealed. *Trots of the mouth,* they called it. An unintentional occupational hazard. Though, if he was honest with himself, Bill Potter frightened him. Something about the way he looked at people kicked Aaron's defense mechanism into overdrive. He became subordinate. Smiled. Placated. Put his foot in his mouth. Too late to turn back now, though.

He forced a grin. "Well, the long and short is we got him liquored up real good one night. It was the minister's birthday, see, and we had a small celebration at Van's, above his store front. Told us a horrific story of how his parish burned to the ground. Couple people died in the fire. Me and Van, we couldn't believe our ears. He was pretty broken up about it. Sort of just fell apart. Kept talking about a redemption only the Pope could give."

"He's catholic?" Potter blinked, surprised.

Aaron shrugged. "I know he said it was at Yale College. Uh... Connecticut."

"He never said how?"

"No. He mumbled something about 'suspicious circumstances.' We had our *own* suspicions, though. Once a week, we would host a card game. Always invited him, but he would never come. In fact, was very adamant about *not* coming, saying he'd never touch a deck of cards again. We figured a man with a personality like his would be itching to take a few dollars from us."

"You seem a smart man, Aaron," Potter said, glancing around at the spooling machines. "I would think someone with your mind might be able to tinker with this thing. I'm certain it *does* something. Maybe try to get it... running?"

"Running?"

"Yeah. Something clearly powers this thing. Time is of the essence here. If not, if you know a market that would buy it, I'd split the earnings with you. But only under the condition you don't mention me or where it came from. Deal?"

Aaron raised a brow.

"Please, Aaron. Those must be my conditions. I appreciate you respecting them."

Aaron bit his lip, avoiding Potter's cold, dead stare. *Better* not *to let a man like him down.* "Right. I mean, I—I could try, Bill."

4

Upon leaving the mill, Potter walked straight toward the church, the other end cap of Missouri Plaza. This town grew more and more interesting each day. Apparently, corruption extended even to the minister. He thought back to his first conversation with Chisum and wondered if maybe he was right about the residents of Missouri Plaza. Thus far, everyone shared some fairly colorful history. One that led them here.

Nowhere.

From under the brim of his hat, he took in the sights. The street maintained its usual calmness, just as it looked upon his arrival. Scant townsfolk moved up and down, carrying out their daily routines. Not a single person looked at Potter as he walked, a notion that could not please, or perplex, him more. His plan to avoid town had proved unrealistic, but he felt more at ease with this strange, tucked-away town.

He just hoped it stayed that way.

On the porch of his storefront stood a man in white, a burgundy stained apron tied around his waist. Charon the butcher. Potter watched him through squinted eyes. If he didn't know better, he'd say someone watched him, too... though that feeling never ceased.

Charon stood, arms folded, a frown painted on his round, glum face. His hair, what remained combed across his balding head, shifted in the light breeze. Potter thanked his lucky stars that he had no incentive to send his son back to the shop. Ever. Should Chisum cease supplying provisions, hunting proved to suffice just fine, even if the game left much to be desired thanks to the semiarid climate and scattered woodlands. Thus far, providing ample meals for the young'uns hadn't been a problem, and most likely wouldn't be, so long as he could keep with the Cattle Baron of New Mexico—*his* kind of people.

Paying Charon no further mind, Potter stopped in front of Reynolds's Buy & Sell. From the street, he craned his neck to peer into the dark window, hoping to catch a glance of the curly haired proprietor standing at her post. Nothing. Perhaps she'd offered a shave and trim to some lucky resident. He considered entering, but he didn't need any supplies or goods. Besides, what would he say? Prior to fleeing here, he hadn't seen many women since Bessie's passing, much less spoken to one. Well, other than his little girl. *Eh, maybe later.*

He carried on. Glancing to the side, he caught sight of a man in a top hat, likely T.S. Quinsberry, sitting on his rocker. The aroma of his cob pipe smoke lingered in the air. Not much business today, Potter supposed.

The church loomed brightly behind a short white picket fence. Potter cautiously crossed a brood of unintimidated clucking hens as if he were in *their* way, hoping to avoid confrontation. He smirked at the thought as he pulled open the right French door; the rusted hinges brayed, echoing through the empty church. He entered and strolled up the center aisle of the dimly lit nave. Quiet. Amber strips of dust-speckled sunlight poured through the few windows, diagonally reflecting off pew tops. He stopped a moment to admire the giant round stained-glass window straight ahead in the rear. Gorgeous. Various blue tones comprised much of the patterned cells, along with purple and pink in Mary's outfit. Red and gold trim lined the perimeter, complementing golden skin tones and the crescent halo over each head. Breathtaking as the window was, he thought it a bit gratuitous... perhaps something specifically wanted by Van, who reminded him of his young self. Lord only knew where that could lead. Van's pal and confidant seemed the opposite: a man of simple tastes and pleasures, analytical, with qualities like a blacksmith. Also, a bit of a pushover. Potter saw the possibilities in such a powerhouse unification.

He crossed over the chancel and behind the Lord's Table, noting a faint red wine stain on the altar's white cloth. *Damn dry town.* Wings fluttered along with faint trilling overhead. Directly overhead, as a matter of fact. Behind a wooden grate, where the belfry loomed. Its bronze bell hung desolately. The lantern, suspended above the bell, flaunted enchanting birds, all elegantly perched along its edges. Strange design, he thought, having the steeple—partially open, no less—in the back, over the chancel. *Good thing they don't get much rain in these parts... though I wonder how often Healy has to clean bird shit off the Table.*

He found Healy sitting in the vestry, a meeting room to the left of the chancel, drinking the holy sacrament out of a large, ostentatiously bejeweled chalice and copying notes from a larger work. Assumedly, the Bible. From the looks of the small room's twin bed and sizable wardrobe, this must be where Healy slept.

Potter coughed. "Minister?"

Minister Healy jolted, glancing up. "Huh, what?" His head spun around until his disoriented gaze reached the doorway. "Mr. Potter! Pleasant surprise, pleasant surprise, yes."

"Well, this wasn't a planned visit. Sorry to interrupt."

"They never are, are they? Well, other than Sunday morning, I suppose." Healy snickered. "So, what brings you in, my son? Confession? Well, you've certainly come to the right place."

Potter cringed. "Uh, no."

Healy felt around his desk, pushing papers around, searching for something. Then he felt his face, realizing that the *something*, his round spectacles, were already in place. "Of course, we'd have to baptize you first. Then, I'll clear my entire schedule. I can only imagine, under that exterior, an entire lifetime of sin, yes?"

Potter glared at the inebriated man. "What exactly would *you* know about it, Minister?"

"Well, don't get your britches in a bunch, Potter! Sin is inherent in every man and woman. You were born with it. No shame in that. It's as natural as bees to a flower. That's what I'm here for. Now granted, we don't really do penance in the traditional sense here in the, uh, Methodist church," Healy rambled and trailed off. "Probably lose a lotta folks, I imagine. I start advising them to share their deepest, darkest secrets—"

"Minister, I'm here cause I thought maybe you might wanna take a look at something." Potter pulled the chain from his pocket. "I, uh, found it among Bennett's things in his study," he added, saving Healy the trouble of asking.

Minister Healy's eyes stretched wide, his mouth gaping as though he beheld the mythical Holy Grail. "Incredible!"

"You *know* what this is?"

"Indeed!" The Minster reached his hand under the dangling cross. "May I?"

Potter released it into his palm.

Healy held the necklace out in front of him with one hand; his other palm cupped around the pendant. "This, Mr. Potter, is the cross of the Knights Templar!" The Minister turned it over, examining the engraving of the date: in the year of their Lord, *1312.*

"*Nights?*" Potter pointed toward the ceiling.

"No, no, no. A knight!" The Minister, gesturing, made his arms wide around his body. "A Knight, Mr. Potter. Metal armored soldiers. Knighthood was an honorary title for men representing service to the monarch or church. They existed in Europe, oh, mostly around a thousand years ago or so. The Middle Ages. Also known as the medieval era, or as I like to call it, *the Age of Faith.*"

The wheels in Potter's brain turned. The theory made sense. Well, only in that he vaguely recalled reading Geoffrey Chaucer's *The Knight's Tale* as a boy, though the book's knight depiction didn't quite match up. But a *real* knight?

Minister Healy pulled an old thick leather-bound book from a shelf next to his desk. He opened, flipping through the pages until he came upon the section. "You see, the Knights Templar were a Catholic military Order, forming in the tenth century. This year—" he pointed at the pendant—"the year of thirteen hundred and twelve, was when the Order disbanded."

"How do you suppose this came to end up in my, uh—study?"

"Well, Mr. Potter, that is indeed the question." The Minister thumbed through a few more pages. "According to the scriptures here, after their dissolution, what was left of the Order fled from Ireland to New England in early twelfth century, see." Healy emptied the wine bottle's remains, filling his chalice.

Potter raised a brow, wondering where Healy got wine in a dry town. "Fled?"

"Oh yes. Mostly to avoid imprisonment. Or being *burned* to death." *Sounds about right.*

"The once powerful Order began a steep decline, losing battles, losing land—the holy land—finally losing support of the countries. Sooner or later, their secret organization had been revealed, and the monarchs sought them out for extermination... kings indebted to the Order, who owed them quite a fortune with no intentions of repaying. The dealings in Europe in those times were quite nasty. Look here." Healy held the pendant for Potter. "The writing. It's in Gaelic."

"Gaelic?"

"The language of the Irish. This necklace proves they made it to America!"

"Well, shit, minister..." Potter, though fascinated, didn't share the same excitement as the minister. "Is it worth anything?"

"Oh, yes."

"Really?" His eyes popped.

"Indeed. To the congregation, it is quite priceless! I would love to have this on display during service. I think it could be very inspiring for the townsfolk! May I hold on to it?"

Potter ground his teeth. With Chisum's accurate sentiment on silver's current value, or lack thereof, melting the necklace down would prove a fruitless venture. And even if the Knights Templar pendant held historical value, Potter had no way to contact an interested buyer, especially not without drawing attention to himself. He should just say *hell no* and throw the damn useless thing in the river.

Instead, he mustered a reluctant, one-shouldered shrug. "Don't see why not."

5

A sign hanging from the front door of the post office read: *Closed. Will be back end of week.* Potter, tapping the envelopes on the back of his hand, stifled the urge to slam his fist into the wall. The letters would now be late, even though he'd planned to get them out ahead of schedule.

The morning had started with such lofty promise, but the necklace turned out to be shit. He harbored doubts about the mysterious black box that Aaron held for him. And now Morgan's coercion mail sat in limbo. One disappointment after another, and not even lunchtime. This trip, insofar, had been a bust. He twisted his head, setting his sights on the grocery.

Upon entering, Potter didn't see Nora at her post. *Maybe this is a bad idea.* He turned toward the door.

"Bill?"

He stopped. Nora had just reached the bottom step of a set of stairs in the back corner, appearing a bit more casual than usual in a floral bed gown, gray petticoat, and blue apron. Her hair shone from under a white linen cap, braided in a long pony, and a yellow kerchief covering her breasts bulged from the gown opening. If he had to guess, she was in the middle of chores in her homestead.

She smiled. She always smiled. "What a pleasant surprise. What brings ya in today?"

"Uh, just, uh... just ran out of potatoes, is all." He had plenty of potatoes. "Just gonna grab a sack, if you have it."

"Sure do, darlin. Came in yesterday, as a matter of fact. Right over yonder." She pointed across the store to where the root vegetables lived, her eyes never leaving his. "That all you came in for, Bill?"

Potter, uneasy, deflected. "Uhhh, actually, I was trying to mail some letters. Post office closed?"

"Yeah." She walked from the stairs along the front of the store to her post. "Van and his father had a meetin over in Albuquerque. His father's a big-time lawyer. They're still workin on some land claim here, I reckon. Been ongoing ever since I can recall."

"Oh. I see." Potter walked up, grabbing the sack on his way. "Well, let me pay you for these and let you go bout your business." He dropped some change, nodded, and walked away.

"Bill," she called after him.

Nearing the door, he turned back. "Yeah?"

"What do you say I cook you and the young'uns supper one of these nights? How'd that be?"

He smiled thinly. Happy, yet saddened in the same instant. He wanted nothing more than to spend a lovely evening in the presence of Nora, but the unknown pervaded, likely disasters spinning through his mind. Associating with him brought risks. The last thing he'd want is for her to be hurt, or killed, on account of him. "That is a mighty generous offer, Nora, but I don't think I'm ready for—"

"For supper," she interrupted. "Surely you must have it every night." As if she thought him sheepish, her tone shifted toward the stern voice one used with a child. "Do you not?"

Potter, fearing her unexpected forwardness meant he'd offended, floundered. "I just mean to accept such an invitation. As much as I'm wholeheartedly obliged."

"Well, I'll leave the invitation open." She emphatically popped open the register, pulled out bills, and began counting. Still focusing on the cash, she added, "Friday, I plan to cook enough food to feed a small village. Call it seven o'clock. You show, you show. If not, Miller and the boys in the café will be mighty happy." She pushed the cash drawer shut and looked up impassively at Potter.

The smile was gone.

Potter offered a slight nod, tipped his hat, and left.

CHAPTER 16

Coffey exited the front door of the main house. On the silver tray in his hand, he balanced a tall glass pitcher of room temperature tea and eight glasses. He just needed to finish up his morning chauffeur duties before changing into his wrangling outfit and commencing the day's activities with Potter.

Walking across the yard, he curiously found the ranch hands, along with his boss, gathered around the stallion pen. From what he could see over their lined shoulders, Emiliano and Gustine were at one end holding lassos. Potter stood a short distance behind. The other boys, Elija, Hiram, and Salvador, watched from along the edges, smiling, giggling, and making a game of their naïve comrades. Chisum stood outside the pen, leaning over the railing, a cigar wedged between his beaming teeth.

Two standoffish mustangs paced the pen, while Potter, standing out of the way, directed the two men on how to tame the beasts. Emiliano, successfully roping his horse, gently brought the stallion down to the ground and saddled it. Gustine lacked his partner's luck. He, instead, cornered his horse, which it most certainly did not like. Not one bit.

"Get that lasso moving," Potter yelled.

Gustine started twirling the rope, staring the beast down as he slowly advanced.

"All right, don't take your eyes off him, now."

NEIGH!

The stallion kicked up its front legs. Gustine twirled faster. Higher.

"All right, you gotta time it just right. Don't be hasty."

The stallion appeared anxious, pacing left to right, unable to escape. Gustine, standing in the middle of the pen, followed the horse's lead, stepping left to right. The tension grew as Gustine moved in, cornering the disgruntled beast. Coffey gaped. Gustine would be trampled for certain. Before he could muster another thought, the beast shot up on its back legs.

NEIGHHHHHH!

"You gotta—you gotta get it—get it right under the knee, there," Potter hollered and pointed.

Gustine swung and launched the rope. The lasso landed around one hoof as it came down, jerking him forward. He lost his grip on the rope, and it tore away, the slack slithering around the horse and out of reach.

"*Nope.*" Potter shook his head and made a quick lateral move toward the gate.

The beast charged Gustine. Wide-eyed and panicked, he turned, screaming, running for the nearest edge of the pen. He grabbed the top of the gate and propelled himself over as the animal bolted forward, cracking the side of the fence where he'd just been standing. The impact launched Gustine over, and he somersaulted to the dirt. Chisum laughed heartily, clapping his thick hands.

Potter exited the pen, where Sandy greeted him, baring gifts. A recently slaughtered woodland creature hung from her mouth. By the looks of it, a mole. She dropped the carcass in front of his boots, and he smiled.

"Looks like ya boys could use a break." Coffey poured a large glass, handing it to Chisum.

Chisum pulled away the cigar, patting Potter on the shoulder. "You're provin to be quite the interestin hire, Potter. Impressive. Quite impressive." Chisum took his glass of tea and walked to the front porch of the main house. Sandy frolicked off behind him.

"Hiya, there, Bill." Coffey grinned ear to ear, handing Potter a drink. "Been real eager to hear bout whatcha found in that well."

Potter slugged his full glass and, with a shaky hand, wiped his mustache and beard with the back of his sleeve. "Just the strangest thing, Coffey."

He paused. In his mind, the words he wanted to say sounded almost absurd. Shit, who was he kidding? It *was completely* fucking absurd.

He sighed. "It's... I think it's a ship. Best I can say it. Almost like an old iron clad gunship of sorts, though nothing I ever seen before."

He studied Coffey's expression, more curious than bewildered.

Coffey seemed to study him as well, likely noticing the tremors. "A ship, ya say. Ya mean from the war?"

"Maybe," Potter said, unconvinced. "You know, I saw one once. It was after we fled Bull Run. In the Potomac. We had to cross the river, which we tried to do discretely. Piled in this small, abandoned lifeboat on the riverbank. Got halfway across, and there it was, just sticking up from the water. Saw the smokestack first. Then, as it neared, we saw the flat gun deck. Canons. Real unsettling to realize that most of the boat was submerged. We made it across unseen and hid behind some trees to watch it go by. Just creeping along. It was eerie as all hell."

"An ya think *that* is buried in ya backyard?"

"Not that one, but... you hear old campfire stories about the USS Merrimack." He grinned, almost salivating. "The ship vanished from Virginia. Rumors say the Confederates sunk it. Others have said it's filled with treasures: gold, jewelry, foreign antiquities pillaged and plundered from mansions, Southern plantations, and such."

"Why? Shit. Huh-how?" Coffey's face twisted as he pushed his wiry hair back. "Seems awful far away."

"I—I don't know. Maybe brought up the Pecos, there? The surface was made of steel, I'm guessing. Like an ironclad deck, you know?" Potter lit a quirley, barely keeping the match steady, and stared off into the pasture, considering whether to proceed. The words slipped out of his mouth before he made up his mind. "I breached it, Coffey. I got inside."

"Well? Well, whatcha see, Bill?"

"You wouldn't believe me, even if I told ya."

"Well, sure I would. Try me."

Potter did his best to stifle a smile, but couldn't help himself. "A treasure, Coffey."

"Treasure!?"

"Yeah... curious artifacts. Antiquities-like." Potter's smile faltered. "An inaccessible treasure. Enclosed behind a clear wall. Impenetrable. Shit, I tried like hell."

Coffey rubbed his chin, eyes wide.

"That wasn't all, though. There was something else down there. Something deceased. You're gonna ask what, but I-I don't know what."

"How can that be?" Coffey gaped, bewildered, though his eyes kept darting to Potter's trembling hands.

"Don't know. It was long dead, whatever it was." Potter took a hearty pull off the quirley.

"An animal? Maybe sumtin they brought in before they buried it?"

"It was no animal. I don't know what it was, but it—it wasn't human, either."

"Sweet Mother of God. Bill, now ya talkin madness, here."

"If I'm lying, I'm dying."

Coffey stared, aghast. "I think we better have more tea."

He poured himself and Potter another tall glass. From his inner pocket, he pulled a silver flask, one from Chisum's collection, and topped off the drinks with brandy. Potter squeezed the glass to prevent his hands from shaking.

"Anyone else know bout this find?" Coffey poured just enough to keep from spilling.

Potter drained his glass. "Christ, no."

Well, the young'uns sure did. Then he thought back a moment. Isaac was down there, too. He hadn't considered his son catching a peek at the remains of that thing.

"Good. I'd keep it that way." Coffey took a long sip. "I know this prolly ain't none my business, but you okay, Bill? Can't help but notice your hands keep shakin."

"Ah, that ain't nothing. Don't worry about it." Potter put the glass down and hooked his thumbs in his holsters.

Coffey took the hint. "So, whatcha think ya gonna do with it?"

Potter thought long on this. Just as he did with McCormac. He knew what he wanted to do. What he should do. Whether *that* was going to happen, he'd just have to wait and see.

He shrugged, giving Coffey the honest answer. "I don't know."

3

The sweats came hard and furiously. Potter writhed and twitched between damp sheets in a pool of cold sweat, eyes watering. His head pounded to the rhythm of an elevated heartbeat inside his skull worse than any moonshine hangover—a feeling dangerously on the verge of cracking like an eggshell. The fever had spiked multiple times throughout the night, then broke slightly. Even with the small reprieve, he refused to move from the comfortable clutches of wrapped sheets. His whole body still burned and radiated as fierce chills propagated through him, shaking him to his core.

A cool breeze circulated the room from an open window, but the night was far from peaceful. Cicadas chirped their clamorous choir of love ballads, infiltrating Potter's brain. He clamped his hands over his ears, too weak to find the window through the blurred darkness beyond the burning candle remnants melting on his bedside table.

Days had passed since his last *special* quirley. With his meager supply now gone, Potter needed to lay off the Juice if he wanted any chance of overcoming withdrawal symptoms. He'd experienced the shakes in the past, a brief spell of unintentional withdrawal due to lack of product; after the Big Flood, substances such as opium all but disappeared as the city entered its reform. But this withdrawal exceeded his tolerance threshold.

He forewarned his children that Pa was *sick*, and they'd best leave him be a couple of days. Isaac had explicit instructions for his chores and overseeing meals, besides keeping a keen eye on his sister. Fortunately, Aaron was understanding and didn't need him at the mill for a couple of days. Potter informed Chisum of the situation ahead of time too, and with confidence; Chisum understood and offered his support should he so need it. Potter had accepted a cut of tenderloin that would last them the week. He felt guilty leaving Coffey in the dark, considering he was literally the only person here—and as he thought about it, maybe in his entire shit life—he'd call his friend. And, for the first time, he worried what Coffey might think. He didn't want pity or concern on his behalf.

Potter leaned over bedside and vomited into a metal pail he found earlier in the barn for just such an occasion. Now, besides burning up, his throat scorched with stomach acid. A pitcher of sterile river water he'd boiled earlier in the day sat out of reach behind the fading candle. He reached defiantly with a shaky hand but fell short, his strength plummeting. The candle flickered in his wary sight, sending up bright floaters in front of and behind his eyelids. He blinked in the dark. An eerie yet familiar sensation washed over him, something he hadn't felt since childhood.

He closed his eyes, but the visions kept coming. A phantasmagoria of images, vivid colors. Red, yellow, orange. A picture book of life that didn't make much sense. Ornate mansions, barking hounds, labyrinthian gardens. Home. An odd powdery aroma of lilies ignited his senses. Things sitting in his subconscious flared to the forefront, all too young to comprehend. The undeveloped memories the naïve mind never retains. Hallucinations. They hastened, overwhelming him before he fell unconscious.

Chapter 17

Tynan and his two marshals sat quietly in the parlor room of the Bennett estate. Claude picked at his dirty fingernails. Grover, chewing tobacco, spat into a copper cup he kept in a satchel tied to his horse. Tynan stared at his open watch. Waiting. The room was quiet. So quiet, he could hear the sweep of the hand *ticking* with each second of passing time. With a gentle swipe of the thumb, he brushed over the inscription on the inside lid. In old English, it read: Dunkin.

Finally, the door opened. A servant entered, tall, black, clad in a black and white chauffeur's outfit. In his hand balanced a silver tray with a silver coffeepot and four porcelain cups. He placed the platter down on the coffee table between the three men, who sat in armchairs around it, before pouring a cup and offering one to each. Grover declined, instead spitting into his own cup as he eyed down the servant with contempt.

"Is your master on his way in, by chance?" Tynan asked, taking his steaming coffee cup from the servant's hand.

"I'm here, gentlemen." Morgan appeared in a refined brown three-piece suit, as if he'd just returned from a day of necessitous business meetings. "I apologize for my tardiness." Morgan took a seat in the fourth and last chair.

The servant nodded toward him. "Cup of Arbuckles', sir?"

"Thank you, Lemrich, yes."

Lemrich smiled and poured a cup. A moment later, after dropping in two lumps of sugar for his boss, he left.

"Now, what is it I can do for you boys? You claim to have information about my son-in-law?" From the table, Morgan opened a cigar box, pulling one from the stack and offering it around.

Tynan put a hand up, shaking his head, as did Grover.

"Well, don't mind if I do." Claude smiled, reaching over to take the cigar. He moved it under his nose, twisting it back and forth. "Mmm, mmm, mmm. I sure do enjoy a fine cee-gar. Quite fancy. Where does one procure such fine quality tobacco? Havana?"

"New England, actually."

Claude's mouth dropped. "This here is from the Yanks up north!?"

"It's considered hybrid. They bred Cuban seeds with seeds from Sumatra in South America to come up with a leaf which derives from shaded soil. It's quite fascinating, the meticulous cultivation methods, when you consider one doesn't necessarily inhale the smoke."

"Speak for yourself, mister." Claude lit his, pulling back, then blew a stream of gray smoke.

"But you gentlemen didn't come here to discuss the growing methods of tobacco." Morgan touched a match to his, twisting while he puffed so the flame would evenly light.

"Please excuse my deputy, Mr. Bennett. He's yet to be properly house trained," Tynan said, ignoring Claude's contemptuous glare. "Sir. We have reason to believe your late daughter's husband is none other than notorious outlaw Joe Griffin. Goes by a number of aliases. Now he's using, or should I say, *was* using, Edward Sullivan. He's wanted on countless war crimes: desertion, armed robbery. Murder." He handed Morgan the wanted poster.

"Yes, this looks like Eddie Sullivan. And no, I'm afraid I know nothing of which you speak."

Grover finally spoke up. "Might I mention, sir, there is quite the hefty reward for the capture—"

"Do I look to want for anything here, boys?" Morgan smiled. "Look around you."

Tynan had looked. He sat in a large parlor room, essentially Morgan's office, in one small section of a large palatial colonial. Just in this room alone, while waiting for Mr. Bennett to arrive, Tynan had spotted obvious wealth. Wealth he wouldn't see in ten lifetimes. The liquor hutch with fine china, the grand piano, the elk head over the stone fireplace, the mahogany desk, they all left a bitter taste in his mouth, even worse than the coffee he sipped.

Claude smirked. "Reckon we can't claim to know if you're privy to this information, but rest assured, if you're trying to help this criminal elude capture, your actions will carry heavy charges of their own."

Morgan's demeanor soured. He dropped his cigar in the crystal ashtray and sat forward. "You dare come into my house and threaten *me*? You've any idea who I am?"

Grover sat up. "We know exactly who you are, Silver Baron of Colorado. Hullabaloo. Your influence don't much impress us."

"To tell the truth, we're a bit curious." Claude leaned forward with a cold smile. "Who else you have hidin in those mines, who might be of interest?"

Morgan stirred in his chair. "I think it's time I asked you boys to leave. Lemrich!"

"Yes, sir?" Lemrich appeared immediately from around the corner, as if he'd been eavesdropping.

"Go run out back and fetch the boys to see these men out."

Tynan sighed. The boys, part of Morgan's security detail, stayed in a compact cabin hidden behind the estate. From Tynan's research, one of them even doubled as his driver.

Lemrich nodded and turned to leave when Tynan's hand went up.

"Now, that won't be necessary. We'll be rightfully on our way. Look. Mr. Bennett. We have no interest in your, uh, how do I say, extracurricular activities. Ain't none of our business," Tynan offered, placating. "I read about your wife and daughter. A genuine tragedy, what happened. That alone would, hell, probably make me reconsider *my* faith. On top of that, you lost two young boys to the pox as well. One can't even begin to imagine what that loss is like. I know I surely can't. You have my deepest condolences." Tynan waited a moment for Morgan to ease up a bit, sit back in his chair. "You have two grandchildren, yes?"

"Yes."

Tynan, sitting up, leaned forward, peering in Morgan's pensive eyes. "It don't bother you—that man, that *monster,* is raisin the only begotten family you have left? Surely, they'd fare better here, at your estate, instead of bein out there. In hiding. Like animals."

Morgan looked over at a portrait on the wall behind his desk: his wife, daughter, and two grandchildren.

Tynan studied him. "Well, hell, I sure think they would. Just think of the education they could have. The life. You say, 'look around here,' and, well, I have. And what I see is their best chance for a future." He sat back. "Because honestly, it's only a matter of time till he's found. If not by us, then by some other outfit. And God only knows how that will play out. You don't want them young'uns in the middle of it."

Morgan, still pensive, puffed his cigar.

<h1 style="text-align:center">2</h1>

Ten minutes later, Morgan stood at his open window and watched as Lemrich saw Tynan and company out the front door. Grover stopped a moment as he exited to give Lemrich a salty glance, then spit on the stone landing next to his polished shoes. Reaching over and snatching a pocket square from Lemrich's breast pocket, he wiped the brown guck from his beard and tossed the dirtied fabric back with a deadpan "much obliged."

The men mounted their steeds. Tynan put a piece of rolled tobacco into his mouth, then turned to his marshals.

"We find Griffin, or whatever fabrication he goes by now." He spat. "You boys best be prepared for what follows. Time's a wastin. Let's go."

Lemrich, overhearing, hurried to Morgan, who he found in a dense cigar haze at his desk. Almost melancholic. His chair faced the window behind, and he sat, staring out to watch the three men gallop down the stone driveway. He sipped an apéritif of Campari, swirling the bright red liquid around his sherry glass as his cigar continued to burn in the crystal ashtray nearby. Smoke billowed.

Lemrich coughed. "Mr. Bennett. Sir."

Morgan looked over. "Come. Have a seat."

Lemrich, brows furrowed, sat in the leather-bound chair across from his boss. Silence followed.

He broke first. "I think them boys is up to no good, sir."

"Yup, I share the same sentiment." He turned to face Lemrich. "There's a letter here I've written, though unsure I would come to use it. Now I'm afraid I have come to no choice. You will take this to the Federal marshal's office this afternoon. I'm not feeling up to going anywhere."

"Yes, sir."

"I know you've only been here a short time, Lemrich. And we haven't really had much of a conversation. About anything, much less about your life in Missouri Plaza. Never talked much about my brother, either. In fact, I never much wanted to ask. To know about his... *lifestyle*. What he was doing down there." Morgan rose. He pulled a textured glass from a collection in a small hutch next to the desk, and with it, the bottle of Campari. Gently, he poured his servant a hearty drink and topped off his own.

Lemrich smiled. "Obliged."

"You've had to live with my brother for how long?" Morgan smiled and touched his glass to Lemrich's. "You've earned it. John... always a strange, strange character. Hard to believe we were brothers. Hell, even harder to believe we were twins!" He sat, chuckling wryly, and took a dip swig. "Just mirror images of one another, I suppose. Who could've thought two people birthed from the same womb at the same time could be so emphatically different. Who knows? I suppose that's one of the few things that separated us. Had he stuck around, though, we've could've taken over this city."

Lemrich raised a brow. By now, his employer was pretty well liquored up. Quite unusual for this time of day, and certainly for this early in the week. Perhaps the information enclosed in his letter brought him some remorse he needed to drown.

Chapter 18

The sign on the door read

"BE BACK IN THIS AFTERNOON."

Thoroughly irritated, Potter shoved the letters back inside his coat pocket. It was the end of the week—a rough week at that—and the postmaster was *still* away from his goddamn post. *Guess that means the bank is closed, too.* He smirked and shook his head.

He stared out over the town, the post office porch offering the perfect vantage point. Right in the middle of the strip, he could see everything. Probably more so from the second level, hell, even the roof. Not a bad way to monitor the goings on, especially if this setup was intentional. Brilliant, if so.

The morning unveiled itself slowly around him, a gorgeous bluebird day in the making. The sun still rose leisurely just beyond the church. Before nine a.m., if he had to guess. He felt fresh, invincible. With the lingering effects of opium withdrawal dissipating, he'd experienced one of the best nights of sleep he could remember, and at sunup, he'd risen and cooked a large breakfast for Isaac and Clara. With some of the leftover tenderloin, heavily preserved with salt and stored in the cold basement, he'd whipped up a tantalizing batch of steak and eggs with fresh bread and sliced apricots, a delicious fruit of which New Mexico had a seemingly endless supply.

Potter took a deep breath of sweet, clear air. Nothing would bring him down today. Nothing... other than the goddamn postmaster.

As he stepped down, he pulled on the hat brim to shield his face from the glaring sun. He could just about feel the fine lines of crow's feet pervading each corner of his squinting eyes. A stagecoach and several horses sat on the otherwise quiet street, parked just outside the mill. He knew Isaac toiled inside, a thought which filled him with pride, and he'd yet to visit the facility during his son's diligent work. Not to mention, almost a week had passed since he left the device with Aaron. Truly, if he was being honest, the device was all he could think about. He lacked any hope in the strange, busted hunk of metal's potential. But that globe. The pulsing, white glow...

He needed to know what progress Aaron made, if any.

Upon entering the noisy mill, his gaze immediately fixated on several men on the right side, standing in an elongated room. The postmaster, Van, stood next to Aaron, along with two gentlemen. One, older, wore a premium beige three-piece suit and matching hat; the other, similar in age, flaunted a uniform with a silver star on his chest. The town marshal.

The racket from the spooling machines stole his attention. The women, hard at work in their long blouses and aprons, kept their faces barely visible under linen caps. Completely ignorant of the office proceedings. He found the placement of the office and the design of the facility as a whole quite interesting. Though odd and unconventional, the layout doubtless served its purpose for Aaron, providing him with the perfect vantage point.

Potter made his way around the floor to the office, appearing in the doorway. Van, facing the door, finally peered up from the huddle of men around the desk, while the others, taking notice, stopped speaking and turned.

"Bill!" Aaron's mouth gaped. "Uh... was not, uh, quite expecting you today." He flashed sheepish glances at the other men, at a clear loss for what to say. "Uhhh."

The words lumbered out of Potter's mouth unwittingly. "Was just looking for the postmaster."

"Hiya, Bill. I do apologize," Van said, nonchalant. "We've been away on business." He turned to the man on his right. "I'd like you to meet my father—"

"Roswell Smith," the man interjected, voice, deep and hoarse. He stepped forth, extending a hand to Potter. "Mighty pleased to meet ya."

Potter shook it. "Bill Potter."

Smith's grip was overly firm and extensive. An attempt to exhibit dominance. Potter held in an irritated sigh. From the grandiose smile to the handshake and attire, this man bore no dissimilarity to any high-falutin politician he had come across. Crooked like an auger, the lot of them. He looked down at the high, exquisite shine of Roswell's black-scaled boots.

Roswell took notice. He boasted a hearty smile, exposing a shiny gold canine. "Premium caiman gator. Straight from a cobbler over in the New Orleans' French Quarter. You just can't get quality like this anywhere else. I'd dare you to even try."

"Bourbon Street," Potter inferred.

"Ah! You've been?"

I shot a bank teller there in the face when he decidedly pulled a gun instead of the bag of cash I asked for. "Just once."

Potter, seeing the man's fascination with the black box, wondered how long until he offered some sort of queer, two-timing horse-trade advance. Surprisingly, out of the two men standing here, Roswell posed the biggest threat to his—*shit, does he know*—

"Have you met the marshal?" Van offered.

"I don't believe we've been properly introduced, Mr. Potter. Dave Mather." The marshal tipped his hat.

Potter, deadpan, nodded. He recognized the marshal from Miller's, and though he could have done without ever making his official acquaintance, he supposed it was time. No need to arouse suspicion through avoidance.

"I must say, this here contraption is quite some interestin piece of equipment," Roswell said. "Ain't never seen anythin like it." He turned to the device. "Where did you say you came across this thing?"

Potter hesitated. The answer *I don't remember saying anything to you, asshole* seemed neither appropriate nor cordial. "I didn't."

"Mr. Potter, If I may… I must say, as a man who studies law, I deal with a clientele who wish to keep things close to the chest, so to speak. You are, for lack of a better word, an outsider of our town here. You don't know any of us. But we are a tight-knit little community. So I understand your reticence to divulge information. I assure you; you have nothing to fear. We *are* very curious. It's my understandin you've been doing a bit of excavatin in your backyard tryin to situate yourself a well?"

Potter fired Aaron an incredulous glance, whose tan complexion flushed rose, looking down at his feet.

Guess he knows. "Yeah."

"I bet there's more out there where this came from. More of whatever it is, this—"

"There isn't." Potter cut him off. "I've dug up much of the land from my house to the river. There ain't nothing else out there. I assure you."

There was a moment of awkward silence until Aaron, archly uncomfortable, finally cut it. "Uhhh, after cleaning it up a bit, I got to playing around with it. I think it is some sort of power supply."

Mather's eyes narrowed. "What you mean, 'power supply,' boy?"

"I could not presume to guess, but, uh, all signs point to it being an engine."

"Like a steam engine?" Mather glared, incredulous. "Boy, this tiny thing couldn't run a locomotive, much less clear water from a coal mine. You been smokin them funny cigarettes?"

Aaron returned a fiery glare.

"It's no wonder that old codger Morgan won't sell!" Roswell smirked. "He's been sittin on somethin up there, hasn't he? I knew it. Did I not say that was the case, son?"

Van nodded, matching his father's shit-eating grin.

Roswell went on, shaking his head. "We should a been up there a year ago, tearin up that property."

"I mean, we couldn't, Pa."

"I know, I know. Now, it's only a matter of time."

Potter gaped. *Tear up the property—only a matter of time?*

"Don't you see, Mr. Potter," Roswell continued, "Whatever this is, whatever's down there—if anythin—it could benefit this whole town!"

"Bill, I'd like to hold on to this a while longer, if you would not mind terribly," Aaron asked sheepishly. "Uh, I think I'm on to something. I would like to try a few things here."

Potter, head spinning, hesitated before answering. "Yeah, sure. Whatever you think." He glared at Roswell. "As for the rest of you *concerned citizens*, this here box, and whatever else is under that ground, is private property of Morgan Bennett, Silver Baron of Colorado. And I'd think twice before stepping an uninvited foot onto his land." He tipped his hat and uttered, "Gentlemen," before turning and walking out.

As he untied his mare, the mill door opened. He looked up.

Aaron skipped feverishly across the bridge. "Bill! Hey!"

Potter mounted up, blood pressure rising. His face had flushed, yet his body strangely chilled, as if he'd just submerged in the winter river. Nothing Aaron could say would make this betrayal of confidence up to him. His rage went beyond mere anger. No. Something more lurked beneath the surface, something he couldn't reconcile.

Fear.

Aaron came to a sliding halt, kicking up a clay dust. "I am terribly sorry, Bill. I know you said not to tell anyone about the box, and I-I had every intention not to, but they—they just showed up, while I was toying with it, you know? I-I did not know what to say. And the marshal... he does not like me very much. Mr. Smith started to ask questions. He-he scares me, too, to be honest. He will soon run this town, you know."

"How's everyone know I'm digging a well?"

"I-Isaac told me about it and I must have mentioned it to Van in passing, you know?"

Silence fell upon them for a moment while Potter glanced off. An idiom he'd learned in his youth regarding excuses and assholes came to mind. *Everyone has one, but the question is always how dirty.*

Aaron looked up, his tone shifting morosely. "You cannot know what it is like to—to struggle. To drift, town to town. Knowing you are not accepted. Where your worth is always questioned. You are constantly looking over your shoulder."

Potter, sitting with reins in hand, stared off into the Pecos. Finally, he turned to Aaron. *Yeah, kid. I know more than you think.*

"My parents died in a fire when I was fifteen. I barely made it out myself. For years I hid out. Worked odd jobs. Lived in fear. Until I met Van and Mr. Smith. That man gave me a home. Helped find me work in this mill. I owe him. At the least, I could not lie to him."

"It's fine, Aaron," Potter finally conceded. As expected, his mood remained unchanged, the anger burning bright in his belly. "I'm just sorry I brought it here."

Without another word, Potter yelled a command and set off, tearing hell for leather over the bridge.

2

Potter arrived home post haste. He jumped down from the horse and began pacing the yard, hitting himself in the forehead with the palm of his hand.

Stupid, stupid, stupid, greedy fuck. Why, why, whyyyyyy? You've gone and fucked it all up, and now you brought trouble, you brought trouble, trouble's coming, how do you plan to get out of this one, Joe, huh?

He needed a drink. Fortunately, Coffey had left behind the remnants of a bottle of brandy from their last spitfire venison cookout.

Potter stormed into the house and found Clara washing clothes in the kitchen sink. After quickly greeting her with a kiss, he grabbed the brandy and pulled the cork with his teeth, spitting it on the counter. He tipped the bottle back, taking a generous swig of the brown liquid. His throat burned as it fired down. Another.

Thoughts of men showing up on his property flooded his brain. If they found the ship, someone was bound to find him. But fleeing Missouri Plaza, the safest, smartest option, would upend the young'uns.

He'd never seen Clara happier; Isaac loved his prosperous mill position. They had a future here. And where would they go, anyway?

The running never stops. Not as long as I'm around.

Apprehensively, he opened the basement door and stared into the open crate of dusty dynamite. The arsenal had the capacity to overthrow an entire city. Not that he'd forgotten. But even with such firepower, Potter knew he couldn't single-handedly protect his property. He was good, but not *that* good.

Another option still remained to him, though being plenty drunk would be the only way he'd go back down there. He sighed, took another swig, and got to work.

3

Potter blinked, letting his eyes adjust to the darkness of the ironclad.

Over several trips, he'd transferred the dynamite to the well, gently dropping separate, smaller packing crates of the material down into the ship. Though he still failed to grasp how, and why, John Bennett had acquired so much of it in the first place.

He glanced around the long, vast hall of the ship. Regardless of Bennett's reasons, he supposed, he was more than grateful for the abundance of materials.

After lining the corridor from the base to the control room and then back to the base, Potter carefully, tediously tied all the ends together in a complete U-shape with a spool of wick, also found in the crate. The brandy coursed through his veins, numbing him to his inexplicable surroundings. Even so, the thought of the control room made his fingers shake... especially knowing what remained behind the control room door. Knowing he soon needed to reenter.

A little more liquid courage can't hurt. He swigged hard from the bottle, then proceeded down the hall.

The ship had numerous nonfunctional doors lining the corridor, leaving Potter curious about where they led. What potential wonders, *or horrors*, lay concealed beyond them? Lacking any concrete notion of the ship's size, he considered the possibility that the dynamite might not obliterate the whole ironclad. His sense of security solely relied on his ability to annihilate the ship, if he wished, in a last resort scenario.

Potter wiped his sweaty neck. Hopefully, even if the explosion didn't finish the job, the devastation and subsequent flooding would keep anyone from snooping around the property.

As he came full circle, tying off the last of the dynamite, he set down the lantern. A small, reflective surface on the ground glimmered against the shadows of the flickering flame. Potter squinted. Propped up against the wall, speckled with dust, sat the opium vile. He dropped his work, walked over, and picked it up, rolling it between his fingers. The euphoric flush of the brandy diminished any inhibitions his sober mind might have raised.

He grinned. *Eh... what the hell?*

4

The colossal carding machine growled and gurgled unusual chatter. Isaac, down to a white tee-shirt and dripping with sweat, stood before it with a large metal fork, head throbbing and ears ringing. He'd stuffed rolled swabs of wool in each canal to dampen the noise, but the trick only worked enough to make the sound bearable, if that.

His suspenders chaffed his shoulders as he shoveled bushels of raw material onto the spiked conveyer, daydreaming of sitting upstairs behind a spooler. Perhaps one of these old maids would kick off, and he could take over. Anything beat the carding machine. He would just about play an infinite game of hide-n-seek with his little sister if it meant he'd never have to feed dirty wool into this ghastly, loud monstrosity again.

The discussion with Mr. Wilburn on his first day lingered in his mind. Those words about "knowing what you *don't* want" returned. And, as he thought about it, he finally knew what he didn't want: to endure the same hardships as his father, returning home exhausted, in agony, and unfulfilled after a grueling day. Thoughts of Grandpa crossed his mind, along with Mr. Wilburn, Ms. Nora, and the other shop owners in town. He recognized that life would demand relentless dedication, but there was a certain sense of fulfillment that came with being in control of your own destiny.

Isaac smiled, then sniffed. Something smelled... acrid?

The noise from the carding machine grew louder, reaching a high-pitched squeal. Puffs of dark-gray smoke discharged from every orifice of the machine. In a panic, Isaac stepped back and quickly glanced over its visibly moving parts. And there it sat: a chunk of wool, stuck at the top of the feeder. Quickly, he jabbed and prodded at it with the metal hay fork, trying to release it from the belt, but the soft fabric just pulled and separated.

5

Aaron stared at the device. The globe in its center swirled with volatile smoky-white mist.

"This thing is fascinating," he muttered, caressing the glass. Energy gently nipped at his fingertips, as if moving through the surface. "You think we can break it open?"

Van knocked on it. "Pretty solid. Why—you think there's somethin inside?"

"All I can say is it feels... alive."

Aaron continued to feel around the globe, the glow reflecting off his spellbound face. His body tingled. The tips of his fingers grazed over little concave imperfections in the glass, three nodules on each side, which he lined up with three of his fingers. He wasn't sure why, but he felt an impulse to turn it. And with much effort, he did. The box slowly shifted and clicked. Van and Aaron glanced at one another.

"Do it again," Van whispered.

Aaron forcefully twisted it another click. Then another. It clicked several more times until he completed a full rotation. Then the globe started blinking, a series of popping and clicking and winding emanating from within. Van and Aaron stepped back and watched as each side of the device mysteriously opened at its center, folding into itself. A silver cylindrical tube appeared with a bright whirring sound, sliding out six inches out on each side. A moment later, all functions ceased. The globe dimmed before finally extinguishing.

"Whoa." Van gaped. "How did you do that?"

"I—I do not know!"

The two stood and stared at the device a little longer, waiting for something to happen. Nothing did.

"I think it could be trying to turn on," Aaron said.

"You mean like a lamp?"

"Well, sort of, I suppose. That is the right idea." Aaron began analyzing the outer edges of the transformed box. "If this thing is what I am thinking it is, I think I might know how to get it running."

"You say, 'runnin?'"

Aaron looked out onto the mill floor. "I believe we might be able to rig it to one of the spooling machines here. And maybe, if it can generate enough friction..."

Aaron quickly relieved the women of their duties, giving them the rest of the day. Despite their clear confusion, they asked no questions, happy to oblige. He stood watching as the last few ambled toward the exit, tapping his foot all the while. *Hurry, hurry, hurry.* As soon as the door closed, he locked the mill behind them while Van carried the device to the closest machine.

Joining his friend, Aaron removed the metal cover, exposing the inner guts and moving pieces of machinery. Cogs, pistons, pulleys, belts, all as familiar to him as the back of his hand. Thin strands of wool stretched throughout, wrapped around the many cylinders until eventually stopping to spool around wooden handles.

After cutting through all the fabric leads, Aaron removed a central shaft connecting two large pulley wheels. No effortless task. He tried to rig the box by inserting the exposed cylinders between the two pulleys, but the cylinders wouldn't quite open far enough.

He gestured to the other side of the machine. "Give me a hand, would you?"

On the count of three, both men pulled at opposite cylinders with everything they had, struggling to extend the opening. Their tug-of-war succeeded just enough. The box slid right inside the widened space, essentially replacing the former shaft in a snug gap between the two pulleys.

Van fired up the machine. With his foot on a paddle underneath, Aaron pumped, generating power within the gears. The pulleys turned—one clockwise, the other counter—and sure enough, the box cylinders turned with it. The movement started slowly, with some clear resistance within the box, but sure enough, the more he paddled, the more everything shifted. The globe fired up with a flash and continued on with its pulsing, ominous glow. It began to oscillate, slowly at first, then faster and faster. Within moments, it rapidly accelerated to a few hundred revolutions per minute, a familiar speed for Aaron's machinery. The bright whirring returned at a frequency that seemed to increase. Tiny red dots of light, the size of a pinhead, lit up the device in the vertical nooks and crannies of its black outer shell. Van and Aaron just looked at one another with pure amazement.

"What in God's name you spose it's doin," Van wondered aloud.

Aaron stared, grinning. "I do not know."

At that moment, the device pieces separated from each side of the spinning globe, sliding apart along a metallic shaft running through the globe's center. The white mist inside quickly dissipated, exposing its crystal-clear core. Myriad flashes like lightning pulsed through it, in vivid colors of blue and red. A current, of sorts. The device contracted once again, then the end side opened, separating, the pieces vanishing as if folding into itself. Standing at a distance, Van and Aaron found themselves captivated by the incredible sight unfolding before them.

With Aaron no longer at the controls, the spooling machine ceased its operation, while the enigmatic box remained active. Primed for its intended use, whatever that may be. The two gaped into the open cavity. Several thick, shiny, cylindrical crystals, the shape of railroad spikes but resembling diamonds, protruded down from the interior mechanical material.

Aaron, with curious apprehension, approached the device. He gently felt the smooth, warm edges of the crystal, gave it a tug, and tried twisting it one way, then the other. Nothing. Something told him to give a push, and when he did, the object clicked and dislodged into his hand—surprisingly heavy for something so small, about four inches long by the naked eye. Holding it to the golden sun piercing the mill window, he saw two places along the shaft where the object, tinted light blue, appeared whittled down with a triangular shaped indentation. As he turned the prism, a spectrum of colors reflected from within its azure body.

6

Isaac rushed to the top of the stairs, desperate for help. The mill, to his surprise, sat empty. Odd, but no time for dwelling. He ran to the office, where Mr. Smith and Mr. Wilburn stood in front of the desk with their backs to him. As he opened his mouth to speak—

"My god, Aaron, you think we hit the jackpot here or what," Mr. Smith exclaimed. "These are like diamonds or gems of some sort, aren't they?"

Isaac saw six shiny, crystal-like objects laid out in front of them.

Mr. Wilburn picked up two, examining each. Identical. He lined up the triangle edged notches perpendicularly with two pieces as if to interlock them, then glanced at the others. "They are too heavy for gems, though they do remind me of something we used to play with back home."

"Yeah, what's that—your grandmother's jewelry box?"

"A Kumiki."

"Akoo-Ma-Kee?"

"*Ku*—miki. It is a Japanese word meaning 'put together.' You know, like a puzzle. Look here, see these notches? They all have them."

"My genius friend, always full of surprises."

Mr. Wilburn fidgeted with the pieces. The puzzle, as it were, snapped together with mild difficulty, though Isaac wasn't surprised. Mr. Wilburn was naturally good with his hands—perhaps the smartest person Isaac had ever met.

Mr. Wilburn held up the strange object. Light pierced through it once again, displaying a brilliant mosaic of color which seemed to flash, oh so subtly, in an intermittent pattern. Completed, it resembled a spiked ball, though the spikes were blunted. Isaac gaped, captivated by the beautiful prism.

"It is a knot," Mr. Wilburn explained.

"A knot, huh?" Mr. Smith laughed. "Strangest knot I've ever seen, but I guess that's where you and I differ, friend."

"What do you suppose it is doing?"

"Can't say," Van said, gazing into it. "Kinda reminds me of the telegraph."

"Like a signal?"

Van shrugged. "Maybe."

A sulfuric scent stung Isaac's nostrils. He blinked, pulling his eyes from the crystal to see sooty smoke drifting in from the basement doorway. He opened his mouth to call for help—

"Potter says this was the only thing he found in his backyard. I don't believe that horseshit for one damn minute." Van stared at the shiny stone, eyes hungry. "Come now, please tell me you ain't that ignorant."

Isaac backed out of sight from the doorway.

"You think there is more?"

"Shit yeah, I do. You gotta lot of brains for a Chinaman, but you sure lack the good sense God gave the common man." He giggled, holding up the prism. "I'm gonna bring this little crystal object to my father. He's got some government connections. I reckon he may know someone who can inspect such a thing. And I tell ya, sooner rather than later, we're gonna find out what in Potter's yard."

Isaac finally panicked. "Mr. Wilburn!" He entered the office posthaste, as if he'd just shot up the stairs, and pointed behind him to the smoke billowing from the stairwell. "The carding machine, it's—it's all jammed up! It's smoking—look!"

Aaron hurried toward the black cloud. "Shit! Come give a hand, Van!"

"What should I do, Mr. Wilburn!?" Isaac asked, hoping for one answer in particular.

Aaron stopped briefly, giving him exactly what he wanted. "Uhh, I think you might be done for the day, Isaac."

He ran out of the office, down the stairs. Van dropped the prism on the desk and sprinted out behind him.

Isaac watched Van's dashing departure, then turned to the sparkling prism. Mesmerized. *Those colors...*

7

With hands in heavy pockets, Isaac briskly walked out the front door and into the warmth of the early summer air. Crossing over the bridge, he started toward the many steeds tied to the long post. To his dismay, Blanco was not one of them. He walked circles around the post in a twitchy fit, hoping he'd somehow overlooked the only black horse in the bunch.

His heart froze in his chest. The post was maybe five feet from the edge of the riverbank. A stupid place to tie a horse. He teetered to the edge of the bank and peered down at the scant plot of land which, barely, harbored the ground level of the mill.

Nothing.

He ambled in lopsided circles through Main Street, which, as his luck would have it, teemed with activity. Carriages and stagecoaches traversed the road or sat stationed alongside storefronts. Horse posts and troughs, previously unnoticed by him, appeared to exist in four places on both sides of the road; horses, of course, tied to all. Brown, dark brown, chocolate, shit-on-a-goddamn-stick; they all looked the same. Starting on his left, Isaac bustled past the seemingly empty assay building along with the vacant bank—*what a peculiar town*—skimming the tied steeds and glancing down alleys as he moved from storefront to storefront. Maybe someone found Blanco loose and tied him up? Or what if someone had stolen him?! His sister would be utterly devastated, and likely reproachful, given that she didn't particularly approve of him riding Blanco. But Pa rode that ancient horse he'd brought home before they moved, and, of course, he explicitly prohibited *anyone* from riding Ma's "temperamental mare."

Isaac walked past the marshal's office and the peculiar furniture/coffin store. The Abraham Lincoln looking gentleman he hadn't met, but assumed was Quinsberry, sat perched on his porch, gently rocking in his chair. Their eyes met, and Quinsberry held Isaac's gaze with a look of contempt as he passed, giving him the collywobbles. Evidently, business was slow.

The alley between the undertakers and Miller's Café provided a glance of a few dark horses grazing under the water tower, but as his patience wore thin, Isaac skipped examining them and carried on across the street to Taylor's Tailor & Clothier. As he did so, he happened to glance inside Miller's. The marshal sat in clear view at a window table with a newspaper in his hands, engaged in conversation with that pretty barmaid. Her hand rested on his shoulder. Isaac smiled. Just about everyone in town seemed so friendly. Maybe if he couldn't find Blanco on his own, he could return here and ask the marshal for help. Curious, Isaac glanced back at the undertaker, still rocking, though he couldn't see his watchful eyes.

The vacant church lot only offered a handful of liberated chickens clucking outside the short, white picket fence. He peered around, then glanced at the busy horse post between the tailor and Ms. Nora's store. Many horses, none black, none Blanco. *Ugh, what a stupid name.*

Walking by, he saw Nora through the wide window behind the counter, tending to patrons. She looked happy. Always smiling. She, like the barmaid, was very pretty; he wondered for a moment whether his pa thought the same. As he passed, Nora glanced out and shot him a hearty Texan grin. He pretended to miss her look, wanting to avoid an interaction. Last thing he needed was talk of a missing horse making its way back home.

He continued past the Farmer's Alliance, busy as well, and found a couple chocolate steeds, none of which belonged to his sister. He passed the post office. Not much going on in there with Van at the mill, though an older gentleman in a white suit stood leaning against the counter with a newspaper in hand, a cigar clenched between his teeth.

Isaac, heart thundering, completed his journey around Main Street, pausing before his last stop. The only one he actively tried to steer clear of: the butcher's shop. The end of the month neared, and Charon's quest to fulfill his sacrament loomed. Isaac had his scruples. Something about the scary man's attention, both recent and peculiar, just didn't feel quite right, and his own tentative agreement to the ritual made him uneasy. With Pa working six, sometimes seven days a week now, they hadn't been back to church, nor had they needed the butcher's product, since Mr. Chisum graciously supplied their meat. He wondered—shit, hoped—Charon might've forgotten about the whole damn deal.

Isaac approached the Alliance, reaching the edge of the wide and porchless adobe brick store front. Closing his eyes, he forced himself to slowly poke his head around the corner. Last store, for all the marbles.

He hadn't the slightest idea what he'd say to explain his way out of this: the disappointment in Clara's eyes, the anger in his pa's. His skin stung as he recalled his singular taste of the end of his Pa's service belt: his punishment when Clara, under his care, had burned Ma's book collection shortly after her death. The second worst day of his life. He couldn't fathom the possible depth of punishment for losing a horse.

Slowly, his eyes pried open and glared ahead. The alley was empty.

His heart thumped, skipping a beat, and dropped into his stomach. Nausea crept into his dry throat as he turned in circles, giving Main Street another desperate once over.

"Isaac…"

Oh, shit.

He froze a moment, then turned to Charon. He stood on his porch, clad in the same stained, filthy apron—fresh blood smeared down the side.

"Exquisite timing, son."

Isaac stood in silent protest.

"My brother, Father Harry, just arrived the other day. He is quite delighted to meet you!"

Isaac narrowed his eyes. *Father… Harry? Was that the right name?*

"Haven't seen you in church, son. Everything all right?"

Isaac nodded.

"Not if you're absent from the house of God, it isn't. Now, what could possibly be more important than your covenant with the Almighty?"

"It's just… well, we're real busy now, sir. My pa is working. I'm now working. My sister needs watching after. And—and—"

"Son," Charon said, moving to the edge of the porch and leaning over the railing a few feet from Isaac. "Didn't I say to call me Charon, huh?"

Isaac took a step backward.

Charon slowly rounded the edge of the porch, stepped methodically down three steps, and stood in front in front of Isaac. "Now, there is always time for the Lord. And you don't necessarily have to go to church every time to accept the Lord, if you make the effort at home. Say your prayers before supper. Practice with your sister. I imagine you own the Bible. Am I right on that one?"

"Uhhh…"

Charon shook his head. "Oh, Isaac. Today has *got* to be the day, son," he said, putting a hand on his shoulder. "You see, it was the work of the good Lord which brought you here today. Ain't no denying that!"

For a moment, Isaac wondered what really brought him here—the divine power of "the good Lord," or some shrewd play by Charon. Maybe he'd hidden Blanco inside the butcher shop. He peered over Charon's shoulders into the front windows.

"Having faith will only get you so far with the man upstairs. That's why it's imperative you commence with the ceremony!"

"I'm afraid I can't right now, you see, my horse is missing, an-and Pa is expecting me back home, see, he works real late, uh… gotta get hunting and supper going."

Charon's neutral expression slipped. His eyes narrowed slightly, his mouth bowed in either disappointment or frustration. "Well, okay. Perhaps another time would be best. You say your horse is missing? Why don't you come inside, and I'll bring you home. I'm expecting Buckley, my driver, anytime now. Supper will be on me. How's that sound?"

The skin on the back of Isaac's neck tightened, the hair stiffening. He glanced around awkwardly, wondering how he'd say no to such a proposal. All he wanted was to find Blanco and go home. He looked toward the mill and the barren bridge, wondering if Aaron or Van might appear and intervene—not that he wanted them to.

"So how about it, son?"

"Huh?"

"I said, why don't you come on in and wait. We'll take you home."

"Isaac," a familiar voice called from behind.

Isaac turned to find Nora at the edge of the alliance. In her hands, she held the reins of a black horse.

Blanco!

"I think this old stallion belongs to you," she said, pulling Blanco across the alley entrance.

Isaac's heart soared, then fell at Nora's aberrant, deadpan expression. In the handful of times he'd made her acquaintance, he'd seen nothing less than a seven-mile smile stretched across her pretty face. Its absence left him disconcerted.

She met Isaac's eyes and handed the horse over. "Be careful, hon, these straps are a little frayed. Found him wanderin up and down Main Street round lunch time. Recognized John Bennett's old nag right away. Had'im tied up round back. Once the crowd died down, I was planning to bring'im back before you finished up the day at the mill, but looks like I'm a bit"—she glanced at Charon and back to Isaac—"late."

"Mrs. Reynolds. Pleasure to make your acquaintance," Charon said with a thin smile, his tone even and indifferent.

"*Mizz* Reynolds." she clapped back curtly, her hands resting on her broad hips. "Thank you very much."

"My apologies." Charon's smile dampened. "Anything I can do for you, *Mizz* Reynolds?"

"No, I'm afraid not, Mr. Dotterweich. Just came over to give the boy his horse and see him off." She turned to Isaac. "Go on now. Go home, darlin."

Without hesitation, Isaac mounted Blanco and pulled back on the reins, squeezing his legs against the horse's ribcage. Blanco lunged forward. He looked back as they set off, catching Nora say one last thing before she turned and tramped away.

"Look, *Charon,* if I may... I don't know what your intention with that boy is, but I think it best to just leave'im be, ya hear?"

8

Not a moment too soon, a red stagecoach pulled up alongside the butcher's building. The elderly man behind the reins gently and cautiously stepped down, bones creaking and cracking, and ambled around the storefront where Charon still stood, watching the boy ride off over the bridge. By the time he finished his short walk, Buckley had quickly and masterfully rolled a cigarette and stuck it between his lips.

Without breaking focus, Charon said, "I want you to follow that boy. Find John Bennett's property and gather any information you can get. Tonight has got to be the night."

Buckley struck a match, lit his cigarette, and nodded.

9

With a quirley hanging from his lips, blue smoke wafting from the tip, Potter stared through the glass. The peculiar treasure of the artifact room beguiled him, staring back through the clear barrier. Concealed. Unattainable. Taunting. If he ended up back on the run, these items might prove highly profitable. Maybe in Mexico or South America. There, they'd live like royalty. His skin crawled at the thought of not being able to access the treasure, much less steal it. Though, if he was being honest with himself, he didn't really want the items at all.

Since his youth, Potter relished taking money. He'd started legally, as a landlord. The eldest of seven siblings, he had the responsibility of managing multiple properties owned by his family in southeast Connecticut. Properties rented by the affluent. Properties he had perpetual access to. He himself was no drudger; as the son of prominent business owners, he certainly never wanted for much. So, what made him steal—boredom, the challenge, the titillation of committing such an act? He thought not. It was a compulsion. Kleptomania... a condition he'd read about in his father's Harvard journals. He knew his parents were likely abreast of the party responsible, too. After years of numerous tenant complaints of neighborhood theft and a looming reputational business threat, the solution presented itself.

The Rebellion War.

Joseph Griffin, in their eyes, didn't qualify for the mere three-hundred-dollar reprieve—the price to buy your way out of conscription. Due to his potential inheritance of their grand estate, Griffin overlooked the comprehensive control his parents possessed over his financial holdings. Three hundred dollars was pocket lint to them.

During the war, he'd pilfered from fellow brothers-in-arms and looted enemy corpses too, of course. *But did that really count?* Rations, ammunition, money. Life. Shortly after, he'd doubled down on such commodities, taking them in larger quantities and usually with excessive force. He took women, though never unwillingly or with much difficulty. After all, he was quite the handsome man. More importantly, he took Bessie for his wife. His most prized treasure of all. And he'd stolen her from the one man no mortal wise dared cross, much to the chagrin of her father.

He'd finally won. Or so he thought.

"Bill!"

Potter blinked. The voice, familiar, echoed from far away. *There ain't nobody there.*

"Mr. Potter!"

Mr. Potter? He dropped the butt of the quirley—one of two he'd rolled, the other tucked under a flap inside his Stetson—and snubbed it with his boot toe. Several more times, his name echoed through the strange ship before he cautiously emerged from the hatch. Of course, he saw only the clay pit wall and, above, a bright yellow ball illuminating the pale sky. Then the silhouette of a man obscured his view.

"Bill!?"

He knew that voice. "Coffey?"

"Oh, sweet Jesus. Glad I found ya!"

Potter climbed from the pit. Now, seeing Coffey up close, he could see the distress in the man's eyes. His cowboy attire, unusual for this time-of-day, piqued Potter's curiosity, though the medley of alcohol and opium kept him pleasantly indifferent. "What's going on, you—you look troubled?"

"Boss sent me down here. We gotta situation over at the ranch. The cattle, they busted out the barbed wire. Scattered all over! Boss needs all hands-on deck, if ya know what I mean."

"Yeah... yeah, I do. Shit."

Potter instantly knew what this meant: likely, an all-day affair. Isaac was still at work, and even in his euphoric state, he didn't feel comfortable leaving Clara alone. Not to mention this fully armed ship. Christ, for all he knew, someone busted open the gated pasture to draw him away. He had no doubt that they, whoever *they* were, had duly informed the entire community about his property. A wave of paranoia and hot flashes swept over him, leaving little means to stem the tide.

He hesitated, wiping his perspiring forehead with his hanky. As he attempted to shove it into his back pocket, it fell to the ground. He didn't want to let Coffey down, nor Mr. Chisum, but he was stuck. His mind ineffectually ran in circles, the opium, though a small amount, comfortably numbing his thoughts. Maybe he should bring Clara to the ranch. But he'd have to tear hell for leather, given the urgency, and he couldn't risk her safety en route. She was safer at home with the crate of rifles.

Fuck, fuck, fuck, fuck, fuck… I can't, I can't, I can't, I can't, I can't…

"Coffey, I-I-I'm sorry, I—"

From the woodlands, Isaac appeared on Blanco's black back.

"Bill?" Coffey looked behind, then back at Potter inquisitively.

"Eh. Never mind." Potter sighed, relieved. Though still not fully comfortable leaving, he climbed Bessie's mare and waited.

Isaac rode up moments later. "Good afternoon, Mr. Coffey. Pa."

Potter quickly looked at the sun's position. "Isaac, you're home early?"

"Yes, Pa. Mr. Wilburn gave me the rest of the day. Carding machine jammed up good. Needs fixing, I reckon."

Again, Potter's mind went straight to that black box, Marshal Mather, and Roswell Smith. *Why… why in holy damnation would a machine just all of a sudden "jam up?" They trying to get us all back to the house together, or just the young'uns? What the hell are they playing at!?* He shook his head. *It's the opium, it's the opium, it's the opium, it's the opium, it's the opium, it's the opium, it's the opium, it's the opium, it's the opium, it's the opium…*

"Bill!" Coffey snapped his fingers.

"Huh?" Potter snapped out of it.

"Ya all right, friend?"

"Uh, yeah. Yeah. Fine. Fine." Potter glanced Coffey up and down, then reached out to touch him. "That's a mighty *fine* jacket. Cowhide?"

Coffey looked down. "Uh. Yeah. It is. Uh, we gotta get a move on, Bill, if we gonna get hold of this."

"Right." Potter turned to Isaac and glared into his befuddled eyes. "Keep an eye on Clara. You hear me, son?"

"Yes, Pa."

"I will be back by nightfall. *Do not* answer the door. You encounter any trouble; you head straight to the basement with your sister and you hide in that weapons cache. No one will come mess with you in there. Just remember, sometimes you gotta throw a grenade. You just never know. Trust me."

Coffey shot Potter a bewildered look. Isaac's poor eyes widened, glancing at both his pa and Coffey.

"*Oh*, and be cleaned and dressed! We're invited to dinner at Ms. Nora's." Potter had only just recalled her invitation. Despite his previous intentions of not returning to Missouri Plaza, now, in his sorry state, the thought of seeing Nora proved irresistible. *I must not know what I'm saying.*

Shaking his head at himself, Potter tugged at the reins, turned, and tore into the woodlands with Coffey.

10

Buckley, near the edge of the property, watched the men enter halfway down, hitting the dusty trail to the meadow where all the trails interconnected. One led to town, another to the Jinglebob Ranch.

From behind a tree, he puffed his cigarette, top hat in hand, his long, wild hair drifting in the cool breeze. He watched with partially obscured, narrowed eyes as the boy entered the house. "Father said curious things, he did. Curious things."

Buckley considered just going in and taking the boy himself, but that idea posed a couple of issues. Not that he couldn't handle a twelve-year-old kid. At eighty-two years young, he remained tough as a workhorse... but there was the sister. And this talk of a *weapons cache?* He didn't like the sound of that. No, sir. Buckley could not reconcile all of what he'd heard, but he'd done as Charon had asked. The details would mostly satisfy him.

It's all in the details.

Dinner at Ms. Nora's.

PART II

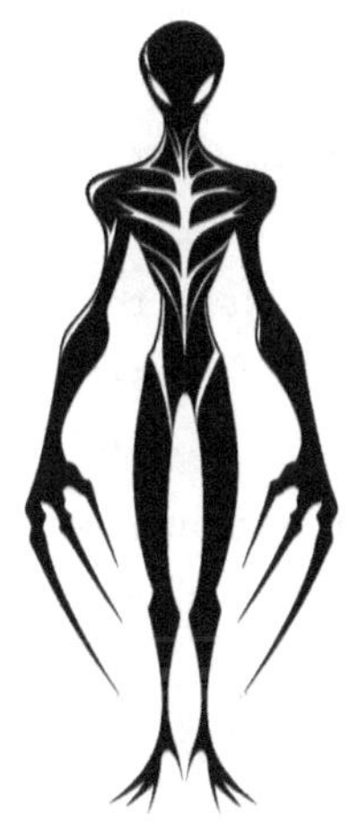

CHAPTER 19

It was only a matter of time before Clara found herself down in the pit, inside the ship. Unintentionally, of course. Though curiosity loomed in her subconscious, she hadn't given the ship much thought until today, waiting in her Sunday best.

They were to have supper in town, but they were starving, so Isaac had fried up a few eggs he'd fetched from the coop alongside the barn in an effort to not spoil their appetite. With satisfied tummies, they had begun an intense game of hide-n-seek, as you did when satiated, energized, and waiting for your pa's return. Isaac had won two games, having successfully evaded his sister's hunt, first hiding, or rather, squeezing, into the oven. The door had barely closed behind him. The second time he'd hid inside the weapons cache, tucked away down the dark path, which Clara had forgotten about. She did, however, look inside the empty dynamite crate. Nothing.

She wanted to quit playing, but she needed to beat her brother at least once. Though her determination was not without guilt. She threw a slightly manipulative tantrum, and Isaac, likely feeling bad, gave her a whole thirty seconds to find the perfect hiding spot.

At first, Clara ran out to the barn. She considered the loft, but the ladder was missing. The tool closet door hung open, but provided a far too easy target. She exited in an anxious flurry, time running out, knowing her brother would soon yell—

"Ready or not, here I come, Clara!" The call rang faintly from inside the house.

Clara looked around. There was the schooner—still covered, but empty. The outhouse. The smelly, gross, fly-ridden outhouse. That scared her. She looked beyond and saw the well pit, immediately running to it. She stopped short at the edge and looked down. Boy, was it steep. The jump loomed, far too risky for someone of her size. And her pretty dress. Oh, Pa would *not* be happy if she got it dirty.

The squeaky hinges echoed as the side screen door flew open. Clara turned to see Isaac explode through the opening. She panicked, glancing around for a place to hide but finding nothing. Her Pa's hanky lay discarded in the grass.

Isaac, paying no attention, headed straight toward the barn. Clara peered into the pit and made up her mind. She grabbed the hanky, laying it at the edge of the pit, then hiked up her dress, sitting on it. With her button-up half boots, she cautiously edged herself over the side and swiftly descended, gracefully landing on her feet. She almost lost her balance, wildly flapping her arms, but she managed to stabilize herself without a sound.

Pa said—commanded, really—not to go inside the ship. But Isaac had been. Why not her? How dreadful must it have been? Her skin erupted in gooseflesh at the thought of what grave things may lie waiting in the shadows. Flutters filled her little tummy, battling against the negative thoughts creeping in. "Faith," she repeated to herself. "Gotta have faith." She was finally tired of being afraid. If Big Brother managed it, then how dangerous could it be?

The entrance of the ship emerged before her, the ladder poking up. She smiled.

She might finally win this game.

2

Isaac exited the barn and glanced around the yard. He pulled away the veil which covered the back of the schooner. No Clara. Not surprising, but he still had to double-check.

The outhouse.

"All right, Clara, good job. You got me. Gross place to hide. And I'm not going in there, so come on out!" He stood and waited. "Clara!"

He pounded on the door, annoyed, then flung it open. Empty. No sign of Clara in the vacant stall. *But where else could she be?* Inside he'd been thorough, checking every conceivable place, even spots he might've hid had it been his turn. Still plenty of nooks and crannies one could stuff themselves into, if you could believe it, but surely Clara should have turned up by now.

Scratching his head, he looked around. Toward the river, he saw the small mounds of dirt around the pit. *Oh, no…* Isaac ran now, certain of her hiding place. The end of his father's black belt flashed through his mind's eye, setting his stomach churning.

"Clara, you better not be inside that damn ship," he hollered as he cautiously crouched at the edge, dropping to the pit floor. He hovered over the open latch. Darkness. "Clara!" No answer. Finally, he came to his rational senses. No way she'd be hiding way out here in this dark, creepy ship. Right?

As he turned from the latch, a hand grabbed his ankle.

"AHHH!"

Clara, giggling, poked her head through.

He glared down at her. "Holy Christ, Clara!"

"Come on!"

"Get up out o' there. You know Pa don't want us in here!"

"Game ain't over till you tag me, stupid," she teased, ducking down inside the ship.

Isaac, though plenty annoyed, hesitated at the opening. Pa's warning rung in his ears. *You do not go into that hole. Ever. Do—you—understand?*

But what could he do? Sighing, he followed his sister down the ladder.

He saw only darkness upon his descent, save for a soft, amber glow pulsing somewhere up the corridor. No sign of Clara. He approached the lighted object, recognizing it as his father's lantern; its flame gently flickered as he lifted it in front of his face. An anomaly against the wall just beyond the juddering reflection caught his eyes. Short, narrow rods lined the walls all the way down the corridor, each suspended in the middle of the wall, bound. When he drew closer, he finally grasped what he saw. *Dynamite.* Though he couldn't fathom why Pa would want to destroy the ship.

A sharp, faint clanking drew his attention down the hall.

"Clara!?" He inched his way down, holding the lamp straight out in front.

That familiar, stale scent slowly pervaded his nasal passages. He didn't like it. He didn't like being down here, and he planned to give his sister quite a tongue lashing when he found her. Ahead, though faintly, he could see the cracked door to the control room. He prayed she wasn't inside, recalling the look on his father's face... something eerily close to fear. Still, the only open doorway loomed, and despite his aversion, he entered.

First thing he noticed was the metal man's remains. Fascinated, he stared at the armored skeleton, veiled in a sheer blanket of intricate webbing. Its skull, fully exposed, leaned to the right; its open jaw brandished a gold-checkered smile. Wisps of long sliver hair, still intact, draped over its armored chest.

An auric brilliance shimmered in his peripherals. The lantern shifted, reflecting against something near the far wall. Moving closer, Isaac held the light high to fully observe the objects behind the transparent structure. He gasped. Pa must have found these buried artifacts but not yet unearthed them. *Maybe that's what the dynamite is for?*

Something slowly moved over his left shoulder, brushing his collar bone. Clara's hand. He turned, rolling his eyes, but the hand was not that of his sister's. Not a human hand at all. Only three fingers, each thicker, longer than any he'd ever seen. The skin, grotesquely wrinkled, brown, and leathery, ended in honed tips. Razor sharp. Something guttural gurgled behind him.

Isaac froze, unable to move. The hair on his neck stood erect. Blood drained from his pale cheeks and settled like cold stones in the pit of his stomach.

A crusty finger crawled up his neck, and that's when he twitched, squirming back. In the scattering light, something stood. Something with a silver oval for a face, a mouth full of tiny holes, and narrow slits for eyes. Eyes staring at *him*. Isaac screamed, backing away; his legs twisted. Tripping, he fell crashing onto the seat of his pants. The lantern came down, gently clanking its metal base as it bounced. The light flickered as if to extinguish, but didn't. His arms shook, bracing for cover, the lamp dangling in hand.

Shrill, familiar giggling followed. Too familiar.

Isaac dropped his arms. Clara, standing over her appalled brother, removed the metal man's helmet, a smile painted across her victorious face.

She'd won.

"What the hell, Clara," Isaac yelled, seething. A moment later, and he would have pissed himself.

"Got you!"

"That shit ain't funny!" He quickly stood, dusting his pants, and shot his sister a scorching glare, noticing she still held whatever touched him. "That a hand!?"

"I don't know. That man had it." Clara pointed to the metal man, unfazed. Then again, she *was* eight.

"Ugh!" Isaac's face, beet red, boiled. "Christ, you scared me half to death"—for a split second he considered the consequence, but the words spilled from his trembling lips anyway—"you, you goddamn gullyfluff!"

Clara's mouth dropped in utter disgust, her little pale face souring. Isaac instantly regretted his words. Gullyfluff was literally the *worst* thing anyone could say to another person.

"Don't call me that!" She shoved him away. Hard.

Isaac stumbled backward into the wall, smearing away an age of dust along with him. Once again, the potential consequences of his actions stunned him. It took everything in him to not smack her, though he'd yet to raise a hand to her in anger.

"That's it! I'm done playing with you!" He shook his fist at her, lantern shaking in his grasp. "And when Pa gets back, I'm telling him you tricked me into coming down here! And he's gonna be so mad—"

"Look!" Clara's eyes widened, pointing to the now dust-free wall behind him. He turned to see that his blazer had revealed the presence of a door. In the pale light, a small square panel shimmered, exposing an imprint roughly the shape of an oversized hand debossed into the surface. A hand with three edged fingers.

Isaac stared for a moment, wide eyed, then shook his head. "We don't belong down here. Pa's going to be back here any minute. You know what he's gonna do to me, he finds us down here!? You remember what happened last time. Now drop that gross thing and let's go!"

"But Isaac!"

He'd heard enough. Grabbing her hand, he dragged her across the room.

"No, stop!" She tightened up, resisting with all her weight.

He yanked at her wrist. "Come on!"

Clara pulled back with such force, she slipped through his grasp, stumbling backward and falling on her backside. "Ouch!"

Isaac's heart sank at the sight of his sister, lying on the ground, her dress dirtied. What if she had suffered physical harm?

"I'm... I'm sorry, Clara," he offered, voice sheepish. "You okay?"

"I'm fine," she snapped, picking herself up and dusting her filthy dress with a heavy hand.

She glowered at Isaac, but her anger lasted only a moment.

"Look!" Hers eyes lit up as she pointed to the clear wall. "You know what that door opens to? A room full of all that! A treasure, Isaac! Do you know how happy Pa would be if we were able to get it for him!?"

Isaac stared at the wall. Perhaps that *was* the answer. Their pa might be angry they disobeyed him, but surely his fury would pass once he saw their spoils. And, as Isaac looked at the wall, he imagined moving away from this new *austere* lifestyle. He was no fool. He knew they didn't move from Denver, from all they knew, so Pa could find work. He hadn't the slightest idea why they were in Missouri Plaza. That questions was best left unasked.

After a quiet yet apprehensive deliberation, he nodded. "Okay. Gimme that thing."

Beaming, Clara complied.

Isaac placed the rubbery hand on the panel. Nothing. He applied some pressure, and as he did, the panel plate compressed a half inch or so. A soft light-gray glow illuminated within the handprint and along the panel edges. Isaac dropped the hand and stood back with Clara. The wall to the right of the artifacts began to grind and shift. Slowly, the door opened, squealing along its dry track like nails on a chalkboard.

The young'uns winced at the noise, grinning all the while. This mystery certainly surpassed hide-n-seek. Hearts racing, they entered.

Isaac led the way, lantern held high, with Clara right on his heels. This room, adjacent to the control room, looked much smaller than the previous space. Much busier, too. He turned a full revolution, getting a bird's-eye view of the layout. No other points of entry or exit. And no treasure. There were, however, four long cylindrical glass tubes situated in the center. At six or seven feet long, their rectangular bases protruded four feet from the ground. The tubes, encased in each, rose up halfway, barely visible through a quarter inch overlay of gray dust.

A narrow counter stood against the wall beyond the tubes. The surface displayed glass panels flush with the wall alongside variously sized and shaped dials, knobs, and switches. Two tall, wide chairs sat positioned in the front, along with a long, semi-clear plate of glass which protruded down from the low ceiling. The glass panels and buttons displayed peculiar, scratch-like symbols.

Isaac and Clara inched their way around the space.

"Isaac, what are these?" Clara climbed the edge of one of the tube bases, brushing away dust with the end of the pink sash tied at her waist. "You think there's treasure inside!?"

Isaac leaned over with the lantern. "I don't know. I—I don't think so." The capsule, though dark, appeared empty. "We shouldn't be in here."

He walked to the control counter, waving the lantern over to analyze its foreign features. Darkened colors of green, yellow, and red faintly appeared under dusted clear buttons; Isaac wondered if they might emit light.

"Isaac!"

He immediately turned to his sister.

She leaned over another capsule, staring down into it with fixated eyes. "C'mere! I need the light."

Isaac held the lantern over the dusted tube. The material inside shimmered, the flame's glow reflecting in the metallic, bronze-like surface. Though its contents appeared solid, the shimmer gave the tube an appearance of motion, almost flowing. Molten. Isaac exchanged a perplexed, awestruck look with his sister.

Clara, using her sash, dusted the surrounding surface of the capsule, exposing several inactive buttons, switches, and small glass panels. At its base, she unveiled a plate with a handprint, like the door entrance. She gasped, looking up at her brother before scurrying out of the door with the lantern, only to return moments later with the mummified appendage.

Isaac stood and watched, chewing his lip. He didn't feel right about any of this. An imagined scene of Pa returning, seeing them depart from the well with a wrathful gaze, replayed over and over in his head.

The hand hovered over the plate as Clara lined it up.

Isaac needed time to think—to figure out how to get his father or maybe Coffey down here instead of opening the capsule by themselves. "Wait!"

Clara mashed the hand onto the panel. It suppressed with a pale glow, followed by distinct clicking. The base also gleamed softly in blue, brightening quickly to a deep azure. Within moments, it began to ascend slowly from the floor.

Together, the siblings backed away from the clicking and popping, Isaac holding the lantern between them.

A narrow stream of icy air rushed upward from several mini ports on each side of the capsule, hissing like steam from a kettle's spout. Isaac could see his heavy breath leaving his mouth. A dense mist filled the capsule as the air depleted, the capsule radiating with a brilliant white light. The base halted.

Click!

The capsule split horizontally at its center, the seal breaking suction and releasing its pressure. Each half slid open lengthwise in the opposite direction. The young'uns stood frozen in the soft glow, vapor seeping out of the opening in a languid escape to permeate the space surrounding them. As the mist thinned, partially dissipating, the capsule's strange, frosty contents gradually revealed themselves: a serpentine, alloy material, though, up close, it appeared lustrous and damp. Soft. The paper-thin layer of veiling frost quickly melted away. To Isaac, the composition looked like an elongated sack of potatoes.

Clara took a step forward.

A whoosh of compressed air slammed into their faces. Isaac grabbed his sister's arm, pulling her back.

The metallic potato sack, deflating, desiccated away around an internal, solid structure. The young'uns turned, eyes bugging, to a gurgling clear tube at one end of the capsule, a dark liquid draining down below the floor. Parts of the sack, which now took on a gelatinous appearance, shifted. Scraping emanated from the inner edges. Something inside... moving. The center of the wet sack rose several inches before splitting open at its gooey seam. Gray condensation misted from the orifice with a clear, viscous fluid oozing down the edge.

Rising from the severed opening came three long, honed phalanges, sharp to the tip. The wet, trembling fingers reached up, cupping the ship's cool, stale air. The young'uns gaped at the hand in motion, then back to the decomposed one in Clara's arms, then back up again. The hand gently splayed its fingers, twisting at the wrist. Ooze dripped as the arm followed, its wet skin gleaming with a gray-blue hue as it reached out, trembling, before falling to the side of the capsule, motionless. Clara turned to her brother, a horror unlike any he'd ever seen in her eyes.

"Let's go, Clara!" Before he could finish spitting out this sentence, Isaac had Clara's hand, dragging her from the chamber.

She dropped the hand, unable to avert her fearful eyes as her brother pulled her away.

The two hauled ass up the ladder, out of the ship, and inside the house, Isaac slamming the door behind them. He stood against the frame, bent over, heaving, trying to catch his breath.

Clara, in tears, jumped onto the couch and hid under a chunky brown hand-knit throw.

"What was that!?" Her pallid face poked out from under the blanket wrapped around her head, her voice quivering.

"Don't... know." Isaac barely eked out the words between deep breaths.

"I'm scared, Isaac!"

"It can't hurt us. I-I think whatever it is... is dead now."

"How do you know!?"

"It—it stopped moving, remember?"

Faintly, in the distance, something rustled.

Isaac backed away toward Clara; they both stared at the front wall.

"It's coming, it's coming!" Clara sobbed, hysterical.

Isaac joined her on the couch, squeezing his arms around his bundled, trembling sister. The noise intensified. Nearing. The familiar sound of hooves pounding dirt.

Through the window, Isaac saw a man in a hat on horseback approaching the homestead.

"It's Pa!" Isaac hopped off the couch.

Clara burst from under the throw, beaming. "Pa!?" Her excitement promptly melted away, and she threw out a hand. "Wuh-wait!"

Her brother stopped.

"You-you can't tell Pa bout what happened in the—that ship!"

"But, what if he—"

"Please don't tell Pa we went in there, Isaac! *Please—pleeeaaase!*" She yanked desperately at his blazer sleeve, tears streaming, terrified.

Looking into her eyes, he knew they both thought of *that* night... the night Clara torched her mother's book collection. The palpable fear of their recent encounter paled in comparison to her current state of terror.

Isaac's mind ran circles. Telling his father was the right option, but he trembled, thinking of the consequence: the feeling of Pa's folded belt against his bare back. His ass. His legs. The image nauseated him as much as the physical pain.

Blinking away the memory, Isaac sized up his sister—her pretty dress now a mess. "Quickly! Go change before Pa gets in!"

Isaac tore off his jacket and began smacking the back, trying his best to clear away the dirt. The azure crystal shot from his interior pocket, rolling across the hardwood floor with a heavy clank. Clara stopped and turned as the crystal brushed by her feet. She picked it up.

"Woah." She gazed into the sparkling, iridescent object, captivated. "It's sooo pretty. Where did you get this!?" She turned the knobby ball in her hands. Translucent shades of red, yellow, and orange twinkled inside its core.

Isaac tramped over and grabbed it from her delicate grip. "You shouldn't touch it!"

"Hey!" Clara scowled. "Well, what is it?"

"I got it from the mill." He glared at it. "But it came from inside the ship. Heard Mr. Smith and Mr. Wilburn talking about bringing a bunch of city men—businessmen, probably lawmen—down here to our land. Coming to get what's in the ground." He nodded toward the pit.

"So?"

"They ain't the good men, Clara," he clarified. "They're the Bad Men."

Clara squinted, her face scrunched with confusion.

"Bad Men gonna come take our land. Come take our pa away from us! You don't want that, do you?"

She flinched, horrified. "Nooo!"

"Don't you worry. I won't let nothing bad happen to us. And whatever *this* is," he added, raising the crystal, "they ain't gonna have it. Quickly now, go change!"

He smacked away as much of the dirt from the back of his legs and coat as he could while Clara scurried upstairs. He knew his little sister didn't quite understand, but nor did she ask for clarification. No matter. He'd evoked the fear of losing her pa, and that was enough. *"All men bear a debt,"* Grandpa had said on his first day in Missouri Plaza, not realizing that Isaac eavesdropped through the dirty window. And Pa would have to repay his, whatever that meant. Although Isaac had never questioned the surname change and sudden move, his intuition told him that these activities were not typical for families.

Isaac, clean and composed, just managed to slip on his blazer as Pa opened the door and stepped inside.

Clara, in a fresh dress with a pink bowtie in her hair, stood mid-landing on the staircase, staring. Pa looked at Isaac, to Clara, then back to Isaac.

Silence.

Pa furrowed his brow. "Uhhh. You kids ready?"

Chapter 20

The Antiquarian regained consciousness, its eyes glazed and utterly bewildered. By this time, the cryogen liquid had drained and the remaining viscous fluid had dried to a semi-solid, tacky substance. Slowly, it sat up, then draped its long, trembling legs one at a time over the side of the cryogenic sleep pod. Taking a moment to fully come to, it let its eyes adjust to the dark. Its nostrils flared, taking in wafts of stale, dusty air.

Gently, it stepped down—a balancing act—taking one wobbling step at a time.

Something was unquestionably awry. The soft white glow of the emergency lighting around the upper perimeter allowed for easy maneuvering through the unusually dark laboratory. At the control panel, the Antiquarian slipped into one of the icy seats and tapped several buttons, dust clinging to its tacky, muscular frame and its honed fingertips. The sharp, resounding clicks of glass tapping glass filled the inexplicably muted research vessel. Frustrated, it tried the sheer computer screen projecting down from the ceiling instead, pounding the icons with more force than necessary.

Nothing.

The craft was inoperable—disconcerting, at best, since, to the best of its knowledge, inoperability should be impossible. Though the damned hyper-drive malfunctioned, *another supposed impossibility*, the moment they entered WL-9768's orbit. For the love of Zurik, the ship was one of the oldest units in the fleet, its days undoubtedly numbered. Not to mention, Earth, as they referred to it here, had proved more difficult than expected.

Still, the being hadn't resented the projected long return home to SH-2-275. With the Earth-time equivalent of a millennia-long inter-galactic conflict, compounded with the economic and financial burden faced by the Antiquarian military—*as well as their species*—it supposed it was lucky to just have a craft and be on assignment away from the mayhem.

All "improbabilities" aside, the craft should at least be awake. Unless if the craft was utterly destroyed, which, insofar, it clearly wasn't... or de-commissioned? But even then, there would be some residual intelligence coming from the Cerebrum. Just enough to get the screen running and possibly access a local map or utilize an external camera.

Unless... *No.*

Eyes fully adjusted, the Antiquarian ambled into the dingy, dust-filled cabin of the artifact room. The armored Earthling, which had been alive and awaiting transport back to SH-2-275 for observation and research, now offered only a pile of bones behind tarnished tin plating. A damn shame, too. Part of the Antiquarians' millennial visit assignment includ-ed collecting artifacts and gathering human specimens to track this new planet's evolution.

Its gurgling curses rippled and echoed through the empty craft. It hadn't returned home. The question now: how much time had passed?

The Antiquarian stepped into the corridor. Moonlight poured into the hatch, illuminating a narrow path. Specks of drifting dust sparkled through the bright stream. Scattered footprints disturbed the thick ash, leading behind the Antiquarian and into the control room. The direc-tion provided little comfort as the Antiquarian entered. Its comrade lay slumped over on the ground. It inched around the corpse's chair, fear becoming a reality before its eyes. The damaged control box in front hung open, the black box—*the Cerebrum*—powering the ship *gone.*

Hurrying back to the cryogenic chamber, the Antiquarian put its hand to a dusted square panel. The wall creaked open three feet, revealing a short, walk-in closet. White compression suits fitted with armored paneling over the chest, shoulders, abdomen, thighs, and shins hung from a long rack which slid out from the inner wall. The suit's color adjusted to the skin tone of the Antiquarian as it slid inside, a cool baby blue with a touch of gray, molding to its muscular form. Imperceivable, yet shiny. It wasn't sure what to expect outside the ship, but up until now, the primitive creatures of WL-9768 posed no imminent threat with their unsophisticated weapons. And the fact that the Antiquarian was still here, alive, meant that not too much time had elapsed.

At least, it hoped.

With one swift bound, it shot up through the hatch and into the pit, then to ground level. It sucked in cool, crisp air through its snout, savoring the freshness in its complex respiratory system before fully exhaling. Thankfully, the Antiquarian's self-regulating body temperature ensured its comfort and warmth despite the planet's unpredictable weather. WL-9768's atmosphere had no adverse effect on its glossy exterior, either, though the dynamic pigment of its skin would undoubtedly continue to adapt.

The Antiquarian stared up at the starry, bright sky. Beautiful, peaceful, and, if nothing else, ordinary, at least in comparison to the rest of this strange, primitive world. What it looked up for, it quickly found—what the inhabitants of this Rock referred to as "constellations" in the celestial sphere. The Earthling's sky unicorn glowed in the distance, but the most prominent feature of this fantastic beast dwelled in its eye.

Home.

The cool night spoke in soft tones. Light trilling emanated from miniature nocturnal creatures roaming the prairie, along with the placid sound of nearby flowing water. A quick scan of the lens observed a plethora of minute movements alongside a central, freestanding structure on this fragment of land, fringed by a partial moat.

Water.

The Antiquarian drank generously, squatting, scooping river runoff into large, cupped hands. It felt as if it had been at least a hundred years since it last tasted something so cold, so clean, so refreshing. Briefly, it wondered whether it had been much, much longer. It kept drinking, glimpsing the myriad tiny amphibious creatures just below the surface, whirling past with the current.

Catching sight of an extensive structure, it ambled toward the building, passing by several tiny, roaming, two-legged creatures that accounted for the minute movements it had detected. The unintelligent beings clucked and hurried away, allowing it to pass, disinterested, to peer into a window of the structure. Although it immediately detected no life-forms, it stood for some time to be certain. As it turned away, it caught movement in its vast peripherals and stopped to do a double take back through the window. Something inside moved. The Antiquarian moved with it, gently, side to side, mimicking its movements. It saw something it hadn't seen in some time.

Its reflection.

A large, ornate, reflective surface hung against the hallway wall. It slid off its helmet and took a longing look at the weathered face glaring back. A lanky finger carefully traced the narrow jawline up over high structured cheeks and under the thin grooves of large, red, striated eyes. The view, though from afar, had unveiled enough.

The Antiquarian sulked. It had seen better days.

Its stomachs growled.

It moved into the second structure, where a much larger, four-legged creature lay on a pile of yellow plant matter. The Antiquarian peered over the little door. The black creature stared back at the being. Its many nostrils flared, taking in the old animal's unappealing scent: a faint whiff of decay.

It walked out.

2

The sun gently sank behind the mountain range into an ocean of orange haze as the schooner broke through the woodlands, nearing the rickety bridge on its approach to town. The temperature had quickly dropped since Potter's return from his emergency cattle herding excursion. He sat behind the reins, wrapped in his dingy brown overcoat; Isaac and Clara sat next to him, also bundled up. Two lanterns gently dangled, unlit, on either side of the carriage, awaiting their use on the return. The ride stayed mostly silent; the clip-clopping of the horses' hooves and the squeaking bench provided the trip's only sounds.

Potter, anxious of the evening's activities, looked down at himself. Coffey had lent him the outfit from Chisum's wardrobe: a white oxford, brown wool vest, and matching tie and dark slacks. Coffey also ran him a warm bath, kindly trimming an inch or so of scraggly, graying beard hair with a pair of shears found in a drawer under the sink. The last time Potter had experienced such cleanliness and propriety eluded him. Though not usually self-consciousness, he suddenly, and without un-derstandable reason, found himself needing to create a profound effect with his appearance.

Life in Missouri Plaza, full of such promise, had changed him. He'd earned the trust of his current employer, Mr. Chisum, quite a feat in itself. With the slowly growing rapport among the other cowboys in the group and his developing friendship with Coffey, he'd begun to experience a sense of acceptance that had eluded him for some time, maybe his entire life. And then there was Nora.

A sinking feeling in his stomach warned him that this wouldn't be a long-lasting situation. He knew the importance of never growing com-placent in a location. All worthwhile things met their sudden end, danger never more than a step or two behind. Why would life here be any different? And as the warm feeling in his chest, what he could almost describe as happiness, dimmed and drained away, he knew, here and now, what his family needed to do. They'd leave, effective immediately.

He glanced at his offspring. He'd need to break the news to them tonight, but the look on their morose faces gave him pause. "You kids been mighty quiet this whole trip."

Neither looked up.

"Isaac? Clara, darling? Something wrong?"

Clara gently elbowed Isaac in his side, biting her lower lip.

Isaac stared at his feet. "No, Pa."

Potter was no fool. "Look here, we're just honoring Ms. Nora's cordial invite for supper. Nothing more. Got it?"

"It—it's not that, Pa."

"Then what?"

3

Isaac, eyes still averted, fell silent.

"Son," Pa pushed.

"Well, it's just that... what are we going to do with that underground ship?"

"Never mind about that ship, all right? Ain't nothing to worry yourself about. You hear?"

Isaac pictured the dynamite sticks lining the long ship corridor. A dryness crept into his throat in anticipation of his father's potential reaction. "Well, I—I saw the empty crate in the basement. The dynamite crate."

Pa sighed. "It's what we call a fail-safe."

"What's that mean, Pa?"

"All it means is that ain't nobody gonna come on our property to harm us. And certainly, nobody is coming for what's buried in that well."

"You learn to do that in the war?"

"No. There was no dynamite then. Mining for your grandfather, though, we used it quite a bit."

Isaac, always curious about his father's wartime experience but too afraid to ask, figured now offered as good a time as any. "Why'd you go to war, Pa?"

"It was our *civic duty*. You fought for your country. For your freedoms. You fought against tyranny."

"Tyranny?"

"Tyranny is a people against your freedoms. The funny thing is, you fought for those freedoms, yet there was no *freedom* in your choice to fight."

"I don't get it."

Pa sighed. "Son, we live in a dark, *dark*, unforgiving world. A world you and your sister have yet to be privy to. You've had it real easy back in Denver. On the farm. Visits to Grandpa's. And it pains me to say it, but that ain't the same world in which man exists. Man is a fiend. His murky heart ain't filled with nothing but guile and savagery. He'll take everything at the drop of the hat. Then kill you dead just as fast for the inconvenience. And in all of my days, I ain't never met one wasn't worth his weight in horseshit."

Isaac squinted. He didn't understand everything he'd heard, but... *Surely Pa doesn't believe that.* He thought of all the days they'd worked on digging the well together under the sweltering sun. "What about Mr. Coffey?"

4

Potter paused, taken aback. "Well, I spose. I spose he'd be the exception." Potter ignored the sudden pang in his chest, instead focusing on his young'uns. "Look at me, both of you."

Isaac looked at his father. Clara continued to stare at her feet.

"You need to protect what's yours. Fight for it. I can only hope living here this past month had an effect on you both. I need you two to be smarter. More vigilant. Life—it ain't easy, especially without your ma here to help guide you two. It's a raging goddamn river, is what it is. Only thing you *can* do is learn a way to navigate it without drowning." *And sometimes those flood waters come rushing in, and there ain't nothing you can do.* Potter knew this truth better than most, but he kept the thought to himself.

"I think I wanna fight when it's my turn, Pa."

"It created a lot of good, but listen to me, Isaac. There is nothing good about war, you hear me? Not a damn thing. Dying for a—a something you don't quite understand. Killing for it. I pray to God you are never faced with that choice. Things were much different for me than they will be for you and your sister in these times to come. What you *can* do: make a better choice. Don't create chaos. Create opportunity. Help those who can't help themselves. That's how you separate yourself from the savages."

Isaac's voice hushed, almost whispering, as if reluctant to ask. "What happened, Pa?"

A loaded question. To Potter's twelve-year-old boy, there'd likely be no acceptable answer or explanation, nor true importance. He supposed he'd explain his past in full when Isaac reached manhood, but he also suspected he'd never live to see that day.

Best stick to the big picture lessons for now, Potter figured. "All I can say, son, is this: my time on this earth has been far from exemplary. What's carried me through were a few, for lack of a better word, *principles*. They sure as hell kept me alive, and they're still worth their weight in bullion. *One*: listen to many, speak to a few. You can learn a lot about the loudest guy in the room. And never offer anything unless asked, or until it's absolutely necessary. Safer having reservations. Keep things tight to the vest. Trust is a precious commodity. *Two*: never loan or borrow money from *anyone*, especially friends. That can get ya killed. *Every time*. Except Grandpa." Potter smirked slyly. "You can take his money *all day*. And *three*, and this is most important, son: above all else, be true to yourself. People are always gonna test you, and how you respond will determine how far they will get with you. Ain't no sense placating these types of people. Always stand your ground, and always speak your mind with what you want in this short life. Course, not everyone's gonna like it. They don't have to. At the very least, no one can take that away from ya."

Isaac nodded, squinting in contemplation. These Shakespearian tenants had served Potter well, and he wholeheartedly knew them to be true. He just hoped his son understood, too.

The carriage stopped in front of Reynolds's Buy & Sell, and they all dismounted. Potter glanced through the window. Nora stood inside, kneading dough on a counter butcher block. He raised his knuckles to the door, trembling slightly, and knocked.

Nora smiled, wiped her dusty hands on her white apron, and sauntered to the loft door, pulling it open. "Bill Potter. I was curious if you'd make my acquaintance this evenin."

Potter flushed as he removed his hat, trying his best not to break eye contact and failing miserably. "Uhh, I apologize for our tardiness, Nora," he said, fidgeting with his hat brim. "I hope we're still welcome in your humble abode."

She stepped back, beckoning them through the door. "You're right on time."

5

"The boy. He's across the street, sir." Buckley, like a good lapdog, proudly rasped in the ear of his master.

Charon, mid-chew, swallowed a hunk of bloody meat, then dropped his utensils on the plate, slightly turning his head to acknowledge Buckley standing over him. Over the blaring instruments of the house band, he returned a curious "Oh?"—as if this encounter had been fortuitous, as if Buckley hadn't been perched on the stagecoach alongside Miller's with explicit instructions to "keep an eye on the grocer's apartment." He glanced at Lamiya, sitting directly across from him. She glanced back submissively from under her pink bonnet as she cut and slowly masticated mousy bites of steak. Compulsively, she dabbed corners of her narrow, clean lips with a bib cloth tucked into her blouse neck, embroidered *Miller's Café*.

Charon smiled. "We will go ahead as planned. You know what to do."

Chapter 21

Elija salivated, glancing at the grave faces of his cohorts behind a diamond flush. The rush of a winning hand, sweet as the chance to dip his wick with a house's best girl, electrified his whole body. It had been so long since his last brothel visit, he'd almost forgotten the feeling.

He raised. Hiram and Salvatore folded. Emiliano and Gustine called.

Elija, brandishing a sly grin, fanned his glorious hand on the round table.

"Nice hand," Emiliano remarked, then fanned his shabby cards. Jacks over aces. "Full house!"

Elija's smile melted away. *Shiiiit.* So close, but no cigar. Oh well. He had a *special* cigar he'd soon enjoy.

"Sonova—*bitch!*" Gustine slammed down his cards, draining his whiskey glass.

Emiliano scooped the pile of red, white, and blue chips across the green felt, then began stacking them by color. The rest of Jinglebob's live-in ranch-hands exchanged weary inebriated glances, enveloped in a blue haze of tobacco smoke. A full ashtray, empty drinking glasses, and peanut shells littered the perimeter between each man's seat while a five-wick candle burned at the table's center, creating ample light. More flickering wicks lined the highly illuminated living room, along with a rip-roaring fire and the amber glow of scorched timber. Chisum had granted the men, plenty exhausted after the long day's haul of chasing cattle, the rest of the evening off, along with a case of rye imported from Albuquerque in a recent cattle barter.

"Your deal, partner." Emiliano dropped the tattered deck in front of Hiram. "You call it."

Hiram, blowing smoke rings, gave the cards a quick thought. "Joker's wild."

Elija, too tired to care about the loss, got up, yawned, and stretched his arms. "I gotta take a piss. Deal me out."

"Be a good cheer, will ya, and grab a bottle from the kitchen to pour us another round."

Elija stepped out, calling over his shoulder. "Ya'll can wait two damn minutes."

He lit a stogie he'd planned to smoke earlier in the day, before the cattle escape. A special stogie he'd cut, emptied, and filled with marijuana he'd picked up in a pharmacy in Lincoln County. The skunky vapor filled his yearning lungs as he held, then exhaled, letting the cool breeze guide his inebriated body in a gentle rock to and fro. At this point, he was plenty drunk *and* high.

Boy, what a bright night tonight. *Must be some moon.*

The urge to piss suddenly escalated, and he carried on down the porch, then stumbled down two steps, his boot heel catching in the space between the stairs. His inattentive, ambling gait brought him to the side of the barn. The outhouse... too far. Not a chance in hell, not when the barn wall sufficed. He supposed the ranch siding would suffice too, but the windows remained open to cool the house, and he didn't need any more shit from the fellers. Plus, tonight, he could actually *see* the barn from the porch.

He unbuttoned and began relieving himself, which, in this moment, proved the greatest feeling in the world. Closing his eyes, he sighed with contentment. But when he directed his gaze towards the barn, anticipating the full moon, his eyes found its radiance obscured by clouds. Instead, something else glowed up there in that night sky. The strangest goddamn thing he'd ever seen—some kind of eldritch glow, twitching in the atmosphere, sort of... just... hovering, stretching along the entire valley. The haze boasted the most vivid greens he'd ever seen, like chartreuse, except the haze was *alive,* and dancing brilliantly across the whole damn sky! He cocked his head back so far, awestruck and swaying, he began pissing on his boot.

He pulled the stogie from between his lips, glancing between it and the green sky, then tossed it away. "Oh, fuck me!" He'd surely overdone it this time.

Quickly buttoning his trousers, he turned in a panic to call the boys. The restless groans of the cattle, carried from the pasture, interrupted him.

Shit. "No. Not again, please—not tonight!"

Wild game posed a constant threat to the livestock. Bears, cats, even vultures. Not to mention coyotes. The goddamn worst, those coyotes. A pasture plague. And something else. Something much worse. They'd crossed paths with some big sonovabitch attacking the herd not one month ago. Certainly at least one of them had shot it, and, with a shrill, bloodcurdling cry, it had vanished into the night. *Christ.*

His ability to rationalize diminished by the second. He glanced between the ranch and pasture, mouth ajar, debating between hollering for the boys or tending to the cows. He couldn't focus. Euphoria took hold, blurring the lines of risk which, under less blitzed circumstances, would have elicited a call for help. Decision made, he drew his sidearm and traipsed awkwardly past the barn, his gait heavily influenced as he followed the misty green trail.

He climbed the wooden gate which led to the pasture and hopped down, wobbling but catching himself. Acres of flatland stretched before him. The pale green glow reflected ominously off the cattle's backs, providing minimal detail as he walked among them. Urgent shuffling in the distance signaled the potential problem as the livestock, *hundreds* of cows, began pressing their one-ton bodies toward Elija. He pushed against the anxious current with his arms up, lantern in one hand, gun in the other. As he reached the end of the herd, the field began to open up, and he crossed a cow on its side. In the skylight he saw its throat cleanly slit and... drained? The ground under his feet remained remarkably dry, considering the gaping chest squarely opened—the ribs cut with precision and removed. Squatting over the animal, he waved the lantern over the cavity.

The heart was missing.

He looked out, noticing, for the first time, his warm breath escaping from his parted lips. Just beyond the steamy respiration, two other cows lay on their sides, presumedly dead, several yards away in either direction. He stood, peering side to side, and saw nothing. Heard nothing, other than the few outlying moos from behind the gate.

Maybe he'd seen wrong, imagined the whole thing. That shit he smoked was *bad*. Did he tell the boys? Yeah, tell them *what*, exactly?

He didn't need this right now. Go inside. Go to bed. Call it a night. He turned for the ranch.

A thud from behind drew him back around.

A straggler cow ten yards out had collapsed to its side, and something else loomed in front of it. Something quite large, something not identifiable as any animal species he knew. And, more than that, something almost... *human?* He couldn't see much over the cow's back, but this *thing* looked busy. The heinous, wet sound of masticating and tearing flesh carried over the distance.

Then, the creature looked up.

Elija froze. The eyes, dark red in this light, blinked in rapid succession, though they were twice the size of his. Two thick, twelve-inch antennae, like those of an insect, curved above each eye and back behind the bald, shiny head, sharpening to a fine edge. It was missing—

No nose. Wait, where the fuck is his noooosse!?

Just slits. Three slits in an odd, triangular shape, which oscillated. Breathing, Elija presumed, by the escaping vapor. Its jaw, thin and split at its center, unhinged horizontally. It crouched over the cow, examining. Eyelids. Eyelids fluttering. Thin, muscular arms flared out, taking in the air, its sharp fingers splayed. Its body reflected the pale green skylight.

Fucking mescaline, that's what he must've smoked! He'd never tested the substance himself, but he knew of its psychological effects and hallucinogenic properties. He stood in incredulity, watching this man-creature *eating* his cows—

That, at least, must *be real. But how!?*

He was clearly going insane. His head spun, watching, until the sound came. An odd distortion.

"What in holy Christ," he muttered.

A strange clicking in brief bursts. Trilling. Raspy. Much like a cricket, though louder and more defined than any insect he'd heard. Slower, too, the cadence disquieting.

The tall man-creature shifted, still crouching. Its arms, legs, and torso struck Elija as human, but other elements also protruded from different parts of its shiny body. Each elbow extended a foot or so beyond the forearm, like jagged bone: knurled, narrowing to a serrated point, and connected to the center forearm by a thin, fleshy material. Its calves and chest bore similar protrusions. The jagged bone curved up and slightly back from the corner of each upper pectoral muscle. Two more extended from its shoulder blades with a thin, veiny film of fleshy material narrowly draping down over each shoulder, almost to the ground. On either side of its waist, protrusions with more of this thin material flared out just over its hips, curving down near its thighs.

Its bluish skin shimmered in the green glow as it worked.

Elija blinked. Irrespective of his current mental state, he at least recognized his obligation to halt the destruction of his boss's property. He slowly raised his pistol, cocking it as his sights locked onto this man... *thing.*

The creature stopped and peered over the dead animal. It raised itself slowly, staring out toward Elija, its mouth smeared crimson. Its chest heaved with each breath of air, condensation wafting from an open mouth. The mandible, split down the center, quivered; warm blood dripped from each edge. Elija froze in his boots, unable to avert his delusive eyes.

The man-creature's head twisted back and forth, antennae shifting as if scanning its surroundings, before it crouched and returned to its meal.

It pulled the cow's steaming heart from its chest, holding the organ above its head.

"Oh, fuck this." Elija holstered his sidearm, turned, and bolted toward the ranch.

He charged through the operatic mooing of the herd and out the gate, letting it swing behind. The herd followed, shuffling through.

With his gun handle, Elija wrapped at the living room window. "Hey, guys! Come on, get out here right quick!" He continued to smack at the glass, taking quick glances behind.

The men inside looked around at one another before dropping their cards and rising from the table. "Fuck, let's go, come on, hurry, god-dammit!"

The men fired out the front door and ran—two with lanterns, all with guns drawn—down the porch and around to the side of the ranch where Elija stood. The desperate cries of the herd resonated from the barn as they charged in, followed by a smattering of simultaneous conversation.

"Fuck, Elija, what's all the fuss about!?" Emiliano heaved, trying to catch his breath.

He could barely force the words out of his mouth. "The-there's some-some—*thing* out there in the pasture!"

"Huh?"

"A-a-a-a—"

"What?"

"A-a *thing!*"

"What's that mean, goddammit. What thing?"

"My GOD, would ja look at that!" Hiram pointed a finger to the sky.

Elija shook his head. "I-I-I don't know. Whatever it is, it-it's killin Boss's cattle, though!"

"What, like an animal?"

"No..."

"The hell didn't ya shoot it!?"

"I-I-I—"

"Jesus Christ, Elija, you smokin that shit again, ain'tcha. What I tell ya bout that!?"

"Holy fuckin shit my Christ, what's all *that* in the damn sky. Will ya look at it!?" Gustine stared, captivated by the shifting haze.

"No—I don't—I don't fuckin know," Elija yelled, panicking. "Forget the damn sky! Look, it-it stood real tall-like, like a man. You know, like you and me!"

Everyone disregarded Elija and stared up. Shock and awe subsumed their faces.

"Look, I seen it tear out its-its damn heart, raisin it up to the sky!" Elija feigned the motion of the man-thing, raising the heart.

"Now, how's that even possible? You—you seeing anything?" The men, finding it difficult to break their sky gaze, intermittently peered the prairie.

"Just... darkness," Salvatore said.

"I see them cows all pourin out the damn gate!" Hiram pointed.

"What do we do—should we alert the boss!?" Panic flushed Gustine's face.

"No. No need to disturb the boss. Go in and grab the torches," Emiliano ordered.

Salvador returned post haste with three, and Hiram lit them with a match. The five cautiously entered the pasture in a side-by-side formation, a distance of five feet between each.

Within moments, the men found themselves in front of the downed cow, albeit twenty feet back. The strange, unidentifiable creature hunched behind, silent. It had stopped its feeding upon the approach of the ranch-hands.

The men, armed, shared bewildered glances, waiting for this thing to make a move, any move, to show itself. It soon stood, eyelids fluttering, and turned its head as if to view its surroundings. The torches' flame reflected from its glassy red eyes. Chilling.

It stepped back. The shoulder blade protrusions moved outward, and the fleshy film expanded another five feet on either side, fluttering as... as...

The creature raised itself several feet from the ground.

"What—what—what unholiness is this," Emiliano muttered, mouth agape. "I think someone now needs to warn Chisum."

"Cristo, es el Diablo!" Salvador crossed himself.

The men's heads fell back, their staggering eyes following the movements of the hovering being: a silhouette amid the green-lighted sky. Its wings vibrated, creating a soft, audible sound.

Elija whipped his head around, ensuring his compatriots saw the same thing he did. "What did I tell ya?"

Gustine, face stricken, slowly backed away. The creature's head followed his movement, locking eyes with him. His boot heel rolled over a stone, throwing him off balance, and he squeezed the trigger as he fell onto the seat of his pants, erratically opening fire. The other men, in a bewildered flurry of solidarity, shot at the creature too, scurrying backward and sideways in a feeble, frantic attempt to keep an eye on their target.

Elija gaped as several bullets tore through the creature's wings. Cylinders emptied, striking its—*armored?*—chest with enough force to knock it out of the sky and into darkness.

2

Coffey, dressed neatly in his black and whites, entered the second-floor parlor room with a silver platter. It held a steaming pot of coffee, a cigar, and two matches. Chisum, as usual for this hour of the evening, sat in his silk robe on a cozy red Victorian parlor chair with a snifter of brandy, entirely engrossed in his current novel: *Vril*, by Edward Bulwer-Lytton. He took a moment to greet his loyal servant while shoving a cigar in his face, subsequently striking both matches, twisting, and igniting the sweet tobacco leaf.

Gun fire blasted in the distance.

"Coffey, once a week. Once a week, I'd like tea. That isn't too much to ask for now, is it?" Chisum blew a plume of silver smoke.

"Course not, Mr. Chisum." Coffey sat the tray down on a side table and poured a steaming cup, glancing up at the window. "Looks like them boys is at it again, huh?"

"Yup. Been a long day, Coffey. They deserve it."

"Reckon that case of scotch might a been a bit too generous." He smiled.

"You may be right." Chisum returned the grin. "You know you're welcome to join them."

"Not really my way, sir." Coffey, as friendly as he was with the hands—or as friendly as the hands were with him—knew his place at the ranch. Better to keep things business as usual. Besides, he knew all too well that fraternizing with these men, white men, particularly, could have consequences. "But I 'preciate the consideration."

"Suit yourself."

Coffey nodded. "Already have."

3

Hiram ran for his life, the harrowing shouts of the fleeing cowboys around him echoing through Jinglebob Ranch.

"Do y'all see it!?"

"Christ."

"We kill it!?"

"I don't see shit!"

"Why you stoppin!?"

"I'm out!"

Panting, Hiram slowed to a halt, standing, intentionally, amid the livestock. Glancing around for the other men, he realized they had ceased running, too. Each man's flame flickering across the pasture provided the only indication of his location. The two with lanterns had placed them down as they crouched, fumbling to reload their Colt revolvers. Gustine, the closest to Hiram, panted and grunted, mouth hanging open as he struggled to shove each quivering bullet into its slot. Saliva dripped from his lips as he heaved over his pistol, blocking the lantern's flame.

He disappeared first.

A blue flash. Hiram twitched; a chilly wind gust washed over him.

Overhead, someone screamed.

Hiram turned. The sound, bloodcurdling, faded in a direction he couldn't quite resolve, though his intuition told him *up*. But that was completely absurd. Beads of sweat dripped down his furrowed brow, the torch in his hand now burning at full capacity. His vigilant eyes darted back and forth between the other flames in the distance.

"What do we do," a distant voice bellowed.

"I say we get the fuck out of here," yelled another.

"Good call!" Hiram, closest to the gate, made a hasty dash for the exit, still blocked by confused, wondering livestock. "Goddammit, get the hell out the way!"

He pushed through the ambling herd. As he exited, a rasping thud greeted him with a splatter of warm blood across his face. Gustine's lifeless body lay slumped backward, impaled by the metal gate. His weight gently twisted the post sideways. A quick wave of the torch over Gustine's vacuous eyes sent Hiram reeling, stumbling toward the nearest building for cover: the stable. Inside, he'd find a pitchfork. Maybe the machete. Given that landing a stray bullet proved difficult, he at least retained enough good sense to consider the use of alternate weapons.

Hiram jerked open a utility closet, grabbed the pitchfork leaning among shovels and other farming tools, and whirled around. He stood center in the soft dirt and hay: torch in one hand, the fork held in the other, tucked under his arm like a jousting lance. *An open target*. His head jerked back and forth between either opening, wondering which side to exit. Bizarrely, he could actually see the rooftops of the ranch and his boss's Victorian under the glowing lime haze as he inched back the way he'd come.

"Hiram," Emiliano shouted from the entryway. Salvador and Elija stood tightly behind on high alert, flashing glances side to side, up, and around.

"Yeah," he called back, spinning. The sound of horses shifting in their stalls sent him in semi-circles of disquiet.

"You good!?"

"Uh." He looked around. "Yeah, I—I think so."

"Come on! We need to get Chisum before it gets into the house!"

Hiram looked behind to a vacant entryway before beginning a brisk pace toward the men.

"Ain't no sign of it anywhere," Elija said, turning and watching.

Hiram reached the exit, heading for the house. "That thing comes back, I gotta little surpriaaAAAHHH—"

From above, two hands latched onto his upper back and neck, driving their nails through his coat and into his flesh.

4

Emiliano locked bone-chilling eyes with Hiram a moment before the poor man ascended, screaming into the dark rafters.

Dropping his torch in the grass, now two steps behind, Emiliano jumped, reaching for his friend. He grabbed Hiram's heel with one hand, holding tight. For a moment, both men hung in the air.

The boot peeled off.

Emiliano fell a foot, stumbling backward. "Hiram!"

The pitchfork plummeted along with the torch, instantly igniting the surrounding hay and sending flames furiously down the stable.

Silence. Emiliano raised both pistols and stared into the void, waiting.

"Come on," Salvador urged. "Let's go!"

Trilling filled the stable with its ghastly reverberation. A moment later, a deluge of warm blood splashed Emiliano's face, mouth, and eyes. He mopped his forehead with both jacket sleeves, clearing his vision just in time to hinder a length of Hiram's entrails, unraveling from the darkness, from falling atop him.

Salvador reached in and pulled Emiliano out. "Move your ass, gringo!"

"Wait!" Emiliano stopped. "Lock the doors!" He yanked the door along its slider, latching it closed... but not before tossing in his torch.

5

Elija gasped. "The horses!"

"Fuck the horses," Emiliano snarled. "Go round the other side!"

Elija and Salvador ran to the back of the stable. Salvador smashed his lantern on the ground, sending a propulsion of flare up a stall wall.

"Wait!"

"Wait!? For what, *coño*!? Let's go!"

Before pulling the door closed, Elija peered around the burning building for his friend, for the creature, for a potential opportunity to free horses—his mare, Fandango, in particular. He'd claimed Fandango three years ago in Tijuana, when he'd dueled her previous owner: an infamous Mexican bandido. Elija, who had been shacking up with the bandido's señora, still held the horse in a sentimental, though mostly trophied, regard.

The smoky haze beginning to engulf the space made seeing not only difficult, but insanely risky. Elija listened instead, hoping for some sign. He heard only the roar of the flames and the neighs and bucks of the confused steeds rattling in their open stalls.

As he began to pull the slider, two figures in the back dropped from the ceiling. One figure, likely Hiram, fell, vanishing into the flames. The other landed on its feet. A silhouette amid the misty vapor. Wings fluttered with a cumbersome twitch, singeing in the expanding heat. Elija, fearing its icy stare, slammed the slider door shut and threw over the latch.

He turned to run, then froze. Salvador had rounded the corner, sprinting full speed towards Chisum's house behind Emiliano, already halfway there.

Alone, Elija stood, staring back at the barn door. That *thing* hadn't seemed too concerned about its surroundings. *What if it survives the flames, somehow?* He wouldn't put such a feat past the creature, not after all he'd seen tonight. But if it survived, then all the horses would perish for nothing.

Surely, the best way to ensure this motherfucker dies is a clean, old-fashioned bullet through the head. He just needed to lure it into the open. Then, he could take his shot and single-handedly save the ranch. *This is crazy—how much booze and marijuana have I had?* But his confidence only continued to rise as he pictured his victory, the money and acclaim he would doubtless earn from Chisum. All senses blunted. He felt invincible.

Slowly, Elija unlatched the barn door.

6

Potter gazed around the parlor room, filled with at least thirty or so paintings. The still lifes flawlessly replicated gorgeous landscapes and structures, most of which he recognized upon his initial viewing: the Pecos River, the mill, the church, even Bennett's house, surrounded by the river with a backdrop of the Capitan Mountains in the distance. Some paintings hung from walls, while others lay stacked in corners, likely waiting for their space in the store. He recalled seeing an easel during supper, positioned in the corner between two windows with square panes in Nora's living room, with the canvas atop it offering a scenic view of the town.

Snip. Snip. Snip.

His panoramic view from the reclined barber's chair reminded him of the Wadsworth Atheneum Museum art gallery he'd frequented as a young boy. *The Eleanor Reynolds Exhibit.* Though these paintings proved much more impressive than anything he could ever recall seeing in Hartford. Courbet, Millet, Daumier... *amateurs.*

He wanted to kick himself. "I still can't believe you're the artist."

Nora, standing behind, leaned in to speak in his ear. "Guessin you didn't see the signature at the bottom of the one I gave you, did ya, darlin?" She took two fingers of damp hair and snipped an inch of mangy, split ends with a pair of shiny shears.

"You truly do have quite a gift."

"Why, thank you. And just so you know, Bill, flattery will get you everywhere."

She giggled. She was always smiling and giggling. This evening, especially, Potter had paid close attention. The ray of light Nora exuded astounded him. Nothing could pull her down from her colossal, effervescent cloud. She possessed a rare presence, unlike anything he'd ever laid eyes upon, and he wondered how this hard-working, unmarried pioneer woman could reside in such a desolate, arcane town while remaining so jovial. Perhaps her grounded semblance mirrored his own, having suffered and survived life's tribulations. Or perhaps, more simply, Missouri Plaza epitomized home for her, much like it did for the rest of this meager community. Though Potter found this idea difficult to fathom; her hallmarks seemed too good for this place. Whatever the cause, however, her surroundings didn't seem to define her.

At the day's end, she is a lady to the manner born.

His face flushed again, at a loss for words. "How, uh... how long have you been painting?"

"Oh, now, just bout most of my life. Barely picked up a brush during my marriage, though, brief as it was. Trying to be a *good little housewife,*" she mocked playfully.

Snip. Snip. Snip.

"At the general store here?"

"Lord, no." Nora giggled again. "If you couldn't tell by the way I talk, I'm a Texas gal, through and through! No, we ended up here on pure coincidence, travelin from Dallas on our way to California. My husband,

Sam, was a very successful city banker. Had quite a way with people. With money. So much so, he got into it with some bad people. Long story short, fearin for our lives, we just packed up and left. Bout all you can do in a situation like that. Just a tad late for the Gold Rush, I reckon." She smiled, then dampened Potter's hair with a wet cloth and began separating sections, snipping away large, matted chunks. "Needless to say, we didn't make it. Fell in love with this little town. Decided it be smart to go by my maiden name, Reynolds, so we did. Sam ran the barbershop and I, of course, ran the grocery store.

"Unfortunately, we were never able to have children, which broke my heart." Her voice softened, trailing off to a whisper. "Tried like hell, though. After five painful miscarriages, we finally called it quits. If it ain't meant to be, it ain't meant to be, I reckon. But I guess it's just as well. He passed from cholera bout four years ago now. Took up paintin after that, more as a salutary way of keepin busy."

"What's a cholera," a voice asked from behind. Clara sat eavesdropping on the second to last staircase step, eating a piece of crusty bread leftover from dinner.

Nora turned and smiled. "Oh, honey, it's a terrible, terrible disease. Mostly comes from drinkin foul water. You go on and eat up, now, don't be shy!"

Clara grinned, turned, and ran back to rejoin her brother in the cozy upstairs apartment.

"We had a similar situation in Denver," Potter said with slight reluctance, uncertain how much he wanted to share. "You heard of the Big Flood?"

Nora nodded as she trimmed away.

"Probably one of the biggest catastrophes I have ever borne witness to. Just a besom of destruction. And mind you, I'd fought in the war. But I'll never forget it. It had rained for, well, felt like forever, anyway. I was stressed. When it rains, there's no work, and no work means no pay. I imagine much of the farmers shared the same sentiment. My Bessie, her mother, and Clara were on their way home from the theater when it happened. Downtown became the nexus for the Platte River and Cherry Creek. They rose with great fury, combining forces, tearing through their banks. My wife, and mother-in-law, along with many others got caught in all the turmoil. Clara saw the whole thing happen."

Nora put a hand to her heaving chest. "*Sweet Jesus.*"

"Wiped out much of the town. I heard sometime after that some plainsmen, mountaineers, had forewarned city officials of swollen creeks, but they largely ignored wild folk. And no one else saw the disaster coming. Needless to say, with the flooding, the sewage overflowed. It contaminated the water supply for months to follow. Trash, manure, *bodies*. Filth. Many families got sick."

Nora finished the cut, bringing the length down to a respectable level of growth, then lathered up Potter's neck for a shave, tidying up Coffey's quick trim job. After, she rubbed a little lavender oil between her hands and massaged it into the fibers and his neck, slowly making her way down his upper back.

"Now, some say Denver was overrun by saloons and gambling. Brothels. They say God smote that town." Potter shook his head, pulled his pouch and its contents from a front pocket, and began rolling a quirley. "Now, I don't know bout all that, but it was dark times for a spell. Certainly, was for me.

"Twelve people went missing that night. I refused to rest until I found my wife, dead or alive. I left the young'uns with their grandfather and, with a few men from the mines, left on a search and rescue. I remember the weather following the storm was absolutely perfect, like something out of fairytales. The birds chirped. The sun was high and bright overhead. Never do I recall seeing bluer skies. It was warm, uncommonly warm for May. Like the storm never was. Just inexplicable destruction everywhere.

"The town itself was under several feet of water for days. Like a ghost town in the middle of an ocean. The only people out were the few with boats. I figured they were all on the same mission. I tell ya, I had no idea how long the Platte was, but we combed that river for two days on a boat my father-in-law had commissioned. Navigating the debris fallout was something to behold. Floating structures. Rooftops. Dead horses. More of those than anything else out there. Bodies and the like. Every one knifed the heart as we pulled them out, wondering. Found one woman, *alive*, just sitting in a tree, bout fifteen miles or so downstream.

"We came upon two tall oaks. Found the stagecoach there, wedged in between, mostly submerged, you know, sort of on its side. The driver, still attached. His leg stuck out of the water, caught in the reins, though the horses were long gone. I wish I could tell you I was hopeful, but I knew before I opened the door. The water inside was murky, but sure enough, there she was. Her gold locket reflecting the light."

Nora leaned over and placed her hand upon Potter's, which restlessly tapped the armrest. "I am so sorry, Bill. I truly am."

"I'll never forget the look on my little girl's face when the Sheriff brought her home and told me what happened. I just broke down... wept like a baby in front of her, Isaac. Selfish and weak, I was. I lost it. That was the only time the kids ever saw me like that. I—I was barely there for them after that. Worked long hours to take my mind off the pain of it all. I don't know. I feel like I failed them. I don't know what I was expecting. A happy ending, I guess. Lord knows I certainly don't deserve one."

"Sounds like y'all were goin through a lot, is all. It's understandable," Nora said. "You're a good man, Bill. I can see that. Saw it on your face the minute you stepped into my store. Coffey speaks highly of ya; I heard bout what you did for him. You stuck your neck out for a perfect stranger. Risked your life. Bad men don't do such things."

He gently squeezed back and looked up at Nora, inches above his face. She offered a wistful smiled, then leaned in, planting her lips firmly on his.

Potter twitched, awestruck. A shockwave ignited every blunted nerve in his numb body, though he barely moved, let alone returned the sentiment.

She kissed him again. This time, his lips parted slightly, tentatively inviting her in. By the third kiss, Nora slunk over the side of the chair, embracing him in an awkward straddle as she pulled back on the side lever. The chair fully reclined. A wave of guilt washed over him, a prickly heat spreading across his skin as he returned the kiss, though his unease softened with each caress of her back.

This is wrong, partner. This is all wrong. This is—

Before long, he found his hands squeezing her backside under her dress. Her hands unbuttoned his pants.

He didn't stop her.

7

Coffey, spotting the blaze from a kitchen window on his way to fix Chisum a snack, rushed out the back door and onto the adjacent porch. He glanced toward the ranch for the boys, eyes darting around the property, the barn, the prairie. Finally, he noticed the level of visibility at this hour in the evening.

He gaped at the dancing green haze overhead. "What in God's good—"

Before he could complete his sentence, Emiliano arrived at the house, darting swiftly past him.

"Hey!" Coffey whirled.

Emiliano was already out of reach. His footfalls pounded up the staircase as Coffey turned back to stare at the ominous sky.

A moment later, Salvador reached the house, rushing past.

Elija, following, hesitated only a moment. "We need to get Chisum the fuck outta here!"

Coffey's head spun. Mouth ajar, he glanced between Elija's panicked eyes, the burning stable, and the bright green sky before turning back to where Elija, now gone, had stood.

The abrupt neighing of distressed horses drew his attention to the stable. A handful of steeds bolted from around the building's corner, tearing past the house and into the dark.

A guttural, trilling sound reverberated.

Once again, Coffey turned to fire. The silhouette of a tall figure stood amid the blazing flames and bright green-navy skies of astronomical twilight. The figure began moving in his direction, smoke rising from its shoulders.

"That *Hiram?*" Coffey gazed at the bluish figure emerging from the dissipating shadows, gradually becoming more prominent. Burgundy eyes rapidly blinked. The trilling escalated.

Coffey's wary eyes squinted, trying to make out its strange features. "Aw hell no, that ain't—"

Before he could finish, a hand grabbed his shoulder, thrusting him backward.

"Let's go!" Elija yanked Coffey spinning through the doorway, then stepped back onto the porch.

Coffey tripped backward, crashing down on the seat of his pants. From the floor, he watched Elija pull both sidearms, quickly unloading all twelve rounds. The bluish figure stumbled backward, falling to the ground.

"YEAH—HAAA! I got the sumbitch! I did!" Elija hollered, panting, struggling to catch his breath.

"Hey, hey, what in God's name is *that!?*" Coffey blinked, picking himself up from the ground and dusting off the back of his pants. "Elija, where's the other boys!?"

Elija's smile vanished. He grimaced as he walked inside, passed Coffey, and headed toward the stairs. "Gone."

Coffey, glancing behind, followed him up to Chisum's parlor room, where his very confused boss stood by his chair. Emiliano and Salvador guarded the front.

"What's goin on down there!?" Chisum glanced at each of his men.

"I think I got the sumbitch!" Elija's elation returned. "I shot him dead, I did!"

Emiliano blanched. "It got out the stable!?"

"What did," Chisum demanded.

"How do you know it's dead," Salvador asked, reloading his pistol.

"I seen it fall!" Elija smiled like a child who'd just killed his first game, spilling out his empty shells, nonchalant, onto Chisum's lavish Oriental pashmina wool rug.

"I don't trust it. That *thing* was no man I ever seen!" Salvador, now posted up against the wall next to the window, peeked out.

"Will someone please fuckin speak to *me*," Chisum snapped.

"Mr. Chisum, we're under some sort of attack," Emiliano finally said.

"What—who!?"

"Never mind that, boss. We gotta get you to a safe place!"

"What—no. I'm not goin anywhere. This is what I hired *you* for. To regulate intrusions and any stealing of *my* goddamn property now. Where's Gustine? Where's—"

"Dead. Both dead." Salvador stared at the incinerating stable.

"I think it had..." Elija hesitated, eyes wide with fear. "It had wings."

"Wings?" Chisum's furious eyes darted between the men.

"What if there's more?"

"Christ." Chisum waved an annoyed hand, his face reddening. He turned to sit back in his comfy chair.

"Salvador?" Emiliano nodded at the window.

"Not seein nuthin."

"Look," Emiliano tried again. "We don't know where it came from or how many are out there."

Coffey stepped in, putting his hand on Chisum's shoulder and looking him dead in his leery eye. "We need to go."

POP!

Shattering glass drew the men's attention to the open doorway of the shadowed adjacent room. Creeping sounds of crunching and popping followed as feet dragged over the shards. The ranch hands cautiously stepped in front of Chisum, guns drawn at the icy footfalls. Each jarring step slowly faded into the silence stifling the parlor room. Guttural trilling shattered the still air, echoing as wisps of gray smoke drifted past the doorway.

The footfalls ceased.

With a sensation of time distending, the men stared at the empty door without moving. Without breathing. Through the dark, three long fingers slinked around the center edge of the doorway, gripping the frame. Its sharp fingertips dug in, the wood creaking and splintering.

"What is it, Coffey," Chisum, wide-eyed, whispered dully.

Something gurgled in the darkness.

"*Nope.*" Coffey grabbed Chisum by the arm sleeve and yanked him toward the exit.

8

"Fire!" Emiliano pulled his trigger before he could even finish the command.

Gunfire rang out in succession, blasting into the floral wallpaper and through the misty opening. A flash shot across, out of sight.

"Get behind the boss," Emiliano ordered Elija.

He obeyed, pursuing Coffey and Chisum—already halfway down the right side of the U-shaped hall.

Emiliano leaned toward Salvador, motioning with his gun as he whispered. "Head on out around to the bedroom door. We got this fucker trapped."

Salvador nodded, sidestepped into the dim hallway, and scurried to the door. Once there, he took cover alongside, awaiting either the creature's exit or his opportunity to join his comrade.

Emiliano, step by cautious step, approached the open doorway, trembling pistols pointing. The heel of his boots softly, unavoidably, clanked across the floorboard, possibly giving up his position... but what choice did he have? He closed his eyes, took a deep breath, and exhaled completely.

Guns blazing, he exploded into the dark, screaming, unloading both Colt cylinders in a matter of seconds. The heedless muzzle blasts provided brief flashes of his horrifying assailant, twisting through the open space in front of the door. He couldn't be certain if any rounds had struck, but when those hammers struck empty chambers—leaving him in darkness—ice shivered down his spine.

9

Salvador waited until the firing stopped and the bullets finished splintering through the door, inches from his face, before turning to face the entrance. With a leg raised, he aimed his heel above the knob and struck the door, shattering it open while pointing his guns into darkness. He hesitated for a moment, uncertain of Emiliano's whereabouts in the shadows.

"SHOOT" echoed from within.

The creature struck out from the darkness, lifting him off the floor while obscuring its own path. Its charge quickly ended at the stairway railing as they both crashed through, falling straight down.

10

Elija, who'd just about reached the bottom, halted as Coffey and Chisum froze ahead of him. The horrifying hodgepodge crashed down before them with such clamor, the bottom steps crushed and splintered under its weight. Without hesitation, the three men fired right back up the stairs toward the parlor room.

Emiliano, standing over the busted railing and emptying shell casings onto the floor, grabbed Elija's arm as he passed. "Hey—hey! Where the hell are you goin?"

"Uhh." He looked at Emiliano, dumbfounded.

"Get after it. Let's go!"

The two ranch-hands crossed the hallway, quickly reloading while beginning their slow, vigilant descent. Salvador's body lay at the bottom, his neck broken. His lower half sprawled on the stairs, while his torso and arms splayed on the floor. A dark red pool slowly expanded around his twisted head.

Emiliano threw Elija an obscure hand gesture, signaling for him to inspect the front half of the house while he moved toward the back.

Elija, quivering so hard he barely gripped his gun, stepped over the corpse, continuing to glance down in between panning the dimly lighted space. He could not avert his focus from Salvador's open eyes, the empty, upward stare.

11

Coffey locked the two parlor room doors behind him and his boss as Chisum poured himself a hefty glass of brandy with a shaky hand, spilling half its contents on the credenza.

"We're trapped, Coffey! Like fuckin rats, trapped, with no means of escape!" He put back a healthy gulp, slamming the crystal down and wiping his wet mustache with a sleeve.

Coffey spun around, looking for the answer to an impossible riddle. The locked doors they hid behind offered little assurance, nor did the fireplace. *Bullets don't seem to work. What good's that poker gonna do?* Climbing the flue seemed impossible, mostly because of the boss's wide hips. His eyes flitted across the mounted deer head over the mantle, the elephant gun next to it. Again, wishful thinking. Probably not even loaded. He looked back at the fireplace, following it up... the roof!

Coffey hurried to the window and slid it open. Sticking his head out, he glanced up and down, ignoring the chartreuse skyline. Inconsequential, compared to the problem at hand. The mansard roof ledge hung above. Below, nothing. The height, though only two stories, still proved quite a drop.

He craned his neck, racking his brain for an answer. Then, he saw it. "The front porch, boss! We can climb out onto it and climb down."

Chisum gazed at him with bewildered desperation, threw back his freshly filled snifter, and nodded.

The two crept down the eerily serene hallway, cautiously tight to the right wall. No noise, no movement. They slipped into the spare front bedroom, brimming with hope, and yanked at the windows.

Stuck. The sills were nailed shut—Chisum's way to prevent thieves from climbing the porch and entering in the middle of the night. In their distressed state, the men had forgotten this minor detail.

"What can we use to break the window!?" Coffey waved the open lantern around, the high flame flickering sideways.

Chisum cringed. "No-no! That thing could hear us! Fuck! Fuck!"

Coffey looked up. *The roof.* "This way, boss!"

He led Chisum back out into the hallway, behind the central staircase, and up narrow winding stairs, leading to the empty, two-bedroom third floor. Upon reaching the window, Coffey, jabbing his palm under the frame, popped it open. He immediately stepped out onto the narrow ledge of the mansard roof, turning to give a hand to Chisum.

Boss peaked his head out, blinked, and backed away. "Nuh-uh!"

Coffey grabbed him. "Boss!?"

"Coffey, you know how much I had to drink tonight!?"

"Well, no."

"Neither do I! I ain't goin out there; I'll fall to my goddamn death!"

"I gotcha, boss. Now, ya need to trust me on this one." Coffey extended a hand, beads of sweat rolling down the sides of his temples.

With grave reluctance, Chisum stepped slowly out onto the ledge, holding the protruding window frame for dear life.

Coffey handed Chisum the oil lamp. "I'm gonna climb down on the porch roof now. I will help ya down when ya ready, okay!?"

Coffey, as a tall man, reached the pitched roof without much issue. He sat on the mansard ledge, then flipped himself over and slid down to hang off the edge. Then he dropped another one to two feet, managing to land quietly on his feet.

Chisum handed off the lamp and tried to repeat what he saw, albeit much less gracefully. He sat, turned onto his belly, and inched his way over the edge until the roof reached his midsection—the breaking point.

His shorter, heavier body slid off the ledge, and he dangled, barely holding on.

"Don't you let me fall, Coffey," he hissed.

"Gotcha, boss." Coffey's words rang hollow in his ears as he wrapped his arms around Chisum's slipping legs, praying not to slide off the roof.

He couldn't say what happened next: whether he slipped on a loose shingle, or if Chisum tore off the gutter altogether. Either way, both men slid down the pitched roof, rolling off the side and crashing, ass down, hard into the hedges under the parlor room window.

12

Emiliano's right hand trembled, completely extended in the forefront. His index finger twitched alongside the Colt's trigger, where it wouldn't accidentally fire. His left hand, gripping its twin, pulled back close to his chest. Passing through Chisum's office, he inched down the somber hallway, the parlor room coming up on the left, and, just beyond, the kitchen. The floorboards gently creaked in the distance. Just Elija, briefly seen from his peripherals. Parallel to Emiliano, though across the house, the other ranch hand headed toward the dining room as they combed the first floor.

Emiliano crossed the parlor room, slowly and deliberately turning to face the opening. Empty. At least, from where he stood. Still, he entered the space with just as much caution as he'd used to creep down the hallway, guns raised, ready to unload both cylinders into this creature and finish the job with the eight-inch blade tucked away in his side sheath if he had to.

To his disappointment and relief, the parlor was clear.

At the same time, he could hear Elija crossing the elongated dining room, pausing—likely checking under the equally elongated dining table—and then continuing on again. From the sound of it, he walked slowly, almost dragging his feet. Evidently, he wanted to remain a few paces behind Emiliano.

With a sigh, Emiliano entered the open entryway into the wooden panel kitchen. The immaculate room shone, thanks largely to Coffey, save for a tea kettle sitting on the back burner of a large stove in the rear. Candles in their half-life melted in silver holders, flickering in each corner and windowsill to cast dancing shadows across the center butcher block island and the many pots and pans hanging from the ceiling above.

A thin, distant creaking twisted Emiliano around. Just beyond the kitchen, the back door and its decrepit aluminum-screened counterpart hung wide-open, gently swaying. Odd. Maybe that thing had left the house. He walked over, hopeful, and looked up at the unsettling sky. Elija, still out of sight, worried him. He'd seen the fear in that boy's eyes.

Another creak echoed in the dark. He glanced to the right front corner, outside the candles' twinkling reach. The walk-in pantry. His blood pressure rose; the pounding of his heart echoed through his ears in the silent void of Chisum's house. At a crawling pace, he inched toward the pantry, his boot heels softly thudding with each step across the floorboard.

In his peripherals, Emiliano spotted Elija, slowly entering the from the dining room doorway. Tension rushed from his shoulders. His partner, still in the house. Still alive.

With Elija at his back, Emiliano drew closer, guns raised. Although he couldn't see the two-way swinging door, he knew it was there. He just wished he'd held on to one of those torches. Holstering his left pistol, he reached for the door, grasping the handle with his fingertips. Elija kept his distance behind, guns raised, as Emiliano stepped into the dark.

His best idea at the moment: kick open the pantry door and open fire. Perhaps just the latter, though he hesitated at the thought of filling Chisum's pantry with bullets. He needed to be certain. Picking up a saucer with three muddled candles melting into each other, he took two brief steps back, raised his right foot, and smashed the door open with his boot heel.

An unearthly screech sounded as a wooly, white *something* clobbered into his chest and, with sharp pins tearing at his flesh, propelled itself off his ribs, sending him backward several steps. Three slashes met his grimy cheekbone, dragging across his nose. He hollered in surprise, dropping the plate of candles and struggling to regain his balance.

The assault abruptly ended, his brain unable to catch up. He spun, glancing around wildly in the darkness. A cacophony of thrashing trailed along the granite countertop; porcelain containers of salt, sugar, and coffee flew to their destructive demise, rattling along the kitchen floor.

The creature, small, hell-bent for leather, slid uncontrollably toward Elija, skidding, slashing, and clawing the floorboard to avoid him before firing back up on the counter and jumping into the sink. A moment later, its pointy-eared face appeared in view near several burning candles. It offered a long, penetrating hiss, jumped out, and backed away into the dark.

Sandy... fucking cat!

The fallen candles rolled into the pantry through the still-swinging door, creaking on its dry hinges. Emiliano, heart jabbering, glanced in and immediately released a chest deep sigh of relief. Empty. He turned to the sink counter, glaring at the last place he'd seen the damn cat. The fallen flames flickered as the pantry door swung in and out, then extinguished.

A thud, which seemed to emanate from the roof, and a subsequent rustling outside the dining-room window snapped his attention away from the hidden feline. Elija gawked anxiously at Emiliano.

Emiliano nodded. "Go check it out."

Reluctantly, Elija turned and entered the dining room.

From behind, the pantry door creaked open slowly. Deliberately. Emiliano's heart dropped into his stomach as his body warily turned, compelled by some sheer force beyond his own rational understanding. He cocked the gun, still gripped in his clammy left palm, under a shaky thumb.

Long phalanges curled around from above the door frame, gripping the edge. Something large dropped from the ceiling, then raised itself to its full height. As his eyes met the creature's terrifying red orbs, numbness radiated through his body, ice in his veins. The chills sent the hair on the back of his neck standing on end.

Elija called out from the other room. "It's Chisum and—and, uh, Coffey! Shit! I think they're headed for the damn stagecoach!"

Emiliano's gun rose with blinding speed.

Not fast enough. Before he could even pop off a round, a sharp edge—similar to the cat's claw, though thicker, heavier even—brushed his esophagus.

He gasped, sharp yet brief. The air refused to pull into his lungs as he choked on the hot liquid filling his mouth. More spewed from under his right hand, which he clasped around the giant slit in his throat. The serrated edge of the creature's forearm lowered as Emiliano stumbled backward, heedlessly squeezing off rounds into the cupboard, the ceiling, and the kitchen window as he fell into the counter.

Sandy screeched, catapulted off the countertop, and shot down the hallway, her wretched mews trailing.

13

Coffey, helping Chisum into the stagecoach parked by the ranch, turned his head toward the house.

Chisum froze a moment, listening to the gunfire reverberate over the ranch. Squealing echoed into the pasture.

Sandy.

His heart broke at the idea of leaving his friend behind. The thought of going back blazed in his mind, but only for an instant. Surely, it would be suicide. A heaviness inundated him; he swallowed dryly and slumped himself into the coach.

"Let's go," he muttered.

14

Elija turned, startled by the gunfire. A thud followed, then silence.

White flashed through the parlor room. Sandy bolted past, scurrying under a Victorian armchair with a plaintive mew.

Again, the house fell eerily silent, save for the sluggish drag of his own heavy breathing. He should make his way back to the kitchen to check on Emiliano, but he now stood alone in this house, with no chance against the unknown looming within.

Hooves trampled outside as the stagecoach tore ass past the house, Coffey hollering commands.

Elija gaped after the coach as it disappeared into the night. "Wuh-wuh-wuh-wait for meee, goddammit!"

He broke for the front door.

15

Sandy, panting, crouched under the chair on high alert. Her coat swelled, the fur on her back spiking and running down her spine. She watched the clobbering of boots jog by, hoping, and succeeding, not to be found.

The reverberations trailed away, and, moments later, a breeze shifted through the parlor by her tail. She knew what that meant: *outside*. All seemed quiet.

Time to make a break.

Staying low to the ground, tufted belly fur to the floor, she scurried alongside the couch, then the floral-patterned wall. The deafening pops of gunfire and bloodcurdling screams stopped her dead in her tracks. Oh, she left too soon. Too soon indeed.

Unable to pinpoint where the sound originated, she followed the source of cool air until the opening stood in her peripherals. She scanned the dark space through dilated pupils, able to see everything through a monochromatic blue hue. All clear.

Sandy made a break for the exit, hurtling through the doorway onto the landing. The fresh air ruffled her long, alabaster coat as she slid to an abrupt halt, colliding with the boot of a fallen man. Slowly, she gaped up with wide eyes at the tall, peculiar, light blue creature standing above.

Her new friend. The one that had crawled inside the pantry while she sat hidden behind a bag of flour... at least until the exploding door scared her half to death.

The creature peered back down at her, then gently squatted and stroked her bulbous mane with a heavy but slow hand.

Sandy recoiled slightly, still petrified, watching its every move.

The creature raised itself and stood at the edge of the stairs, staring out over the vast, green, moonlit valley.

16

Smiling, Potter wrapped his arms around Nora's waist, hands inter-locked. Both lay, mostly, fully dressed, with Nora awkwardly on his lap.

"I'm sorry, I feel like I cut you off before," Nora murmured. The right side of her face nudged against his left, brushing against his nicely trimmed, oiled beard.

"It's okay." Potter inhaled. The faint scent of lavender oil lingered. Soothing.

"You just—you just look so sad, Bill. And if I'm bein completely honest, I've been hopin for quite a bit of time you might take the initiative. But as we got to talkin, I got worried that was never gonna happen." She gently slipped a hand under an unbuttoned shirt slit, running her fingers through his graying chest hair. "You just seem a bit, well, shy. Which ain't terrible. Actually, it's quite refreshin, meetin a man who ain't just shootin vile, crude remarks out their childish mouth, or worse, tryin to just get me in the sack. You'd be surprised by the things I hear day to day from people just passin through the store. Anyway, I hope I wasn't oversteppin."

Potter's grin slipped, a familiar, leaden weight returning to his stomach. "You're probably right. I'm certain I wouldn't have made a move on you."

"You really loved her, didn't you," she asked, tone even and genuine. "Your soulmate."

"I do."

She gently rubbed his chest. "How'd the young'uns take it... the loss of their mother, that is?"

"Clara, going through her own, rebelled. She'd 'forgetfully' leave the gate open so Bessie's cranky mare would roam off. Came home one night, late as usual, to fix em supper, and found a barbeque in the back-yard of my wife's book collection. She just torched them all. I whipped Isaac good and hard with my old service belt for not keeping an eye on her. She didn't speak to me for... well, a long time. She's bout as stubborn as her old man, I reckon. But those days were a bit of a blur for me. A drunken opiate induced haze I was hoping I'd never snap out of. Morgan found me, had me locked up to dry out before the funerals. At my wife's burial, he told me he wanted custody of Isaac and Clara. Damn near insisted. That was never going to happen."

"Why on earth would he want to take your children?"

Potter slid his hands away, a fire in his belly beginning to blaze. Memories of that day, the day he put his wife to rest, burned into him. His invariably disapproving father-in-law. Bessie, pulled from a submerged carriage. Staring into her empty, opaque eyes, her pallid, cold flesh against his face as he hugged her for the last time.

"Please, excuse me." Potter sat up.

Nora slid down, now perching on his lap. Rising to stand, Potter supported her as she climbed to her feet. Then he walked out onto the porch and leaned over the railing. Main Street appeared mostly desolate, the townsfolk scarce. Two carriages traveled in opposite directions on either side of the road. The faint drumming of a piano offered jaunty tunes, brimming from Miller's Café across the way along with the savory scent of smoked beef ribs from the chimney.

The cool, dry air cooled his flushed face, refreshing him as he leaned out to overlook the town. Lighting his quirley, he pulled back a deep breath of bitter smoke, holding it a moment before exhaling its vapor and watching it slowly dissipate. The night seemed bright. Brighter than usual, even with the amber glow of the streetlamps. He looked up, expecting a pale-yellow moon high above the town, and did a double take. An eldritch green glow loomed in the distance, dancing in sync to the rhythm across the illuminated skyline.

17

Nora stepped out. Standing next to Potter, she plucked the quirley from between his two fingers, which hung limp over the railing. She took a drag and exhaled, gray smoke spilling from her nostrils.

She grinned, relishing the sensation. "Can't tell ya the last time I had one of these smokey treats."

"Delicious, ain't it," Potter asked, staring out at the sky.

She glanced up, following his gaze. Her mouth dropped, along with his smoke.

"Sweet Jesus, Bill." She pointed at the twitching haze, its alluring green color fluctuating with faint shades of red and purple. "Ya-ya seein that? What is that in the sky there, huh!?"

"Dunno." he said dreamily, almost nonchalant. "Never seen such a thing in all my life. It carries a strange elegance, don't it?"

"That don't concern you, hon!?" She gaped, staring between the haze and Potter before glancing up and down Main to see if anyone else bore witness to this disquieting event.

He shook his head, leaned down, and picked up the smoke, ripping another drag.

Her gaze settled on him. "You all right, Bill?"

"Gonna be fifty-five end of August. *Fifty-five.*" Potter enunciated his age, almost in bewilderment, still gazing at the haze. "That's older than most people live by a decennium or more, you know that?" He smirked. "Hell, I should've bought the farm when I was Clara's age. Eldest child to seven siblings. All dead. Postmaster with the Pox showed up at our front door with mail, and that was it. I was the only one who didn't get sick. Then, the war. Then—" As if unwilling to finish his thought, he hung his head. "Lived two lifetimes, Nora. One privileged, bullshit existence followed by one of barbaric, utter savagery."

"You also lived one as a father. A family man. Am I right?"

He turned to her. "There're things you don't know about me. That no one knows about. Terrible things. I—I thought the kids and I would be safe here. The middle of nowhere. I was wrong. Must've been out my damn ignorant mind to think such a thing. To think *anyone* is safe in this world."

She blinked. "What are ya sayin, Bill?"

"I actually came here, much to my chagrin, to tell you I'm sorry and—and to say goodbye."

"Bill, slow down. What are ya talkin bout?" She reached out her hand, wanting to brush her fingers over his shoulder.

"HEEEYAAAA!" The distant, frantic shouting, along with the pounding of galloping hooves, broke the awkward tension between them.

CHAPTER 22

Charon and Lamiya stepped out of Miller's luncheonette and gaped at the chartreuse skies above.

Charon crossed himself. "Sweet Holy Mary, mother of our Lord Jesus Christ."

They had been in a delighted mood only moments earlier, thanks to their evening of dining and entertainment inside Miller's. Although their idea of entertainment was complaining at every little thing that went wrong: as usual, everything. Charon's porterhouse, which he'd sold to Miller, was grossly overcooked with a warm red center. Christ, didn't he ask for it *rare*! And Lamiya, her poor ears. The three-string trio blared far too loud, especially from where they sat. Then that savage barmaid Sheyenne had offered them a table further back, which they'd obviously refused with disgust. How dare she ask them to give up their usual table, where they'd sat every fourth Friday for the better part of the last six months? And the band—oh, *they* couldn't tone it down!?

When Charon and Lamiya stepped out of Miller's and saw the disconcerting green skies, however, their cheery disposition shattered. They'd failed to follow through with their equinoctial sacrifice, unable to coerce the Potter boy to their farm, and now the full weight of their incompetence bore down on them.

Sometimes, late at night, Charon actually wondered if *God's Work*, something he wholeheartedly believed in, was all just a bunch of hullaballoo. He'd cared little to find out. He'd just thought, maybe, he had more *time*. But, as he looked up to the strawberry moon peeking brightly from behind a cloud, he knew.

The day of reckoning had arrived.

"Sir." Buckley, standing on the porch smoking, nodded across the street.

Peering over at Reynolds' Grocery, Charon grinned. *There's still hope.* "Buckley, get to the carriage. Quickly!"

2

Coffey yanked on the leather reins wrapped around his fist. The horses skidded over gravel, bringing the stagecoach to a screeching halt. Without a moment to spare, Chisum swung open the cabin door and helped himself down before Coffey could dismount.

"Where the hell is Smith," he demanded.

Coffey glanced around. "I don't believe he's here, boss."

"Well shit, Coffey, I can see *that!* Find him, for God's sake!"

The men walked through the tight alley alongside the building between the hardware store, coming to a narrow set of stairs leading to the second level. Chisum huffed up the flight, out of breath and out of shape, and rapped at the door with the side of his fist.

Van opened the door, evidently nonplussed at the sight of John Chisum standing on his landing—likely the last person he'd ever expect to show up at the post office, much less his front door. Coffey, who had collected Boss's mail for years, figured Van could just about count on two hands the few times he'd actually spoken with Chisum in his many years in Missouri Plaza.

"Mr. Chisum? Coffey?" Van glanced back, then returned his gaze, still perplexed. "What—what can I do for you's?"

Chisum pushed his way in before Van could finish speaking, leaving him holding the door open. Coffey waited on the landing until Van invited him in, which he did with an almost imperceptible nod.

Coffey strode into the kitchen behind Van. As he glanced around, he discovered the cozy apartment, though quaint, lacked in offerings. It comprised only two rooms with a partial wall divider. For some reason, he'd expected to find piles of mail all over the place, as if Van would've taken work home with him. He supposed Van hadn't much need, since he lived above his place of employment. The kitchen housed a small, round table, where Van's father, Roswell, sat with a bottle of red wine with two glasses.

"John?" Roswell raised a perplexed brow at the interruption, wiping his wine-stained mustache with his pocket-square handkerchief. Standing from his chair, he quickly brushed his cream-colored slacks, part of his matching three-piece suit, before extending a hand to greet Chisum.

Chisum, in inadvertent disregard, walked around the table until both Smiths stood in his view. "Where's that fancy telegraph machine of yours?"

"Uhhh," Van dribbled, his brain too slow to process.

"We need to send for help right away. Well, for God's sake, boy, don't just stand there with your britches in your hands. Point me in the damn direction!"

"It's, uh... it-it's downstairs," Van stammered. "I-I don't quite understand—"

"Some *thing* attacked my ranch! Set it ablaze and killed my damn men!"

"Wuh-what?" Van's eyes darted back and forth from Chisum to Coffey.

Chisum turned to his servant. "Coffey, am I speaking goddamn Chinese over here!?"

Coffey stifled a crooked grin. "Sure ain't, boss."

"All hell's broken loose! Come on, you fool, get a move on!" Chisum grabbed Van by the arm and led him out the door.

3

All the way from Nora's porch, Potter watched, and certainly heard, Chisum's alarm. Moments later, his employer, the postmaster, and the postmaster's father ran *into* the post office. Curious, yes but mostly nerve-wracking. He couldn't shake his paranoia, the fear he'd been found. He could only imagine the bounty on his head. Maybe he should have just skinned out of town that afternoon.

"Whaddya spose is all that about," Nora asked, glancing back from Potter to the post office.

"Don't know." He stepped off the porch.

"Bill, where ya goin!?"

He didn't answer. Nora quickly stepped behind, catching up with him near the post office. Together they entered the dark lobby and followed the soft glow of lanterns and surly chatter in the back room. The gas-powered wall lamps, set low, provided about as much insufficient lighting as the hand-held options, illuminating the strange scene before them.

Van, sitting at a mahogany, roll-top desk in front of a telegraph, tapped away on its round morse key knob, a square device with a spring-loaded lever attached. Chisum had already lit a fresh cigar. He spoke, pacing back and forth behind the desk, and Van tapped out his words. Clicking echoed through the space.

"This is John Chisum. Cattle rancher of Missouri Plaza, New Mexico. Eighty miles south-east of Lincoln County, New Mexico and two hundred miles north-east of El Paso, Texas. The Jinglebob ranch is under attack by an unidentified assailant. It has killed livestock and several of my help. Please, I urge you to send reinforcements immediately."

"Now what?" Chisum looked to Van.

"Now we just wait for a response, I reckon."

"Well, shit. How long's that gonna take, Van," he asked, as if Van knew and had merely decided to withhold the answer.

Van, sweating profusely and struggling to maintain eye contact, just shrugged his shoulders. His eyes stopped on the doorway, staring at Potter.

Coffey, closest to the doorway, turned. "Bill!" He grinned and shook Potter's hand with ecstatic enthusiasm.

"Everythin all right," Nora asked.

Chisum pulled the cigar from his face. "No, everythin's not all right! Did you just hear? My ranch is under attack!"

Potter narrowed his eyes. "Who?"

Maybe bounty hunters had discovered his employer. Bennett's land was definitely *off grid*. Few people, other than the odd and mysterious residents of Missouri Plaza, even knew their homestead existed.

Chisum shook his head. "Not a who, Bill. A-a *what*."

Potter raised his brows as Coffey struggled to explain the events of the last hour. The details proved vague at best; Coffey and Chisum had seen very little. Potter couldn't reconcile the story for the life of him. Madness, surely.

He looked back and forth from Coffey to Chisum. "I don't understand."

"Not much else to it, Potter," Chisum shouted. "Some vile thing swooped in and tore through my men like they were sheets of water-closet paper!" He turned to Van. "You got any weapons in here? A pistol, a rifle, a-a-a-a goddamn cannon?"

"Uhhh, I, uh... well, I don't, uh—" Van's damp forehead looked like it might explode under the pressure.

Roswell interjected, voice dripping contempt. "Let's not jump to any conclusions, John. Where's Mather? We should consult with him first while we wait."

"Aw hell, anyone rowin with both goddamn oars in the water knows where Mather is. Or should I say, *with whom*. Only question is how close is he? Barracks locked up? Surely, he's got weapons inside."

POP, POP!

Gunfire rang out somewhere in the distance.

The group hesitated, staring atwitter at one another. Gunfire, though uncommon, was hardly unheard of, especially on a weekend or special event. But today was no holiday. And with news of Chisum's "intruder," Potter thought it felt too coincidental. He turned for the doorway as, through the gunfire, the faint, guttural screaming began.

"Wuh-wait! Don't go out there!" Chisum pleaded. Beginning to sweat, he removed his Stetson and blotted his beading forehead with a pocket square.

Potter briskly made his way to the front lobby with Nora and Coffey in tow, gaining a hazy look out the dusty window. Under the dim glow of a gas streetlamp, a tall man with an eye patch and a top hat hopped around a lopsided stagecoach. Unable to see more through the grit, Potter pushed halfway out the door.

Coffey grabbed his arm. "Bill, I seen it my with my own eyes. He's right. Ain't no animal I ever come across before."

Potter could see the raw fear in Coffey's white, wary eyes.

The screaming continued intermittently, louder now, much more disconcerting. The sound, the uncertainty, drove Potter out the door despite Coffey's warnings; he skipped down the steps and feverishly scampered up and across the street toward a busted stagecoach. By this time, some of the other townsfolk had gathered around, forming a shallow barrier near the alley. Most spilled from Miller's, having heard the commotion.

Potter pushed through the growing crowd. A body lay sprawled on the ground, a pistol clenched in his bloodied grip.

4

"Isaac..."

Isaac stared at the crystal knot, gently turning it over in his hands. Like peering through a kaleidoscope, he thought, save for this one didn't require looking through the window of a long wooden tube. Vivid shards of color reflected throughout as it moved.

Faintly, in the distance, the voice echoed again. "Hellooo?"

Isaac barely even heard them. The glow twinkled in his palm, captivating.

"ISAAC!"

Isaac gasped, jerking back so hard, he nearly dropped the crystal. "Huh—wuh-what!?"

Clara glared at him. "What are you doing!?"

He blinked around at the small yet cozy apartment, comprised of a family room, kitchen, and tiny bedroom, barely adequate to house a full-size bed. Dimly lit wall lamps provided much of the lighting, along with half-burned candles slumped in their gooey, waxen bases in windowsills, on side tables, and over the fireplace mantle. He and Clara sat on one of three different shabby sofas enveloped in front of the crackling fire.

For a moment, Isaac had no idea where they were. Then, he spotted the small, square table in the kitchen, still covered in the remnants of a devoured feast. *Ms. Nora's.* The bones of a stripped roast chicken sat on a carving board in the center; the savory aroma still lingered in the toasty quarters.

He inhaled deeply, tension easing from his body. "Nothing. What do you want?"

"I said, where is Pa and Ms. Nora?"

"Busy." Isaac shrugged, returning his gaze to his new toy, now wondering if his forlorn father was, in fact, cozying up with the proprietor of Reynolds's Buy & Sell. During supper, he had noticed Pa offering Ms. Nora that same soft stare his ma used to own.

"Why's it taking so long for a haircut? I went down before, and they were just talking!"

"AHH—OWW!" A muffled scream drifted into the apartment.

Clara and Isaac pulled their attention away, peering up and around.

"Oh Lord, somebody please help! Oh, it hurts. It hurts quite badly!"

Isaac jumped from the couch and ran to the window. In the road below, a woman lay holding her ankle around a black, calf-high boot, crying out in pain. He glanced around the street, finding not a single soul to help. He *had* expected to see his pa or possibly Ms. Nora exit the barber shop.

"Oh, please, somebody! Please! I'm in tremendous pain, I couldn't possibly get up!"

"What is it," Clara asked with moderate interest, sitting upright.

"Nothing, just some lady. Looks like she fell or something. Ain't nobody out there to help."

"Ohhh, heavens, ohhh," the lady cried out.

Isaac waited and waited for his pa to emerge and help the poor woman as she wailed. Nothing. "Aw, hell. You stay here. I'm gonna to go find pa."

"Don't you leave me," Clara whined.

"Here." He tossed her the crystal knot. "You can hold this till I get back."

Clara caught the toss easily, her eyes lighting up as she sank back into the cozy couch.

Isaac skipped down the steps, walked behind the store counter, and cautiously ducked his head in the barbershop's quiet doorway. Empty. His mind stirred, wondering where they could have possibly gone, and why he and his sister were left behind. The lady uttered another cry and, without further hesitation, he proceeded through the vacant room, exiting onto the porch.

The woman shook and bawled from under a pink bonnet. "Oh, please, son, won'tcha come give me a hand? I—I've fallen and twisted my poor ankle!" She sobbed in a fetal position, holding her foot. "Surely, I can't make it up on my own!"

Isaac, once again, glanced the empty streets, then stepped forth toward the woman. She looked up and extended a white-gloved hand. He reached for it, but the dancing green skies stopped him dead in his tracks. Maybe she'd tripped while looking up. Or maybe she fell while running away from something and—*that face,* now clear in the skylight. Where'd he seen it?

Before he could muster another thought, he felt the pressure of two bracing arms. One wrapped around his upper body, and the other pressed firmly over his mouth. He writhed and tried to scream as something swept him backwards, heels dragging painfully across the dirt, his resistance only slightly delaying the inevitable.

He fell backward into a stagecoach, someone already sitting inside on the left. The hurt ankle lady?

A man plopped down across from her and pounded on the wall, slamming the door behind him. "Let's go!"

A command fired from the driver, and the horses took off with such force, Isaac rolled backward into the lady's legs. Impulsively, he tried to rise, but the lady dug the heel of her black mid-calf boot into his neck, holding him down.

"Hello, son. You never came to see me," Charon said dryly.

The butcher's glacial stare terrified Isaac more than anything. Heart thundering, he fought to breathe, but Mrs. Dotterweich's pressing heel restricted his airways. Pain stabbed at his lungs, his vision blurring.

5

"We're running out of time," his wife pleaded. "You saw those skies. We must prepare *Capacocha!*"

Charon glanced away from the boy, meeting Lamiya's gaze. "You want us to do the ritual here, darling? Would this satisfy your insatiable desires?"

She nodded. "Now. Now, for our Lord and Savior, before we lose it all!"

"Well, so be it then." The coach would have to suffice for the ancient Incan ritual. The sacrifice must be made. And Charon would once again ferry over an innocent soul to the other side. From his inside blazer pocket, he pulled a small black leather-bound book and tossed it to Lamiya. "How quickly can you read the scriptures?"

She flashed a sly smile.

Charon looked down at Isaac. "Sorry, young chap. I suppose I must dispense with the theatrics before the missus' knickers get all twisted."

From a leather sheath which hung from his belt, concealed by the black blazer, he produced a butcher's knife. The long silver edge shimmered in the flash of pooling light from a passing streetlamp. Isaac quivered. Charon slid to the edge of the seat, then slowly leaned in, lowering the blade, the boy watching it near his throat.

Everything fell silent.

6

A blur of white light flooded into the carriage, much like a dream. A living nightmare. *"Keep hold of him!"* faded into the background, along with an incoherent babble of what Isaac guessed was Bible verses. A barrage of pleading—*please, no*—fell from desperate lips, which he soon realized to be his. Then the cabin shook violently, and before he knew it, the nightmare ended.

Almost.

The horses skidded to a halt as the right rear side dipped, the wheel shattering with a shriek of wood. Mrs. Dotterweich flew up from the seat, smacking her pink bonnet against the hard roof and chomping her lower lip. Squealing, she grabbed her husband's blazer for support. The knife fell from his hand as he grasped the roof, though his head still smashed against the window, cracking the glass.

Isaac rolled from the attempted assault and exploded from the stagecoach door, jumping over a pothole and bolting down the dusky alley. His heart thudded inside his narrow frame as he struggled to suck down the fresh, cool air into his wheezing lungs, pumping his legs as fast and far as he could. Stairs leading God-knew-where on either building side tempted him, though the idea of getting trapped on some roof or patio quickly deterred him. Keg barrels. Stacked box crates. Headstone and... coffins? Not inside a coffin, not tonight.

A side door! *Please, please open.*

He eagerly met the knob, twisting. Nothing. After pounding at the windowless café door, he glanced behind. Charon stepped clumsily from the stagecoach. It was dark, but with this misty sky, Isaac knew he re-mained somewhat visible down the alley. *No, no, no, no.* His head spun around, gaze landing on the one probable place of salvation.

The water tower.

7

"Oh, Charon!" The blood dribbled down his wife's chin as she reached for his pocket square.

"Buckley, you blind old sonovabitch!" Charon yelled, waving a fist.

This wasn't the first time his driver had caused an accident in as many months. He let the reins slip through his grip one stormy night in January, sending the stagecoach into the shallow creek, runoff from the Pecos, near their home.

Goddamnit.

Charon reached back into the cabin and pulled a revolver from under the seat. He glanced at the busted wheel, half of its rungs snapped clean off, and stooped down to check the axle. Bent to hell. Hopefully not damaged to the point where the carriage wouldn't make it home, though hardly his most pressing issue at the moment.

"Heaven's sake!" Lamiya threw open *her* side door before Buckley could reach the handle. As she climbed out, she slapped away the trembling hand he extended. "I got it, I got it. Back away! Back away now, you fool!"

Buckley did so, lighting a pre-rolled cigarette he pulled from his outer suit's chest pocket with a wooden match struck on the wheel. "Sorry, ma'am. Musta missed it is all, I suppose."

He shifted around his leather eye patch as if *that* had caused his lack of perception. Lamiya glared with contempt, holding the handkerchief to her swollen, bloody lip.

No time for this.

Turning, Charon jogged down the alley. "You come back here, boy. There is no place you can run that I won't find you!" He stopped, raised the revolver, and popped off two rounds.

Lamiya yelled from somewhere far behind. "Careful now, darling. You can't kill him yet!"

8

One round struck the cafe door, eminently close to Isaac's face. Wood splintered off, slicing his cheek as he fumbled backward. He pivoted toward the utility shed under the tower, partially hidden by its high stilts and elaborate, lattice structure. Maybe he could climb the tower and scream over the town from above. Surely, someone would hear—his pa, hopefully, from wherever he'd vanished. He knew the butcher's gun likely had four bullets left to dodge, though the tower should make shooting much more complicated. He glanced back. Charon, already halfway down the alley, ran with shocking speed for someone of his bulk. Isaac, flustered and lacking alternatives, ran under the lattice and rounded the corner behind the shed—

FWAP!

He collided face first with something solid. The force sent him off his feet, tumbling backward onto the seat of his pants and stealing from him what little breath remained. Gasping for air, he peered up at the object that sent him down.

Something stepped forward from dark, the bright sky casting bars of light and shadowy lattice across its body. A warbling cry gurgled from its darkened face, an unnerving, loud screech that echoed through the valley.

Frozen to the ground, Isaac had no wind with which to scream. He just stared up, unmoving, at the shimmering creature they'd awoken.

9

Charon slowed to a brisk pace as he met Isaac. "Oh, the Lord, he sure works in mysterious ways, does he not?"

The boy, sprawled on the ground, didn't bother looking back. He just stared up, past the shed's corner. Charon followed his gaze, and what he saw dropped his jaw.

"My God." He locked onto those burgundy orbs. "It's you... the Prince of Darkness... here, in the flesh!"

He crossed himself, then dug behind his necktie for a chain, pulling it out and kissing the hanging crucifix. He raised the gun back in a futile surrender, knowing bullets offered no match for Old Scratch.

The devil's slanted lids fluttered, gaze following Charon's movement as he began taking deliberate steps back. Its eyes dilated fully, the red lenses rolling back into its head.

With an almost unperceived quickness, it lunged.

10

Potter approached the one-eyed man in the top hat, leaning over the dead man and a hysterical woman in a pink bonnet. She sprawled across the body in a grieving embrace, her ferocious sobs forcing onlookers to back away while exchanging ghastly expressions. The man's face resembled split sausage casing, flesh bulging through three deep, parallel slits. The wounds began at his forehead and cut diagonally across to his chin, splitting his nose and lips down the middle. One eye socket, hollow, oozed burgundy; the other stared directly back at Potter. Only the man's size and thinning comb-over identified him as the angry church patron and butcher, Charon Dotterweich.

Nora rushed up, brushing against Potter's side, Coffey just behind her.

"My god, Bill. What—happened?" She covered her mouth in horror.

Lamiya, panting for air, choked out a scream. "IT ATTACKED HIM! IT ATTACKED MY CHARON! OH, SWEET JESUS, IT CAME OUT OF NOWHERE, IT ATTACKED HIM, OH MY GOD!"

The crowd whispered among themselves, gaping at one other. A barrage of words, all variations of the same question, spewed from their lips. "What attacked him?"

"I DON'T KNOW, I DON'T KNOW, I DON'T KNOW!"

"I ran down and pulled him out, I did!" Buckley assured the townsfolk, proudly puffing a cigarette.

"What was it, Buckley?" Nora asked.

"I ain't saw nothin." Buckley glanced down, ashamed.

Nora squatted next to Lamiya, putting a hand on her twitching back. "What'd you see, Mrs. Dotterweich?"

"It—it-it wuh—was dark-darkness!" Wheezing and sobbing, Lamiya turned to Nora, grabbing a fistful of her blouse. "I-I tell ya, it-it-it wuh-was that *God damned Satan himself!* Come straight up from the river of fire and brimstone! He's come, Nora. He's come to SMITE THIS TOWN OF PERPETUAL SIN AND EVERYONE IN IT!" Spittle flung from her puffy, bleeding lip, hitting Nora's face in between wails and gasps for air.

Potter pulled Nora from Lamiya's clutches, and the distraught woman fell back upon Charon's remains. He turned his head and peered down the multihued, sparsely sky-lit alley.

"Wait here." Potter reached behind his blazer and unhooked the leather enclosure strap over each holstered LeMat revolver.

"What..." Nora, aghast, glanced from Lamiya to Potter. "Where ya goin, Bill!?"

Potter didn't answer, nor look back. Entering this alley was the absolute last thing he wished for, but some odd, sheer force of will compelled him to do so. The thin strip of streetlight vanished from under his boots as he entered the darkness. His eyes, quickly adjusting, could just about make out a set of stairs against the side of Miller's on his right. The stenciled outline of empty wooden barrels and stacked pine crates sat beneath. To his left, Quinsberry's tapered pine boxes leaned vertically against the side, a blank square top and oval headstones resting alongside. He didn't miss the odd irony as he ambled towards his possible death.

Hearing a commotion, Potter glanced back. Marshal Mather fumbled out of Miller's and down the porch side in a slightly disheveled uniform, adjusting a lopsided gun belt. Gray chest hair stuck out the top of his brown collared shirt, the top two buttons undone. Gus Miller, wearing his usual bartending garb, followed several steps behind Mather, towel in hand.

"Look out, look out, everybody!" The marshal pushed his way through the crowd, voice raising an octave higher each time he spoke. "Make way, please! Come on now, coming through!"

The stout marshal, diminishing under the twenty or so townsfolk, finally broke through. "Mrs. Dotterweich, you all right? Now what pray tell is—*oh sweet, heavenly Jesus!*"

The color instantly drained from his cheeks, and he clutched his stomach. Potter figured the poor man hadn't seen a dead body in over a decade, much less one with a violently mutilated face.

"Look out!" Thrusting himself through the few stragglers alongside the edge of the alley, Mather bent over, gripping the side wall of Miller's, and vomited in the dirt. Fine particles of dust billowed from the splash.

Miller peered at the remains through the break in the crowd. "Oh, for fuck's sake, lad!" Wincing, he turned his head, crossed his chest, and kissed the tip of his thumb. "Terrible, terrible way to go, I think."

Potter, halfway down, spun back to the water tower directly ahead. He stepped lightly but confidently, ambling into the void, his palms resting over each LeMat handle. A cool gust of wind picked up, ruffling under his blazer. A dry creaking startled him, drawing his attention upward. Just the windmill beginning its oscillation, the fantail gently twisting behind. A bluish gray strip of moonlight crossed the revolving fan blades diagonally across the wide water keg. He glanced over the half-exposed moon, which rivaled the green glow. Behind, the cries of the hysterical Mrs. Dotterweich carried down the alley alongside the marshal's retches.

Reaching the end of the alley, Potter turned and looked back at Main Street. Though the alley wasn't terribly long, perhaps half a city block, the circle of townsfolk seemed infinitely farther away.

A sort of warbling sounded ahead, almost birdlike, albeit sluggish and quite unsettling. Loud. Gritty. Like those Denver katydids, except with a busted instrument.

Before Potter cocked his head fully around, he whipped both pistols out and up, clenched in his fists, hammers cocked. His eyes darted in the dark, struggling to see. A glimmer of moon and green sky spotlit the meadow just beyond the lattice of the tower. Empty.

The sound stopped and started, intermittent. It echoed all around him, almost through him, a reverberation fluttering his nerves. *Nothing's out there... right?*

He stood perfectly still, firing shallow glances right and left, waiting for something to emerge from the dark. The warbling suddenly stopped. Something shifted behind him, a scraping, followed by a bright squeal. Potter quickly turned to a small box crate next to Miller's, a shadow scurrying across.

Goddamn rat.

Another sound, ahead, caused him to look up. Just the windmill, now cranking.

To the right, something shifted in his peripherals. He did a double take. Tough to see, similar in contrast, but there it stood, perched on the low-pitch roof of the water tower, gleaming periwinkle in the twilight.

Goose flesh crawled his skin, up his arms, and down the back of his neck. The creature glistened, chest heaving, *breathing*, standing tall. The eyes, dark, almost bug-like, stared out, overlooking the town with most of the villagers in its peripherals. Its jaw opened down the middle, revealing a mouth with rows of razor teeth. As the bitter chill of the New Mexican evening air pierced his thick, weathered skin, Potter realized where he'd seen that ghastly face before... or, rather, one he recalled as heavily decomposed and long deceased.

Little worried him, much less terrified him in his half century walking this earth. Even with the looming burden of McCormac's untimely arrival, he remained relatively unfazed. Three thousand redcoats blasting muskets in his general direction on a muddy meadow in Prince William

County, Virginia, had been the closest he'd felt to true fear. But at least then, he'd known what he was up against. And of course, in his twenties, he'd been invincible.

That was then. This was now.

Potter glanced down, gently holstered his guns, and stepped backward, not taking his eyes from the creature, which he was now certain came from his pit. Finally, it moved backward, fading into the void. As he turned for the alley, the creak of an opening door drew him back. The utility closet flung open and out came running—

Potter gaped. "Isaac?"

"Pa!" His son reached for him, grabbing his sleeve.

"Isaac, what-what are you doing out here?" He glanced around. "Where's your sister?"

"Ms. Nora's—Pa, I saw it! I saw it, I saw it up close!"

Potter scanned his boy, looking for injury. He cupped Isaac's face, brushing over his thin cheek cut with a thumb.

"It didn't hurt me, Pa, it didn't! It leaned over me an-and looked at me with these *brilliant* eyes an-and I think sniffed me. I was so scared, but it was okay—"

"We need to go, come on." Potter took one last look around, then placed his hand on Isaac's back, shuffling his son up along the alley.

11

Van, still sitting at his desk staring at the telegraph, shouted to his father and Chisum. "Hey, so what's all the commotion out there? Can ya see anything?"

The men, who monitored the lobby window with the restless anticipation of a people awaiting imminent attack, glared at the glass.

"I don't like it. I don't like it one bit, for Christ." Chisum spoke out loud to no one in particular, though Roswell stood nearby. "By God, Mather finally made an appearance."

The sound of the telegraph sprang to life, startling Van. Although he sat in anticipation of a response, mostly to avoid whatever occurred outside the post office walls, he surely hadn't expected one to arrive this evening, much less this fast. From the transmitting device in the desk cubicle, a narrow strip of paper generated, discharging from the loud mechanism.

"Hey—hey, guys! We got a message! Come quick!" Wide-eyed, Van held the strip of paper with two fingers as it pulsed from the telegraph. With his other hand, he began to decode with a lead pencil, scratching the words onto a used manila envelope.

Chisum burst into the room and pulled the soggy-tipped cigar from his mouth. A trail of saliva followed. "Christ, boy, what's it say? What's it say!?"

For a moment, Van just blinked at the envelope. "Uhhh, it says they've already a dispatched unit en route. Two days ago, from Fort Hood, Texas."

Chisum's brows crinkled, dumbfounded. "Fort Hood? Well, how the hell can that be possible? I thought you sent word to Albuquerque?"

"I—I did."

"Smith, you ain't making a whole lotta sense to me."

"Uhhh, best guess? Fort Hood alerted authorities in Albuquerque of their actions; they might be closer in proximity. Or maybe they was already there, passin through on their way down here?"

"What, uh, why they coming? They say why, boy?" Chisum fidgeted with his mustache. The fresh look of panic in his eyes matched the one he'd worn when he'd first entered the post office.

The Smiths weren't *directly* privy to the wheeling and dealings at the Jinglebob Ranch, or with the others in town, but they hardly needed to be. Van had heard enough old maiden sewing circle conjecture about Chisum, and he knew when a man looked jumpy. And Chisum? Well, he walked like a cat upon a hot baked stone.

The front door opened.

Van jerked to his feet, he and Chisum both poking their heads into the lobby. A breeze of cool, arid air met them. Roswell stood in the doorway, staring down the street.

"Pa," Van called. "What's goin on out there?"

"Looks like some sort of accident. We should check this out, John, see if they need a hand or something."

"Are you out of your mind!?" Chisum approached Roswell. "Did you not hear a good goddamn thing I said!?"

Roswell put his hand on Chisum's front shoulder. "John, you need to just calm down. I understand you're under duress—"

"With all due respect, Roswell, you ain't seen the shit I've seen tonight." Chisum clenched back down on the wet stogie. "So, if you wouldn't mind takin your goddamn hand from my shoulder, I'd be much obliged."

Roswell dramatically removed his hand, placed it up as if to wave goodbye, and walked out the door. Van hesitated, unsure if he should stay or go. Chisum's twisted face ignited the fear in his gut, but this would soon be his old man's town. *His* town. In front of Pa, and the townsfolk, he had to maintain a strong façade. Appearances carried weight. Looking back at Chisum, then to his father, already halfway down the street, he stepped out the door.

Chisum ambled out behind him, muttering audibly all the while. "Christ, they're out of their damn minds."

12

Closely guiding his son in front of him, Potter side-stepped around the spectating Main Street crowd, still hovering over Charon Dotterweich. He glanced over the many heads.

Standing behind the sobbing Lamiya, Buckley hunched over the corpse, chain-smoking rollies. He fidgeted with his eye patch and muttered incomprehensible, repeated lamentations. "Damn shame, I tell ya. Damn shame."

From across the crowd, Nora locked eyes with him. His gut told him to snap the fuck out of it, to get Clara and skin out of town, but that warm gaze tugged at some corroded, temperamental strings inside him, hindering his departure.

Roswell and Van arrived beside him, peering over shoulders to get a glance through the tightly huddled spectators.

Chisum, in tow, moved at a brisk pace so as to not be left alone. "Did ya see it, Potter," he shouted from afar, huffing.

Potter fought back a groan as the crowd turned to look at him. Leaving *quietly* was, at the moment, out the window.

The marshal, wiping the acrid remains of vomit from his bushy mustache with a paisley handkerchief, glanced back and forth from Chisum to Potter. "Can someone please explain to me what the hell is goin on here?"

Lamiya looked up, then stood to face Potter, wiping her swollen red eyes. "You saw him, didn't you!?"

"Who!?" Mather, bewildered, glanced away, attempting to avoid Charon's remains.

Lamiya eyed the marshal with utter contempt. "The God damned Devil himself, you sinful troglodyte. That's *who!*"

Mather, noticing his shirt, hurried to fasten the remaining buttons.

Van stepped forth. "We're under some sort of attack, marshal!"

"A-attack," Mather stammered with utter incredulity. Clearly, in his cozy little town- appointed job as an official, he hadn't faced an "attack" of any kind.

Miller pulled a tarnished silver flask from his back pocket, unscrewed the cap, and tipped it into his mouth. He swallowed hard, wincing, and wiped his mouth with his backhand before offering a sip to Potter.

He blinked at the outstretched flask. "What's that?"

"A lil Number Nine, Red Eye, eh."

Potter raised a bewildered brow.

"Gin," Miller clarified.

"I thought you didn't sell liquor?"

"I *don't* sell it, mate! Never said I didn't *'ave* it."

Potter grabbed the flask, took a healthy swig, and handed it back.

Chisum, heaving and breathless, finally arrived. "Did ya see it, Potter!? Did ya?"

"What was down there, Bill?" Nora, now at his side, slipped her warm hand around his.

Potter, giving a quick glance down the alley at the vacant water tower roof, didn't answer, instead squeezing Nora's hand. She opened her mouth to speak—

"We need to go." He began pulling her and Isaac away.

"Wuh-where we headed, Bill," she asked.

He didn't respond.

"Bill?"

He dragged them beyond the onlookers, around the busted coach.

"Bill... *William Potter*!"

Potter stopped partway in the street and looked at her.

Bennett's house. Everything left in their world was in that house. Every penny saved from the Jinglebob Ranch. Food. Clothing. His scattergun. And, of course, those seemingly unattainable artifacts. But if that thing came from the pit in his yard, then his place was definitely out of the question. God only knew what else dwelled in that ship.

"I don't know." He peered up at her second-floor window. "We gotta get Clara. I know *that*. Your place."

"NO! No-no-no, that thing can get into *any* place!" Chisum appeared from around the coach. "I'm tellin you, it *jumped* through my second-floor window, for Christ's sakes!" He pleaded. "No place here is safe. No place!"

"I gotta get my daughter, John."

"The mill!" Van interjected. "It's a big place. Plenty of space to hide out till the authorities arrive."

"That mill?" Chisum pointed. "The one on the opposite side of town? We'll all get picked off on the way."

Potter looked down the street. The mill was a good idea, but Chisum was right. A helluva walk to the tail end of Main Street, and not one he wanted to risk.

Van glanced around. "Oh, the church!"

Roswell shook his head. "What good will that do, son? It'll just follow us there."

"No, the basement! We—we can hide in there."

"We can't fit the whole goddamn town into a..." Chisum shot Van a bewildered look. "There's a *basement* in that church?"

"Oh yeah, yeah, trust me, it's uh... we—we—"

"Can someone please tell me what in Sam Hill is goin on round here!?" Mather joined the party, eyes darting from Van to Chisum.

"We ain't got time for all that, Mather," Chisum exploded. "Help is on the way, but we can't wait! There's some unholy thing stalkin this village, an unstoppable sumbitch. Killed all my men, and we need whatever firearms you can muster up. Now!"

The marshal gave a tentative nod. "Then let's go, son. Gonna need a quick hand."

"Uh." Van's body shifted toward the church. "I wanna make sure everybody gets down there safe and sound, you know."

"Your father can lead em down. I need someone with some strength, some vigor, if we get into a tight spot now."

"Why don't you take, uh, Coffey?"

Coffey took a step forward.

Chisum raised a hand to block his path. "That I can't abide, Smith. Coffey doesn't leave my side."

The marshal didn't argue. "Time's a wastin, son. Come on then."

Mather and Van began a feverish pace toward the office, though Van kept glancing back at the church. Mather, more focused, only tore his eyes from their destination to scan the strange skies.

Potter followed the marshal's gaze, hoping against hope not to see something watching them all from above. The pale face of the strawberry moon made its primordial appearance, finally slipping from behind its clouded veil to commingle with this eldritch chartreuse haze. Current situation notwithstanding, he and the rest of the townsfolk standing on Main Street could at least agree on one thing.

Tonight was something to behold.

13

Roswell glared at Chisum. Surely the servant should have gone instead of his son. But he couldn't argue here about why Van's life mattered more than Coffey's. Bad for the optics. Better to focus on formulating a plan, getting everyone to safety. Coming out on top. He just needed to think of a good alternative to the chapel. He agreed with his son about needing to hide, but a space with so many windows posed unnecessary risks. Besides, who knew how many people would even fit in this alleged basement?

He turned to Miller. "You have some space, a-a-a room? Somethin with no windows?"

"Aye, pantry in the back. Where I store the dry goods, though it's plenty filled with cases o' Schweppes Ginger Ale and that retched Doctor Brown's Celery Tonic." Miller's mouth twisted in disgust. "Tell you, I couldn't give that shite away to a thirsty Chinaman crawlin in from the railroad."

"All right, listen. Get everyone inside in that pantry. Lock all the doors. You have any protection in there?"

"Ya betcha, I do."

Heads turned in the crowd, and chatter among the townsfolk increased. Panic quickly elevated, and as it did, Roswell stepped forth to face his people.

"All right everybody, please listen up." He held up his hands in the air, gesturing for quiet. "Many of you know who I am, havin met me over the years. Perhaps you shared a cup of Arbuckles' or a meal with me in Miller's, or we exchanged amusin anecdotes. Some others I am less familiar with, but that will change, I assure you. The name's Roswell Smith. I am the father of Vance Smith, your humble postmaster. This wasn't how I was plannin to announce my candidacy for office; however, now's as good a time as any, I reckon. I will be soon appointed as your first Mayor of Missouri Plaza. And as your mayor, I can assure you that I will let no harm come to you and your loved ones."

He spoke with confidence, making eye contact with as many as he could, and the crowd, mostly, listened. They trusted him. And if he led them through this crisis, his mayoral office was all but guaranteed. He struggled to stifle a furtive grin, especially as he caught sight of Chisum glowering in the background, angrily puffing his cigar. He wafted away swirling smoke with a lazy hand.

"Please, all of you, go on back inside Miller's with haste," Roswell instructed, keeping his voice even to encourage calm movements from the crowd. "Do not stop for anythin. Stay vigilant and protect yourselves and your families until we figure out what exactly is goin on here. I assure you, there is nothin to be concerned about. We've just received word that the proper authorities are en route. We expect them any time now. You folks, the powerful community that is Missouri Plaza, have no fear."

The townsfolk exchanged apprehensive glances as they began filing back into the café.

Roswell smiled to himself, glancing over his obedient flock. Lamiya and Buckley remained unmoved.

He walked over to the grieving widow, kneeling over her husband's remains. "Mrs. Dotterweich, Ma'am, I am terribly sorry for your loss." He leaned in from behind and placed his hands on her shoulders in an effort to help her up. "If you would please just follow the others—"

Lamiya shuddered, shrugging him off. "You get your filthy, swindlin hands off me, *mayor*." She scowled. "You don't think we know what you're up to here?"

"I—I, uh, I'm sure I don't know what you mean, ma'am."

"That shrewd son of yours and that no good Chinaman friend of his planning on smuggling in the Devil's water and poisoning the whole town. Oh, yeah... my Charon overheard all of it!" She stood, her face twisting in a snarl. "*You*... you and the other sinners of this town. Satan has returned to smite you all. Before he's done laying down his retribution, you all are gonna look back and wonder how you had it good for so long and pissed it all away." She smirked, stood, and walked to the stagecoach. "Let's go, Buckley!"

Roswell watched her slam the door, Buckley ambling into the driver's seat behind her. The cabin wobbled on three wheels as the horses made their slow departure down Main Street.

Chapter 23

Van glanced around the marshal's office, a small, one-story building with two rooms still dimly lit from before the marshal left for Miller's. Not much to see in the forefront. A visitor's bench lay against the window, and two desks faced each other on either side of the room. One sat completely bare, veiled in a thin layer of fine dust, perhaps with the idea of introducing a deputy. The other, Mather's, looked bare as well, save for a filthy coffee mug and a cup full of sharpened pencils. Behind rested a dust-laden, mostly empty bookcase, and in the corner stood a coat rack with a long trench, which looked as if it had yet hold a coat. One could argue the space was not well utilized, especially considering the lack of crime, but that didn't stop Mather from holding his post as the marshal of Missouri Plaza.

Against the wall, behind Mather's desk, a rack hung with two rifles. Mather grabbed one, tossing it to Van, then grabbed the second. Opening his desk side drawer, he pulled out two boxes of rounds and a gun belt with two pistols buttoned into each holster.

"You familiar with how to use one of these, son," Mather asked, feeding bullets into the iron receiver on the rifle's side.

"Uhhh, not really." Van turned the heavy, foreign steel over in his hands, grimly staring at the intimidating streak of silver reflecting in the amber glow thrown from the wall's gas lamp. Though he'd held guns before, he'd never fired one. He supposed tonight he'd learn.

"It's real simple. You shove the bullets in here..." Mather snapped back on the handle, loading a round. "You pull back on the lever action here, aim, and fire. And you pull back on it again, son."

Van considered the pair of rifles and pistols. "This all you got, Marshal?"

"Hell no." He smirked. "Got a cabinet in the back full of rifles."

Just as he finished that statement, a chilling noise rattled through the room. Both men spun to face the back wall toward the open doorway, Mather holding the rifle out. The retched sound, though distant, increased to a deep, guttural warbling.

"What is it, Marshal!?" Van whispered, mouth ajar.

Mather hesitated, staring.

Van's hands began to tremble; his stomach soured in icy knots. He wasn't ready for this. "You-you think it-it-is comin from out-outside?" Outside. Safer out there, for sure.

Mather wheezed an inaudible snicker, shaking his head. He released the rifle's hammer and lowered it. "Awe, shit."

Van, slowly struggling to load his rifle with trembling fingers, stopped to gaze at Mather. "Wuh-wuh-wuh-what?"

"Got some drunkard passed out in the cage. Can sure grind the gravel, can't he?" He shook his head. "Hope he ain't married. Poor woman."

Van sighed with relief, wiping his forehead with his sleeve. "Who?"

"Uhh, I dunno. Says his name is Julian Haynes? *I dunno!*" He emphasized those last two words, as if Van had asked a stupid, irrelevant question. "Some lawyer feller from New England, I guess. Bridgewater, Massa—Massachusetts? Got his whole life story. Hell, the whole damn café practically did, the way he carried on." Mather pulled each sidearm from its dry holster, checking their full cylinders. "Anyway, he was causin such a damn commotion in Miller's earlier, lookin for a, a sherry cobbler. Damn fool. Told'im it was a dry town, but of course, he don't listen. Gave him plenty warnin. Then he started gettin handsy with Sheyenne, so, you know, I hauled his ass right in. Swear to Christ, it was like he *wanted* to get tossed in a cell. Sumbitch passed right out. Guess all he needed was a bed for the night. Feller looked like he had enough forty-rod to kill a goddamn horse. That boy's gonna need the Gold Cure when he's finally brung back from the dead."

Van knew of forty-rod. Some cheap, dank, bathtub whiskey strong enough that, if one drank it, they'd just about stumble forty rods—about an eighth of a mile—before finally collapsing. Needless to say, Van had never tried it. "Gold Cure?"

"Strychnine, arsenic, and atropine. Looks like pure gold when they stick ya with the hypodermic. Be in fine fettle after that, I assure you."

"Ain't some of those poisons?"

"The *poison* is what's runnin through that boy's veins. Be right back with them rifles, son." Mather turned to walk, then spun back to Van. "Somethin comes rappin at that front door…"

Van gulped. "Yuh-yeah?"

"Don't answer it." Mather's mouth twisted into a sardonic grin as he continued across the room to the open doorway on the far right.

2

As Mather neared the cage, the retched warbling increased, as did his smile. He could relate to the current state of Mr. Haynes, though he himself was now ten years sober. *At least* someone's *having fun tonight.*

He entered the dimly lit back room and took the corner. Half of the room, similar in size to the front, contained several interconnected metal cells along its length. Haynes, in the furthest cell, lay slumped over a wooden cot on his front side, mouth open, spittle clinging to his lower lip and dribbling down his brown three-piece suit. His curly blonde locks formed a parasol, veiling his wretched face, while his leg and arm draped over the same right side.

Mather smiled and shook his head as he stepped in, fumbling in his pocket for the cabinet keys. *Oh, to be young and stupid.* He looked up, stopping dead in his tracks.

Directly in front of him, in front of the cabinet, loomed an unfathomable creature. The tall, shiny blue figure peered into the cell, next to a wide-open window—one which Mather realized he'd never closed after the afternoon heat.

The creature stared at the man on the cot, head gently cocked to the side. Its figure looked slender, though quite muscular. Sinewy. He could just about see every fibrous thread of its long arms resting at its side. And tall. Taller than any man Mather could recall ever seeing. It briefly reminded him of the Tallest Man Alive at P.T. Barnum's show, which he'd seen some twenty years ago.

Its skin glistened with a strange yet beautiful metallic sheen, an iridescence which shifted in varying color in the soft pool of the wall lamp glow behind. Cerulean. Sky blue. Gunmetal gray. Slate.

With its backside to Mather, it displayed another fascinating oddity. A design, of sorts, slightly darker than its dynamic skin tone, yet still noticeable. The pattern stretched across its upper back, around its neck, and along its shoulders, quite like the designs of different indigenous peoples he'd encountered over the years. Intricate patchwork, thick, a weaving of infinite curved lines and pointed edges. He imagined the tribal art wrapping around the thing's chest, though he couldn't quite tell.

The branch-like projections emanating from this creature's upper back and hips, however, disquieted him. Forearms. Calves. Similar to the body art, they too had curved, pointed edges. Frayed, singed pieces of what appeared to be some gossamer material, almost translucent, clung to the branches. Its chest heaved lightly, shoulders rising just so with every gurgling breath.

The "snoring" sure as shit wasn't this Haynes feller. It rattled from the unholy *thing,* apparently capable of taking out Chisum's regulators.

The creature raised its arm, gently slipped between the cell bars, and smoothly slid the door open, instantly popping the locking mechanism.

Clank! Clink-clink-clink.

The fucking keys slipped through Mather's shaking hand. He squeezed shut his eyes, heart stopping. Breathless.

He exhaled fully, prying open his lids. The blue creature turned slightly, blinking at him. He stood quivering, now staring into those dark red orbs. Its lids fluttered opened and shut on an angle. The lower left met the upper right at dead center.

Once Mather—*partially*—regained control of his faculties, he did the only thing he knew he could do.

Panic.

Fumbling and inadvertently firing his rifle, he stumbled backward out of the doorway, whirling feverishly into the main office. Van, loading a Colt pistol, nearly jumped out of his seat.

Mather paused, gripping his riffle in both fists. "Son, I don't think those rifles are gonna cut it."

"Huh?" Van, befuddled, peered between Mather and the back entryway.

Mather looked behind, too. Long, shiny fingers slid around the door frame with ghoulish languor, followed by a gripping blue hand. The sharp tips dug into the wooden panel, cracking.

Mather slammed open the door and broke out into a full—

"RUN!"

3

Potter swung open Reynolds's Buy & Sell's door and stepped back outside with precipitating caution. Though he struggled to watch his every step, clumps of dark curls obstructed his view.

Clara, nestled in his right arm, held tight around his neck with her head buried in the nook, almost under his coat. Nora followed directly behind, Isaac's hand gripped in hers.

Potter, safely descending the few steps, swung right, the church in his veiled sight. Distant carriages hauled ass out of town, vanishing into the void of night along with the fading stride of trotting hooves tearing up the loamy earth. Evidently, not everyone trusted the new mayor's advice.

With the last coach disappearing into the horizon, Main Street stood barren, save for the remains of the ghastly, inexplicable scene involving the Dotterweichs and their broken stagecoach.

The omnipresent, vile trilling reverberated throughout Main Street, interrupting their stride with halting trepidation.

Christ, where—where's it coming from? Fully exposed, Potter spun about with no means to tell, craning his neck to glance up and down Main.

"What is that, Bill," Nora muttered.

"I don't like it," Clara, groaning behind her pa's head, emphasized each word with utter dismay.

Potter charged ahead, forging their path. "Keep going."

The church neared, the faint shimmer of the lamp casting its scanty glow over the double doors. Potter, breathing heavily from an open mouth, trudged forward, condensation drifting before him. A chill hung in the air, the temperature gently dropping as the night sky crept forward. Beyond the church, the canary moon loomed, large and ominous, dwarfing the Capitan's jagged green silhouette below. The mountains appeared eons away from them, from any neighboring civilization. Potter had never felt so alone.

The left door of the church swung open. Coffey leaned out, holding the door with one arm while waving them in with the other.

Potter grinned and picked up the pace to an almost full-on jog, racing to enter the house of God. Now, knowing that hellish monsters existed, the unbeliever in him wondered if maybe... just maybe the Man upstairs did too. *If we're safe anywhere, it has to be church. Right?*

They hurried through the door. Safe.

Coffey's eyes scanned Main Street, now in his full view, before cutting the town off from their world with a quiet click of closing doors. Potter lowered Clara; she slid like a lead weight from his grip.

He turned to his friend. "What's the plan, Coffey. Where's Minister Healy?"

Coffey shrugged. "Bout to get a rude awakening."

4

Roswell, refusing to shelter inside a tight pantry with his potential abettors, found himself in the rectory with Chisum at the foot of Healy's cot. *The mayor can't be seen hiding in a time of panic and despair. The mayor solves problems.* To his dismay, the mayor hadn't another option.

Healy, oblivious to the world's happenings, lay cold in his white pulpit robe, now disheveled. A twisted green stole wrapped his forefront, and drops of purple stained the white clergy collar peeking through his black collared shirt. On the dresser rested an empty bottle of the holy sacrament and a stained bronze chalice. The woody aroma of fermented fruit pervaded, seeping from the pores of the unconscious minister.

The two men exchanged vexed looks.

"Wake him," Chisum said.

Roswell leaned over and clapped in his snoring face. "Healy! Come on, wake up! Hey, Minister! You in there!?"

The minister's mouth, locked open, expelled a cacophony of wretched snores filtered through a stench of stale burgundy strong enough to just about wake the dead.

"Oh, fuck this." Roswell grabbed each shoulder and shook the hell out of the minister, forcefully pumping him into the firm cot. "HEALY, WAKE UP FOR FUCK'S SAKE!"

"BAHH!" Healy's eye snapped open, and he shot bolt upright. "Wuh-wuh-whu-what—what's going on, for the love of all Holiness!?" Panting, he rubbed his eyes with his palm heels, glanced around to verify that he remained in the house of God, and blinked at both men in front. "John? Roswell? Well, what-what time is it, gentlemen, for crying out loud—"

"Time to get up," Chisum demanded, cutting off Healy. "We got a situation."

5

Mather fled the office posthaste, cutting straight up Main.

"Marshal, wait," Van called from behind.

Mather, panting and out of breath, turned to see Van sliding to a dust-plumed halt in front of Miller's illuminated café. The boy pointed to where its proprietor stood behind the counter.

The marshal shook his head, dumbfounded. "Why the hell we stoppin, son!?"

"Miller—I remember him sayin he's got weapons!"

Mather glanced at the church, right in his grasp, then looked back at his companion with a raised brow.

Van's face twisted with incredulity. "He-he's just standin in there. Out in the open."

"Okay?"

"Polishin... glass."

Mather, wanting nothing more than to beeline it to the church, groaned under his breath. They could undoubtedly use whatever weapons Miller possessed. Sheyenne, too, came to mind.

He wanted to ensure *her* safety: this Apache woman who'd taken possession of his old ticker. And the timing couldn't have been worse, now that he'd have to answer to the soon-to-be appointed mayor. *Kiss that silver star goodbye, son.* Hell, for all he knew, he'd soon be shackled in his own jail for miscegenation. An Indian was considered persona non grata in these parts, and the law strictly forbade engaging in relationships of a sexual nature with them.

Marshal David Mather, having never previously broken a rule, again wondered how and, furthermore, *why* this forbidden fruit tasted so delicious. Yes, she was younger, much younger, with her striking features and tawny skin. She certainly lit up any room through which she breezed. But that wasn't it. Not all of it. There was something arousing in the fact that an old stickler such as himself, a pencil pushing slough, could have this secret edgy side. But who was he kidding? Any man playing with at least half a deck had to assume.

He took one longing look back at the church before jogging strenuously over to Van.

They entered together, the butterfly doors swinging behind the men on its squeaky hinges. Miller, not even looking over, poured two-fingers of some pale-yellow liquid into a rocks glass. The sharp aroma of botanicals permeated, assaulting Mather's sensitive nostrils; he immediately identified the gin, despite the many years since his last encounter.

"What, uh... what are you doin, Gus?" Mather sauntered toward the counter with an incredulous glance.

Miller threw back his glass. "Jus 'avin a wee bit o' drink, Marshal. You gonna *haul* me in, eh?"

"I'm, uh"—Mather swallowed—"afraid the jail is fully occupied. We don't have access to our firearms."

"The mad drunkard you arrested got em, eh?" Miller smirked and threw back two more fingers of gin.

"Whatever that *thing* is that decimated Chisum's ranch, it's inside my jail."

"Might I interest you in a tot?" Miller poured the shot before finishing the question.

Mather hesitated, staring longingly, then looked up. "Better make it a double."

Miller's eyes lit up, and he flashed a crooked grin. His gold teeth twinkled as he poured Mather the glass, then offered one to Van, who politely declined with a raised hand.

Mather threw the double back, the familiar burn igniting his senses.

Miller kept his focus on Van. "You sure, Smith? You look a bit peelie-wally."

"No. Where are the other folks?" Van swiveled his head around the empty café.

"Storage room, 'idin. Jus like you said."

"What! Why? I said to get everyone to the church!"

Miller shrugged. "Your father felt differently, I suppose."

Van's face twisted. "Huh."

Mather glanced up, sensing something in Van's tone. "What is it, son?"

"Nothin, never mind. Are they at least safe here?"

"Aye, bout as safe as a twenty-year-old can o' tomatoes, I reckon. Which, incidentally, I've got."

"I don't know how I feel about old tomatoes. Why ain't you in there with them?"

"Don't like tight spaces. Besides... I've lived a long time, fellers. Lived in many places. I can tell you this: if there's one thing you can be certain o', is that you can't stop what's comin for you. You can't cheat fate, nae, sir. Nae matter 'ow long you run an 'ide. Best to stand up, face it 'ead on, I say."

Mather wondered if Miller would keep that sentiment if he knew exactly what the threat entailed. "Sheyenne with them?"

"Aye."

"Good, good." And for him, that was enough. "Uh, look, Gus. I know I've never asked, but I can only assume you have protection here. God willin, you do. We could use every weapon you've got here."

"I'm sorry, Marshal. All I've got is my twelve-gauge be'ind the counter." Miller pulled it out along with a box of shells. "Whatever this is, I'll be joinin the fight, if you don't mind."

"Then let's get to the church. The others are waitin on us."

Miller killed the lights, and the three crept out the door with a gentle stride across the porch, down the steps, and onto Main Street. Amber streetlight reflected in ten small pools on either side. With the eldritch glow over the valley, Mather could just about see the entire strip.

He glanced up and down. All clear. "You two stay close behind. Keep vigilant, ya hear me? Let's cross."

And they did. Slow, deliberate steps. The loam crushed under each boot heel. Beyond the resounding footfalls, only the rumbling of a working windmill behind broke the silence, twisting in the breeze. Not that Missouri Plaza was known for its nightlife—it wasn't—but Mather couldn't remember the last time he saw the streets so empty, especially at this hour. Still, a good feeling warmed his whole body as he approached the church, now in sight. All looked fine in the west. Though hilariously under-armed, they would be safe once they reached the basement. Only a matter of time until help arrived.

A slow, sonorous trilling shattered the crisp air and swept up Main, rattling the men. They stopped, only halfway across the street.

Miller gripped the shotgun to his chest, peering up and around. "What's that, Marshal?"

"Somethin that's risen from the depths of hell."

"Is-is-is it near? It sounds near." Van's raised rifle trembled in his armpit crook.

"Don't—nobody—move," Mather muttered. His torso spun in a creeping semi-circle, rifle held high at the ready. His shifting eyes froze halfway. "It's right behind us."

"Oh, oh, Christ," Van whimpered.

"Standin in front of my office."

"What do we do?"

"I have a strange feelin, fellers." Mather racked his brain. "These bullets we got ain't gonna do it. However, they may be enough to slow that thing down and give us a head start. When I say 'when,' we fire and run down that alley, there." He nodded ahead. "Maybe we can divert it away before we reach the church."

Miller and Van exchanged an affirming glance.

Mather nodded. "Ready... *WHEN!*"

Mather turned and fired his rifle, then took off full pelt for the alley between Taylor's Tailor & Clothier and Reynolds's Buy & Sell, watching over his shoulder. Seconds later, a conservative blast from Van's three-round shotgun echoed through the air. The creature instantly recoiled to the side, seemingly before the first squeezed trigger, leaving the delayed shot from Van's rifle to blow out the marshal's front window.

Still looking backward, Mather's boot caught the jagged edge of a rock. A popping sound filled his ears, and a jolt of pain shot up his leg as he lurched into a sideways somersault. The impact knocked the wind clean out of him. Miller slowed and grabbed the marshal from behind by the collar.

"Don' fuckin stop, mate!" He yanked until Mather returned to his feet.

Van, right behind, shoved him onward, causing Mather to actually scream in pain. They took the corner around the back of the clothier, Mather in full limp, and backed against the wall.

"You-you think it-it-it-it saw us!?" Van, at the edge of the building, turned to give shallow glances up the alley.

"Shit, my damn ankle! I—I think I twisted it!" Mather placed a hand on Miller's shoulder, preparing to put weight on his foot.

"Can you walk on it, mate?"

"I-I think so. Not very fast, though." Mather gently increased the pressure, a whimpering moan escaping him inadvertently. Agony.

Trilling reverberated over Missouri Plaza, averting their attention to the town's walls and the valley sky.

"I say we make a stand 'ere," Miller said. "Wait for it to come, and we ambush it before it follows us to the church!"

"I think thuh-that's a-a bad idea. They say it..." Van gulped. "It killed all Mr. Chisum's men."

"Well, 'ow the 'ell can that be, mate!? What we talkin about 'ere—it's just a damn man, ain't it!?"

"What I saw ain't no man." Mather panted; his face twisted in revulsion.

His simple plan to take a few men and arm them with the town's meager weapons stockpile had gone horribly awry. Roswell, in his first, albeit mostly unofficial act of leadership as self-appointed mayor, had managed to vaguely lull the naïve townsfolk into a false sense of security. But *he* was marshal. Missouri Plaza was still *his* town, and keeping its people safe was *his* duty.

He shook his head. "But you're right, Gus. I don't know if I can make it, and we can't lead it to the church."

"Well." Miller pumped the shotgun. "So be it, mates. You boys ready?"

"No!" Van squeaked in protest, shaking his head.

Mather nodded. "Okay, fellers."

Miller jumped out to face the alley, Mather hobbling behind. Van simply twisted around the corner and hung by the edge.

An empty, silent street met them.

The three stood perfectly still, guns out, staring at their own breath dissipating into the shadows of the muted alley.

Miller shook his head. "I don't see nothin, Mather."

"Muh-muh-maybe it-it-it's gone," Van muttered, inching backward behind the corner.

"And where do you suppose *you're* 'eaded, Smith?"

Van craned his neck, eyeing the church. "I-I-I can't do this."

Mather gaped, lowering his rifle. "*What!?* Pull yourself together, son!"

"I-I-I got this-this here town to consider. Muh-me an-and muh-my old man. I-I-I can't die here. Not like this. Sorry fellers!" Van turned and began an apathetic sprint toward deliverance.

Miller shook a fist. "For fuck's sake, Smith!"

"Smith!" Mather hobbled out of the alley in a feeble attempt to stop him. "Smith!"

6

Miller, the last man standing, peered up the vacant alley, giving a last inspection before backing out. He turned the corner.

Three black serrated edges sliced through the flesh under his jugular, shredding the windpipe. Fast. Clean. Deep. The sensation resembled that of a paper cut, swiftly replaced by the chilling embrace of the breezy, arid night. A surge of warm liquid followed, splashing his puffy white arm sleeves still out in front, holding the shotgun. Mouth agape, he struggled to pull in shallow gasps of air, choking.

The blue creature, which had dropped from the roof, reached into Miller's open mouth and pulled out both gold teeth with ease.

Stumbling back, Miller tripped on Mather's rock, firing the clenched shotgun into the creature's chest. It rocketed backward into the dirt before he fell away himself, both swallowed up by the alley's shadows.

7

Mather shuddered and turned toward the jarring shotgun blast. "Miller!" He shouted at the shadowed alley.

Impenetrable darkness. Nothing but the agony of Miller's desperate, dissipating gasps echoed back.

Mather turned to Van and did a double take. The coward was halfway to the church already.

"Goddamn it!" Mather hesitated, looking back for any signs of the downed creature... for Miller, who could be heard no more.

Chapter 24

Chisum wiped an age of grime down his slacks, swearing to himself. The hanky from his blazer pocket lay draped over a pew upstairs. Of course. Sweat beaded his flushed face, and dark ovals formed under the thinning pits of his white Oxford shirt.

He glanced around the peculiar basement, making sure they'd gained all the leftover materials from when Van and Aaron had completed their renovation job several years earlier. In a corner of the six-foot high room, amidst the shelving of unused Christian artifacts owned by Healy, sat additional sheets of scrap wood along with limestone blocks and granite stones, ones used for the front steps and foundation. Nothing that would help them now, though.

He handed off the last of the wooden panels from the bottom of the basement stairs to Roswell, squatting above. Then he climbed back up the ladder and crawled from the opening, previously hidden by a sliding platform built into the chancel which held the Lord's table. Shaking his head in disbelief at the underground compartment, he turned to glance about the church.

Potter and his son worked one side of the nave, boarding up the row of three narrow windows. Potter held the long, awkward panel while the boy hammered away using a chipped limestone brick. Coffey and Ms. Reynolds worked the opposite wall. Potter's little girl sat in the front pew, wrapped tightly in her coat and staring at some glass toy in her lap. She turned it over in her delicate hands, adrift and largely unnoticed. At the back wall, Healy kneeled, swaying, deep in inebriated prayer, facing a five-foot cross of southern yellow pine suspended in front of the vivid stained-glass window with Our Lady of Grace.

Chisum studied the glass before turning to Roswell. "How're we gonna board *that* up?"

Roswell, also down to a white button-down, looked up indifferently, narrowed his bushy eyes, and shrugged.

The double doors shook violently. Everyone stopped, the sound drawing the current congregation from a focused fortification effort to an exchange of befuddled glances. Healy stood hastily and turned, almost tripping over his own feet under his discombobulated robe. He habitually crossed himself.

"Christ Almighty, it's here, ain't it. It found us!" Chisum gripped his hat with two fists. Beads of sweat rolled down over furrowed brows. "We need to get inside the basement now!" He glanced at the opening, then back at the entrance. Even the notion of the basement brought little comfort, considering what he'd witnessed tonight.

The doors heaved back and forth, threatening to rip from their dusty hinges, but a two-by-four plank wedged in between the handles prevented their opening. Barely. The shaking ceased, immediately followed with—

RAP—RAP—RAP—RAP—RAP—RAP—RAP—RAP!

Coffey, closet to the doors, looked back to a deadpan Potter. The little girl shoved the crystal into her coat pocket, turned, and kneeled on the pew, leaning over the backrest to view the commotion.

The doors shook again.

RAP—RAP—RAP—RAP—RAP—RAP—RAP—RAP!

"Hey, hey, fuckin open up in there, Christ," someone called from outside. "Come on—quickly, quickly!"

2

Coffey ran to the door and slid out the two-by-four. Van exploded inside, flinging the doors open so hard, they almost snapped back shut. Coffey grabbed them just in time and prepared to reseal the entrance, but distant shouting halted him. He peeked his head out through a narrow opening. Mather, tearing ass from the dark, came into focus.

"Wait for me, goddammit!" Mather's heavy frame shook as he shuffled up the stone steps, panting past Coffey.

Coffey glanced out at Main Street, now empty, before shutting the doors and replacing the barrier.

"Vance!" Roswell stepped toward his son. "Praise Jesus, you all right? What happened out there, son? Tell me!"

Coffey could see the haunted look in the boy's eyes, a reflection of the same hellish encounter that he himself had narrowly escaped. He watched Van lean forward between the first set of pews, hands resting on shaky thighs, head shaking; he couldn't catch his breath to speak.

"What happened?" Chisum repeated, incredulous. "*What happened? How bout 'where are the goddamn guns, Mather!?'*"

"Guns!?" Mather howled. "That *thing* out there just picked off Miller, for God's sake! Forget the shittin guns, there ain't no guns!" He grabbed a handkerchief laid on a pew and, with the whistling sound of the Union Pacific, wiped the mucus running from his nose into bushy salt and pepper whiskers.

"What do you mean, 'picked off,'" Nora asked.

"Dead, Nora. It just swept in and snatched the life from him like"—Mather snapped his fingers—"*that.*"

Nora's face twisted in horror; she reached an arm around Potter's waist and leaned into his sleeve to hide watering eyes.

"Did-did you see it, huh? Where is it now?" Chisum demanded.

"I—I don't know." Mather's head shook. "Out there somewhere. Miller hit it with the shotgun, and it fell to the ground."

"Is-is it dead?" Roswell perked up.

"It took a close-range twelve-gauge blast to the chest. I'd say it ain't doing too well, wouldn't you say?"

Roswell hurriedly panned to inspect the room. "How's the windows?"

"Other than the stained glass, it's done," Potter said.

"Then let's hope the fact it can't see in saves all our hides. It's time to go below. Wait for the authorities."

3

The nine strolled up the center nave toward the chancel, Roswell in the lead. Potter paused where Clara waited in the aisle for her pa, taking her hand.

Strange squeaking, high above, broke the brief solace. A faint chirping. Potter looked up, but beyond the wall lamps, only darkness veiled the ceiling.

Clara, walking alongside, squeezed his hand. "What is that, Pa?"

By this time, all nine paused, heads staring up. A shadow finally emerged and fluttered into view. Small. Birdlike. It shot over the group, vanishing again.

"Just a bat, darling, is all."

The group resumed. As they neared the chancel, two more bats swished down from directly above. A moment later, two more, then immediately three.

Potter squinted. "They must be coming from the bell tower."

Tough to see. Only a large, square vent separated the cupola from the church. Through its wide cracks, a black cloud of screeching bats suddenly poured into the sanctuary, erratically firing in every direction over the group. A deep scraping followed, sharp and scattered.

"Get to the basement!" Chisum squawked.

Potter scooped up Clara, scurried into the sanctuary, and climbed up onto the chancel behind the minister, his employer, and the soon-to-be-appointed mayor. Nora and Isaac followed. The open basement loomed beneath; above, an unrestrained grinding amplified to a thundering clatter.

"STOP!" Coffey shouted from behind.

Potter turned his head. His friend threw back one arm, blocking Vance and Mather, and reached out with the other for the group ahead of him, as if his determination alone could stop what happened next.

The tower bell plummeted through the vent. Potter twisted and fell to his knees, shielding his daughter as the bell fell straight into the basement hole, wedging itself in the opening. The clapper, which hung inside, struck the bronze edge, casting its final, yet sonorous—almost deafening—carillon pitch. Roswell and Chisum, mere inches from the opening, braced themselves; the impact sent them stumbling backward from its path of destruction. Everyone covered their ears under a thick plume of dust.

The moment the ringing settled into a dull roar, and hands began to unfasten from ears, a resounding shriek filled the sanctuary. Potter quivered at the startling yelp of his daughter, still embraced. Slowly, he looked ahead.

The creature stood atop the bell, chest heaving, almost pulsing in and out. Its eyes blinked, surveying the group.

Nora, now by Potter's still kneeling side, grasped his shoulder tightly. "Bill, what—what is that!?"

Healy, behind the bell, staggered to his feet and pulled the cross from under his robe. He held it out in front and began taking small steps backward, reciting prayer. "Let the Lord be our protector against the wickedness and snares of the devil! May the Lord rebuke him! Prince of the Heavenly Host, by the power of the Lord, thrust back to hell Satan and all the evil spirits who wander through the world—"

The creature hopped down in front of the gaping Healy, wrapped a hand around his clergy collar, and squeezed his throat to lift him two feet from the floor. Cross still out, shaking in his chubby fist, Healy continued reciting through gritted teeth and strained breath, his face beet red. The creature's head, mere inches from Healy's, turned slightly and blinked at Healy, his terrified, bowed reflection reflecting in those giant red orbs. Its jaw separated in the middle, just enough to expose rows of tiny, serrated teeth, pinchers on each end, tips clicking. From deep within came the guttural warbling, rippling through the church. The creature's moist nostrils flared, seemingly taking in Healy's scent. The man's body unstiffened only slightly, eyes fixated and still brimming with unmistakable fear.

Potter gaped. *Is this communication?*

From behind—way behind, between the middle pews—Mather and Vance held their rifles out, sights set.

"When you get a lock on, son," Mather said, one eye closed, staring down the barrel with the other, "you shoot that sumbitch. You got it?"

"No." The rifle trembled in Van's grip.

"No, wait." Coffey, standing in front of the two men, put both arms out. "You'll hit the minister!"

The creature warbled again. With its long hand tucked under the minister's fleshy jowls, it gently twisted his head side to side and glanced the heavyset man up and down.

"Wuh-wuh-what," Healy eeked out.

The being dropped Healy on his heels; his legs gave way under the weight of his body, sending him falling backward.

Potter pried Clara from his neck and handed her off to an unexpecting Nora, still staring in shock and awe at the monster before her. "Take Clara. *Hide!*"

"Huh," Nora turned, and, without consideration, found Clara already in her arms.

"*Noooo,* Pa!" Clara reached for her father's neck instead, grabbing a fist full of coat collar as she squirmed from Nora's grip.

"GO! NOW!" Potter gave Nora a firm nudge, yanking his coat through Clara's clenched claws.

She wailed, arms stretched out in Nora's tight grip as she ran left past the front pews, around the sanctuary, and toward the rectory.

With one last glance at his retreating loved ones, Potter pulled his pristine LeMat pistols and moved quickly backward down the center, firing at the creature. Muzzle blasts emerged from close behind as Mather and Van joined the assault on either side, exchanging intermittent rounds at the blue devil. Aiming while moving proved difficult in the dim lighting; only one or two bullets struck the creature's back through its shredded wings. Red eyes narrowing, it fully swung around to face the firing squad.

Potter stopped and squeezed off four rapid shots, hitting its chest.

Christ, he nearly overlooked the thrill, the electric surge of energy pulsing in his blood when harnessing such brutal authority. It wasn't the expungement of another soul, no. You bottled that remorse, stored it away, and hoped the cork stayed plugged. But despite Warren's appearance, haunting Potter's subconscious, killing the man and his brothers had rekindled something in him. A rather onerous, for lack of a better word, *pleasure*. Perhaps it took more than dipping a toe back in that murky water to believe this sensation wasn't a fluke. Despite the sentiment, in the end, the crux of the matter always came down to one thing: prevailing.

He paused, noticing a strange anomaly. Each bullet that struck lit up the creature's torso, radiating a brief glow, a shockwave that lasted only for an instant. Almost unperceivable. Jagged lines, cracks, perhaps, displayed too, at least momentarily. If he saw true *damage,* maybe they could put an end to this thing after all.

"Potter," Mather shouted. "What are you doin!?" Rounds fell from a brimming pants pocket as he fumbled to reload the Winchester.

The blue being lunged over the bell, over the sanctuary, landing ever so gently in the aisle between the front pews. It stepped slowly forward, advancing the men, driving them backward as Van and Mather fumbled to reload. Twenty-five, thirty feet away. With a clear view of his target's head, Potter opened fire again, heedful of his limited capacity. Though how many more shots would they *possibly* need? Head shots always guaranteed death.

With unrivaled speed, the creature crossed its face with both arms. Bullets struck its serrated forearm protrusions, ricocheting each round. One bullet zipped by Potter's head. Another struck a pew.

Shit.

4

Coffey crouched through a row of pews and scurried up the side to join Chisum and Roswell, working on the situation behind the mayhem. The bell, now wedged in at a forty-five-degree angle, was, of course, no ordinary bell at all. Van's father had specially ordered it, just like the stained-glass window, from the Vanduzen Bell Foundry in Cincinnati, known for their large, ostentatious ringers. The impressive four-foot-wide bell, a representative of freedom and an echo of divine power, now blocked their only passage for escape.

Coffey, squatting gently behind, wrapped his hands around the crown's edge on the bell's upward slant and pushed with all his might. Roswell and Chisum bent over either side, hands under the lip, and pulled too, trying to dislodge the mouth. Their crimson faces twisted with every pained grunt. Roswell kept counting to three and shouting *"lift!"*

"Together, gentlemen! Together! Count of three, let's go!" Roswell shouted again. "One, two, three!"

The men tried again. Chisum's sweaty grip faltered under the narrow lip; he slid right off, falling backward. Coffey fell to his knees, panting, out of breath.

"It's stuck! What are we gonna do now!?" Chisum patted his dripping forehead with a hanky.

"Uh," Roswell stuttered, looking around. "We break the window, make a run for it!"

"What good will that do? That thing will just hunt us down!"

Coffey peered back at the blue creature walking down the center nave, its singed back protrusions twitching irregularly. He shuddered.

5

Clara lay on the church floor, watching the men.

Ms. Nora had forgone the rectory idea, instead dragging Clara around the sanctuary and past the stained glass. There, they'd found Isaac huddled behind an armchair in the east corner. Ms. Nora had grabbed him, and they'd all slid to the floor together, swathed in her warm arms.

Peering out from beneath the pew, Clara strained to make out bits and pieces of the conversation at the other end of the church. *They can't move the bell on their own.* Ice gripped her heart as she glanced over to an oil lamp on a mantle between windows her pa and Ms. Nora had boarded up. She knew what she needed to do if only she could just muster the strength to rise... to overcome those nasty collywobbles coiling in her belly. She truly believed in faith over fear. Faith, thus far, had triumphed over fear in each instance since arriving in New Mexico. Pa had been right all along. Fear *was* poison—a slow killer which consumed its victim over a lifetime. She resisted its hold on her.

Clara burst up from the ground, Ms. Nora reaching to grab her and falling short. Ignoring shouts for her to "get back," Clara broke free and ran down the side of the nave, heading straight toward the mantle.

6

Potter, Mather, and Van neared the barricaded front door, their assault coming to a disquieting end. Potter, down to two rounds—his buckshot—conserved as much ammo as he could, holding off the blue being while Mather and Van struggled to reload their weapons. Still, the creature advanced slowly, meeting them halfway down the nave.

Movement drew Potter's eyes away from the creature. His daughter stood, nearly adjacent to the blue being, along the right-side wall. *No...*

Breathlessly, he watched her grab the lamp. Barely reaching it on her tiptoes, she managed to slide the base toward the edge, gripping the bottom to carefully lift it down and extinguish the flame.

Mather continued to fumble, loading the Winchester with the last of his pocket's contents. Van filled his last cylinder and snapped it back into place. Now the three of them watched in spine-tingling horror as Clara turned to make her way back.

The creature paused with a slight twist of the head.

Potter's previously pounding heart stopped in his heaving chest, plummeting into his sour gut. *This thing's field of vision must be vast.*

It turned to Clara, also watching. She gaped up at the creature, the lamp clutched tight against her chest. The blue being blinked at her. Its head slowly cocked to one side, then the other, looking her up and down.

"NO," Potter murmured, prayed, watching the exchange.

It took a lengthy step in her direction.

BOOM!

Potter's buckshot hit the back of the creature's neck, chipping away some material that fell, rattling across the hardwood floor. The blue being belched a shrill squeal, followed by a low, gritty grumble as it turned back. Its shimmering, azure skin tone suddenly darkened several shades, seamlessly blending with its tribal body markings.

"Hey, you sonovabitch," Potter screamed. "We're over here, come on!"

The blue being leaned in and ripped a pew from the ground, launching down the aisle. Nowhere to run; no time to duck. Potter struggled to lift his arms, barely able to brace himself. Van, now on his Colts, kept firing. Shots ripped into the pew before the wood smashed into both him and Potter, clotheslining them, and instantly taking them down.

The pew barely missed Mather, who began firing his rifle once again, getting off two rounds.

The bench landed awkwardly, partially leaning on the end armrest of one pew; the other end fell atop Potter. The impact to his head—though mostly blocked by his arms, now in tremendous pain—threw off his equilibrium, giving him instant spins. He glanced around at the pews, now furiously twisting and swirling around him.

The creature bounded to the marshal, grabbed his fleshy neck, and lifted him from the ground. It looked him straight in his bulging, blood-shot eyes, blinking almost inquisitively. Analytically. Its nostrils flared.

Van, on the opposite side, crawled from under the pew and reached for his pistol. From the ground, he fired his last rounds, striking the creature in the lower back and tearing into its silky flesh. A green, viscous liquid splashed from the wound.

A high-pitched squeal belted from the being. It flung Mather backward, landing him perpendicularly across a row of back pews. He yelped in agony, his spine audibly crunching down on the top edge as his heavy body rolled onto a bench.

All around Potter, the world danced.

7

Nora watched from the pews as Clara ran to the bell men, the lamp in her small hands. Opening the base with tiny, quick fingers, she poured the oil down the wedged edge of each side of the basement opening.

Despite her terror, Nora beamed.

Chisum, too, watched in wide-eyed awe. "My god, is this Potter girl brilliant! Why the hell didn't *you* think of that, *mayor*!?"

The three men resumed their work. With much effort, they dislodged the heavy bell, rolling it out of the way.

Chisum instantly sprung down the basement ladder rungs, picking up Clara as he made his descent.

Coffey turned, waving for Nora. "Come on, Miss, Isaac!

Nora pushed Isaac ahead, running close behind him. He descended first.

She hesitated, looking around. "Bill! I don't see him!"

"Ain't no time, Ms. Nora," Coffey said with a gravelly tone.

"Ms. Reynolds, let's go now. Down the cellar!" Roswell stood in front of her, beckoning toward the opening. "We'll check on em. Don't you worry bout that, now. Quickly, ma'am!"

Anxiously, Nora peered beyond Roswell. He held her back, obstructing her view and coaxing her toward the opening. But, past his arms, she saw the only thing standing: the creature.

Holding back sobs, she descended.

8

Van jumped onto a bench and ran down to the side aisle. The creature lunged toward him, thrusting the pew from its path and knocking over those behind. Van hopped down just in time. Running up the aisle, he turned, fired two shots, then clicked several empty chambers at the blue being, which swiftly bounded diagonally, now facing him at the front of the nave.

His father, behind him, called out, "Come on, boy!"

Van stood unmoving, staring at the creature. "What about the marshal? Mr. Potter!?"

"Ain't no time! Vance..."

Van hesitated. Potter, under the bench, barely moved in a languid toil. Mather, out of sight, appeared to be down for the count. He swallowed hard, mouth bone dry. A ghost of a chance he'd make it to the basement.

He glanced down the row of pews next to him. On the ground, halfway down the center aisle, lay Potter's LeMat pistols. The creature stood an equal distance in the opposite direction.

He could do it. Oh, yes. If he could get close enough, he could do it. It bled. This, he knew. *And if it bleeds, it dies.* He knew one of those guns still had a final shotgun shell in its chamber. He stared at the creature, which stood, breathing, waiting—waiting for something only *it* knew.

"VANCE," his father screamed.

Van looked back toward the basement.

"Come on—let's go!"

In some deranged consideration beyond his own rational comprehension, he looked at the gun again, then shook his head. Suicide, surely. What in Sam Hill was he thinking?

The squeak of the pew drew his gaze from his departure. Potter. He pushed the pew off his chest and slid out from underneath, slowly, on his hands and knees. The creature turned.

Now. His chance to make it to the basement. He peered back at the gun, then to his father. Salvation loomed, waiting for him.

The creature moved toward Potter.

9

Potter glanced over at the vertiginous being. It whirled in dreary semicircles along with the dimming church, all obscured in the shadows of fading light. Still dizzy. *Fuck.* He scanned for his pistols. Mather's rifle lay within reach, ten feet away. Without thinking, he crawled toward it.

The creature moved in.

Potter reached for the rifle, narrowly grabbing it, and spun on his back. He snapped back on the action lever. The creature leapt forward, straddling him, leaning in. With a clear shot to the throat, he pointed the barrel, squeezed his eyes shut, and pulled the trigger.

Click!

Numbly, he unclenched his lids.

Those unsightly red eyes leaned in, two feet from his own. His curved reflection shined in each glossy orb. The three nostril slits fluttered with each dampened breath, taking in the scent of its prey. Cold exhalation washed over Potter' flushed face.

The creature snatched the rifle from Potter's grip, almost tearing off his fingers—still secured in the lever action loop—with it. It turned the weapon over in its long hands, caressing every curved edge; its eyelids flickered oddly. Admiration? Bewilderment? After studying the rifle's craftmanship, it cast a perplexed look down the barrel.

Potter recalled the Templar Knight's sword. If this thing dated back to the twelfth century, perhaps it had never encountered such power.

The creature snapped the riffle in two like a twig, throwing each half in either direction.

THWAP!

An empty rifle cracked the creature in the back of the head. "HEY!"

The being turned to Van, standing behind.

"COME ON! COME AND GET ME!" Van paced backward, waving at the blue creature.

It followed, though hesitantly.

"Come on, you sonovabitch!" He stepped slowly, firing quick glances back.

His father stood from the ladder halfway down the basement, watching with horror.

"I'm right here," he yelled. "Come on!"

The creature slowly but surely followed, now fifteen feet away.

Potter turned to Mather, face down, slumped across the bench. His mouth hung open, spittle dripping, and his arm draped off the edge of the pew.

"Hey, hey, Marshal!" Potter grabbed his shoulder, shaking him. "You alive!? Christ, Mather!"

"AHHH! Ughhh, careful, Potter—I'm awake, I'm awake," he said gravely, though his closed eyes begged to differ.

"Come on." Potter grabbed his arm, lifting.

A shrill, bloodcurdling howl fell from the man's wet lips. "I can't move, Potter. Everythin—everythin's numb."

"Mather...?" He glanced up the nave.

Van and the creature faced off at the other end of the church. Roswell's shouting voice echoed from the back. Slowly, he looked back to the marshal.

Mather struggled to open a tearing eye. "Best guess? Back's broken, son. You go on. Get out of here while ya can."

10

The creature inched closer to Van, now at the top of the aisle. Terrified, shaking, he stared up at its face, just as Potter did. His reflection stared back in those glossy red orbs. Possibly the last thing he'd ever see.

Regret flared in his gut. He'd given up a straight shot to the basement, and the rest would soon be headed toward salvation. Well, most of them.

But the marshal and Mr. Potter still had a fighting chance, if he could just drive this creature away.

He steeled himself. *They* had Plans. Van and his father. And with Plans, you needed people you could trust. They both liked the malleable marshal; there was history, there. And knowing Mather's "secret" would soon have its advantage. Potter—the unknown, the wild card—remained at the bottom of the Long List, but they figured they'd eventually dig up something, pun intended, from the man's past. No doubt, he would choose to repay his new savior in dividends, not to mention *property*, which would likely be theirs in time, anyway. 'Sides, Mr. Potter looked like a man you'd want working for you in the event of an unsavory element breezing through town. Van wanted, *needed,* to keep them both safe.

Plus, if he pulled this off quick, he'd be the savior of Missouri Plaza.

"I'm sendin you back to Hell!" With a clear shot to its vulnerable throat, Van pulled the LeMat tucked in his pants behind him—the hammer already all the way back, engaging the lower barrel—and squeezed the trigger. The Hammer cracked down with a short *ping*.

A puff of smoke.

The creature stood before him, unmoved.

Misfire.

Van's mouth dropped as the blue being approached. With one hand, it wrapped its long, pointed fingers around his throat and lifted him straight up. With the other, it squeezed Van's hand, still wrapped around the pistol. It crushed the carpels before twisting his arm around to complete a revolution. His shoulder tendons tore seamlessly inside of his shirt sleeve, his bones popping and snapping with ease. Before his brain could fully process the pain, long before it even signaled his mouth to scream, the creature tore his arm clean from its socket. Dark arterial blood surged from the opening.

Van groaned, gaping down at the void where his arm once lived. Blood beaded his face and open mouth. It tasted warm.

"NOOOOOO!" His father, twenty feet back, began to claw his way from the basement opening.

Van struggled to focus, to signal him to stop. *No...*

Coffey grabbed his father, straining to hold him back. Pa fought tooth and nail until one of them lost footing, both plunging back into the basement. Screams for "my boy" echoed up from below.

Van smiled, relieved, turning back to his reflection in those giant red eyes. Crimson spray from his shoulder showered the Antiquarian's cobalt body and bug-like face as it launched him straight back through his father's imported stained glass.

Colored shards rained down the basement opening below.

11

Potter glanced around for a viable weapon. Nothing. Well, almost nothing. He looked down at a glassy-eyed Mather.

The marshal returned his desperate gaze. "Help me up, son."

He hollered, eyes rolling tears as Potter pulled him from the bench and leaned him upright.

Mather pulled his pistols and, with trembling arms, raised them straight out. "I'll cover you—get to the basement."

Potter looked at Mather and nodded. He crossed the pew to the side aisle and paused as the creature turned around. Mather unloaded from each gun. Several bullets struck the Lord's table; a few more hit the pulpit. None hit their target.

The being darted its head about in confusion, peering around the back pews before it purposefully plodded down the center aisle. Potter, slunk against the wall, watched as it walked right by him toward Mather. With a sigh of relief, he took one gentle step to his right, toward his destination.

It stopped. Slowly, the creature turned its gaze toward Potter, standing against the wall, frozen between two boarded windows. The being bounded right over the entire row of pews, landing five feet to his left, head slinking around.

Potter's terror-stricken heart hopped and skipped as he fought to control the fierce, shallow breaths expelling from his lips. He gaped up at this creature's perplexing actions, struggling to anticipate its next move. His arm twitched as he recalled Van's ghastly groan of fear and incredulity, over and over, the sound forever singed into his brain.

He had no intention of having his own limb ripped from his shoulder socket.

His head finally stopped spinning, giving him a clear vision of their assailant. Foot by foot, the creature shifted closer to him. Its deep blue skin glistened and shimmered in the glowing eminence of the wall lamp behind Potter. It looked practically identical to the deceased thing in that inexplicable ironclad buried in his fucking back yard, except the living version was far worse. Hideous. Nothing short of horrific. It reminded him of an insect, a sort of praying mantis, though much more evolved. Humanistic.

It crossed directly in front of Potter and just... hovered. He stared at the chameleon-like body armor which wrapped its chiseled being. Quite different from what the Templar Knight offered. The armor changed color, similar to the being it protected, but it appeared to be wearing very thin with imperfections. Cracks. The back collar, Potter guessed, looked shredded away from his buckshot. Only a matter of time until it failed.

At least, he hoped.

The creature's head slowly shifted. Left. Right. Looking at either side of his head? Wet nostrils flared, breathing. Snuffing him out.

It cross-blinked rapidly, several times.

These peculiar mannerisms, impossible to grasp, utterly disquieted Potter. Was the creature studying him, or just toying with its prey like a wildcat? Potter once again saw his reflection in its eyes. Its jaw separated at the center, exposing pinchers on either end; a viscous, clear mucosa stretched with it. Behind, rows of tiny, serrated teeth gleamed.

One of the creature's arms stretched out sideways, its hand meeting the wall. It dug its fingers into the surface, tearing into the panel and slowly running along it. The opposite arm reciprocated, both inching toward Potter, both aligned with his throat.

Potter's mind drew blank. The last thing he wanted to see before his end were the eyes of the horrifying creature who did him in. He clenched his lids shut, the thumping of his jabbering heart nearly drowning out the grating of dragging claws. Nearly.

POP—POP—POP—POP—POP—POP!

Potter twitched; his eyes popped opened. Mather, slowly but surely, had reloaded his Colts.

The creature squealed and turned for Mather.

"Bill," someone shouted in a low tone.

Potter looked over.

Coffey, partially emerged from the basement, waved him in. "C'mon!"

Potter inched his way in Coffey's direction, keeping a close eye on the creature's pursuit of the gunfire.

Mather dropped one gun and, using the top lip of the pew as a crutch, fired four more rounds, all striking the creature's upper body. Still, the blue being quickly neared. Its back protrusions shifted, outstretching its obliterated wings.

Potter, halfway to the basement, stopped in his tracks, heart pounding as he stared through the frayed fabric of the creature's wingspan at the marshal. Yet he couldn't ignore Coffey's urgent cries coming from behind.

Mather stiffly inched his way down the row toward the center nave, sheer agony engraved on his red face. From the opposite end of the aisle, the creature locked eyes with Mather and thrust both pews flanking him apart. His broken body hit the ground with a scream. Before he could open his eyes, the blue being straddled him. He glared up at his empty, defenseless hands, the last gun inches out of reach.

The creature reached down for Mather. Its narrow fingers gripped each edge of his silver star, sharp tips clinking as it made contact, and pulled it off his shirt. It waved the metal under its active nostrils before its mouth quivered open, pinchers clanking against the steel. A moment later, the blue being slid the star into a concealed thigh-side compartment.

Curiosity furrowed Potter's brows as his mind drifted to the artifact room.

With its hands once again free, the creature lifted the anguished marshal horizontally into the air, pressed straight above its head. The ungodly sound ripped from Mather's lungs almost shook the Lord's table. Between those strange, pressing hands, his body began to bow, forming a slight U shape; the sound of his spine snapping and crumbling under pressure reverberated through the nave. A moment later, Mather fell silent. His head slumped over; his arms dangled, limp.

Potter couldn't tell whether the marshal had passed out from pain, but he suspected, hoped, the poor man had departed to meet his maker. He did know this: Mather and Van had saved him from meeting his own. No time, however, to ponder whether their sacrifices were in vain, though he doubted he would've stepped up the same, if the boot was on the other foot.

A hardened tug of his arm sent him off balance as Coffey yanked him backward toward the basement. The man didn't say a word, didn't even glance at the horror behind. Before Potter knew it, he found himself at the bottom of the ladder.

Roswell sprawled on the cold floor directly below, wailing into his palms between slightly incoherent mumbling. "My boy's gone, my flesh and blood is gone! I can't believe it—I can't believe it!"

Potter just stared up as Coffey slid the Lord's table overhead, sealing them below.

CHAPTER 25

Four wooden panel walls surrounded a clay-dusted hardwood floor, now heavily tracked by sinuous boot prints. The basement, though far less than half the size of the church, stretched large enough to serve as another livable space. Scattered effects from the minister's past back east, all kinds of intriguing items, occupied much of the tight, subterranean dwelling.

Artifacts. Wooden shelving lined one side wall, along with the entire back wall. Rows of small crates on the bottom, a reliquary of sorts, contained colored robes, lockets of hair, bone fragments. Strange shit. Large rubied crucifixes lay interspersed throughout, likely of catholic origin, Potter figured, since Methodists didn't so much subscribe to crosses with a crucified Jesus.

Sitting in the darkness, he took in his surroundings. Three rows of shelving stored dust-coated statuettes: random nativity characters and farm animals, Jesus praying, Jesus carrying the cross. Mainly, it presented an homage for various versions of the Virgin Mary and baby Jesus. One curious statue of Mary showed her straddling a serpent between her legs. The shelves above and below held more various sized crucifixes, silver and bronze candelabras, books (bibles, or maybe hymns), wine—bottles and bottles of wine, some empty, most corked—incense sticks (quite aromatic), drinking glasses, goblets, chalices, Saturn hats, and birettas. An upper shelf held a crate filled with, oddly enough, children's shoes.

But Potter found the paintings most interesting. Fourteen small canvases, stations of the cross, lined one section of bare wall, about three feet of space between each. Stacked paintings lay in the corner, too. Larger works. What appeared to be The Holy Family, The Last Supper... mostly religious subjects, but all exquisite works. Potter was no historian, but he'd been to the Wadsworth Museum. He knew a Rembrandt when he saw one. *The Return of the Prodigal Son.* Holy. Shit. Next to Rembrandt was Poussin's *Extreme Unction* and Vermeer's *The Allegory of Faith.* He could only guess what others.

Potter had seen a few such paintings visiting Saint Patrick's Holy Trinity in Hartford as a young man. Such cathedrals of exceptional merit would, from time to time, bring in significant works depicting a religious nature, splashed on canvas by the world's greatest artists. These pieces of art provided material for study and reflection by the fortunate few blessed with a classical education. At some point, Potter suspected, the paintings before him must've been on display for public viewing. If he was still a betting man, he'd put silver dollars on Yale College.

One corner of the basement stowed a rusted-over twin-size cot with a bare mattress and pillow; it squealed and squeaked as Healy kneeled beside it. He faced a large cross on the wall, elbows on the cot, his hands together in silent prayer. Every so often, he'd begin speaking aloud, his voice barely audible.

Next to the cot stood a mahogany credenza, presumably filled with clothes. A rocking chair sat in another corner, occupied by Chisum, who gently rocked up and down. Three chairs, possibly part of a kitchen or dining room set, lay scattered haphazardly, as if they'd been dropped and forgotten about. One held Coffey, sitting hunched over. With elbows resting on his thighs and hands tucked under his chin, he stared at the ground. Nora sprawled beside Potter on the floor, both their backs against the wall. Isaac and Clara sat nearby, playing with the holy figurines.

The oil lamp, the room's only meager light source, flickered in the center of the room, perilously low on fuel.

Coffey and Potter had boarded the hatch with the last of the stored paneling upon entering. Now, he wondered what good their barricade would do. Faith among the group had diminished since trapping themselves below. Only a matter of time until *it* found them.

Coffey's words, spoken just as they'd pulled the Lord's table shut behind him, echoed in his mind. *"I thought you was a goner. You's a real lucky man, Bill. Real lucky."*

Lucky... yes. Potter's entire existence had been built around the theory of luck. He possessed an incredulous and presumably innate ability to walk, hell, *parade* through the valley of the shadow of death with a big *fuck you*, continuing to elude Azrael, the pale rider... not that he actually *believed* in the archangel. But luck provided no answer. Not this time. The creature had cornered him. Toyed with him. Why? Its actions made little sense. Hell, none of tonight did.

But everyone else who crossed paths with the creature had suffered the same quick, violent fate.

Healy began again, barely audible. "Lord Jesus Christ, display your power in the world. You are a miracle-working God. Give us the strength to follow you and help us in time of trouble."

2

Clara maintained the farm, the nativity animals all gathered in a circle, protecting the baby Jesus. She stopped and glanced at her brother. Isaac held Joseph and Mary, running a thumb over the handcrafted curves and grooves of each piece.

"I'm scared," she admitted, her words barely a whisper. Mustering courage in the face of peril was one thing. This felt like something else entirely. Anticipating the inevitable, her faith began to falter. "Aren't you?"

Isaac looked up at her with confidence. "Na."

"What!?"

"Pa ain't gonna let anything happen to us. Never has. Never gonna."

"But *how* do you know?"

"You remember how he handled the Bad People that tried to hurt Mr. Coffey? Now they're best pals. And in return, Mr. Coffey got him that job protecting Mr. Chisum's ranch." Isaac smiled. "Our pa, Clara, is the toughest man you'll ever know."

Clara, recalling her father's heroics in the face of danger, nodded emphatically. The memory brought her a small sense of hope. A belief that they could escape the church basement alive.

She glanced over to where Ms. Nora and Pa sat hand in hand. They appeared happy, despite the evening's horrific events. She wondered how long their happiness would last, with that thing up there looking for them. Not to mention the Bad People.

Her stomach churned as she remembered her earlier conversation with Isaac, their secret misadventure into the pit. The nativity lamb shook in her hands. Now that the monster hunted them, Pa needed to know where it came from. But *that night* still haunted her. The whip of Pa's belt. Isaac's screams.

Unable to stop shaking, Clara dropped her porcelain sheep, walked over, and curled up next to her pa. No matter how much she upset him, she knew he'd never hurt her. And, in a tiny room full of people, her brother would be safe from his fury.

At least, she hoped.

3

Potter draped his arm over Clara. "How's my little girl?"

"Scared, Pa." She squeezed him tightly. "The monster is coming for *us*, Pa."

"Remind me of the truth of your power," Healy droned on. "Surround us so no one can pluck us from your hand. Remove our fear and replace it with faith in you, God. To you be all glory and power, forever and ever."

Potter's eyes narrowed. "Don't be silly, darling. You have nothing to fear, okay? I won't let anything happen to you, you hear me? None of us down here will."

Clara's eyes watered; she blinked tears. "Now that the monster wakened, the Bad People are gonna come take you away, aren't they?"

Chisum and Roswell both sat up in their chairs.

Potter tilted her head up with a finger under her chin so their eyes met. "What are you saying, Clara? What *Bad People*?"

She gave him a wistful, crooked smile. "The Bad People who want what's in that buried ship,"—she hesitated, then morosely added—"where we woke the monster."

Potter looked over at Isaac and said, loud enough for the entire room to hear, "what's she talking about, Isaac?"

Isaac's mouth dropped. "Uhhh..."

"Talk to me, Isaac," Potter commanded. "What's she talking about, *'Bad People?'* What *monster* did you's wake?"

"We-we-we was playing, Pa, an-and we went inside the well, and—"

"You did *what*!?"

"We-we-we didn't mean to, Pa! Honest, we didn't!"

Potter blinked. "What—did—you—do?"

"I'm sorry, Pa!" Isaac shuddered, beginning to cry.

Potter's face burned red. He stood and marched over to his son. "What I say, huh? I told you, boy, I told you to keep you and your sister out that goddamn pit!" Potter grabbed Isaac by the shoulders and shook him. "Didn't I!? Huh!?"

Isaac's crying flooded into a full-on bawl. The boy wheezed and shuddered with violent spasms, no longer able to form a coherent sentence.

"Don't, Pa!" Clara shouted.

"Bill!" Nora cried.

"I gave you one simple job while I'm away at work, boy. Just the one! She's just a little girl, for Christ's sake!"

Nora stood. "Bill, you stop that! Unhand that boy!"

Potter glared at his trembling son, then forced himself to let go and step back. He turned to find all eyes on him, mere shadows around the lantern's glow.

Clara stood fearfully latched onto Nora's waist. Horror... unmistakable horror filled his daughter's eyes as she spoke. "I'm not a little girl anymore."

Potter blinked at his daughter. Perhaps she spoke true. After tonight, he knew one thing for certain: she'd earned her seat at the table.

Healy broke from prayer and, in a loud but stern whisper, shouted, "Please, keep it down! That *thing* can hear us." He glared up at the boarded ceiling.

"What's your boy sayin, Potter," Roswell demanded.

Potter expelled a deep, guttural sigh. "We found something buried in the backyard. A ship of sorts."

"A ship," Chisum spoke up. "What kind of ship?"

"I—I don't know. I think it's an old ironclad gun ship. You know, from the war."

"Well, how the hell is that possible?"

Potter's eyes narrowed. "Came down the Pecos, I reckon. Figured that was obvious."

"But *why*?" Chisum, more inquisitive than irritated or surprised, turned to his right-hand man. "Coffey, you know bout this?"

Coffey sat straight back in his chair; he looked back and forth from Chisum to Potter. "Uhh, I, uhh—I—"

"Coffey didn't see anything," Potter interjected. "Me and the boy found it."

Roswell's face seared red, visible even in the dim lighting. "I recall, back at the mill, you sayin there was nothing else you found out there, right?"

"Look, I didn't want to draw any unnecessary attention to my property. And, frankly, it's none of your goddamn business what's buried in my yard," Potter said evenly.

He could've lied. Once, he'd devised various scenarios at the drop of a hat. But he knew none of his words would provide solace to Roswell, and, at the immediate moment, he didn't give much of a shit.

Roswell charged up to him. "Unnecessary! You failed to mention it was harborin fuckin monsters!"

Instinctually, Potter reached for his sidearm, shocked to grab a handful of air.

Chisum stepped between the two men. "Roswell."

Healy held up his hands. "Gentlemen, gentlemen, please. There are *other* powers at play here. Forces that are beyond—"

"Stay out of this, Padre," Roswell interrupted, still glaring at his opponent. "I'm the mayor of this town, Potter. Everythin is now my goddamn business, you'll be sure of that! We get out of this hole in the ground, you'll have a lot to answer to. Believe you me."

"What was in that ship, Potter?" Chisum, curious, pulled a half-smoked cigar from an inner pocket. Maybe he intended to light it, though he just rolled it back and forth between his fingers.

"Some gold trinkets, of sorts. Maybe some silver. Strange things. I don't know. Stuff from another time period, maybe."

"Just who the hell are you, Potter, huh," Roswell growled. "You show up here mysteriously. I've been solicitin Morgan Bennett for that property for years, to no avail. You show up in it and bring a whole heap of trouble to this small, quiet town."

Coffey stood. "C'mon now, boys, ain't no time for fightin. We got much bigger *things* to worry bout, here."

"Oh, piss up a tree, Coffey. I don't recall askin a no-good cotton-pickin spade's goddamn opinion. Only reason you're here and not upstairs with that thing is because of your association with this man right here." Roswell pointed to Chisum.

"Hey!" Chisum stepped in.

"Gonna be a lotta changes round here when this all is all over, I can promise you—"

"Hey, wait a minute, goddammit!" Chisum's round face reddened. "Now you're gonna watch how you speak to my *associate*, Smith. Ain't no cause for that kind of talk, you hearin me? And as for Potter, well, he's employed by me. A man of high character. Now we're terribly sorry your boy's gone. We are. He was a good kid. But that don't give you the goddamn right—"

"*The right!?* You wanna speak to me about *rights*!? As of this week, I am mayor of this town. And you better watch it, John Chisum. 'Cattle Baron of New Mexico.' How bout I order an investigation of *your* dealins? How'd that be? I'm sure some of those faces round your property might be the same ones I saw on a stack of wanted posters in my office."

Chisum's voice fell deathly quiet. "I am the largest, *cheapest* supplier of cattle from here to Santa Fe, east Texas, all the way to New Orleans. Puttin me out of business will piss off quite a lot of people who depend on my product. I don't think you'd want to contend with those consequences, *mayor*."

"Your product can stay. Anyone can herd cattle," Roswell declared. "I'm cleaning up this township when this is over. I'm no fool, John. You don't think I'm aware this little commune is chock full of degenerates? The dregs of this great commonwealth? Hell, it fuckin evolved from some disillusioned, Seventh-day Adventist Church outcasts runnin from whatever troublin nonsense they caused in Missouri! Accepting *anyone* who strolled on in. Talk about dregs. And where're they now, I ask?"

"We don't stop that thing upstairs, they'll be no town left to be mayor of." Coffey turned gravely to Potter. "Bill, what are we gonna do?"

Potter, standing stoically, glanced around. Expressionless. *Hell if I know.*

"We wait," Chisum answered. "The cavalry should be here in no time, I presume."

Potter glared at his employer. "The *cavalry*?"

"They've been dispatched to Missouri Plaza. Strangely enough, I was told they were already en route."

"Huh." Potter blinked.

"Who knows when, though? Could be days before they show, if they even show at all with those egregious green skies and whatever's in them. More of those... *things*? This could quickly become a widespread situation," Roswell spewed, still enraged. "And we haven't *any* recourse for such bizarre circumstances! And not to compound the problem, but we have no food. No water. We can't just get drunk off wine and hope for the best. We're trapped here like goddamn rats!"

"We need to put a plan into place. We need more weapons. Can we get to the marshal's office?" Chisum, in a cold sweat, patted his glistening forehead with his hanky.

"No, no, that's too risky. I don't wanna see anyone else hurt," Nora pleaded, hugging Clara in her arms.

"Besides, whatever the marshal's got won't be enough." Chisum finally shoved the cigar in his mouth, patting his jacket and waistcoat pockets in search of matches.

Potter barely heard them. *The cavalry.*

"Pa, what about the basement?" Isaac spoke up.

"Huh?" Potter glanced at his son.

"The rifles!"

"What's he sayin, Potter," Chisum asked.

"There's, uh, a stockpile of guns and ammunition buried in my basement." He looked at Isaac. "That's brilliant, boy."

Chisum cracked a smile. "I knew that old crackpot Bennett would finally prove useful! Sumbitch, sittin right on an arsenal cache under everyone's noses." He shook his head, finally found his match book, and struck a flame.

Roswell, still fuming, paced the room. "For God's sake, John, you're not gonna smoke that down here, are you?"

Potter blinked at Chisum's frayed cigar, remembering the old cigar Coffey had unearthed during their dig. The puzzle pieces shifted in his brain, clicking together. "My God."

"What is it, Bill," Coffey asked.

"He knew. Bennett. He knew all along." Potter turned to Coffey. "He didn't deliberately forgo the use of a well in his backyard. That sonovabitch knew! That was *his* cigar we found in the pit. He dug the well just as *we* did and found the ironclad. He was scared, Coffey. He feared what was down there, so he collected all those weapons."

Coffey's brow furrowed. "Ya think he got inside?"

"I-I-I don't know. Maybe. I mean, it was pretty easy for *me* to break in. Perhaps he blew it open, then did his best trying to seal it back shut. I don't know!"

"Bennett was a loon," Roswell spat bitterly. "And let's face it, he was *no* saint. Who knows what sordid things *the general* did during the war. Oh, I remember him and his *servant*. Saw them in town once, at Miller's, actually. Quite chummy, they were. That was also, incidentally, the last time I saw him. Anyone saw him, I might add. I'm willin to bet dollars to dog shit he ripped off those weapons after the war and stashed them away in case they came for him."

Ignoring Roswell, or perhaps wanting to spite him, Chisum struck his match and lit his cigar. "Regardless of his intentions, the question now is how the Christ you plan to get them."

Potter's head sunk.

I've no fucking clue.

4

Hours. Hours must have passed, surely. Exactly how long, Potter didn't know. An eternity?

The dim flicker of a fading oil lantern singed in the center of the silent basement floor. Any moment it would extinguish, leaving them in complete darkness. He stared at it from his seat on the floor at the back of the room, pleasantly surprised by its endurance. Nora sat next to him, head leaning on his shoulder.

Potter looked over at her, barely visible in the dim light. Shadows concealed her eyes, though patches of sun-kissed cheeks remained visible in the gloom. They glistened, wet.

"How you faring, Nora," he asked softly.

She sniffled. "I'm okay. Can't believe Van is gone. And the marshal. I've known them a long time. Good men, ya know? I don't understand any of this, Bill. Ain't you worried?"

"I think we'll get out of here."

"Not what I'm referrin to."

Potter sighed, needing no reminder of the authorities en route. He held little to no chance of passing unrecognized. Every unsavory bounty hunter had doubtless crawled from the squalid crevices of society to try their luck at seeking him out.

Potter shrugged. "They find me here, they find me here. I was stupid to think I could hide in Missouri Plaza."

Nora squeezed his hand. "What will they do to ya?"

"More worried about what they'd do to my family to get to me." A vision of hostages gunned down on the Kansas Pacific flashed before his eyes. He looked over at his children, sitting on the cot. He needed to find a way to get them out safely. "I've made a lot of poor decisions, Nora. Hurt good people to sustain my own precarious survival. I always knew, though; I'd never outrun it. All I wanted was enough time. Time to do right by them."

"I don't know nothin bout all that, Bill. All I've seen is a man who'd go to the ends of the earth for his children. That's all."

Potter offered a tentative smile. He wasn't so sure, but he wanted so much to believe her.

"You know you ain't the only one, either."

"Huh?"

"This town's full of people who don't wanna be found. We're most of em."

Potter shifted his gaze towards Nora, struggling to meet those captivating blues in the dim lighting.

"We ain't never gonna let anyone take one of our own, ya hear? If need be, we'll shove you and the kids down here till things cool off." She smiled, putting her arm around Potter's shoulder.

Coffey sat forward in his chair, looking up. "Things is mighty quiet up there."

"We should check it out," Chisum said. "See if that thing is gone. Besides, I gotta take a piss. Don't know bout anyone else."

"Good idea," Roswell said. "I vote Potter."

Potter stood. "Why me?"

Roswell rose too. "Well, because you are the reason we're all down here. And I don't think the rest of us deserve to suffer the consequences."

"Fine," Potter ground out through gritted teeth.

Coffey climbed to his feet as well. "I'll give ya a hand, Bill."

Potter climbed the ladder while Coffey held it steady. With the back of the claw hammer, he gently pulled each of the twenty or so nails. When he reached the final few, Chisum joined Coffey to support the hanging edges. Finally, the three men pried free the awkward board and gently lowered it to the ground.

Potter removed his hat and climbed the ladder once again, pulling the resistant hatch back. With some force, he dragged it less than a foot. *Time to grease these tracks, Healy.* He stuck his head through the narrow opening, where a cool breeze of welcome, fresh air ruffled his disheveled locks.

At first glance, he saw nothing. The low lighting made viewing anything beyond the Lord's table difficult. A few blue shards remained along the radius of the round void where the stained glass once lived. No sign of life in the green sky, however.

He glanced around again. Nothing in the church, either. His only obstruction was to the right, where the Lord's table lay, but he couldn't imagine the creature hiding there. Maybe it *was* gone. Maybe he had a real chance to make a break for it—grab the kids and get a head start before the cavalry arrived.

He dragged the table back over his head, his face twisting as he did so, and turned to the entire room, staring up at him.

"What is it, Bill," Coffey asked.

"Nothing. Just heavy is all. Didn't see anything, but then again, I could only see so far."

"That table sure slid over pretty easy for me."

"Huh." Potter looked up at the one thing, the stupid table, which separated them from the creature. "Well, I'd say it's right above us then."

"Christ! Christ on the goddamn cross!" Chisum began pacing the basement. "What are we to do? We can't stay down here all night!"

Coffey dug grime from under a long fingernail. "We dig."

Chisum stopped. "Huh?"

"Ya know, this ain't the first time I been stuck in the ground. Trapped, like. Course, it's been bout twenty years or so, but that don't change nothin. When the Rebels came an blew Fort Pillow to high heaven, they took bout eighteen or so of us colored men back to their camp. Dropped us all in a great, big hole. Sealed the gate above. We figured they had no intention of ever letting us out, so we took to diggin. In turns, ya see. Some dug, while the rest watched for the guards above. We was down there a good long while, prolly days, I'd say, before we realized they had abandoned camp. Left us for dead. Like animals. Only reason we knew that was cause we was being hunted." Coffey looked up, staring through the ceiling. "Black vultures circlin above. Some chewin their way through the wooden latch over top, tryin to get in."

He sat back down in his chair. "Not all of us survived down there, see. Bodies of our feller brothers began to pile up in one corner. Them birds lookin to feast on em. Waitin for the rest of us to go, ya know. Jus watchin. Waitin. And the quiet. Sooo quiet, it was. Hadn't heard silence like that since... since ever, I think. We managed to tunnel ourselves almost to the edge of the river before the Union troops showed on up."

Chisum gaped. "Christ, Coffey. I'm sorry you had to endure such a horrific thing. Can't imagine, but you're not seriously suggestin we *dig* ourselves out, are you?"

Potter gasped. "Tunnel! Shit, that's right."

Nora looked at him. "Huh?"

"Van. I overheard him talking to Aaron about tunneling under the stores for—"

Potter bit down on the words. Van was gone, and, assuming they survived the night, he saw no reason to implicate Aaron for something now irrelevant.

"Uh... some private project, I reckon." Potter jumped down from the ladder and turned three-sixty, staring at the walls. He grabbed the dying lamp and held it where he and Nora had leaned earlier.

Knock, knock, knock.

Solid.

"You know bout this, Healy," Roswell asked.

Healy peered, wide eyed, around the group in astonishment. Clearly, he hadn't.

"You, John? You know?"

Chisum's befuddled look matched Healy's. "No. Absolutely not. How would I?"

Though Chisum was evidently uninformed about the finer details of the new operation, Potter remained unconvinced by his employer's reply. He wondered if the man's poor cover irked the new mayor. *Even your kid's got secrets, Smith.*

He took a step back, surveying the room once more. "Everyone, clear the shelves!"

The group quickly and quietly removed the items, placing them in the center of the room. The shelving followed. Knocking reverberated from anxious fists, everyone trying to find the hollow wall as the eight of them spread along the perimeter. Next to Potter, Chisum banged the surface with the side of a fist.

Coffey called from the corner of the back wall, next to the stations of the cross. "I, I think I got somethin!"

Potter walked over, felt around. He knocked at the wall to the left of the stations. Solid. But in between, the sound almost echoed. He stepped back for another look. The stations... in the shape of a door.

Pulling station ten away revealed a sliver of darkness. Potter pressed his hand to it. A thin, cool breeze greeted his fingers. Station nine and eleven came down next. Four, five, and six followed. Another sliver. He had expected a latch or a hole, something to open. Nothing. In fact, the wall behind each sliver, which ran from ceiling to floor, proved solid.

Potter, analyzing the wall, reached back, wriggling his fingers. "Someone grab me the hammer."

A moment later, Clara placed the tool in his hand. Swinging back, Potter drove the head through the wooden panel, leaving a quarter-size hole. Cold air smacked his face. With the claw end, he split the hole down the center and used his boot heel to penetrate the panel. It tore away easily. With the palm of his hand, Potter smashed out the upper portion, revealing a narrow, dark passage.

With the deteriorating lantern, essentially useless at this point, the group entered the pitch blackness.

"You *sure* you didn't know this was a door?" Chisum shook his head, directing his frustration at Healy.

The minister shrugged helplessly. "I, I just thought it was poor carpentry."

5

The Antiquarian crouched low on the large table, silent and still. Listening. Watching.

Its mosaic, three-hundred-and-sixty-degree vision saw everything through thousands of miniature hexagonal lenses, and saw it with depth. Based on the poor aim of these Earthling creatures, it knew its eyes also saw a higher frequency of light, its field of vision only narrowing once the analytical eye below exposed. Unfortunately, its spectacular optics heavily relied on motion for accuracy. Still objects appeared two dimensional—flat—and anything living just seemed to blend into the background.

Though, just now, it *saw* nothing. Heard little. Smelled everything.

What a stench. The repugnant scent of Earthling creatures had faded some, but as long as the smell lingered, it knew the primitive beings hid somewhere close by.

The bleeding finally stopped, the wound clotting relatively quickly. As expected. Soon, the Antiquarian would resume its hunt.

A patch of cuticle formed from within the clot, creating a fresh layer of exoskeleton, bonding and strengthening its neck wound and lower back. Its neck, still healing, would most likely never return to one hundred percent. And it would be days before it completely healed.

Most vexing of all, its wings were gone. What pieces of membrane remained, singed and frayed, twitched uncontrollably in an awkward attempt to flutter. Painful, but ultimately inconsequential. Upon its return to Sector SH-2-275, a team of military medical technicians would administer the transplant. Until then, its vertical leap and honed fingers allowed it to climb structures, which had served it well up to this point. Still, the Antiquarian should never have allowed itself to get trapped, to get injured. The long sleep must have thrown off its internal mechanisms, though the transitory nature of its weakness didn't make its failure any less dismaying.

Its mission parameters, three, to be exact, remained far from complete. It knew this. But its success remained imperative, regardless of how much time passed in returning home.

Time. If only it knew. These Earth *things* were far more advanced today. Their weapons, more powerful. They—

Ugh, the Antiquarian couldn't think anymore, not with this Earthling stench. Eventually, it would find the Cerebrum. Then it could start the repairs.

Too much time spent here. Too much. It wanted off this miserable rock.

It sensed something else, too.

Close.

It waited.

6

Single file, the group ambled their way in the cold, dark unknown. Potter led, slightly crouched, lantern dangling out in front. His other hand interlocked Nora's, who trailed close behind. Isaac followed, then Clara, with Chisum, Healy, and Roswell in the middle. Coffey closed the end of the chain.

The tunnel structure proved quite primitive, poorly dug out. Two-by-four support beams stood on either side, running across the ceiling every ten feet or so in a desperate and feeble attempt to hold the passage together. Cobweb silk clung from above, gently swaying as they passed. Nora, with a free hand, pulled away clumps from their path. The walk reminded Potter of traversing the narrow, unfamiliar trails in Bennett's claustrophobic mines, the type where one might carry a caged canary with them as a precaution.

The tunnel stretched on, impressively long. *Must be beyond Nora's storefront by now, maybe even past the hardware store. But how much farther to the mill?*

A ladder emerged in the lantern's glow, though the tunnel stretched onward. Potter handed the light to Nora and ascended the steps halfway. Above the carved-out dirt lay a wooden trapdoor, which he pushed up on, opening the hatch and flipping it up and over the rug it lay hidden underneath.

"It's the post office." Potter peeked around the back room, then descended. "I'm guessing this trail must go all the way to the mill. Follow it there."

"What will *you* do, Potter," Chisum asked.

"Grab the arsenal. I'll be back as soon as I can. Isaac, Clara, come on." Potter guided his young'uns up the ladder. If that thing found the tunnel, they'd be sitting ducks. Better to keep them safe himself… keep them close by him, too.

"You'll come back for us now, won't ya," Nora said, inches from Potter's face. Her words rang strong, more of a statement than a question as she peered up into his narrow, weathered eyes.

He wondered, knowing what little she knew of him, how much of his intentions she suspected. She was certainly no fool.

He stared back down into her pretty blues, just long enough to seal them into memory. "Get everyone to the mill and sit tight, okay? Help is coming."

She kissed him hard on the lips and stepped back, watching him ascend.

"'Scuse me, miss." Coffey squeezed by Nora, stepping on the ladder. "I'm comin witcha, Bill."

"No, no. I need you here with the others. I need someone to look after Nora and"—Potter nodded his head behind Coffey—"*them*. I'll be fine. I got the boy here. We're going to be like lightning, ya hear?"

Coffey nodded. "Whatever ya say, Bill."

"You be careful out there, ya hear me," Nora commanded, her eyes slightly glazed.

He nodded and climbed from the hatch, shutting it behind.

Alone in the post office, Potter squatted in front of Isaac and Clara, squeezing their shoulders. "Now stay with me, you understand. Do—not—leave—my—side. You got it!?"

They nodded vigorously.

The three filed out onto the road. Streetlamps gently flickered, accompanying the glazed skies and lambent glow of the waxing moon washing down over Missouri Plaza. The entire town sat visibly illuminated under a lime green haze. With the increasing number of obstacles ahead, Potter paid the strange sky little mind. He stepped off the porch, glancing up and down the street. Empty, save for Charon's corpse, still lying under a lamppost beside Miller's. Quiet. Too quiet. The church loomed in the distance, also silent.

With caution, they paced up Main Street towards Reynolds's Buy & Sell, where Potter's schooner rested in front. McCormac's nag and Bessie's mare awaited. Potter's blood pressure rose as he reached the carriage. Though they stood a great distance away, the church sat too close for comfort. He kept a vigilant eye on the Lord's house, hoping their actions remained inconspicuous as he and the children climbed into the schooner.

Once seated, Potter pulled up and back on reins with a gentle side to side shift. The horses backed up until the church pulled out of sight. He directed them around toward the mill, keeping a keen eye behind. God willing, the creature wouldn't hear the quiet sound of rolling wheels in their slow and methodical departure from town. So far, as often said in New England, smooth sailing.

When the ambling carriage reached the mill bridge, however, the horses hauled at a faraway sound. A vast and vehement howl. The cry swept through Missouri Plaza from everywhere across the valley. A second howl followed it.

"Pa, did you—" Clara began.

"Yeah."

He gazed up for the first time at the strawberry moon, and, for a moment, he found himself engrossed in the brilliant rock's sentient appearance, adrift, way up there, at the streaking heels of sinuous, green sky. In fifty-five years of scouring this earth, he'd never seen something so... the word *beautiful* didn't do it justice. *Spellbinding*. He wondered how such a sight existed in this cruel world. Once in a lifetime, he supposed.

He held onto the hope that this wouldn't be the final chapter of their lifetime.

"I did." He gave the reins a couple of firm tugs, followed by a command.

The horses began their brisk trot over the bridge. As they crossed, he caught the distant sound of prodding hooves. He craned his head to peer around the schooner canopy.

"Jesus Christ." His mouth dropped, and he swore under his breath. "Who am I, Billy the kid!?"

The whirlwind is here.

Chapter 26

Twenty bestraddled soldiers puttered in from the cold desert void, gently silhouetted by the lime-washed valley sky as they entered Missouri Plaza. Fifteen traveled in two-by-two formation with one man at the helm. Two small, lantern-lighted carriages flanked them, covered in white canopy, with four soldiers behind the reins and one soldier inside a carriage.

Lieutenant Colonel Foster, leading, raised a hand, stopping the troop under the hanging sign. The soldiers, clad in cavalry standard navy-blue wool sack coats—with gold patch and piping and matching forage caps—halted at once. From under a golden horsehair plume dress helmet, the lieutenant colonel noted the shattered stained glass church window just beyond the dimly illuminated reach of a nearby streetlamp.

Four a.m.

Earlier than expected. Much earlier, though, the navy skies of nautical twilight loomed with the threat of dawn, creeping up right around the corner. Lieutenant Colonel Foster hoped the sun held off a while longer. He preferred to slink in discreetly. Covertly. Long before breakfast, long before the residents of a town even woke, leaving them none the wiser as he acquired his target. Less chance of contention or an all-out gunfight. After all, today he sought only one man, albeit an egregiously dangerous one. An outlaw who now harbored two young'uns.

The lieutenant colonel, a father of seven himself, predicted minimal casualty of his own men, if any. In his experience, these wanted men—*animals*—generally ended the threat of apprehension in one of two ways: death by their own volition or by the hands of authority. At the very least, they left their offspring behind, unharmed.

The broken church window disquieted Foster, however. He stared at it, stroking his white handlebar mustache. Likely nothing, though a souring sensation trickled in his gut. Could he be too late?

His paranoia, along with a hardy compulsion to leave no stone unturned, prompted his decision to investigate. Following a commanding hand gesture, fourteen soldiers dismounted; seven taking immediate cover by their horses, rifles raised at the ready. The rest deployed in an organized scuttle around the church. Three ran toward the rear, and four separated on either side of the building, with two at the side windows and two around front. Two front men trampled scattered shards, crushing and snapping under calf-high Jefferson Davis boots, before propping themselves up on either side of the broken window, where jagged triangles of blue stained glass protruded outward.

Sergeant Vincent, on his way, stopped and shouted back, "Lieutenant Colonel, we have a body!"

"Windows are boarded up on the inside!" The side-window soldier shouted.

A call came from around the opposite side. "Here as well!"

Sergeant Woods, up against the building on the side with the broken window, grasped his rifle in the crook of his arm and carefully peered in. After a long look, he shouted over his shoulder. "All clear here!"

"The front doors seemed to be jammed up. Possibly sealed from the inside," said Sergeant Morris, coming up from the front.

The lieutenant colonel unmounted and approached the troops. His saber gently swayed from his hip as he stepped. Kneeling next to the face-down body, in the small radius of dirt not saturated with blood or covered in broken glass, he reached around the neck with two fingers and felt for a pulse.

He looked up at his men. "This man's alive. Let's get him over!"

The two soldiers closest rushed to their commander, kneeling around the young man, each grabbing one of three limbs. The fourth, an arm, was conspicuously absent from his bloody shoulder socket.

"Easy. Easy now, fellas." Foster looked up at the caravan. "Lieutenant Harvey, Brooks, bring the med kit. Hurry, now."

The men turned over the body.

The lieutenant colonel, behind, leaned over the pale boy. "Son, can you hear me? I'm Lieutenant Colonel Eugene Foster of the First Cavalry Division, Fort Hood, Texas."

The young man, eyes barely open, glared up at Foster.

"Who did this to you, son?"

His white lips parted and trembled, eyes drifting. "Cha—cha—cha—"

Foster looked back. "We got that kit coming!?"

Harvey and Brooks arrived posthaste with a large canvas bag. Brooks unzipped it, revealing its contents of bandages, dressings, and instruments. Harvey pulled out a roll of gauze bandaging and held it to the boy's torn shoulder socket. Harvey exchanged a look with Brooks, one cognizant of a much futile effort.

"Just relax, son, we're gonna take care of you," Foster prompted. "I need you to try and tell me what happened here, okay?"

"Cha-cha-cha-cha-cha—" His head and remaining arm trembled, gently raising from the dirt. He waved a shaking finger at the broken window. "Cha-cha-church-ch-ch."

His arm dropped, and his head hit the dirt, eyes rolling to the back of his head.

Foster checked his neck for a pulse, then stood. "He's gone. Surround the building!"

The remaining men unmounted and joined the troops at the back of the church, forming a semi-circle, rifles raised. Vincent and Woods approached the window and peered in.

"What do you see," Foster called.

"The church appears to be in complete disarray, Lieutenant Colonel," Vincent said. "Uhh, I see another body. Other than that, nothing." The soldier lowered his rifle, squinting. "It—It's tough to see, lieutenant colonel. Based on the uniform, perhaps it's the town marssSSH-HAAAALLLAAAAHHH—"

Nineteen men watched the sergeant-major disappear through the window.

Grisly screaming trailed.

2

Abruptly and without breath, Aaron Wilburn woke in a chilling sweat to a snapping and whirring sound. His eyes fluttered, attempting to adjust to the darkness and make sense of his damp surroundings as he panted, heart juddering against his breastbone. *Where the hell am I!?*

Didn't matter. This—*anything*—was better than wherever he'd just been.

He twisted his head around, drawn to the portentous pink glow of the center globe in the black box sitting on his credenza. Red sparks of electrical current fired from its core, gently kissing the crystal surface, illuminating the corner of his bedroom. Magenta flashes pulsed from the center to the inner edges. Internal sounds resembling brief gusts of wind propagated within the device.

How good to be home.

Days and restless nights had passed since Bill Potter had placed this peculiar device in his hands. He'd felt the need to conceal it in his bedroom once he jumpstarted it—once the azure crystal somehow disappeared from his desk.

Tonight, though, something finally dawned on him. He felt drawn to this black box in a mystifying way he couldn't put a finger on. As if this all had been preordained—*a calling,* so to speak—to sequester this device.

This energy.

His studies of the machine, surely not of this world, left him in a perpetual state of wakefulness. A harrowing meditation. Tonight, however, the device proved most evocative. Mesmerizing. Bewitching. A trancelike state had swept over him, enveloping his mind like a dream. Ethereal, even. Though, now that he'd awoken, it seemed more a vivid, hellish nightmare.

He gazed into the box, remembering.

A battle had ensued over Missouri Plaza. A battle under great, green skies. It had started at a ranch, John Chisum's, most like, with men attacking him as he fed in the pasture. Raw meat. He savored the tangy, coppery taste of warm blood on his lips. Lots to feed on. Satiated. However, the ranch hands' act of unmitigated aggression had to be met with a defensive strike, tantamount to theirs, and with extreme prejudice. Aaron felt the flame's heat ripple up his back in the engulfed barn, causing him to soak his sheets with sweat as he drifted on.

He furthered upon Potter's young boy in town, hiding in fear. The innocence in that boy's eyes when Charon, the butcher, appeared and pulled a weapon on the boy. Aaron had zero tolerance for such aggression, and Charon quickly met with the same fierce fate as Chisum's men. Though the boy, he wore a familiar scent. Aaron suddenly knew, though he didn't know how, that this child had been in his craft, perhaps responsible for his awakening.

Felicitations, young boy.

Aaron smelled something else on the boy he couldn't quite place. The boy *knew* something. He'd have to consider this, however—

Oh, my. What is that?

Aaron picked up a pungent scent and quickly drifted on into town, over the crowded strip of Main Street in this strange, tiny village. In Marshal Mather's jail cell, he met an interesting individual locked away. One with, oh, such great potential. The Beast within. A goddamn travesty, wasting away in this cage, when the fine specimen suited one of his mission parameters just fine. Of course, as he tried to acquire this delicious specimen, he was once again thwarted, this time, by the meddlesome marshal himself.

Now the Beast roamed free, he supposed, thanks to the lock he'd opened. But with that smell, he'd surely find it again.

Perhaps the most disquieting sequence for Aaron was when his friends ganged up, carrying an all-out assault to put him down. Little did *they* know. Their weapons, impressive yet primitive, proved no match for his species. And now, it was too late for them. He hunted these cowardly men down, and they posed no challenge. Easy targets. He found himself savagely killing the proprietor of Miller's Café, along with the town marshal, and, of course, Van. There was something so satisfying, yet equally atrocious and gut-wrenching, about staring into his best friend's terrified eyes while his arm broke free from his shoulder socket, then tore away from the body. The potent scent of urine stung Aaron's nostrils before he tossed Van, like trash, out his overpriced window.

They had it coming, these creatures. And if Aaron was honest with himself, they *all* did. *We're all the same, aren't we?* Legionnaires... once, maybe. Dogs of war, that better suited them. And that other man, the one that got away. Potter. He had something interesting about him. Something to offer.

Suddenly, his assailants were gone. Hiding, perhaps. Somewhere. Not far, Aaron knew. He could smell them. Taste them. His ship. The young boy, *and* the young girl. She wore the scent, too, perhaps more so. What could it—*oh*. He perked up. They *had* something. Oh, indeed they did. He smiled. But had they *activated* it?

Aaron, finally catching his breath, shook his head. He couldn't make heads or tails of the vile vision. Was he in someone's mind, reading their thoughts? Or did someone, some *thing*, invade and pillage his own?

Unable to fathom a return to sleep, he carried the device up to his office. There he sat with a bottle of Miller's bathtub gin, a glass, and a book, watching the ominous black box which lay before him on the busy desk.

3

The group, now led by Nora, finally reached the end of the tunnel, which concluded with a wall of dirt. Just as on the opposite side of the church. Nora waved the lantern across, inspecting the wooden surface with her free hand, nudging each edge to see which way it opened. Every side proved solid as she laid into it with the heel of her hand. Maybe something obstructed the entryway on the other side. She had spent little time in the mill herself, maybe visiting once or twice for fabric. She couldn't fathom what the basement might hold.

"What's the problem," Chisum called from behind.

"I—I can't budge it. Might be jammed up." Nora pushed again, panting with effort and frustration. "I don't know?"

"'Scuse me, miss."

Chisum squeezed his slightly rotund body around Nora's frail frame, squishing her against the cold clay. Running his hands up and down the wall, he nudged the surface with his palm heel, feeling for a weak spot. The left side gave slightly. Chisum nodded, stepped back, and thrusted himself into the wall, nudging it open a few inches. He hit it again, widening the crack a bit more.

He turned to Nora. "Can you get in?"

Though tight, she managed to squeeze through the narrow opening, her dress catching and tearing on a serrated edge. Unable to see past a two-foot radius, she stood blinded in near total darkness.

She waved the lantern in a circle. Around her sat storage crates, some of which blocked the hidden passage. The secret doorway, which she had entered from, lay behind wall-to-wall stacked shelving, which housed spools of multicolored twine from floor to ceiling.

Nora pulled with two hands while Chisum pushed from behind. With a scrape of the floor, the blocked door rigidly slid open, just enough for everyone to pass through. Coffey shoved it closed behind him as he entered the mill.

They moved cautiously, staying close together through the busy, narrow maze of the basement floor around Isaac's monstrous wool separator workstation.

Upon reaching a long hallway, Roswell spoke up. "This is familiar to me. I believe Wilburn's domicile is this way."

Roswell led them down until they reached a door at the end of the hall. Despite his best efforts, pounding on it and shouting urgently, their unexpected arrival went unnoticed.

"Well, where in Christ could he be!? He's bout the only one that *wasn't* on Main Street tonight," Chisum said.

Roswell glanced overhead. "Upstairs."

The five, led by Roswell, walked single file up the stairs onto the illuminated manufacturing floor and around the corner to the central office.

4

Aaron, hearing footfalls, looked up from his book to find the disheveled townsfolk standing, in the middle of the night, at the door to his office.

Slightly tipsy, he stood and staggered. "Mr. Smith...?" He glanced around with tired eyes, feeling the sedative effects of the gin. "Mr. Chisum!? Minster Healy—wuh-what-what's going on?"

Chisum pushed his way through, bumping Nora and Roswell from his path to approach Aaron's desk. "I don't know how to put this, son, other than to just come out and say it: some ungodly creature is out there in the night, and it's tearin up the whole town!"

"Wuh-what!?"

"Where the Christ've you been, son? Haven't you heard all the damn chaos out there tonight!?

Aaron cast a befuddled glance over the group.

"It's killed the marshal," Chisum bluntly stated before dropping his gaze. "And... some of the others."

"What are you saying? What killed the marshal?" Aaron watched silent eyes fall upon him. At that moment, the vision returned—the nightmare of his friend, torn apart before his very eyes. He glared at Mr. Smith. "Wuh-where is Van?"

Roswell removed his hat, bracing it in two hands as he stared at the ground.

"He didn't make it," Nora said somberly. "I'm so sorry, Aaron."

Roswell just shook his head.

Mouth agape, Aaron popped back down in his seat, staring off at nowhere but somehow seeing everything. "I, I just don't understand," he muttered. "Can someone please explain what is going on here?"

Chisum approached Aaron and put a hand on his shoulder. "Look, son, we need the place to lie low till help arrives. Got it?"

The black box, relatively quiet since Aaron brought it into the office, began revving up. A deep whirring issued from within, and a brilliant white light flashed with intermittent pulsing throughout the globe. Everyone put up a hand to gently shield their eyes as their vision adjusted, drawn into the beacon.

Chisum shook a finger at it. "That, uh, supposed to do that?"

"My God, would you just have a look at this?" Healy, gaping from behind splayed fingers, sauntered over to it. "Incredible!" He looked at Aaron. "What is it?"

Aaron, still in a dense haze of shock and incredulity, stared into the globe as if he could see beyond its intricate depths. *The device.* He glowered at the box, vaguely understanding that it played some inexplicable part in tonight's events. "Oblivion."

"You figured it out, you sonovabitch, you! You got this runnin." Roswell approached it, unable to avert his wide eyes. A white glow reflected from his bemused face. He reached out, letting an open, trembling hand hover an inch from the pulsing light ball. "This thing is generating light, goddamn *power*, without the use of heat or an internal combustion. How's this possible, Aaron?"

Aaron finally looked up. "It's *not*."

Coffey pointed to the windows across the mill floor. "I think I see somethin outside!"

Healy crossed himself. "Please Lord, please say it's not that thing. Is it!?"

Coffey didn't answer. He scurried from the office to the window, lifting it open.

"What is it!?" Chisum shouted.

Coffey beamed, returning a hearty grin. "Help!"

Chapter 27

Potter and his young'uns made it back to the house at near break-neck speed, or at least as fast as two decrepit horses dragging an unwieldy carriage with three people could run safely in the dark woods without colliding with a tree or losing a wheel. Clara, sitting in the middle of the bench, gripped tight to the back of her brother's and pa's coats so as not to roll backward into the carriage. Perhaps she just feared the backsplash coming from the rear of McCormac's nag as the horse defecated her usual muddy nightmare manure. The smell, beyond heinous, smacked Potter in the face, adding insult to injury on a night that undoubtedly couldn't get much worse.

He yanked back on the reins, the horses sliding to an abrupt halt, and threw out an arm, bracing his kids against the bench back to keep them from toppling over the front. "Let's go!"

Hopping down, he scooped Clara under the arms, lifted her to the ground, and threw open the front door, stepping inside with Isaac and Clara right behind. With a shaky hand, he put the carriage lantern down on the counter, then continued to light a couple of the wall lamps, barely holding on to each match he struck. Cold sweat ran down his temples, his stomach churning as nausea washed over him.

He wiped his face with a handkerchief and turned to his children. "Listen to me. Listen. Grab everything you need, *only* things you need, right now. Get loading them into the carriage. Clothing. Food. Only the necessities." Potter paused. *Delegation—otherwise chaos will ensue.* "Clara, you are on pantry duty. Grab a couple crates from the basement and start filling them, okay? Isaac, grab you and your sister's belongings. Start packing them right now. *Right now,* you got it!?"

Isaac turned to Clara with a muddled look. "But Pa, what about the basement? Aren't we going to—"

"Never mind that, Isaac. Do as I say. *Please.* Go, now. And when you're done, help your sister!"

The room suddenly began to gently sway left, then right. Potter clenched his eyes shut, pinching them with two fingers, waiting for the dizziness to pass.

Isaac nodded and ran down the basement stairs to retrieve the luggage.

Clara peered up at Potter with that curious emerald gaze. "Pa, aren't we going back to the mill?"

He fought the urge to shout, barely grasping his last remaining morsel of patience as he looked at his daughter. He got down on one knee—eye level—and cupped his hands around her shoulders. "Change of plans, honey. Now, I need you to hurry and pack up the kitchen, okay?"

"What about Ms. Nora, Pa? And Mr. Coffey? We have to save them from the monster!"

"We *cannot* go back there, honey. It's not safe for us." His focus on her began to falter as he struggled to shut out the shifting living room behind.

"But Paaa—"

"You and your brother's wellbeing are *the—most—important—thing* to me. To Grandpa. It's the *only* thing that matters now! And I need to get you's far away from here. Do you understand, do ya? Do ya grasp what I'm saying, Clara?" He realized his grip had tightened, jostling her while he spoke, and he forcibly relaxed his fingers.

Clara, morosely, shook her head.

"No, no, no, no," Potter mimicked, shaking his head. "None of this. Please. Go."

He turned her around by the shoulder and gave her a gentle shove. She stopped, shooting him a sad, narrow glance over her shoulder. The dagger of her disappointment pierced his heart.

Isaac returned, lugging three large trunks. He handed one off to his father.

Potter grabbed it and went upstairs without a second look.

2

Isaac turned to his sister.

Clara stared up at him with sad eyes. "Pa says we ain't going back to town."

"I had a feeling we weren't. I think those cavalry men want Pa."

"To help?"

"To take him away."

"Why!?"

"They're with the Bad Men, Clara."

"I don't want them to take Pa!" Clara's eyes glassed, tears immediately shedding from their corners.

"Then we need to hurry and pack our belongings so we can get out of here."

Isaac took a step toward the stairs, but a strange sound stopped him short.

He turned to Clara. Her coat pocket vibrated with a fierce hum. She blinked at him, then pulled a lit-up prism from her pocket, barely gripping it as it shook up her arm. The various hues inside the core flashed. Sparks of bright, colored light flashed inside, brighter than those new incandescent electric lamps he'd seen once in Denver. The multicolored projection from the tiny crystal illuminated the center of the house.

Clara, nearing the basement, paused. "I don't want this anymore." She glowered, heading for the outside door.

"Wait," Isaac blurted. "Where are—what are you doing!?"

Clara opened the door and launched the knot into the dark.

Slamming the door, she turned back to Isaac. "The Bad Men can have it."

3

Potter quickly shut the door behind and leaned up against it, eyes closed. *The Attack,* best he could ever describe it, was coming on. The walls closed in on him, spinning. An unbridled suffocation tightened his throat, swift and inexplicit, leaving his sanity to dangle at the frayed edges. *Is this finally the end?*

The first attack had presented itself during the Rebellion War, lost up in those mountains. Upon his descent, he'd mostly managed to keep the episodes at bay, but they had returned with a furious vengeance after Bessie's passing. The chink in his otherwise impervious armor, a slow and methodical attempt to engulf him completely. Physically. Emotionally. Utterly incapacitated, he awaited his final breath, which never seemed to come.

He knew only one cure for his malady. One he had recently chosen to suppress despite the ecstasy, the *rapture,* it delivered. Or, he supposed, fabricated. Though the consequences of its use remained dire, they paled in comparison to all he faced now.

He packed quickly—not a whole hell of a lot to his wardrobe—and changed from the restricting blazer and tie to something a bit easier to move in. Slacks held up by his lucky red suspenders and a weathered white long-sleeve Henley served just fine. From under his hat, he pulled the special quirley, the one reluctantly tucked away for that *what if* moment, and lit it. He smoked half, pulling deeply and letting the toxic vapor penetrate his seasoned lungs. The opiates struck all the right nerves, instantly soothing him. His hands mellowed to a dull tremble, an almost imperceptible quiver, though he still noticed it. He sat in the near dark on his bare bed, the window open, letting the cold night wash over him.

Oh, did he feel swell.

Floating away...

4

Trilling, deep and guttural, echoed from within the church, breaking the breezy silence as cavalry soldiers slowly closed in on the broken window. A bewildered Foster stood behind his men, his tall, shining saber raised high in the air, tentatively preparing for a fight against God knew what. He'd never seen a man pulled straight off the ground before, and by the sound of his screams, something had tossed him around like a rag doll.

By the time his men inched their way over, silence fell once again. Actually, come to think of it, the whole town seemed strangely quiet. Deserted. The night had reached its darkest phase, right before dawn, but still, in his experience, a saloon or a café should be in operation. Maybe some entertainment, some music. At the very least, someone would drift along the street.

Something wasn't right. He wondered about their intended target, just how dangerous of a man they sought.

Were they too late?

From the round hole behind the church came the sergeant-major, flying out backwards, hitting several troops and toppling them over. He lay sprawled in their arms, eyes open. Throat missing.

Foster stared at the mutilation in horror. Certainly not work of the outlaw for whom they came—not the work of any man, for that matter. The threat before them left him at a complete loss for words, save one: "FIRE!"

Thankfully, they'd come prepared. Eighteen men fired aimlessly into the broken window until their chambers emptied. Then, once reloaded, they fired again, plunging .45 caliber slugs into walls and pews. Their shots tore into the Lord's table and podium, ricocheting off the busted bell with ringing *pings*. Bullets flew back out of the church; one hit a soldier in the shoulder, another in the thigh. One shot struck the gas lamp between the side windows. Flames propelled from the shattered unit, furiously propagating up the wall and across the ceiling.

"They're firin back," Jensen shouted.

"Take cover," Foster commanded.

Most of the troops dispersed on either side of the window and alongside the burning church, out of the line of fire, clutching their rifles between boarded-up windows and the front doors. Now surrounding the perimeter, they stood in silence, awaiting their unknown assailant. Only a matter of time.

In mere minutes, the famished flames consumed the dilapidated structure. Black smoke billowed from the empty cupola and wafted from the broken stained-glass window, fanning around the corner and crossing the cavalry men. Deep warbling spilled from within, a withering groan rising above the sound of crackling fire.

Foster scowled. With the church interior fully illuminated in the burgeoning flames, he gave the command to advance the window. Six troops, led by Brooks, surrounded the broken pane, rifles at the ready.

"FIRE," yelled Brooks.

The soldiers fired into the church, again and again, seemingly not ready for the scene that greeted them.

"Fall out!"

The six men backed away to the caravan.

"There's somethin inside, Lieutenant Colonel," Brooks called as he approached.

Foster peered through the thick smoke, unable to make out anything at this distance. "What is it, Brooks?"

"I—I don't know. It's big. It ain't a person, Lieutenant Colonel, and it ain't respondin to ammunition. It doesn't appear armed."

"What's it doin?"

"Just standin on a table. Watchin."

Foster moved in toward the window, wafting away the dark smoke with a white glove. He stopped feet out from the church, just far enough to see inside.

A tall, terrifying creature stood on the Lord's table, staring back at him. Its reflective skin glittered in the light of the surrounding fire, which now consumed much of the nave as the flames advanced toward the chancel.

The monster's jaw separated; its mouth opened. Trilling poured from within.

Foster dropped his saber down to his side, placing it in his left hand in order to cross himself with the right. "My God." Still maintaining eye contact with the creature, he yelled behind for the grenades, commanding the rest of the men to return to the caravan.

Sergeant Jensen and Sergeant Lariviere ran back with a rectangular crate of Ketchum grenades, pulled from under the carriage canopy. Foster, without speaking, pointed his saber to the window.

"Take cover," Lariviere yelled to the troops, launching a grenade in toward the creature before running to join his comrades on the outskirts.

The grenade detonated on impact. The explosion folded the steeple in on itself; grinding down, it crashed through the roof onto the chancel. Plumes of smoke and ash spewed upward through the gaping hole and from the back window, most of which now covered the north end of Main Street, effectively blotting out the moon above. Flames crawled the exterior, the church now completely engulfed.

"Good Christ, look out!" Foster, continuing to back away to avoid pieces of singed drift, peered up at the raging blaze. "I'd say whatever it was, it ain't comin out no more, gentlemen!"

5

Potter, regaining a bit of composure as his nerves settled and the sickness mostly passed, sat up gently on the bed. His new friends, his *only* friends, eagerly awaited his return... depended on him, more like. Coffey. Nora. Their last grave gazes from the tunnel's shadows stayed vivid in his mind. Hopefully, they'd found Aaron and were now safe inside the mill. The cavalry would likely be enough to protect them, but even the military seemed ill-equipped to face this formidable force. At least with the Army potentially dismembered, Potter supposed, he and the young'uns would have a leg up on making their escape.

But how much farther could they—*he*—run? The idea crept into his bones and nestled, weighing on his soul. He no longer bore resemblance to the man his wife had married; and for the first time, he was glad Bessie wasn't alive to see what remained of this feeble bastard. He had the audacity to preach to Clara about faith before fear, and yet here he sat, tail between his legs, once again ready to skin out of town. Christ... the gut-wrenching look on her confused little face tonight.

Every problem he'd ever fled from had invariably worsened in his absence: his childhood thefts, his unit in the war, the train robbery. The image of Mrs. Frohrmann's pallid body suddenly resurfaced, hanging, her empty gray gaze meeting his. He shuddered.

Maybe it was the drug's euphoric effects, but he felt something wash over him. A sense of clarity... or stupidity. Regardless of which, he needed to see this through until the end.

Potter swallowed dryly and stood. With the help of the boy, they could quickly pack the dynamite, the grenades. The Tarpley rifles were mostly useless, though he supposed they'd make a sturdy club. He knew the fate of Missouri Plaza rested in the hands of every armed, able-bodied person willing to defend it. The town needed *him*. He'd deal with what remained of the cavalry after. Hopefully, he and the young'uns would make a quick slip before it came to that.

If he survived.

He walked downstairs to find the boy returning from loading crates into the carriage. "Slight change in plans, son. Where's your sister?"

Isaac wiped his hands on his trousers. "Uh... don't know."

"I thought you were helping her?"

"I—I was busy packing, Pa. I told her to do the same. So, she went."

So much for staying relaxed. Potter charged into the kitchen to find a suitcase-sized crate partially filled with what little remained in the pantry. Canned goods, coffee beans, root vegetables, dried herbs. No sign of his daughter.

"Clara!?" Potter spun around the kitchen. A moment later, he met Isaac by the stairs. "Go up and check for her!"

Potter grabbed the lantern, opened the basement door, and skipped down the steps, grasping the railing with his free hand for support. Nothing but sheet-covered furniture and—*the ammunition cache*! What if she'd tried to retrieve the rifles and hurt herself falling into the pit?

He yelled for Clara again, swiftly yet cautiously heading toward the hidden storage hindered by his limited visibility of the floor. As he neared, he immediately noticed the gate still open from when he earlier retrieved the dynamite. He hovered over the hole, lantern outstretched, and yelled for Clara two more times. Silence. From his hunched position, he saw the crate and barrel lids lying open, exposing the arsenal beneath—some of it, missing.

No-no-no-no-no-no-no-no...

Potter fired up the steps, exiting the basement, and collided with his son in the hallway, scaring the shit out of them both.

Isaac, bouncing backward, gasped for air. "She's not upstairs, Pa, or anywhere in the house!"

Potter glanced at his son. "Wait here."

He exploded through the side door and rushed into the barn, charging over the hay-covered sediment toward the dark stable. Hoping. Praying. Rounding the stall wall to the opening, he saw exactly what he dreaded.

Blanco was gone.

He squeezed the lantern handle in a trembling hand, inches away from smashing it and setting everything ablaze. "FUUUUUUUCK," he howled from the top of heaving lungs, voice quivering, throat burning.

Only the sedative effect of his earlier quirley grounded him. Out of breath, with spittle clinging from his beard, he hung his weary head.

"GRIFFIN!" A familiar voice shattered the cold, dry air.

Potter shuddered; the lantern rocked loosely in his faltering grip, almost dropping. He shot around, reaching for his hip. His right hand slapped against an empty holster.

A tall figure stood before him in the barn entryway, silhouetted by the moonlit sky.

"Who-who's there?" His voice trembled. A rhetorical question, however... because as soon as that gravelly voice rippled through the barn, he knew the answer.

The dark figure stepped disjointedly toward Potter, spurs clinking with each slightly incoherent, stiffly footed step. Potter, petrified, just watched the shadow lumber inside, threadbare clothing gradually emerging in his light. The rib cage, the only distinguishable contrast among the drab clothing and infused dirt, peeked through a partially open flannel. A dead man walking. He waited for Warren's grotesquely decomposed face to shift into the lantern's amber glow.

"She's gone," the ghost said, face still hidden by shadows.

Potter squeezed his lids shut, feeling a dense chill propagate through his sedated nerves. He pulled in a slow, deep breath, expelling it with an internal count. *One, two, three, four, five.* "I know you're not real, I know you're not real, you're not real, you're not real, you're not really—you're not really here, you're not, you're not, you're—YAAAK!"

Warren's boney carpels dug into the corners of his throat, lifting him straight off the ground. Instinctually, he dropped the lantern and grabbed the man's wrist. Brown, malleable flesh squished in his grip as he dug his fingers into the space between the corpse's forearm bones. His eyes opened, now looking down inches from Warren's gnarled face, which loomed inscrutable under a shabby Stetson. By this time, the little skin left to him had long since molded over, spotted dark brown and black. Where his mouth once lived, a tarnished, perpetual smile of yellow-brown bone around two gold fronts remained. A mocking, haunting grin.

Potter glared into Warren's frosted, sunken eye, inexplicably intact. Next to it, the formerly vacant socket squirmed generously with maggots; they dripped onto his cheekbone as he spoke.

"You didn't listen," he grumbled, speaking each word distinctly, separately, as if they came from someone, or something, else.

Desperate to breathe, Potter pulled at the unbudging wrist with one hand while clawing into rotted flesh with the other. Strands of black, sinewy muscle peeled away, breaking apart under his fingers.

"I warned you to rid yourself of that box, Joe. I warned you, but you just could not overcome your own pridefulness, could you? Not even for the sake of your own children." A hardy chortle gurgled from deep within Warren; his body heaved and swayed, his mouth ajar.

Sardonic laughter, Potter figured. A cluster of black widow spiders fled from in between teeth in its gaping smile, scattering in all directions. Many scurried up Warren's tattered coat sleeve; Potter, eyeballing them, squirmed.

"And here it is. Your downfall. Your painful acceptance of a meaningless existence, to drink from the same pompous trough as the rest of us deplorable lost souls. Though *your* fate is something far worse. Cognizance is your curse. To savor that knowledge, that pain, before your demise. Then, like us, scour the earth in perdition. Absolution?" He shook his head. "I can tell you; eternity is a mighty *long* time. Now I ask you, Joe... what would you trade that pain for?"

Struggling to pull in air, he looked down at Warren's smug, rotting face.

I... I'm not sure.

"It is reassuring, isn't it? To know that some people, people like us—the venal, the blindly arrogant—we never change, do we."

"I—killed—you," Potter squeezed through gritted teeth. He could no longer breathe. His face flushed, burning; his eyes bulged from their weathered sockets. "You—are—not—REAL—MOTHER—FUCK—ERRRR!" With both hands, he dug his fingers in between the bones and yanked, snapping Warren's forearm away in two pieces. Freed from agony, he fell to the ground, gasping for air.

"Do you think saving your friends, the town, can redeem a life of debauchery, Joe? No matter where you run those soldiers will come for you." Warren looked down, his one eye on Potter, dust and bone fragments spilling from an empty coat sleeve.

"I got time." Potter choked out, spittle hanging from a quivering lip.

"We all think we do." The corpse chortled again. "Men like *us* even more so. Each of us surprised to find we are *all* wrong."

Potter, still gasping, reached for the lantern and picked himself up. He glared at Warren.

"Try as you might, you cannot cheat death. And that hourglass of yours..."

Slowly regaining his faculties, Potter backed away toward the door, lantern swaying in hand.

"The only thing you will find along the narrow edge draining the sands of time is the life you lost."

Potter exited the barn, keeping Warren in his eyeline until the ghost disappeared from his light. He turned to the side door of the house.

POP!

Potter screamed as a slug tore into his thigh, sending him sideways. He smacked into the side door, sliding onto the seat of his pants. The lantern fell, this time smashing. Its flame extinguished. He sat, gaping, astounded.

He was shot.

He brushed his fingers through his hair, pushing it from his face, his head strangely, oddly, naked. His hat had fallen away, though where it went, he couldn't see. The pain subsided almost instantly as cold laced his body.

<h1 style="text-align:center">6</h1>

Townsfolk began pouring out of a café. Miller's, the sign read. They made their way across the street in a bewildered state of panic and awe, gazes flitting between the U.S. Army and their burning church. A couple of men tipped their hats low, standing back behind the crowd. One woman walked backward all the way, almost tripping over the body in the street before turning and fading into the alley.

Foster, astounded, gazed at the townsfolk in wonderment. Where had they all come from—surely not all from this little luncheonette?

At the south end of Main Street, two gentlemen briskly emerged from the dark, heaving as they approached. The nearby flames cast bright amber light on their disheveled appearance.

"Oh, thank you. Thank you, God, you're here!" The one in the cream-colored suit extended a hand, panting. "Roswell Smith. Mayor of Missouri Plaza. Did you kill it? Please tell me you killed it!" His eyes made brief contact with the man with the sword, his gaze drawn instead to the inferno.

"I'm Lieutenant Colonel Eugene Foster of the Seventh Cavalry Division. Fort Hood, Texas." Foster slid the saber back into its sheath and shook Roswell's hand. "Can anyone explain to me what in Sam Hill is goin on here? Did we kill what, exactly?"

"Hell, you saw it, didn't ya?" The other man, hunched over with his hands on his thighs, struggled to catch his breath. "Your goddamn guess is as good as ours. We're under invasion, here." He glanced up. "Look at the damn sky! It's fuckin green, you see that!?"

"And you are?"

"John Chisum. Cattle rancher in these parts," he said, decidedly vague.

"John Chisum of Jinglebob Ranch, right? I've plenty heard of ya." Foster shook Chisum's hand and looked up. "It's happenin all over the country. Got reports of that from the north two days ago. That in the sky there, they're callin a solar storm passin on through."

"Solar storm you say? And it twitches in the sky like that, *green*!?" Chisum, flabbergasted, glared over the valley.

"That thing inside there has killed a number of our residents, Eugene," Roswell continued. "My son, Van for one, postmaster of Missouri Plaza. Miller, the proprietor of our café. We lost the marshal, Dave Mather."

About fifteen yards back, an Apache woman wrapped in a shawl turned and blinked. Foster met her gaze for an instant, just long enough to see the firelight reflecting in her glassy eyes as she covered her open mouth with a quivering palm.

"Christ, I can't believe it. Can't believe this nightmare is finally over." Chisum incessantly blotted his damp forehead, cheeks, and neck with a hanky. "You know this evil sumbitch took out all my ranch hands in one fell swoop!? Destroyed my house, killed my cattle, burned down my goddamn barn. This thing is gonna to leave me in ruins!"

"I offer my condolences, but I have questions," Foster said. "What exactly *were* you dealing with—"

Chisum, ignoring the lieutenant colonel, turned to Roswell. "Ruins! You mind tellin me, *Mr. Mayor*, what our great *Land of Enchantment* is gonna do bout rectifying this situation?"

"Now John," Roswell interjected, "I reckon a man of your stature is mighty well insured. Ain't that bout right?"

"Well, my cattle sure are, but my men *ain't*! Those were good, hard-working boys, trustworthy boys! There for you in an instant." Chisum snapped his fingers. "You just can't put a damn price on loyalty nowadays. Families—"

"*John.*"

"I guarantee you, some of them had families. You know they're from right over the border, there. Who's gonna compensate them, huh? I can't be the only party responsible to foot the bill—"

"Enough!" Roswell barked. "Just cut the bullshit, now! You lost your men, your cattle, bah! I lost my boy tonight, John. My son is *gone!*" He shook his head. "*'Foot the bill,'* you arrogant sonovabitch. You think I'm ignorant of the many accommodations the *Land of Enchantment* has afforded you? I'd say you took to the state's tourism quote quite literally. Unwarranted tax breaks. Illegal bartering. Shifty land deals. Not everyone's got their eyes closed. We *all* lost tonight, with one helluva mess to clean up. Hell, we could all be goddamn dead right now! You understand we'd *still* be living this nightmare if the Lieutenant Colonel hadn't showed up here in time, John." Roswell's bewildered brow furrowed. "Foster, you and your men arrived here awful quick, I'd say."

Foster's eyes narrowed. "Quickly? We were dispatched several days ago."

"Several days ago," Chisum staggered. "Well, how the hell's that possible? We just sent a-a-a-damn telegraph."

"We were sent here on strict orders comin from Denver, Colorado by Governor James Benton Grant—"

"*Colorado,*" Chisum interrupted. "Now, what in Christ would they want all the way down here?"

Foster dug into a coat pocket and pulled out a folded piece of paper. "Chiefly on account that we're the foremost and direct unit in proximity. Santa Fe's Ninth Cavalry Division of Fort Union is away on assignment, I'm told, and this is somethin of an urgent matter."

Foster handed the unfolded paper to Roswell, who stared at the drawing under "WANTED."

"And I'll tell ya," he continued, "I had never heard of this *Missouri Plaza,* and I certainly had my doubts over whether this village actually existed. Sure enough, here we are. We're looking to apprehend a largely wanted criminal, whom we have reason to believe has taken residency here in your town."

Chisum took a step backward, eyes darting from Roswell to Foster. "Uh, who-who might that be?"

"Goes under several aliases. Joseph Griffin of Norwich, Connecticut. Edward J. Sullivan of Denver, Colorado."

"Ain't no man here by those names, Eugene," Roswell said.

"How bout a William Potter?"

Roswell looked over at Chisum, who returned a tentative glance. Foster narrowed his attention to Chisum.

Sweat beaded his brow as the man gaped, mouth hanging open. "Uhhh—"

WHOOOOOOOOOOOOOOOOOSSSSSSHSHHHHHHHHH!!!

A fierce gust swept through Main Street with hurricane-like speed and power. Though lasting mere seconds as it blew by, the wind thrust hats from the three men, the throng of troops, and the girding townsfolk, all of whom grasped up at empty air, barely missing their fleeting head-pieces. A low, deep, and almost indiscernible sound resonated, trodden on the heels of the vicious, careening whirlwind.

Foster, along with the rest of the crowd on Main Street, looked up.

Something soared overhead. Something *massive*—bigger than the church. Hell, quite possibly bigger than the whole town. The dark object, airborne, whirred by a hundred or so feet above the stores, blotting out the night sky and casting a black aura over the street below.

"My God." Foster gaped, watching this unidentified flying object glide swiftly above the town for a moment before dissolving over the crest of tenebrous woodlands.

Chapter 28

Tynan yanked back on the rifle's action lever, quickly expelling the spent round and loading anew. He took aim once again, this time blinded by darkness. "Shit."

"What the Christ is you doin, Tynan!?" Grover, ten yards away on the right, hollered over. "We sposed to take'im alive, goddammit!"

"Shut—up!" Tynan, at his wit's end, crowed back.

Tired. Hungry. After several days of travel and camp with these two knuckleheaded bigots, he considered turning his rifle on them.

This was the end of the road.

They had taken camp thirty yards out from the house, setting up at the edge of the woods before the girding river. Too far away, especially with the middling gust shifting through from the prairie on the west side. But that's where this corner of the Bennet house faced, and it offered the best possible vantage to acquire their target.

Tynan had considered hiding inside the home, but such a plan posed too much inherent risk—not only to his men, but to the young'uns of his intended target, whom he had been explicitly instructed (threatened, more like) to avoid harming. Not to mention, he had no knowledge of the potential gang the outlaw ran with today. In no way did Tynan want the bloodbath that would ensue from being trapped inside with Griffin, two innocents, and the possible resurgence of the Cowtown Marauders.

And no. The harrowing outhouse reeked of something far worse than the natural scent of decay.

No, the only option in this situation relied on distance. A besiegement. Tynan prided himself on outwitting his opponent, and he'd be damned to give some abhorrent outlaw the opportunity to get *his* number. Hunting the likes of William H. Bonnie, Sam Bass, and Henry Newton Brown had taught Tynan the cowardly nature of criminals. And cowards *run*. He smiled, remembering the gratification of emptying a double-barrel shotgun, close range, at Brown not two months earlier, as he ran from lynch mob justice in Missouri.

"He's unarmed!" Claude shouted, ten yards over on Tynan's left side.

"He look dead to you?" Tynan spit a wad of tobacco juice, wiping his lip with a leather finger. "Besides, we don't want him runnin, now, do we?"

The boy appeared in one of the dimly lighted windows, lifting it and poking his head through. "Pa! Pa, where are you!?"

An answer rose from the barn. "Isaac, you get away from the window! You stay inside, son, and hide, you hear me?"

"Joseph Griffin," Tynan shouted, "you are surrounded by deputy marshals. Do not move from where you are. We know you're injured. Throw out any weapons on your person now, and no further harm will come to you or the boy."

The boy vanished.

Silence.

The marshals held their positions.

"Griffin, you hearin me? I ain't gonna ask again!"

2

"I ain't got no weapons!" Potter returned, staring out into the dark as if he could identify his assailants.

Oh, he should've known. In the middle of the night, that's when *they* get the drop on you. But who the fuck were they? The voices echoed, too faint, for certain, to be close. Pure *luck* they hit him at all.

He took several deep breaths, back against the wall, and braced himself. With his left leg, heel wedged in the ground, he pushed himself up, using the house as a crutch to slide himself upright. Blood trickled down his leg, nothing more than a faint warmth. He reached over with his left hand, feeling for the doorknob, finding it, and twisting the door open. The pain buzzed, oddly minimal, though his brain still registered something off. With a heavy, limping gait, he stepped with injured leg back into the house.

3

"I heard the door. I think he's back inside," Claude said.

"Well, so what? We was in there; he ain't got no weapons." Tynan stood and reloaded. "Let's go get him."

Grover picked up a lantern he had previously hidden with his satchel and joined Tynan and Claude. The three, rifles at the ready, began their cautious trek toward the quiet house. From afar, the marshals could see somewhat into the two living room windows, albeit narrowly with the hazy, sparse wall lamps. A gilded wall mirror. The back of a couch. No outlaw. They'd lost their mark, and now Tynan stood poised on the edge of walking into obscurity. An outcome he had actively tried to avoid. Even with a thorough sweep of the house, nothing was certain. Still, he liked his odds: three armed men facing one injured man with, at best, a butcher's knife.

POP!

Tree bark shattered behind Grover's head. The gunshot immediately sent the three men ducking for cover.

POP! POP!

Grover's lantern shattered in his hands. The three took a knee and returned rapid, aimless fire at the house.

"Where the Christ is that comin from," Claude shouted in between shots.

Their .45 caliber bullets tore through the Bennett house's thin interior walls like paper, shattering the front and side windows. Griffin, evidently sitting underneath a now broken pane, ducked forward in an awkward tuck and roll. Using his momentum, he pulled himself up and scurried, limping, through the living room, arms up, feebly shielding his head as gunfire burst through from all angles. He flung himself over the armchair, turning it over, barely safeguarded from the stray shots which heedlessly tore into the fabric.

"I see that sonovabitch!" Tynan quickly reloaded, scanning the yard. "It ain't comin from Griffin."

Maybe the schooner? He recalled seeing the three enter the house, the little girl tearing ass off the property shortly thereafter. Now he wished he'd sent one of the deputies behind her. They could've used the girl as bait. The upstairs windows looked closed, though tough to see. Mostly dark, save for the dim wall lamps. He scanned the grounds beyond the property. There, off the front right corner of the house, way off, a glimmer of light emanated from the—

"There!" Tynan pointed. "The ground!"

"Huh?" Claude, trying to look up and reload, fumbled ammo between shaky fingers.

Tynan huffed. "It's comin from the... it's, it's the damn kid!"

4

Isaac had loaded several of Bennett's single-shot Tarpley rifles and posted up at the end of the tunnel inside the weapons cache, each gun in arms reach. The hatch, partially ajar, had revealed Grover's lantern, which he luckily hit on the second shot. Not a moment too soon.

Bullets hit the ground in front of him, sending in dirt and grass. Some grazed the hatch, chipping wood. Isaac ducked down the ladder with a rifle, climbed from the cache, and dashed through the basement and up the stairs. He found his pa struggling to gain his balance behind the armchair.

"Pa!" He tossed three rifles, followed by a box of ammo.

5

Potter caught each gun separately. Breathless, he mustered only an astonished gaze of appreciation, wiping his damp forehead with his back-pocket hanky before the beading sweat could sting his proud eyes. Isaac returned a warmhearted nod of understanding and ran back downstairs.

Potter hobbled to the grandfather clock between the busted front and side windows. With his back against it, he closed his eyes and took a couple swift breaths, basking in this brief serenity. The clock, silent, had ceased functioning, likely taking a bullet somewhere behind its face.

Time stopped.

What followed happened in a matter of mere seconds. Had anyone been on the property and blinked, they'd have missed it.

Or died.

The rapid gunfire recommenced. Potter crouched and waited, hoping to avoid being struck while the clock took the brunt, and stole glances at the muzzle blast locations. Slugs tore new holes through the front and side façade. Wood splintered from the front door. The Gilt mirror shattered. Whiffs of dust billowed from the couch with each imploding wallop.

Potter figured three. Three men, at least. Since *they*—assuming *they* were marshals, however many there were—likely fired standard issue Springfield carbines, he knew they had maybe thirty bullets among them.

He waited.

And the fools spent them all.

The second the firing ceased, he swung around to the open window and unloaded one gun, dropped it, and picked up the next, popping off the second round. Then he grabbed the next.

6

Grover, who'd taken a knee, crowed, taking a nasty .50 caliber slug to the arm. He fumbled his rifle, falling backward on the seat of his pants.

Tynan, nonplussed, watched Grover tumble into the dark, then glared back toward the house. That wasn't the kid... and now *they* were surrounded.

"*Griffin*," he muttered. "FALL OUT!"

Claude, closest to the hatch at thirty yards out, glanced at the moaning Grover. "Awe, fuck it. *I'll* take the kid!" He dropped the spent rifle and pulled two holstered Schofields, making a mad dash toward the hatch and squeezing off round after .45 caliber round.

Tynan stood, shook his head, and sprinted toward the outhouse, away from the gunfire.

7

Isaac, back on the ladder, tentatively held his position. Bullets zinged inches from his head, striking the earth and ricocheting dirt chunks and wood splinters in his face.

He took a deep breath and closed one eye, taking careful aim before squeezing the trigger. The blast echoed as it tore from under the hatch, his right ear instantly ringing. A ghastly, high-pitched scream caused him to wince, and his eyes wrenched open with a relieving exhale. He saw the Bad Man stumble backward, arms flaring, but he quickly regained balance despite a stunned glance at the hole in his left shoulder.

With his last preloaded rifle spent, Isaac snapped open the breechloader latch on top of the rifle case, discharging the round, and loaded anew. The case stuck, refusing to shut. Jammed. In a panic, he yanked back and forth while keeping a scarce eye on the silhouetted marshal. Damn old rifle!

With as much saliva as he could muster from a nervous, dry mouth, he spit repeatedly into the small brass hinges of the breechloader, jostling it. The Bad Man, fifteen yards out, looked down directly at Isaac, now clear in his sight. He smiled, and with a quick right, his pistol rose. Isaac winced, and the lever snapped down.

Two gunshots rang out.

Isaac shuddered, opening his eyes. The marshal, now in partial view, still stood, holding his gun. Almost swaying. The man, mouth agape, stared down at the hole in his chest, directly under his bandana, now trickling blood.

He fell backward. Dead.

8

From where Potter stood across the living room, he only caught a glimpse of the marshal falling away. Though unable to see the hatch, he grinned, proud of himself and his boy.

Isaac...

The silence disquieted him. *Surely, he isn't...*

"Isaac!" Potter stepped from the busted clock to cross the room.

POP!

"UGGHH!" Potter stumbled backward, the rip and burn from another slug hitting him in the left upper chest. The impact sent him off his feet and onto the living room floor, smacking his head.

The rifle slid away, out of reach.

Potter slumped over on his belly. Lifting himself on all fours, he attempted to reach for the last rifle. A sharp pinch, though not horribly painful, prevented the movement; his arm wouldn't extend beyond ninety degrees. *Thank God for opioids.*

Sitting back on his heels, something else pinched. He glanced down.

A whiff of smoke plumed from inside a dark red hole in his shirt. He felt the warmth oozing down his chest and back; the smell of charred flesh wafted past as he reached behind his neck. The bullet had torn through under the collarbone, clean out the backside.

9

Everything fell oddly silent, save the gentle gust of prairie wind shifting over the Bennett property. Breathless and nauseated, Isaac hung almost perfectly still on the second ladder rung, his rifle still tucked in the crook of his armpit, aimed at darkness. His arms trembled with every attempt to keep their firm grip at the ready. The cool breeze caressed his sweaty face, rushing under the slightly flared latch.

He shot the marshals. Killed one, for certain. That man's soul belonged to him now. The thought, previously regarded as gratifying or even valiant, now sickened him. After tonight, Isaac wished to never pick up another weapon again.

He needed to leave the tunnel to check on Pa, but... no. Wiser not to tempt fate. Though near impossible to see anything, he still possessed the perfect vantage if either of those men moved.

The hatch came down hard, cracking his head and knocking him off the ladder. He flopped on his back to the floor. Breathless, he blinked up, vision swimming.

A fancy looking fellow in a top hat and round glasses squatted over the open hatch. He bent forward, smiling close-lipped under a twisted mustache. The amber glow of Isaac's lantern reflected in the man's ominous black specs.

"Don't move, kid."

10

The front door exploded open along with part of the door frame, a marshal's boot stomping it against the wall. Potter's head turned on two blazing pistols entering. He rolled out of the line of fire, grabbed the rifle, and slid onto his side, firing back. The marshal ducked behind the couch. Potter, veins brimming with adrenaline, instantly shot up and crossed into the dining room, taking cover behind the door frame. He dug a paper cartridge round from a hip pocket and loaded the carbine.

The marshal erupted from behind the couch and fired two rounds, one from each gun. Potter pivoted and returned fire, then backed into position to reload once again.

The .50 caliber round grazed the marshal's ear before plunging into the wall. He yipped and ducked back down. "Give it up, Griffin—ain't no way outta here! We don't wanna kill you, ya hearin me? It don't gotta end this way."

Potter could barely hear the man's panting over his own breathless heaving.

"Oh?" He reloaded. "My other option is to be stoned to death outside a courthouse after being starved, shackled, and dragged cross country by you for a bunch of miserable days, huh?"

"That's for the state to decide. That's your best chance here. But let's face it. Even if you don't end up at the end of a noose by the week's end, you'll likely have to contend with the lynch mob. They'll come for ya first."

"You're making my decision real easy."

"I'll give you one chance, Griffin. You throw out your weapon."

Potter couldn't keep this up, and he knew it. How many bullets remained in his pocket? Didn't matter. He was outmatched. He needed another weapon. Could he make it to the basement? Maybe Isaac—*shit, where's my boy?* He hoped to Christ his son was safe. Maybe he escaped the tunnel and rode on off after his sister. God willing.

The marshal, still positioned behind the couch, shouted back "Well, what's it gonna be, Griffin!?"

"Okay. Okay." Potter glanced around the room. "I'm, I'm coming out. Don't shoot!"

"Throw out your rifle!"

Metal clanked across the hardwood.

"Okay," Potter called, "I'm coming out!"

The marshal stood.

Potter appeared in the doorway, rifle raised, pointed at his assailant. The marshal glanced at the ground, where the fireplace poker now lay.

Both men fired at once. Potter struck the intruder in the upper chest. Had there been another round, the marshal would have been a dead man.

Instead, he stumbled back, hitting the side of the house. Using the wall as a crutch, he raised both pistols and fired back at Potter.

The marshal's zingers missed his head by inches as Potter ducked back behind the door frame. A cold sweat touched his forehead; he panted, flushed, his heart pounding against his chest like galloping hooves on hard earth. Unable to conceive his next move, he glanced down at the silver-dollar pools of blood circulating on the hardwood beneath his boots. Although he hadn't been struck in any danger zones, he was losing considerable blood and needed to consider his options. *Cauterizing... painful as all hell, but feasible.*

He continued to hold the gun, though empty, then crossed through the dining room into the kitchen. Maybe he could circle back to the living room and reach the basement. First, he stopped in the kitchen and waited, watching for his assailant to follow.

The marshal emerged in the dining room doorway, holding a bandana to his bleeding chest and following Potter's trail of blood with slow, shallow steps, tiptoeing to prevent his boot heel from audibly connecting with the floor. He paused a moment, then backed out of the room, waiting for Potter to emerge from the other side.

Potter had already anticipated the marshal's course of action. Reaching the basement was impossible, at least with these sonovabitches alive. And Warren had fucked him—fucked him superbly. *Thanks for the warning.* Potter stared at the dining room doorway, wondering if the pale rider waited on the other side. Maybe this really was the end.

No. Not tonight, it isn't.

Potter backtracked through the dining room and peeked around the corner. The marshal stood, guns up at the ready by the corner, while the basement door loomed several feet behind him. Any further movement would surely give Potter away. This was it. Rushing forward, he tackled the marshal from behind just as he began to turn toward the sound of Potter's clopping boots. Both men propelled into the wall and bounced backward, falling to the ground; the marshal's guns dropped, sliding away.

Potter yelped, feeling a sharp jab in the side of his injured thigh as he tried to roll away. Shards of glass littered the surrounding floor.

With youth and agility, the stranger quickly rolled atop Potter, pinning him down and wailing on his face with a closed hand. Slow. Messy. His own affliction was affecting his aim and power, something evident to Potter as he lay, taking wallop after wallop, each slower than the last. The marshal struck him, slapping him with everything he could muster, until each sapped arm lolled by his side, his mouth huffing halitosis stench onto Potter.

Potter felt every blow, but mainly just skin on skin contact. Blood poured from stinging, flared nostrils and busted lips, coating his mustache and beard, his nose doubtless broken. But the pain was mild at best. Mostly swelling. The marshal managed one more feeble strike, a left hook that cocked Potter's head toward the coffee table.

His eye lit up at the sight. *How grand is this?*

He glanced up at his assailant and returned a crimson-lined smile of stained teeth. The marshal grimaced, then leaned in and dug into Potter's chest wound, twisting in his thumb. Potter felt *that.* He returned a shrill yowl, then spit a mouth full of blood in the man's face.

The marshal winced, closing his eyes momentarily. He opened them to a shard of glass tearing through the side of his neck. Blood surged instantly from the clean slice. He rolled off Potter, clutching his neck in a feeble attempt to stop the gushing from between fingers, and lunged for his discarded gun five feet away.

Potter, who'd grabbed a shard of busted window glass during his assault, rolled to his stomach and crawled to the coffee table. His scattergun lay underneath; he had forgotten he'd even hidden it there. He turned over the table, grabbed it, and rolled on his back, aiming at the marshal, now fifteen feet away on *his* back, pointing a Colt.

Both men fired.

"AHH-UGH!" Potter screamed as the slug penetrated his right shoulder.

The buckshot from the sawed-off hit the marshal's face in a scattered pattern. The bulk struck his forehead, sending brain matter and dark, viscous fluid far back against the basement door.

"Ain't no flies on me," Potter whispered with bated breath, watching the man's lifeless body slump backward and spasm for several moments thereafter. He'd forgotten the intricate oddities of the human body after a violent death.

Lowering the gun, Potter lay against the backside of the table. Beads of sweat rolled down his wrinkled brow, matting his soaked hair. He brushed damp strands from his line of sight, panting. He was far too old for this shit. The air hung, silent for a moment as the literal and proverbial dust settled. He only appreciated *how* far the silence stretched when a crescendo of distant footfalls sounded from below.

"Isaac," he muttered.

The basement door slowly creaked open an inch or two. A rifle barrel peeked in. The figure emerged cautiously, peering over into the living room. Tall. Careful. Cold.

Though Potter's vision skewed slightly, eye swelling and dizzy from the assault, he immediately recognized this person was *not* his son. His heart stopped in his chest. *The third assailant.* Before he could suck in his next breath, he hoisted the now cumbersome sawed-off—his shoulder preventing any speed or accuracy—and popped off its last round.

The man ducked as soon as the hammer cocked back with a click, milliseconds before it snapped the firing pin. The final projectile ripped a cannon-sized hole through his top hat and the edge of the door, inches above his crown.

The last marshal stood upright, turned, and viewed the damage with incredulity before looking at Potter. "Mighty fancy boom stick you got there. The problem with them is they only carry two rounds." He picked his hat from the floor, turning it over in his hand before firmly placing it back on his neatly coiffed brow. "You shot my favorite hat, partner."

Potter exhaled deeply and dropped the gun.

"Don't remember me?" The man entered the living room, rifle pointed at Potter. "Name's Dunkin. Tynan Dunkin." With a leather finger and thumb, he tipped his top hat.

Potter stared narrowly, trying to focus his good eye on the well-dressed man in the black overcoat, violet three-piece, and dark green ascot. Tinted specs concealed his gaze.

"Oh, I remember you," the stranger mocked. "Washington Street. 'The Triangle.'"

Home. Though decades had passed since he'd returned, Potter still remembered the Triangle, as the tri-street area had been coined. Washington Street, Broad Street, and Broadway had comprised much of the town's wealth. By the time he'd been drafted, Norwich's residents had accumulated more wealth per capita than any other city in the country, if you could believe it. At least, if one believed the types of pretentious statements lauded at town-wide gatherings and events. As the halfway point, as it were, along the Shore Line Railway from Boston to New York, the town quintessentially embodied the affluence and corruption Mark Twain illustrated in his public work, *The Gilded Age*, one of the many books of Bessie's that Potter recalled reading.

"Course, I thought you was dead." Tynan smirked. "Look. At. You. Beaten down. Defeated by life." He removed his specs, revealing piercing gray eyes. The eyes of a Great Plains wolf.

"I-I-I don't know you."

"Oh, come now, Joe. You Griffins owned half the damn neighborhood! Right? I believe your family commissioned the Otis Library, did they not? Shit. Money. Education. *Arrogance.* The good life, remember?" Tynan grabbed a wooden chair propped against the wall and dragged it over to Potter. He sat, leaning in, and twisted the end of his mustache. "My family was, of course, less fortunate.

"Father was a watchmaker. Not a bad trade. Honest. Skillful. Don't pay a helluva lot. But with eleven mouths to feed, there's no turning away when that letter comes. *You* remember. Then they rounded us up like cattle. Transported us straight to hell. Or Virginia, depending on your preference. Served under McClellan, remember? Another yellow coward. Let General Lee walk away after the slaughter in Antietam. Almost cost us the victory. Our lives. Let *you* walk away, though. Along with hundreds of other cowardly men."

"You, you got the wrong man. Please. Please—wuh-where's my boy!? Did you hurt him? What'd you do to him?"

Tynan shoved a roll of tobacco into the pocket of his right cheek and began to slowly gnaw at it. "Now do *I* look like the monster here?" He spit on the floor. With a right hand, he reached into his vest pocket and pulled a gold watch. The lid popped open as he gently dangled it in front of Potter's eyes.

"Father gave me this before I left for war. Said to me, 'Son, the world is a finely tuned instrument, like this here watch. Seasons, they come and go. Animals, they migrate, same time, same place, each year. Like clockwork. The world runs in a predictable, ordered way.' Do you know the precision it takes to build a time piece, huh? Every wheel, every screw, every spring has its place. A balance, if you will." Tynan grinned slyly, giving his mustache a slight twist. "Thought you could run forever, couldn't you, Joe? Murderer. Train robber. Deserter. Your time has expired." He snapped shut the lid and slid the watch back in his pocket.

"Please, I need to get to my baby girl! She-she-she rode off. Back to town. Everyone there is in grave danger. They're being hunted by some sort of evil. I-I swear to Christ—"

"Shut it, Griffin! You think I ain't heard horseshit before? The only evil is sittin right here in front of me." Tynan spit again, this time wiping the spittle from his lip with a white handkerchief pulled from his inner coat pocket. "Tell me, what type of gutter trash lacks the human decency God gave the common man, huh? The type who kills innocent, helpless men, women, and children! Children, Joe! Like yours. How have you lived with yourself all these years?"

A chill rose in Potter's shaky spine. A wince. Maybe a natural reaction to the accusations Tynan spewed, or else the result of a loss of blood.

Clearly, this man knew who *he* was, though Potter possessed no recollection of *him*. Didn't much matter. He wasn't wrong.

"You want for atonement; I can see it," Tynan continued. "This here is it. Your opportunity for repentance, right here, right now. Account for your sins, and I'll make this quick and easy. Bullet in that hard head of yours. Besides, I have doubts you'll even survive the trip to Wichita."

"I did what I had to do. I made peace with it. Long ago. Maybe you should do the same. Whatever grievances you hold."

"A murderer! And besides, my *grievance*, as you so succinctly call it, is something a man like you could never understand. It's woven in the fabric of my being, so to speak. Somethin that can never be satiated. But that don't concern you. My purpose now is huntin pieces of shit like you to the ends of the earth and back. Without which, I may as well not even exist. Thankfully, there's enough of you out there, I'll never have to worry bout that."

Potter grinned a mouth full of red teeth. "I was a murderer the day they sent me off to war. And you and your mislaid sense of righteousness, pointing that gun? Judge, jury, executioner. You think you're any different!?"

Tynan reached down, grabbed Potter by his shirt and suspenders, and pulled him up from the ground. He backed him into the side of the room, slamming him against the wall.

"I sure a shit ain't *you*!" He drew close to Potter's face. "We savvy?"

"Please, please, please, listen to me. Thuh-there's some-something terrible out there, in that town! People are being slaughtered!"

"I bet they are, Griffin. Ever since *your* arrival!"

"No! No-no-no-no, you don't understand—"

"No, *you* don't understand! You know, they offered a twenty-five-thousand-dollar bounty to bring you in. Alive. Retirement money, Joseph. Ten dead. You, pile of shit, don't deserve another day on Earth, let alone the wait for a trial and hangin. My luck, you'd actually survive the trip. I'll tell ya, when I heard it was you, I decided ten grand'll do just fine." Tynan stepped back and pulled his silver Colt. Opening the barrel, he checked the full load, doubtless for dramatic effect, and spun it closed.

"You know, I was in over in Giddings, Texas for the hanging of Wild Bill some few years back. Oh yeah," he added, as if attending was some great, enviable honor. "You know what his last words were?"

"Please, please," Potter pleaded, reaching out with a desperate hand. "No!"

"Nope! He said, 'I deserve this fate. It is a debt I owe for my wild, reckless life.' I ain't never heard such a thing from a man bout to meet his maker. He took responsibility and atoned for his sins. Very honorable. Right? I tell ya, *I* was surprised. Don't reckon I'd expect the same from you, though." Tynan pulled back on the hammer. "What will yours be, Joseph Griffin?"

The fervor of Tynan's pious gray eyes bore into Potter's soul. In this moment, knew he wasn't leaving this house alive. His stomach churned, cold and hollow. Fear? No, not quite. A burning frustration engulfed him, tearing him apart internally, filling his jabbering heart with rage. His *only* fear was dying and leaving the fate of his children uncertain... and the fact that this creature remained out there, wreaking havoc in town, with nothing he could do.

His last words?

Potter thought it through. He looked up at Tynan and froze, deadpan, squinting to focus his fuzzy vision.

"Well?"

"I used to think there were two kinds of men in this shit world." Staring off behind Tynan, Potter spat a thick nugget of dark blood on the floor, leaving a string clinging from his bottom lip. "The man who loses his life. And the man who takes it."

"Uh-huh." Tynan's gray eyes narrowed inquisitively.

"Though this last month has convinced me otherwise. At the day's end, there's only one." Potter thought back to his terse conversation with McCormac. *No one truly walks away.*

Tynan spritzed brown tobacco juice to his side, wiping his lip dry with a leather index finger. "And which man is that?"

Potter smirked.

With his raised arm, he pointed a bloody finger up over Tynan's shoulder. "Behind you..."

Several long appendages emerged from the darkness. Arms. Legs. Quick movements, almost twitchy. *It* had laggardly entered the open door and crawled the frame up onto the ceiling, obfuscated in the shadows of the wall lamps. Halfway into the dark room, the green inhuman body reached straight down with four long arms and gently dropped to the floor.

Deep *trilling* filled the living room.

It stood.

Tynan, bewildered, turned, glaring up in unequivocal horror at the large, shiny, dark orbs of the creature towering before him. Tobacco fell from his slack mouth. "What the f—"

Potter reached down and yanked out the narrow piece of jagged glass sticking in his thigh. "Hey..."

Tynan turned back. Not fast enough. Potter shoved the shard up, stabbing into the marshal's throat. Potter's face writhed into a snarl, twisting in the glass, slicing his own flesh in doing so; he could feel it scraping the bones behind the marshal's clenched jaw. Warm blood jetted down Potter's hand; the metallic tang filled the air as his burning gaze, like hot coals, pierced Tynan's shocked, slaty eyes, wide with disbelief at either the creature or the realization that America's Most Wanted had outwitted him. Wet gurgling sounds escaped him, his instinct to breathe overridden by the inability to do so. His hand sputtered, spitting out two rounds in quick succession into the wall.

The bright muzzle flash and screaming discharge sent the creature reeling. Potter launched Tynan into the towering creature, causing it to lose its balance as it seized him.

Breathing heavily, Potter paused to recompose himself, to savor this moment. A small smirk played on his quivering lips. Once again, he'd prevailed. Though he knew it remained to be seen whether he—*they*—would survive the night.

"Isaac..." Potter whirled toward the basement door.

KAAA—BOOOOMMM!

The wall, six feet behind, exploded in a brilliant, blinding flash of heat, debris, and shrapnel. A snap of yellow flare kissed Potter as the blast sent him, airborne, across the living room.

11

When Potter came to, he found himself slumped against the adjacent wall.

Silence fell, save for the high-pitched tone flooding the inside his head. Like someone covered his ears, drowning out most sound.

He rolled over, choking on dust, trying to catch his breath through a haze of dense smoke. His gaze blurred, burning—not just from the clouded room. The vision in his left eye had severely diminished. He could only see some scattered debris that had entered on impact, all grainy.

With sooted hands, he brushed away the wood, plaster, asbestos, and other insulating materials partially covering his body as he swiveled his head around in confusion, scanning the massive frayed hole in his living room wall.

He froze, a vision more terrifying than anything he had yet to see emerging through the hazy, gray mist.

The creature resembled the blue being from before, but it moved unequivocally faster. More vicious, and somehow, much more advanced. Its body looked broader, stockier, with a bulk of covering around the torso. Body armor, perhaps. It possessed six appendages, as opposed to the blue being's four, but the two additional arms seemed different. Smooth, undefined. Still, its fingers projected like talons from the torso armor, honing to equally sharp points. Its coloring also differed from its blue counterpart, an iridescent, teal green that continually shifted as it moved.

With a nearly unperceivable flutter of its buzzing, quad-structured wings, the creature drove Tynan against the wall, nearly blocking the basement. Potter, petrified, lay watching in horror as the creature reached in with its middle appendages. It swiftly eviscerated Tynan, spilling his guts across the ground.

Potter gagged and retched, eyes watering at the sight, the smell. With everything he had left inside, he pulled himself from the floor and bolted. Moving as fast as his shaky, limp leg could carry him, he headed straight down the hallway past the study, rounding the kitchen toward the side door. Maybe he could enter the basement from the outside tunnel.

The windows imploded on each side, shooting shards of glass at him. Two more green creatures propelled inside the openings behind. One landed on the sink counter, fiercely grasping onto the ceiling to keep from sliding off. A stack of Bessie's fine porcelain plates came crashing to the ground. The other planted onto the kitchen table, claws grasping wood. A guttural warbling emanated from both.

Still in a near sprint for his injured condition, Potter slid backward, fighting forward momentum as the two things touched down. He stumbled around the corner into the dining room, barely avoiding a collision with a wall, and stopped briefly to grab the doorframe, clumsily regaining his balance.

Evidently, *outside* was out of the question.

He needed to reach the goddamn basement, though. Creeping through the dining room, he posted up against the door frame and, painstakingly, peeked around the corner. The fluttering creature stood with its back to him, continuing to tear a suspended Tynan to pieces. The marshal hung, lifeless, over his own entrails. His gold timepiece fell to the floor, bouncing away with tattered pieces of purple waistcoat.

Potter crept with deliberate movement toward the creature. Toward the basement. Back against the wall, he silently begged not to be seen.

Five feet from the gruesome evisceration, he reached the slightly ajar door and slid into the opening.

The ringing in his ears subsided slightly; he could hear shattering glass and the thudding sound of violently shifting objects, likely furniture, above. He peered up the dark stairs, assessing. *They* must be coming in from all angles.

Potter hastily descended the stairs, his boot sliding on slick blood. His, Tynan's, who even knew. The liquid drove his limp leg out from under him, slamming him on the seat of his pants as he slid all the way down and landed at the bottom. He hesitated there, sprawled on the ground, taking a moment to catch his breath and appreciate his still, somehow, unbroken neck.

Another explosion rocked the house, shaking the foundation. A growing pattering sound reached his ears. A smattering of varying gunfire outside, likely the source of the explosion. Rifles popped off in the distance, along with the rapid, terrifying fire of a Gatling gun reverberating. Faint voices yelled commands, commands he knew all too well. And as he thought about it...

A fucking cannon. The weapon had torn a hole straight through his living room wall.

Potter found himself on the battlefield once again. But instead of Virginia, the horrors of an all-out war erupted on the Bennett property. And those creatures were here, in his *house,* taking cover.

"PA," a familiar voice called.

Potter thrust himself up and glanced over. His son stood in the pale lantern light, arms cuffed around the basement pillar.

He ran over, kneeled, and brushed his hands over his boy's quivering body, checking for injuries. "You all right, boy—huh?! You didn't get hit or nothing, did ya?" He cupped his hands under Isaac's cheeks.

"I-I'm all right, Pa." Isaac looked up. "What's going on outside?"

"You wouldn't believe me if I told ya, son. What matters is *I* got you now, and we're gonna make it out of here, you hear me?" He spoke with conviction, although his words rung hollow, even to him. A vision of the dissipating hourglass flashed before his eyes, the dwindling sands spilling its remaining granules. He at least hoped Clara and Isaac had a chance.

KRRREEEEEEEEAAAAAAAAHHHHH!

Potter and Isaac glanced up. A shrill screech tore through one of the upper levels, unlike anything either had ever heard before. Inhuman. Several more vociferous, wretched cries followed in succession, varying in tone and length.

"Pa," Isaac said.

The look of fear and despair on his son's face broke Potter's heart. *It's not going to end this way,* he told himself, fighting back the creeping guilt of disappointing his young'uns. *Not like this.* He could still make it right, get them away from here.

Potter eased himself down into the cache and grabbed a rifle, loading a round into the chamber. He returned to Isaac. "Spread apart your hands. Keep the chain taut."

"Wuh-wuh-what!?"

Potter took aim. "And don't. Move."

Isaac winced behind the pillar. With a loud bang, Potter shot the chain, freeing the boy from its restraints.

"Isaac." Quickly, he embraced his son, squeezing him long and firm; the soot and dried blood on his face smeared against Isaac's cheek. He couldn't recall if he'd ever hugged his boy like this before. *Just one of my many shortcomings as a father.* The thought saddened him. He'd make it up to both his children, if they survived the night.

If he still had time.

Isaac stared up at him. "I do good, Pa?"

Potter looked his boy in his eyes. "You did good, Isaac. You did real good! I'm proud of you, son. Today you became a man, you understand me? A man!" He wiped his bloody nose and mouth on his wrist sleeve.

"Your face!" Isaac pulled back, eyes wide as he spotted the glistening burgundy leading from Potter's chest to his head. "You... you're shot, Pa! You're shot bad!"

"I'm fine, son. This blood ain't all mine."

"That man. With the top hat." Isaac froze, horror filling his face. "What was he saying up there, Pa? Terrible things he said about you!"

"Listen to me. Listen to me, son. No matter what happens, no matter what you may hear about me, you remember this: you *know* who your father is. All right?"

Isaac's eyes glassed over. He nodded and hugged Potter once more.

"I'm gonna need you to do me a favor. I'm gonna need you to cauterize this wound up here." He swallowed hard. "Both sides. Can you do that for me?"

Isaac nodded, eyes fearful. "How, Pa?"

Potter glanced around. *The busted handcuffs.* He removed the lantern's glass cover and held the metal bindings over the flame.

"We're gonna get this nice and hot. All right? When it's ready, you are gonna press this to the wound, *very hard*, till it stops bleeding." Potter panted, barely forcing out the words. "Then you will repeat on the back. Got it?"

Isaac's face contorted. His head nodded yes, but his mannerisms screamed reluctance. "Pa..."

"Shhh-sh-sh-sh." Potter shook his head, then glanced up at the disconcerting noise within his home—what remained of it.

The mayhem continued above them. Gunfire, explosions, unearthly screaming and trilling. Only a matter of time until those things discovered the basement.

"We don't have a lot of time, son. I need to find your sister. Here, it's ready." He handed the edge of the handcuff to Isaac, the opposite side charred black. With his shirt torn and his gun belt discarded next to him, Potter lowered himself to the cold earth, quivering, clenching his holster between his teeth. Looking up at Isaac, he nodded.

Isaac slowly, begrudgingly, pressed the hot metal to his old man's upper chest, holding the brand firm.

Agony. Whiffs of smoke dissipated before Potter's eyes as his skin seared like beef on a cast-iron skillet. He screamed through clenched teeth, eyes instantly tearing.

With a wince, Isaac let up.

Potter spit out the holster. Rolling over, he coughed, gasping for air on all fours. Spittle clung to his quivering lip. The pain, incredible. Unimaginable. *Christ.* He might have lost consciousness, had he not been partially sedated.

Now for the second hole.

The branding lasted an eternity, or so it seemed to Potter, his mouth watering from the sweet, putrid aroma of charring flesh. He clenched his throat, forcing back vomit. When the torture finally concluded, he needed a few moments to catch his breath and sit up.

"Payback is a real sonovabitch, eh?" He wiped tears from his eyes, offering his traumatized child a grateful nod. "Thanks, son."

Isaac strained a smile. "What now, Pa?"

"I'm going to get your sister. Alone. It's not safe for you up there, outside." He glanced inside the artillery cache. "We'd better thank your Great Uncle Bennett for digging out the basement. Get in."

"Huh?"

"You're gonna hide inside the tunnel. Wait for me to—"

"No!"

"Isaac..."

"Pa, please! Take me with you!"

Potter squatted in front of his boy. "Nothing will find you down here. Okay? Worse comes to worst, you have rifles. Load em up. You have grenades. And if you need to get out, you know where the hatch is. There is no better place to be right now, okay?"

"That ain't it, Pa."

"What is it, boy?"

Isaac's eyes welled.

Potter ruffled his son's hair. "I ain't gonna leave you, Isaac, if that's what you're thinking. I'd never leave you behind. Ever. And I ain't gonna die out there either, you hear me?"

Isaac, struggling and failing to fight back tears, nodded.

"Come on."

Isaac climbed down. Potter painfully flipped over the hatch, jumping in before it slammed down. They crawled to the edge of the tunnel together, Potter wincing with each toddle. The pain had finally begun to set in. Gently, he opened the hatch an inch and peered out.

Bedlam, even from his minimal viewpoint. Torches burned around a caravan of troops. Cavalry men interspersed the edge of the woodlands, some running, some taking cover behind two carriages, all firing at an unseen target. One carriage, as he expected, held a cannon; the other, a Gatling gun.

"Come here." He hugged Isaac once more. "I *will* be back, okay?"

The boy nodded.

Potter grabbed a grenade in one hand, the explosive awkward and heavy. In the other, he clasped a more familiar weapon: a rifle. He looked up at the hatch before shutting his weary eyes to take two deep breaths. *Just get to a horse.* He prayed for one of his to be alive.

With a disquieted sigh and a shake of the head, he climbed out.

Chapter 29

Minister Healy, Aaron, and Nora stood in silence behind the factory floor window, staring out in dismay over Missouri Plaza. On the opposite end of the street from where they stood, flames engulfed the church, an amber beacon illuminating the top of Main Street.

Nora knew one swift gust of wind could send embers fluttering over the stores, setting them ablaze. Taylor's Tailor & Clothier would go first. Then her place. Then, quite possibly the whole town would follow. Gone.

Bill was gone, too. She knew this. The weariness in his eyes had revealed it to her. The only man she'd grown to care for over the long, lonely years in this quiet town and he up and abandoned it; more so, he abandoned her. She wondered, a knot of anxiety tightening in her chest, if she could muster the resolve to start over again. Even if she did, where would she go? Back to Texas? She supposed it had been long enough. Who'd dare take up with this vagrant old spinster? Tomorrow would bring clarity on whether or not she had to cross that bridge.

She glanced at her companions—two men directly affected by the evening's events. They had it much worse. Healy's face, gazing at the ghastly flames, evinced the torture of a man who'd lost everything. His church, his home, his stolen paintings. Gone. A singular tear fell from his eye. An utterly morose Aaron just hung his head, unable to watch anymore.

She placed her hand on the boy's upper back. "I know, darlin.""

"I can't believe he's gone," Aaron said. "Just saw him earlier tonight. I ate supper with him and his father. I—I just don't understand any of this. You say that thing came from the pit in Bill's backyard?"

Nora nodded.

"That means it came from the same place." He turned and pointed toward his office. "The device."

"I, uh, reckon so, Aaron. First I've heard of it tonight. He-he never mentioned it." This, somehow, didn't surprise her.

Aaron returned to his office. Nora, puzzled, lagged but followed. The device on his desk softly pulsed, producing a faint, gravelly noise. A crescendo. Iiiinnnnn; oooouuuut... iiiinnnnn; oooouuuut... a sparse glimmer of red current gently fluttered around its core.

Nora joined Aaron's side. "Why?"

"That thing... what if *it* was here, looking for this?"

"Guess it's possible. Don't matter much now, does it? By the looks of it, the cavalry took care of it."

A *WHOOOOSH* washed over the mill, shaking the building gently. Nora grabbed Aaron's arm for support as they both looked up.

"My God!" Healy crossed himself, backing away from the window.

Nora turned, troubled. "What is that!?"

Healy didn't answer. He stood, mouth agape, still facing the window, staring up at the ceiling.

Nora stepped from the office. "Minister Healy, what was it!?"

"In-in-in the sky!" He pointed upward, then turned to Nora and Aaron. "Something... something just *flew* over the entire town!"

BANG—BANG—

"AHH!" Nora squawked, almost leaping out of her own skin.

BANG—BANG—BANG!

The pounding came from the front door. The three exchanged concerned glances.

BANG—BANG—BANG!

Aaron moved with caution to the side window, peering out. "It's—" He turned to Nora. "Bill's daughter... Clara?"

Nora's breath hitched, hand flying to her chest. *Bill's still here!* But why had his daughter returned? Surely Bill had no plans to come back, but they hadn't even departed. *This can't be good.*

Aaron unlatched the door and opened it. Clara stood with a weary smile, holding several rifles in her small hands.

She handed Aaron the guns with a glance back at Blanco. "I also have something called a grenade back in the satchel."

"Uh, come in." Aaron moved, allowing Clara to enter the mill.

Clara glanced toward Aaron's office. "Ms. Nora!" Excited, she ran to her.

"Clara, you made it!" Nora picked up Clara, wrapped her in her arms, and peered at the door, expecting Bill to follow. "Where's your father, sweetheart?"

Clara glowered. "He ain't coming."

"What do ya mean, he ain't comin, darlin?"

She placed Clara on her feet. Before she could answer, the mill door thrust open. Roswell and Chisum briskly entered, breathing heavily, faces in a pale sweat.

"We need to vacate town," Roswell barked. "Immediately!"

The look of disquiet returned to Aaron's sullen face. "What is happening?"

"Some mammoth airborne ship just sailed over the damn town! That's what for Christ is happening, Wilburn." Chisum's head spun around. "Wuh-where the hell is Coffey!?"

"We thought he was with *you.*"

"Well, no, he ain't with us. Shit, shit, Christ it all to hell!" Chisum stomped and threw his hands up in an erratic panic.

"Did they kill it," Healy asked, his tone deep. Resentful.

"Blew it to *highhh* heaven, minister. Pardon the pun. Ain't nothin survived that blaze, I can tell ya that." Roswell smirked and nodded, proud of himself. Noticing the look of disdain on the minister's face, he changed his insensitive demeanor. "We're, uh, sorry bout your church, Minister. Truly."

"Don't matter a hill of shit, now does it? You saw that thing in the sky. What do we do if there's more of those"—Chisum tried to gesticulate a large, ambiguous creature with awkward hand movements—"*things*, and they come into town before Potter returns? You know how *hard* it is just killin *one* of those sumbitches!?"

"Oh hell, John, he ain't comin back!" Roswell threw a hand up. "You heard Foster, same as me."

Nora stepped out of the office. "What're ya'll talkin bout?"

"The cavalry came for *him*, Nora. He's skinned out of town by now, I'm sure of it."

"The-the cavalry?" Nora stammered, taking a step back. An icy chill swept through her. *My God, Bill what've ya done?*

"If not, then he is in a lot of trouble," Aaron said. "Whatever those things are, I am almost certain they are headed there."

"I believe we should round up who's left," Healy said, still morose. "Immediately vacate town."

"You think those things won't get us on horseback!?" Chisum patted his coat, frantically searching for a cigar. "I vote we let the cavalry do their job, and we wait it out here. Board up the windows. It's a big place. We can survive here for a spell, I reckon."

Aaron shook his head. "What if they cannot, Mr. Chisum? Then what?"

"Well, maybe... maybe send another one of those telegraph messages out! Tell em what's going on down here, get some more cavalry boys out this way. You know morse code, Wilburn, right?"

"I do not."

"FUCK!" Chisum pulled his hat off and slammed it down on the floor.

Nora's mind spun in a dozen directions at once with all the bickering, each thought colliding with the next, overloaded with this new revelation. She craved a glimmer of hope, a single positive detail to break through the wall of negativity that surrounded her.

Not a moment later, the door swung open. Coffey radiated happiness as he entered the mill, beaming from ear to ear. "Sacked the marshal's office!" He nodded to his arms, in which lay Mather's stockpile of rifles, ammunition, and a couple lanterns.

She supposed this would do just fine.

Chisum's twisted face, a shade of beet red, lightened several shades. He even managed a sly grin. "My brilliant, brilliant boy." He met Coffey, pulling a cradled rifle and turning it over in his hands as if just handed a piece of gold. "I don't pay you enough, my friend."

"I saw that thing in-in the sky." Coffey looked at Clara, standing in the office. "Has Bill returned?"

"He ain't returnin." Roswell interjected.

"Ain't—ain't returnin?"

"I'm afraid he's gonna have to," Nora said, looking at Clara.

The little girl stepped from the office.

Roswell turned. "What in eternal damnation is she doin here?"

"She came baring weapons, Mr. Smith."

Roswell stalked to the office. Nora followed.

"Weapons!? It took a whole damn army to kill just one of those things. What's a few rifles gonna do, stave off our inevitable demise?" Roswell glanced at the device sitting on the desk. "And what's the deal with this thing, Wilburn," he shouted across the mill. "Has it done anythin new since it kicked on?"

Aaron shrugged. "Not that I have noticed."

"There's another piece," Clara offered.

Nora's face momentarily went blank. She squatted so she was eye level with Clara. Though things looked bleak, a sliver of hope remained. "What other piece, darlin?

2

Clara bit her lip. She didn't want to get Isaac in trouble, but she needed to help save Ms. Nora and Coffey. "My brother took it. He was worried about the Bad People coming to take Pa."

"Other piece?" Aaron blinked. "The crystal, that's right!"

"What's she talkin about, Aaron," Roswell demanded.

"The box." Aaron walked to his office and glared at the black box. "I noticed earlier. I thought maybe Van took it. He talked about bringing in higher authorities to inspect it. Inspect Bill's property. Makes sense. What if that is why those things are here? If we just bring it to Bill's house—"

Clara perked up. "Yes!" She'd tossed the crystal into the yard, where she'd left behind her brother and Pa, who now faced grave danger from these things likely searching for it and the black box. She figured once it was gone, the Bad People would leave them alone.

"Nuh-uh. Nope." Roswell shook his head, joining them in the office. "That thing stays here. I have plans for it once this is all over."

"No! We need to bring this to my pa!"

"Look little girl, you have no idea what you're dealin with here." Roswell bent forward, hands on his thighs, reaching Clara's level. "You let the adults handle this, ya hear?"

Clara glared fire at Roswell, then at the device. Its globe, once slowly pulsing, kicked up in a dull, hypnotic roar: *iiiinnnnn—oooouuuut—iiiinnnn—oooouuuut.* She reached for it, gripping the edges, dragging it toward her.

"Now don't you touch that, sweetheart," Roswell condescended.

iinn—oouut—iinn—oouut—inn—oouut—iinn—oouut—iinn—oouut—iinn—oouut

Clara glowered. "I'm not your damn sweetheart!"

She yanked back on the device, sliding it off the table. The weight of it jerked her forward. Roswell reached for the other end of the black box, barely catching it before it hit the floor. Clara, in an attempt to strengthen her grip, grabbed the globe with her right hand—

BIZZZAAAP!

A bolt of red current shot from the core into the surface of the globe, entering Clara's hand. The force lifted her off her feet, and she plummeted backward, slamming her head on the floor.

Her limp body slid across the office.

3

The lights... so bright. Potter put up a shielding hand. Dazzling. The colors, every shade of the rainbow.

"Great—Scott!"

His mouth dropped as he stared, awestruck. He'd stepped out into something fantastical, far beyond the bounds of rational thought. A juddering green halo enveloped the languishing full moon while strips of translucent lights flashed in a semi-circular, steady stream across the valley, now fully illuminated. All coming from some sort of *airship* parked behind the Bennett house at the edge of the Pecos.

Potter's worldview expanded around him, strangely infinite. Unsettling. He hadn't unearthed an ironclad warship at all, he realized suddenly... though his mind still struggled to grasp the fact that *this thing* had lived down there, beneath the ground, for *centuries*. He shuddered.

KAA-BOOOOMMM!

The sound of the cannon tearing into his house snapped him back to reality. He ducked and ran, arms up, shielding his head. Another blast exploded several feet in front of him, sending chunks of mound bursting in his face. Dirt and grass particles rained down. He pivoted and ran in the opposite direction, around the side of the house and toward the back of the barn, where he tripped over the body of a fallen cavalry man. Decapitated.

Trilling sounded from above, and he glanced up. The creatures stood on the roof. Some gently hovered, their lusty wings humming. Others emerged on foot from the dark. From the sky.

An infestation.

"aaaaaaaaahhhhhhhhhAAAAAAHHHHH!"

From somewhere afar, the sound of screaming burgeoned. Potter looked up. A cavalry soldier fell from the sky and plummeted into the front lawn with a *thud*, ten feet from Potter, bouncing twice. The body convulsed, blood bubbling from his gaping mouth. A look of surprise and horror flooded his gaping, empty eyes.

Potter didn't hesitate. He picked himself up and ran, rounding the corner at the edge of the barn. He took the corner—

SMACK!

He collided right into a swiftly moving object, bouncing him backward. The creature caught him by the throat, lifting him from the ground, forcefully backing him against the barn wall. Its fingers, smooth, sharp, slid under his scruffy jawline, applying just the right amount of pressure to cut off his circulation without causing pain. Potter winced as his head cracked against the wood. He tried hopelessly to pull in a breath, choking through obstructed airways.

The creature's narrow, red eyes blinked erratically at Potter, sweeping up and down with its haunting lids shuttering on angle. Its facial features, too, seemed narrower, almost sharper than the creature back at the church, though the jaw line looked thicker, more defined, bulging from the forefront of the creature's face. Potter gawked at the hideous monster's mannerisms. What did it *want*!? He didn't know if he was food or just an indiscriminate slaughter on a path beyond his understanding.

Below his own suspended body, he could just about see the creature's other set of arms hovering around his midsection. Its mandible separated at the center, opening to reveal rows and rows of tiny, sharp, twisted teeth. The oozing pinchers at each end clinked.

"HEY," someone yelled.

The creature turned its head.

POP!

From his fading peripherals, Potter saw a cavalry soldier standing off to his left with a rifle barrel in the creature's mouth—though only briefly. The blast, which didn't quite exit the back of its shielded head, still sent the creature slamming onto its back.

Viscous, green mouth spatter hit Potter full in the face. He slid down, thumping on the seat of his pants. With a yelp and gasp of anguish, he sat, staring at the twitchy creature, waiting for it to get up.

It didn't.

A bullet through the damn mouth. Christ, he wished they'd considered that move.

The soldier reached out his hand. Potter hesitated, staring up into the young man's eyes.

"Come on, mister," the stranger urged.

Reluctantly, Potter grabbed his hand, and the soldier yanked him to his agonizing feet. Wincing, Potter bent to pick up the rifle and grenade and, with haste, followed the soldier into the barn entranceway, each taking cover behind the wall on either side of the opening.

"You Joseph Griffin," the young man asked.

Potter hesitated before answering. "Yeah?"

"I'm Lieutenant Brooks. Herbert Phillips Brooks of the First Cavalry Division of Fort Hood, Texas."

Christ, this kid's a baby.

Potter glanced down at his rifle in one hand and the Ketchum grenade in the other. His head spun. He wasn't prepared, nor in any condition, to kill a cavalry soldier, much less a child. Still, he needed to keep his guard up until he understood what Brooks wanted.

The disquiet squealing of the creatures, either raging or dying, reverberated in the distance.

Lieutenant Brooks continued to speak across the wide entryway, shouting over the surrounding discharge of rapid gunfire and cannon blasts. "I'm afraid we've come with some unpleasant news, sir. The United States Army recently received information of your whereabouts with subsequent orders of retrieval several days ago. We're here to take you into custody, along with any other faction of your party."

"Okay?" Potter retorted, though the words dribbled out more as a question, waiting for the *but...*

"Uhhh, it appears there may be a slight change of plans. Any chance you have an explanation for what is happenin here!?" Brooks peered outside, then looked over at Potter.

Screams ricocheted in the distance.

"I'm afraid I'm at a loss myself, Lieutenant Brooks." Potter peered out. He needed a clear path to his horse. "Look, I—I don't have a lot of time. What little I have I need to use to get to daughter. She's in town."

Brooks looked him up and down, barely visible in the moonlight. "I assure you, we've got our hands full here, Mr. Griffin." He removed his Kepi cap and wiped perspiration from his forehead with a sleeve. "I bid you farewell in your journey. I'll cover you best I can from in here."

Potter nodded, silently thanking the young man who'd saved his life.

Exiting the barn, he scurried across the yard, close to the house, slightly crouched. Bright lights flashed in his peripherals, though he did his best not to look. Only three things mattered in this moment: finding a clear path to the horses, preventing the U.S. Cavalry from indiscriminately shooting him, and avoiding detection by these giant, flying anomalies. He succeeded in his first objective as he rounded the corner of the house, though, to his immediate chagrin, what he found proved less than satisfactory.

The schooner, dragged across the property, lay turned on its side, its contents scattered about. Luggage and spilled box crates littered the yard along with his overcoat. In front of him, a yellow pamphlet caught his eye. The edges of the playbill for *Foggerty's Fairy* fluttered, ruffled by the breeze.

Clara...

McCormac's nag, still tied to the bridle, lay twisted behind the carriage backside, her body laden with bullet holes. Dead. Potter ran to the corpse, taking brief cover.

He squatted, stroked the nag's mane, and peered into her open eye. "Sorry, old girl."

His only prayer now was the tentative survival of Bessie's mare. He glanced up and around. Though tough to discern in the chaos, he spotted movement at the edge of the woodlands. A horse, yes. Whose didn't matter.

Carefully, he crept around the carriage front, just far enough to access the small compartment situated under the bench. Rifles sporadically fired in the distance, muffling the shouts of cavalry men calling to one another.

Potter placed the grenade and rifle down and reached over, lifting the latch. His old bayonet lay inside, waiting. He hoisted the weapon, turning it over in his hand. The old blade still produced a silvery luster, though sparse under its bronzing patina. He thought about the last time it served its purpose—to defend young Henry, the poor flag boy he failed to protect, right before he skinned out for the mountains.

A disquiet trilling reverberated through every fiber of Potter's being, twisting the cold, unapologetic dagger of fear back into his guts. He froze, gripping tightly onto the bayonet. The noise, too close for comfort, left him paralyzed, unable to turn and look.

The wagon wheel, three feet behind him around the edge of the carriage, spun with a creak, sending chills through his weak, tired core. Without moving, he glanced down at the rifle and grenade, neither of which offered a viable option.

Too late.

From the corner of his left eye, he watched the creature creep behind him, its head slowly turning, looking, examining. Its eyes erratically blinked, almost vertically.

Beads of cold, pink sweat ran alongside Potter's temple and down his lacerated cheek, the salt stinging his gash. Compliments of the marshal. He had seconds, if that, before this thing grabbed him... but a sharp, rusted surprise awaited the creature if it did.

The strange being, in its slightly crouched defensive stance, inched closer to Potter. He side-eyed the hideous lifeform. Its oddly shaped snout contorted, quavering in quick succession as it sucked air in and out of its tri-hole nostrils, no doubt smelling the savory scent of blood. He swallowed dryly, attempting to hold his breath as the creature stepped toward him.

It stopped nearly six inches from his face and sniffed around, its warm breath tickling his face with a coppery odor. Potter followed its every move with a bulging side eye as the creature gently squatted and reached, feeling for the spot from which the bloody scent emanated.

Something blocked its path.

With a splayed, boney hand, it caressed the warm, silky remains of McCormac's dead nag, perhaps considering a meal. But, almost immediately, it recoiled slightly, as if smelling something not quite right. A moment later, it rose, expanding its lustrous wings—*at least six feet on either side!*—and shot straight up, vanishing into the night.

Potter exhaled a deep, guttural gasp, remembering Clara's nature book. Her *"arth-roo-pods."* He shook off his near brush with death, for the third time in the last half hour, and considered the impossible.

The realization dribbled out as a dumbfounded whisper. "It couldn't see me."

Without sparing another second, Potter grabbed the carriage lantern and his coat from the scattered debris and scurried across the property toward the horse, successfully avoiding the ever-decreasing gunfire. The cavalry remained at least a hundred yards out on the other side of the property, growing farther and farther away with every step he took. Potter smiled. He'd accomplished his second objective.

As he neared the edge of the woodlands, however, three creatures landed in succession in his path, twenty yards ahead. Potter slid to a halt. They stood guarded, slightly crouched, arms raised. Ready to attack. That eerie, goddamn trilling warbled forth from them, standing Potter's hair on end. In a similarly defensive stance, he slowly moved in reverse, step by step. The creatures followed suit, inching forward, wings twitching.

He glanced to his left, toward the cavalry. The gunfire had ceased. Those left alive had taken cover behind the two carriages, the Gatling gun and cannon left unmanned.

Potter, now alone, had failed his third objective. *No way around but through.*

He looked at the unfamiliar device in his hand, his only means of dissolving the obstruction between him and his horse. Although he'd never thrown a grenade before, he possessed a general idea of what to do. Hopefully, that would be enough.

He supposed he'd soon find out.

Gripping the barrel shaped instrument of destruction, he cocked his arm. Pain seared through his shoulder as, with the last dregs of his strength, he launched the grenade into the air. The device took flight, tail spinning. Its heavy body quickly spiraled down between the creatures, the gunpowder igniting on impact.

The explosion and flash of light sent the screeching creatures reeling. One projected backward, losing a limb in the process. The two remaining nearby took flight, vanishing above the treetops. Clear.

Potter limped into the woodlands where, to his astonishment, he found Bessie's mare quivering behind two thick trees. She peered over, locking eyes with her master. He approached her heedfully, slowly reaching for her headstall and pulling gently. She, resisting, snuffled and neighed, pulling back.

"It's okay, girl. It's okay. I'm here. You're safe now, girl, you're safe. C'mere." He closed in, caressing the side of her face, running his fingers through her coarse mane. "I need you, Bessie. I need your help to get our daughter back. I promise, this is the last time."

He stood, slumped, panting, and closed his eyes. The pain viciously returned; his leg, his upper body, and his face throbbed and burned. Only the hodgepodge of drugs and adrenaline prevented him from falling where he stood. *Just as long as I keep moving.* He could make it. He had to make it. He had to.

With a gentle turn, the mare nudged Potter, rubbing her face affectionately against his hair and beard.

He raised his head. "Good girl."

He pulled his sluggish, fragile frame over the horse's back, gripping the remains of the frayed carriage harness, and slid the rifle into a handle grip along the shoulder strap. With no time to spare, he started the trek through the dark woodlands trail to the mill. To the river. Shortcutting the water offered the only straight, clear shot to town, though the exact strength and depths of the rushing river, far from shallow, remained unknown to him. Maybe not for long, he reckoned. With a nudge of his boot heel, reigns in hand, Potter raced off.

4

Land. This strange land—vast—tall structures everywhere—bridged, many mammoth bridges, over surrounding river water, lots of water—oh my, there's an ocean, a vast ocean, big boats, white boats, no sails, shiny—so many tall objects—so strange—giant bridges, hundreds of odd stagecoach-es traveling, thousands, *maybe—giant statue—a god—a guardian, she stands over the land of high towers, like buildings, their surfaces shiny, shiny like mirrors, reflective, pretty—large surface panels with moving objects, moving pictures!? Oh the colors! Our species, they roam this land, so familiar, yet so peculiar, so many colors, they roam like cattle—and stage-coaches, many, so many stagecoaches—peculiarly shaped—smooth, shiny, they move without horses,* with-out-horses—*they move on land—they move in-in the sky—flying stagecoaches,* flying-stage-coaches!? *Fast, fast moving, above and below—*

White light, flashes, trembling, SHAKING, like an earthquake, ground clouds, rising, yellow light, orange, so bright—too bright—pour-ing into the sky—orange, red, like fire—a strange fire—rising, all ris-ing, tall structures flying apart—stagecoaches falling from the sky—every-thing—everything is red—the sky is red—the guardian, she falls from her perch—burning—everything burning—this strange land consumed by flames and haze—a dark haze—can't see—can't see anymore—

Clara's eyes wrenched open. She gasped and shot bolt upright, reach-ing out as if to grasp something out of reach. A rib-shattering resistance prevented her from propelling forward. Her heart sputtered in her chest, walloping echoes pulsating between ears as she panted for breath, gazing around in confusion. Wood, drenched in dirt and dust and darkness, surrounded her. *Strangely... primitive.* She didn't belong here, wherever this was.

Blinking erratically, she noticed slightly blurred figures standing before her. Familiar, though still not quite right. She struggled to ease her breathing and partially regain her faculties, to clear her throbbing head. Put the ever-so-simple pieces together. She was back in the office. But how? She must've been gone for—for—

Hundreds, maybe even thousands of years... shiny towers. Flying stagecoaches. Moving pictures across panels.

She'd spent hours strolling that vast city. *Hours.* Some civilization poised precariously on the brink of a horrifying downfall.

Looking down, she saw Ms. Nora's arms wrapped tight around her. She lay in her lap, on the floor. Aaron and the minister stood over with warm regard. Bickering echoed in the near distance.

Ms. Nora squeezed her from behind. "Baby, you all right, huh? Ya gave us all quite a scare there for a second!"

"Wuh-what happened," she asked, still slightly dazed.

"That box. It gave you quite the shock! Knocked you clean off your feet, honey. You were out a few minutes or so." Ms. Nora probed through her matted curls. "Gotta massive lump on the back of your head, here, too, so you be careful sittin up now. Take it slow."

Clara winced, stroking her bumped head. Shockwaves of pain issued through her skull, only exacerbated by the shouts outside the office.

5

From the open office, Aaron could hear the old men bickering on the mill floor. He stood fuming, spectating over the mid-wall. Glancing over his shoulder, he saw Clara, still cradled in Nora's arms. Then the box—the air around it shimmered as if it radiated. Fully active. He couldn't shake the feeling that a part of him, however small, was still tethered to it. The hairs on the back of his neck prickled, sensing a menacing force on the Bennett property. And yet, somehow, he knew Potter was still alive. The haunting vision of Van's violent demise replayed in his brain. Although just a vision, it left him feeling burdened with responsibility.

"How are we gonna get that hardware out the door now, for Christ's sake," Chisum barked.

"We don't. Nobody touches that goddamn box. I'm lucky it didn't kill me!" Roswell patted down his blazer, as if checking everything remained intact.

He was right, Aaron thought, glaring at the device. Handling it now could prove deadly for human hands.

"Potter ain't gonna be too happy to find out you killed his daughter, Smith!" Chisum warned.

"You think that wanted man is returnin for his daughter? You must be just as crazy as he is. Hell, even if by some damn miracle the United States Army happens to triumph over this here menace, he still ain't comin back. He's as good as dead or captured."

A moment later, Aaron found himself between the two with one of Coffey's rifles, slamming the butt down on the mill floor. "I have heard enough bullshitting!"

"'Scuse me, boy?" Roswell, taken aback.

"No! You have caused enough of a stir here!" Aaron realized he stood inches from Mr. Smith's face. The words tumbled out of his mouth, unexpected and shocking, but he couldn't stop. "Now, I am taking this here rifle, and I am headed over to the Bennett property. Back up the cavalry. Who will join me... you, Coffey?"

Coffey nodded. "Let's get on. Time's a wastin while our friend, Bill Potter, is in trouble."

"Friend!?" Roswell scowled. "That dirty, no-good outlaw brought all this chaos here! For all we know, those things came for *him*! No. We stay and wait this thing out. Let the Army deal with it, then salvage what's left."

"What's left!?" Chisum turned. "This is where we're at now? Reorganize, start over, *if* we survive?"

"Van and I had big plans for this town, John." Roswell's tone softened. "All this. Everythin we all started here. It was just the beginnin. I—I can't lose sight of that now that he's gone."

"We don't make some sort of stand, there ain't gonna be no goddamn town left, Smith. And ain't none of us gonna be here to run it!"

"Your 'big plans' will have to wait." Aaron glowered at Mr. Smith. "You can all sit and argue, but I am headed after them." He turned to Coffey. "I'm ready."

Coffey smirked. "Right behind, Mr. Wilburn."

"We'll all fit in my stagecoach," Chisum said, looking directly at Roswell. "There's room for those lookin to fight for the future of this town, Smith." He picked up a rifle and looked over at the office. "You comin, Minister?"

"Uhh, I best stay here and look after the ladies. I don't believe I'll be of much use out there, Mr. Chisum. May Almighty God be with you all." He blessed them. "The Father, and the Son, and the Holy Spirit."

"For the best, padre." Chisum gave a wry, crooked smile. "Probably just slow us down, anyway. You stay and tend to the ladies. Say another one of those prayers for us." He nodded.

Aaron glared at Roswell. "Last chance, Mr. Smith."

He shook his head. "I'll be fine right here, thank you very much."

"Suit yourself, *Mayor*." Aaron, stepping toward the door, turned back. "You know, your son was like a brother... I am grateful he took me in and for what we built here together. His sacrifice cannot be for nothing. I could not forgive myself If did not at least try." He hung his head a moment, then looked back at Mr. Smith. "I never knew *you* to be so cowardly. You enjoy these next four years. If there is a town left." Aaron walked out behind Chisum and Coffey, slamming the door behind.

6

Nora reached out her hands in support.

Clara, slightly wobbly, rose slowly to her feet. The little girl rubbed the back of her curly head with a wince.

"Careful, honey." Nora gently held Clara's shoulders, ensuring she wouldn't fall. "You think you're all right to be standin? Maybe you oughta just take it easy."

She hesitated. "I'm—I'm okay."

The words rang hollow in Nora's ears. She shook her head. "How bout we go back to my place, getcha cleaned up a bit. Somethin to eat. Whaddya say? Come on."

Clara nodded absently, staring off at the ground.

Nora figured if the place did decide to go up from those pesky embers, she could at least salvage a few things—mainly her art. "We'll take the tunnel. I think it'll be safer than crossin Main Street. God only knows what's goin on out there."

"I don't think you should leave the mill, Ms. Nora, unless we absolutely have to," Healy objected. "Not until we get word from the cavalry that it's surely safe."

"Oh, Minister Healy, I think we'll be just fine. Ain't that right, Clara?" Nora stroked Clara's disheveled locks. "We won't be gone long, gentlemen. I mean, y'all are welcome to come along, if y'all like," she offered, a hint reluctantly. Extending the invitation to Roswell made her somewhat uncomfortable.

Healy glanced around, then glared at the pulsing black box. Red sparks fluttered the globe's perimeter. "Uhh, yes, perhaps I should go with you. Make sure you get there safe and sound."

Roswell glowered. "I think I'm fine right where I am."

Nora gave him a shrewd glance, her glare lingering a moment as she guided Clara ahead of her. "Come on, sweetheart."

"What about the box," Clara said, her voice slightly strained. "They didn't take it... the Bad People will come."

The Bad People. Nora finally understood. Unfortunately, the "bad people" *had* arrived. Many of them. They faced a new threat on Bill's property. "Baby, don't touch that. Let's worry bout this a little later, okay?"

Clara mustered a sullen nod.

Nora took Clara's hand and led her from the office, around the corner, and down the stairs, Minister Healy in tow. The basement wall lamps gleamed fully, illuminating the busy maze of stacked crates and woolen dust bunnies drifting in their path as they walked past a monstrous machine. Upon reaching the split wall, Nora glanced up and down the surface, trying to determine how to open it. No doorknob; too obvious, she supposed, for a secret door. She grabbed the spooled wool shelving and gave it a tug. It began to lumber open, scraping along the floor.

With a crack, the spooling shelf slammed into her forehead. She yelped, stumbling backward as the secret door fired open. Healy, standing five feet behind, caught Nora as she collided into his open arms. Clara sidestepped, barely avoiding Nora's fall as an eddy of tepid air swaddled the three of them. A shrill scream discharged from the girl's tiny throat. Healy looked up. Nora dismissed the pain, fixing her eyes on Clara.

In front of her, the razor edges of long, knobby fingers and two ashy gray hands slid between the narrow door and wall frame opening, pulling in its ghastly figure behind it. Plumes of black smoke coiled in from the tunnel, escaping around the partially charred blue being. Steam rose from its muted body. Its armor, remarkably still intact, seemingly protected its vital elements. Its tri-nostrils fluttered; its charcoal dusted lenses scanned.

Nora, using Healy's robes as an anchor, pulled herself up. "Clara, *RUN!*"

Clara turned and bolted back the way she came, Nora following right behind.

Reaching the stairs and hearing a thud, Nora glanced behind and stopped. The creature straddled Healy on the floor, its chest heaving in and out. Healy, arms raised, quivered uncontrollably, staring up at the being's unholy red eyes. Reaching into his robe, the minister pulled out a beaded necklace, its pendant, a gold crucifix. With a shaky hand, he held the cross straight up and muttered the prayers of the rosary, starting with the Apostles' Creed.

Nora turned to Clara. The little girl stood on the third stair, waiting for her.

"Go on, get up the stairs." She smiled, though her eyes stung, tearing up involuntarily. "Get out of here, go hide back at my place!"

"Noooo," Clara yelled.

"I'll be right behind you, honey, I promise you. Now, *go!*"

Clara hesitated, tears welling. Then she spun around and clambered up the stairs.

With a relieved sigh, Nora turned and scanned the cluttered space, frantic to find something—anything—before it was too late.

7

Clara, heaving at the top of the stairs, spun her head around wildly. Mr. Smith stared blankly out the window down at Missouri Plaza, looking toward the smoldering remains of the church. Did he not *hear* all the screaming? In his right hand, he held the barrel of a rifle, almost like a crutch, the butt resting on the floor.

Barely huffing out the words, she pointed and yelled, "The monster's here, downstairs!"

Mr. Smith turned with an impassive "huh," teetering on apathetic.

She ran to him, grabbed his arm, and tugged with one hand at his cream-colored jacket sleeve while flailing her other arm, waving him toward the basement. "We need help, Mr. Smith! It—it's got the minister! It's got him and Ms. Nora, I said! Come"—she yanked—*"on!"*

She stared up at his grave face, tears running down her cheeks.

He bent forward and put a hand on her shoulder. "Clara, is it? Now listen to me, young lady. It's *too late* for our friends down there, you hear? If we want a fightin chance to survive, we need to leave here posthaste. You understand me?" He straightened, took her hand, and stepped forth.

Clara pulled back and dropped her grip. A newfangled incomprehension staggered her, something she couldn't quite describe—an unrefined feeling which had eluded her since the Big Flood took her ma and grandma. Pluck. The last vestiges of fear, a cold knot in her stomach, dissolved into nothingness as a powerful, almost tangible presence, gave her comfort and strength. She knew it was the guiding influence of Ma beside her.

Mr. Smith just stared into her glowering eyes and slowly backed away. "Come on, honey," he said, picking up a brisker pace toward the door. He stopped halfway to grab a lantern from the ground, glancing at the smoke billowing up through the doorway to the basement before looking back at Clara. "I'll take you home, back to your pa's. How'd that be?"

Clara, astounded, didn't move, didn't say another word. She stared vacantly at the cowardly mayor.

Without another word, Mr. Smith walked out the door.

8

Bessie's mare tore up the trail alongside the river, Potter tightly behind the reins. His heel firmly nudged her hind as they dashed toward the cemetery behind the fruitless bank and assay building. Up ahead, two ominous lights dangled, one seemingly suspended in midair, both separated by several feet of black space. They shuddered in the chilly night.

Potter pulled back on the reins, the mare slowing a bit as they drew near. The large object began to take shape, slowly revealing itself: a stagecoach turned on its side. Potter's narrow field of view homed in on a splash of silvery-white hair on the ground, a face-down head, followed by an unfurled body. *A runner.* Though he didn't get very far. A top hat tumbled past, brushing up against an oval headstone.

The mare trotted further. As the stagecoach crept into view, Potter saw two dead horses, still attached. He paused alongside the undercarriage, the doors torn clean off along with one shattered wheel. He leaned over just as far as his injured body would allow, swallowing back the pain, and peered into the dark cabin. Lamiya Dotterweich, or what remained of her, lay sprawled along the bottom. Her twisted body held its arms up, almost defensively, in the shallows of pooling blood. By the horrific expression engraved on her mangled face, she'd stood no chance against her assailant. Her throat appeared *chewed* out, leaving her head crooked backward, mouth agape. A ghastly mess. Her silver dollar eyes glared up at Potter.

Leaning back, something twisted around the busted door hinge caught his eye. Something oddly familiar. He reached over and pulled a tuft of yellowish fur, rubbing the silky material quizzically between his forefinger and thumb. *Chisum's barbed wire fence.*

A distant door swung open and shut, drawing Potter's attention. The mill on the riverbank stood clear in his sights, illuminated by gas lampposts on either side of the bridge and one over the mill entrance. A man on the bridge, wearing a cream-colored suit, mounted a horse tied out front. Likely Blanco. That bastard politician Roswell looked to be making a mad dash.

The horse bolted over the bridge.

For the first time, Potter noticed his body quivering, most likely the effect of shock long set in. Excruciating pain wracked his body, the efficacy of the opiates almost worn off completely. The full, debilitating weight of his afflictions, his face, his bullet wounds, all of it set in.

He exhaled, watching the misty warmth of his breath dissipate in the night sky. The air, cold and quiet, hung with eerie calmness, the sporadic sound of faint gunfire fading out. Potter looked up.

On the left side of town, black smoke wreathed above rooftops. By the fitful crackle of smoldering embers, he identified the remnants of the church. Behind him and to the right, a circular band of multicolor lights glowed vaguely over the woodland treetops. Home.

He exhaled, watching the misty warmth of his breath dissipate in the night sky.

9

Nora crept through the shadows.

Healy, trembling on his backside, mumbled and stuttered his way through "Our Father," barely keeping the cross steady in his shaking hands. Rosary beads clanked together along his tight knuckles. The creature leaned in with calculated ease, gently reaching down with a hook grip until its sharp middle finger, forefinger, and thumb slid around the shiny gold pendant. It yanked back, snapping the rosary from Healy's wide neck, and analyzed the jewelry up close for a moment before tucking the piece away in a partially charred compartment along its thigh armor.

Sensing her moment, Nora sprung. "Get the fuck off him!"

The creature turned, catching a monkey wrench to the face. Healy lifted his legs in an attempt to roll out from under it, and the off-balance, steaming creature stumbled sideways, falling into a pile of stacked crates.

Nora ran over, reaching out her hand. "Come on, come on, quickly!"

Healy grabbed her forearm, and she pulled him up. In a matter of seconds, they both flew up the stairs. Clara stood waiting in the office, staring at the black box.

"Clara, honey, I thought I said to get out of here and hide!?" Nora stepped in, though Clara remained unresponsive. "Clara. Whatcha doin!?"

"We need to go!" Healy stood staring down from the top of the stairs, waiting for the creature to emerge. His round, red face glistened with sweat.

"What about the box," Clara asked, still not pulling her gaze from the strange contraption.

"Never mind that damn thing!" Nora grabbed Clara by the shoulders, twisting her around face to face. "Hey, hey, hey! We need to go!"

Nora heard a scream from behind, followed by a loud *thud*. She turned to see Healy sliding across the floor as the creature emerged from around the corner. Nora stood behind Clara and embraced her, both watching the blue being. It stared at them, ten feet from the office entrance. Nora glanced behind, calculating the distance to the front door. *One minute, maybe two.*

The creature bounded forward into the office. Screaming, Nora scurried backward, pulling the shrieking Clara with her behind Aaron's desk against the half wall and vacant office window.

The creature stepped forward, then stopped. Its red eyes lit up. No, not eyes. The red lenses rolled back into its head, revealing the round oculi of the lifeform underneath. Situated in the forefront of the large oval socket, they appeared almost human: black pupils and bright violet irises surrounded by a thin, white sphere. Those eyes gaped down, pupils dilated, locked on the black box.

Nora bent down to Clara's ear. "I'm gonna lift you over the wall, very quickly, and you're gonna run out that door and hide, don't matter where. Ya hear me!?"

Clara nodded, unable to avert her eyes from the creeping creature, which squatted and lifted the black box from the floor. The globe stopped pulsing, instead firing blue sparks from its core. The creature placed the device on the desk, running its bony, azure hand, now a lighter shade of robin's egg under its soot-speckled skin, over the glasslike surface. Blue current met its fingers, following their outline as they moved. The creature glanced up and closed its eyes a moment.

10

The power of the box, linked to the multi-lensed internal monitoring system, played back the preceding events. In mere seconds, the Antiquarian saw *everything*.

Prior to their departure home, upon entry of WL-9768, the hyper jump had malfunctioned. Efforts to repair proved fruitless. They'd known that, upon returning home, the superannuated ship was scheduled for decommission. Still, they'd hoped for one last safe trip.

The captain had activated the internal tracking system, signaling a need for rescue. The azure crystal offered little console, however. With the war raging on, all available reserve teams were prioritized elsewhere, and with the device on the blink, the tracker's operability remained tenuous at best. Who knew if or when the signal would reach Command.

No options remained but the long way home. The Antiquarian had thus entered cryostasis for the lengthy return journey. Once in orbit, after programming the ship for its tentative voyage, the captain was meant to join as well.

Evidently, that did not happen.

The Earthling creature, clad head-to-toe in metal, dislodged the artifact room handprint panel with its long weapon, shorting out the circuit and opening the door. Something that should've been impossible.

The creature rewound.

Everything was on the blink. Some internal bug—corrupted semiconductors, CPUs, bad wiring, who knew—created shorts all over the craft. Doors opened, closed; screens powered on and off; landing gear stuck, wings locked before fully expanding; none of this was good.

For a moment, the Antiquarian considered the fact that the cryogenic chamber could've failed as well. Thank Zurik it had not!

Then, there it was. The artifact wall partially opened, just enough for the metal creature to retrieve its weapon.

Needless to say, the Antiquarian saw the climax before it happened.

The captain, impaled by the long, sharp object, clung to life, maintaining control of the ship in a feeble attempt at a safe landing. The craft gradually plummeted from the atmosphere until it hit the riverbank, twice its size at the time, in the lower part of the planet's northern hemisphere. Unfortunately, the captain expired shortly thereafter.

The Antiquarian fast-forwarded.

The Earthling creature in metal woke from an unconscious state, eventually discovering the handprint panels. It lopped off the captain's hand, using it to open doors. Some opened. Some didn't. The freighter door was jammed, either due to the internal malfunction or the pressure of the water. Either way, the metal creature knew its fate. It sat for some time staring out the window, watching the little amphibious creatures moving back and forth through the water. Before giving up completely, in a fit of rage, it tried to break the clear flight pane with its long weapon, among other objects, to no avail. It then forged a destructive path, smashing everything in the control center, including the helm. The long weapon spitefully plunged back into the captain before the recorder went blank.

The black box must have suffered a blow, cutting the majority of its internal power flow. From what the Antiquarian deduced, the metal man most likely perished from lack of nourishment.

The Antiquarian looked up. The little Earthling creature moved toward the door, the bigger one close behind.

It snapped its red lenses shut, and with the device in its hands, it bounded through the open office window, smashing through the support dividers. Its bony, sharp toes plunged into the floorboards, landing mere feet away from the two.

11

Nora yelped in terror, stopping mid-stride as the horrifying creature, at least forty feet away mere moments ago, leapt suddenly into her face. "GO, GO!" She shoved Clara by the back, thrusting her toward the door as she stared up, eyes fixated in absolute horror.

The creature languidly leaned in, its moist nose working, twitching, taking heavy whiffs of Nora's hair and skin. A chemical smell emanated from its burned flesh. She gagged, desperate whimpers squeaking from her cringing mouth. Icy lead filled her veins, immobilizing her despite her desire to fight back. She tensed up, body trembling fiercely, before finally clenching her eyelids shut to shield herself from the imminent end.

The moment stretched out, an eternity of stillness, until the sudden clamor outside shattered the silence. She opened her eyes to an empty room.

12

The horse with no name rounded the corner onto the bridge. To Potter's bewildered delight, he saw his daughter explode from the mill's entrance and run out onto the dusted bridge.

"Clara," he yelled.

The horse slid to a halt ten feet from his girl, who turned, startled. Her eyes, though highly distressed, immediately lit up at the sight of him. "PA!"

He smiled thinly, happy she was not only safe, but easy to find. He reached out his hand. "Come on, honey, we need to go. Take my hand!"

"But Pa, the monster!" She jumped up and down, waving a pointed finger at the mill. "IT'S INSIDE!"

"Baby, please, we don't have time for this—"

"But Ms. Nora and Minister—"

"Clara."

"Healy are trapped inside and I think he's—"

"Clara."

"—hurt. The monster's got Ms. Nora, she needs help—"

"CLAIRE, get on the goddamn horse!"

She blinked, taken aback. Her mouth gaped, and she began slowly stepping backward.

Oh, no-no-no-no-no.

Potter unmounted and stepped gently toward his dismayed daughter. Although concerned for Nora's safety, and, he supposed, Minister Healy's, he trusted them to take care of themselves. If his hunch was correct, and if they didn't do anything stupid, they'd survive the night. Besides, in his condition, he could barely stand, much less defend against the supernatural. He had one priority now, his children's safety, and he refused to fail.

The creature barreled out the door, snapping the wood back off its hinges. It held the black box tucked under its right arm.

Clara turned with an expression of hopeful enthusiasm, likely expecting Nora. She shrieked in horror instead. The mare recoiled, Potter clutching the reins to keep her from fleeing.

The creature skidded to a stop at the side of the bridge, just before toppling over the side, looking at Clara, then Potter, then back to Clara before something else struck its fancy. It peered into the night sky, studying the illumination over the woodlands.

Potter, as quietly as he could, whispered, "Don't move a muscle. Stay perfectly still!"

Nora exited the mill and stopped short, eyes locked on the creature across the bridge. Clara lit up and gasped, taking slow, methodical steps toward Nora.

"No-no-no-no-no-no-no," Potter muttered to himself, watching fretfully. Chills crawled his spine.

The creature's dreamy distraction broke; it glanced around, eyes landing on the bridge and then his daughter. Clara, panicked, dashed for Nora. The blue being looked down at the black box, then back to the girl, and with swift, lithesome movement, it reeled in between her and safety, grabbing and scooping her from the bridge.

"NO-NO-NO-*WAIT!*" Potter watched in horror as the creature bounded into darkness with his daughter.

"Bill!" Nora ran straight into him with an embrace that jogged him off balance. "We need to go after it!"

Potter grimaced, a groan escaping his lips involuntarily.

Pulling away, she scanned his damaged face and body, her eyes catching where his blood-soaked shirt peeked through from under his coat. "Dear God. Bill, you okay?"

Healy stepped out the busted door and glanced over.

"Yeah, yeah, I'm okay. I got ambushed at the house." Potter grabbed Nora's hand and turned to the mare.

"I-I can't believe I— *WE*—made it out of there alive!" Healy crossed himself and looked at the sky, gaping. "Those lights!"

"I'm sure it's cause you're unarmed, Minister," Potter reasoned. "You weren't a threat to it."

"Not true. I was armed with the Power of the Almighty, Mr. Potter." Healy turned from the sky, staring directly at him. "And you. It didn't even acknowledge *you*. I saw the whole thing—it—it—"

"It couldn't see me. Come on, I know where it's headed." Potter slung himself over the horse and reached for Nora, pulling her up behind, wincing. "If you can find a horse alive, follow the lights. After what I've seen tonight, I must say... I now believe there's a greater power out there in this universe. Good, evil, whatever that may be. We can use all the help we can get, Minister, divine or otherwise."

The lingering green mist, alongside the waning full moon and the flickering airship illumination, lit the path home. With a nudge of his heel and a command, Potter propelled the mare into a gallop—albeit briefly. She slid to a halt near the end of the bridge. Gasping, Nora gripped Potter's waist to keep him from tumbling ass over teakettle.

"Woah, woah, woah!" Potter hollered.

The horse's head shook, followed by a shrieky neigh as she stepped backward.

A low, guttural growl materialized.

And there, emerging from the shadows, traipsed a massive golden wolf. The broad-shouldered beast paused, staring from afar, its growl rippling down from curled lips and salivating chops. It crossed the pool of amber light, spilling from the corner lamppost, wrenching its face in a sinuous sneer that bared long, pink teeth.

"Wuh-wuh-wuh-what is that, Bill, huh?" Nora trembled in Potter's ear, squeezing him tightly. "*What the hell is it!?*"

Potter held tight to the reins, keeping the horse steady, staring at the beast before him. Its bulbous mane gleamed a pale-yellow green under strange skies, the same color as the fur from the carriage.

His heart plummeted into his stomach. "No-no-no-no-no-no-this can't be fucking happening."

He glanced over at Healy, petrified in the mill doorway as the wolf stepped slowly forward, stopping twenty feet away. A low growl rumbled like a puttering engine from its quivering lips. The mare drew back, snorting and blowing, the wolf turning for them.

Those eyes... striking blue eyes, like Indicolite, bore through him and Nora. Strangely... familiar.

He looked down at the tucked rifle in his bridle, knowing they had one chance. A snowball's chance in hell, but their only one nonetheless. He waited.

The wolf lowered in a brief crouch that Potter recognized as an oncoming assault, preparing to launch. As fast as his tired arm could reach, he pulled the single-shot Tarpley from the leather handle. Bessie's mare twisted in a recoiling spin, and Potter saw the golden beast in midair coming straight for them, mere feet from a full tackle. He jammed the rifle into the crook of his arm, took tentative aim with his one clear eye, and fired.

The round struck the beast in a baby blue. Howling, the wolf hit the bridge deck with such force that it bounced sideways, rolling over the edge and into the river.

Potter threw down the rifle and spun the mare around.

They were off.

Chapter 30

The stagecoach squealed to a gradual halt just as it broke through the woodland clearing. Coffey, behind the reins, slowly stood from the tufted leather-bound bench.

The boss threw open the wagon door, gaping in disquiet as he stepped out. Aaron followed; they joined either side of Coffey. Together, the disconcerted men stared out over the oddly tranquil Bennett property, taking in the bedlam and remnants of a swift yet indiscernible battle. One which appeared to yield no victor.

A gaping hole exposed the living room of the Bennett house, or what remained of it. Two cavalry carriages sat decimated outside; they looked as if they'd been dropped into the Grand Canyon, leaving nothing but kindling. Pieces of shredded canopy trailed the property like little white flags. A possible attempt at a surrender, ignored with extreme prejudice. A morose cannon lay turned on its side, quite a distance away from its wagon, wheels shattered. Bodies of cavalrymen and horses lay haphazardly strewn about the scattered debris. Among the wreckage lay several twisted bodies of creatures, assumedly deceased. No movement came from anything on the property.

As spectacular and inexplicable as this gruesome battlefield appeared, all three jaw-dropping men stood powerless in their efforts to avert their eyes from the strange craft—*the docked airship?*—behind the river. Its brilliant vermillion caul cascaded beyond the vivid green, moonlit land which surrounded it, emanating a strange and unholy aura that promised anything but salvation.

"My God, Coffey," Chisum said gravely, "what are we lookin at here?"

Coffey offered a bewildered shrug. "Ain't got the slightest, boss."

The men heedfully walked through the abandoned war zone. Coffey scanned the dead among the property, praying not to see his new friend, Bill Potter. A man he realized, in this moment, he'd proudly call a brother. Pieces of human flesh trailed everywhere they stepped, a maze of indiscriminately torn limbs and visceral matter. All three gripped tightly to their rifles, despite grasping the futility of their weapons.

The mangled, drab-gray remains of a creature sprawled ten feet away from their path toward the open living room. Its mandible pinchers sat flared open, exposing rows of subsequent choppers, while the eyes, once a dark shade of red, deepened to a defunct graphite. Its arms and legs lay splayed in the lawn with two new, central limbs—seemingly mechanical to the creature's natural makeup—sticking up. Its fingers clenched, suspended, as if reaching for something.

Dark green liquid oozed from holes in its throat, arms, and face. Pierced armor left its body spiderwebbed like shattered glass. *Maybe a .58 caliber Gatling gun round?* Coffey shuddered. Easily the scariest weapon of the War, with six hundred shots per minute.

Chisum bent down for a closer inspection. "Would you just look at this unsightly sumbitch, fellers? Christ! This thing is much more horrifying than the—"

"REEH, REEEH!" A ghastly squeal discharged from its orifice, while the mandible pinchers twitched. Its grim pair of centralized arms followed, the three-clawed fingers on each trembling.

Chisum nearly jumped out of his skin, recoiling backward and bumping Aaron. The three swung their rifles over in an effort to fire, but the creature quickly returned to its expiration.

The men stepped into the friable hole, entering the disarray and treading sprightly through the debris with the utmost caution. Blood, everywhere they looked. Two more bodies—Coffey thought, anyway—graced their path. Non-cavalry bodies. One, almost torn in half, trailed entrails down the hallway.

"Jesus Christ." Chisum pulled his handkerchief and covered his nose and mouth, turning away from the nauseating sight and the coppery smell of pooling blood.

"I pray to all that is holy, none these men is Bill," Coffey said, glancing at the unsettling remains.

Aaron squatted next to the torn remnants of a man on his side, pulling back on the violet overcoat breast. The silvery glint of a star, attached to the shredded waistcoat, reflected in the flickering wall lamp above. "Looks like a marshal. Mr. Chisum, would you mind checking the other gentlemen?"

"Christ, no!"

"But you are right there!"

Coffey nodded. A valid argument.

Chisum winced. "Aw, hell." Reluctantly, he squatted and threw back the coat, which revealed a similar badge. "Yup."

Two black barrels, mostly covered in pieces of wall fragments and glass, caught Coffey's eye. He bent over and brushed the debris away.

"What is it?" Aaron asked.

"Bill's boom stick," Coffey said somberly. He looked down at the scattergun, then up at the other men. "I do sure hope he's all right."

Another ten feet into the room, something glinted gold. A watch. Coffey picked it up, turning it over in his hand. With a thumb depressing the tiny plunger at the top, the lid snapped open. The face was cracked in a funny, uneven "Y" shape. Under the tarnished face, the hands of time sat, stopped.

"Ain't nobody could've survived this," Chisum stood. "I say we head back to the post office and signal for help. If those things are in that airship out back, we're sittin ducks."

"We should keep moving." Aaron, ignoring Chisum's remarks, stood and paused at the basement door, peering into the buckshot hole and up into the shadowy unknown. He held his rifle gripped tight to his chest.

"Christ." Chisum's head shook.

Coffey led the way with Aaron behind, following the uncoiled length of intestine and unidentifiable organs down the hallway until the spatter dissipated.

Creaking sounded ahead.

"I—I think I hear somthin." Coffey stepped into the kitchen entrance.

Looking back, he nodded his head sideways, signaling the sound originated from within. Guns at the ready, they entered, shards of glass gently popping under cautious boots.

Something creaked again, but this time, Coffey caught it. He pointed to the pantry on the far right, just beyond the stove. Aaron crossed the kitchen, leaving Chisum in the middle and Coffey on the left as they closed in on the pantry. The floor creaked loudly under Chisum's heavy foot. A moment later, the pantry door swung open. Four men pushed through. Cavalry men. They pointed their rifles, ready to fire at the three.

"Whoa, whoa, whoa!" Coffey lowered his weapon with one hand and surrendered with the other.

"Christ." With slight reluctance, the white-haired man gently lowered his weapon, expelling a deep breath of relief that flared his white mustache. "You just about gave me a heart attack," he said, panting, as if still considering the possibility. "I'm Lieutenant Colonel Foster. They still out there?"

Coffey met Aaron's and Chisum's eyes in a silent, discontented exchange. *You mean... there's more?*

Only Coffey responded. "We ain't seen nothin."

The immediate sound of another creaking door somewhere drew everyone's attention. All seven men turned in unison, guns up, pointing down the hallway. Coffey, closest, leaned his head just enough to take a peek at the opening basement door. A rifle and the top hair of a man, a *boy*, crept from around the corner.

"Isaac," he called.

The boy dropped his gun and ran to Coffey, throwing his arms around his midsection.

Coffey, surprised, reciprocated with a grin. "Thank the Almighty Lord, you all right, boy. Where's your pa, now?"

Isaac pulled back, eyes downcast. "He... went back to town."

Shrill cries reverberated from somewhere in the near distance, closing in on the house. With tense looks, the group rushed out the kitchen side door.

Coffey's eyes narrowed, trying to identify what exactly scrambled through the shadows. Finally, something paused at the turned over outhouse.

A whisper fell from his incredulous lips. "Impossible!"

The clicks of cavalry gun triggers drew him around.

"NO, NO—" He lowered his rifle. "WAIT!"

The creature glared back at the men, now lined alongside the house. It held Clara slumped over its shoulder, crooked in between its neck and gnarled chest protrusion. A black box sat tucked under the other arm.

"Unhand that child," Coffey shouted.

The creature just stared. Red eyes narrowed, its chest heaving in potential exasperation or exhaustion.

"Take aim," Foster commanded.

Coffey, in front of the unit, dropped his rifle entirely and flared his arms to the side. "No, don't! Ya'll hit the girl!"

"We haven't got the slightest what we're lookin at here, boy. It took out my entire unit! I will tell you this, we ain't lettin it out of our sights. One way or another, we need to take it out! And if that means takin out some girl too, then so be it."

"That's my goddamn sister you're talkin about, mister!" Isaac turned his rifle on the lieutenant colonial.

"Whoa, whoa, whoa, sonny boy."

Two unit subordinates turned their rifles on Isaac. The third, whose uniform patch read "BROOKS," stood mystified, seemingly unable to choose a side.

"Hey, goddammit!" Chisum turned his rifle on Foster.

Aaron and Coffey followed suit, Coffey glaring at the lieutenant colonial. *Great time for a standoff.*

"You out of your goddamn minds," Foster seethed, his pale face not only returning to its natural color but quickly singing red. "You understand you're pointin a weapon at the United States fucking *Army*!? That comes with a charge of lifetime imprisonment, minimally—generally punishable by death."

The men stood, fingers grazing over hair triggers, waiting. In the distance, trotting hooves signaled the approach of a horse.

2

Bessie's mare came to a steady but gradual halt about fifteen yards from the standoff. The Missouri Plaza crew, with their backs to the path, craned their curious necks but held their ground.

Nora quickly dismounted, Potter pausing behind the reins. The pain, sharp, seared in his joints, his bones. Although his skin was cold to the touch, his insides prepared to self-combust at any moment, his breathing labored. He was just fucking tired.

"There he is, men," the mustached man shouted.

His men averted their rifles.

"Seems we got much bigger things to deal with here, Lieutenant Colonial," Chisum mused, steadfast. "You ain't takin Potter, Griffin, whatever the damn man's name is, even if by some holy miracle we all make it out of this alive!"

3

The Antiquarian stood for a moment, confused by what it could only assume was a conflict among the Earthlings. The youngling squirmed, held tight in its grip. It had everything it needed. As it began to turn, the ground under its feet hummed, emitting a fine vibration along the property.

A piercing blue light emitted from the well hole, radiating straight up from the dusky earth and dissipating as it merged with the colorful, moonlit sky. With the glowing red aura of the airship and the blue light of the well, the river shimmered splendidly. The disruption drew its attention as it did every Earthling in the yard, putting a swift kibosh on the bickering.

With obscurant and unsettling motion, one after another, eight creatures on six legs crawled from the ground orifice, their chatoyant wings neatly tucked behind their bodies. Swiftly, they scuttled to the outhouse, surrounding their comrade. They were the remaining fleet of Antiquarian, a new generation, and they stood, frightfully taller, in solidarity.

The Antiquarian turned toward the lighted well as the little Earthling's bright screams sliced through the chilled night.

4

"NO!" Potter swung his leg back and over, sliding clumsily off Bessie's mare. He half limped, half trotted after his daughter, calling her name in a cold, broken voice.

The strange beings stepped forward and, as they did, every man behind Potter brought their rifles to eye level, cocking back their hammers in unison.

Potter stopped, throwing an arm back at them. "No, don't!" Turning to the departing creature, he shouted with every ounce of breath remaining to him. "*SSTTOOPP!*" He stood slightly hunched, holding himself up with his hands pressed firmly against his thighs.

The creature stopped.

"Please, please let my baby go. You got want you wanted."

It stood a moment, perhaps considering the possibility. Its head moved in a slight, slow nod, sizing Potter up and down. Without further thought, it turned once again toward the well.

"*No-no-no-no-no-no-no. Please—please!*" He began an awkward lurch after the creature.

The fleet stood their ground, waiting. When Potter approached in his feeble attempt to advance, two of the magnificent beings on either side held out their dominant arms, holding him back with little effort.

The creature stopped again, turning to a distressed Potter. It communicated something in a quick, warbling sound, and the hands dropped, freeing him. He paced toward the creature until he stood face to hideous face. An oddly serene silence followed as the two stared at one another. Potter, whose mental fortitude vanished completely, waited passively for it to offer up his daughter. Instead, the creature untucked the device, holding it against its chest. The initial proposition came in the form of the black box.

Potter stared back, dumbfounded. The globe began to sputter blue sparks from its core. The creature held out the box, the orb almost touching Potter, his face reflecting a blue sheen behind it.

The creature's red lenses slid back, revealing wide, shimmering, violet eyes. Then its mandible opened, delivering two guttural words. "Touch. It."

Potter, wide eyed, looked from the creature's bright gaze to the globe. He raised a shaky hand and, with slow regard, placed his palm upon the device. The glass warmed his palm, followed by a jolt through his hand and up his arm, encasing his body as the current jumped from its core to the surface. His head flew back, images flashing across his eyes.

He snapped back with an audible gasp.

The creature—the Antiquarian—bent forward, sliding Clara from its shoulders.

"Pa!" She turned and immediately threw her short arms around his neck.

He painfully squatted down to grasp her tiny frame, planting kisses on the side of her face. "It's all right, sweetheart. It's all right. Everything's gonna be all right." He pulled back just far enough to peer into those pretty green eyes, Bessie's eyes, before looking up at the waiting creature.

She saw that look, turning to the creature, then back to her pa. "*Nooo...*"

"I'm sorry, baby."

"Pa, no-no-no-no, you-you can't!"

He looked her up and down, eyes watering from not only his painful state, but a place deep within. A place beyond remorse. "My beautiful, beautiful, brave young lady." He smiled. "You truly are your mama's daughter, you know that? Spitting image and all."

"Don't go, Pa! Please, please don't leave us!" She blinked, sending tears down her flushed cheeks.

"Listen to me, baby. You and your brother are the best things to ever come into my life. Hear me? Each and every day since has just been a—a gift. And I never dreamed in my life of getting to love anything more." With a thumb, he wiped away a stubborn tear drop from her cheekbone. "My beautiful, brave little lady," he said once more, tears rolling from each bloodshot eye. "Faith over fear. Hold on to that."

Potter looked up to find his boy running over to him. About halfway, Isaac stopped, almost tripping on something below his feet. Potter's hat. He picked it up, ran it over, and stood, dolefully peering into his pa's tired eyes.

Potter pulled him into his chest, hugging his boy for the last time. "You're the man here now, Isaac. You take care of your sister. You're gonna need each other."

Isaac nodded as Potter pulled back to look at him. A face full of tears emerged.

The Antiquarian turned toward the well and reached its open hand to Potter in a *time-to-go* gesture.

Potter nodded and stood, glancing one last time toward the house—shit, what was left of it, anyway. Nora stared back at him. She smeared fingers under each eye, presumably wiping away tears he couldn't see. A small smile graced her closed lips, and she blew him a kiss. Potter placed his Stetson upon his head, nodded, and tipped the brim, returning her smile.

The fleet of Antiquarian dispersed with brilliant, gossamer wings extending from the long, gnarled stems protruding up their shoulders and around their hips. Taking immediate flight, they retreated to their airship like insects to the glowing nest.

Isaac stood behind Clara, arms hugged around her shoulders as if to keep her grounded. Their sullen faces stayed fixed upon their pa's, mournful sniffs hastening to spells of unrelenting sobs.

Potter, once more, looked down at his children longingly, offering a warm smile. The smile of a proud father.

Turning, he followed the Antiquarian into the pit, back to the goddamn ship. A fucking *space*ship.

Now everything made absolute sense.

The upper perimeter squares, which once only glowed, now illuminated fully, wrapping the corridor in piercing blue floodlight. Potter spun his head in bewildered awe, taking in as much as he could with one eye still impaired. The walls, too, shimmered like the iridescent bodies of the Antiquarian. Hard to believe that he stood in the same corridor. And the busted latch was... *repaired*?

The Antiquarian, tall enough to reach the ceiling with its long, thin arms, snapped the latch firmly closed. Its once glossy body, now a matte dark blue, had clearly been through hell and back. The sinewy skin, encased behind finely darkened fissures and jagged lines, took on the chiffony, web-like appearance of shattered glass. Singed slivers of wing fragments whisked from the slightly charred, bulky stems protruding from its equally charred backside.

Without regard for its captive, the Antiquarian proceeded down the corridor to the double doors, which slid open horizontally from its center and vanished into either side of the wall.

Gaping, Potter followed it into the fully lighted bridge.

5

The Antiquarian held the Cerebrum over the helm. The complex, all-knowing technological system formed the Artificial Intelligence which powered their ships, controlled their satellites, and warned and protected against extraterrestrial threats. Most importantly, it governed their society from within the Cloud. The Antiquarian knew little of its superpower, save for that it interconnected *all* things. Biological, mechanical, electrical. A living device. Most interesting of all, however, this little contraption used cultural and historical data from a civilization, combined with a complex series of calculations, to virtually predict the survival of a species... and how to save that species from dying.

The Antiquarian slid the Cerebrum into place.

6

Potter gaped as the device's sides expanded. Pieces formed outward in thin air as if completing an intricate puzzle; miniature bits snapped together to connect into the helm and, subsequently, into the ship. When the cover closed behind, the Antiquarian tapped a few flat, glowing buttons on the glass panel top.

Something tumultuous rumbled from under Potter's boots, stretching across the cockpit and shaking the bridge. He leaned against the wall, thrown slightly off balance. Though, in his current condition, he supposed knocking him around took very little. The tremors quickly narrowed, whining down to a gentle, almost unperceivable purr.

The spaceship awoke.

More lights. Everywhere. Squares of clear glass lowered from the ceiling in front of each unpiloted seat, a panel of sorts, glowing a soft blue. A larger, rectangular piece of glass lowered to a more centralized position in front of all seats. These panels lit up with strange objects, shapes, and lines, some seamlessly moving, flowing. The large one produced a series of oddly shaped geometrical masses, all connected. It took Potter a moment, but it reminded him of a continental map, with a tiny red indicator blip marking, he assumed, Missouri Plaza. The panel map quickly shrunk down, though strangely increasing its overall size, until the map turned and twisted into a ball that popped off the screen!

Earth, in a semi-transparent blue luster, gently spun before them in midair. Potter brushed a trembling hand through matted hair and lumbered forward, staring at the wondrous little ball that held, literally, his whole world. It was not unlike the vision he'd just experienced touching the globe—albeit utterly fantastical—though this seemed real. Almost tangible. He reached out, bracing to touch it.

The doors behind him slid open. The Antiquarian stood waiting, a knight's sword in its hands. Pulling himself from the beautiful globe, he followed his captor into the Artifact Room.

Inside, the knight's somber remains still sat reposed against the wall. This time, he noticed its head, fully exposed and cocked slightly on its side. Threads of long, white hair whisked down from its skull, framing either side of the face. Next to it, against the wall, lay the long-decomposed body of the captain.

The Antiquarian walked to the far door, one Potter hadn't noticed before, though it stood open. One touch of its long hand to the wall plate imprint lit the device blue, sinking it gently inward. Then, with a clockwise twist of the wrist, the Antiquarian turned the plate.

The artifact wall slid outward with a low hiss, stretching slowly but smoothly forward in varying sectional lengths, like automated credenza drawers opening from a massive glass wardrobe. The farthest container stretched ten feet and held some of the smaller items, while the larger items stayed closest to the wall.

The Antiquarian opened the top hatch on a long, horizontal drawer filled with weapons, placing the sword inside. The wall gently closed, now displaying its new artifact front and center. Apparently satisfied, the Antiquarian turned and walked back out of the room, the door sealing shut behind it.

Potter followed, digging his sticky, bloodied fingertips into the groves of the sliding door. With everything he could muster, he pulled, and pulled, and pulled. Trapped. Breathlessly, he fell to his knees, the pain intensifying in his shoulder. His leg. His face. Everywhere. As he picked himself up, standing in disconcerted malaise, quarter-sized drops of blood gathered around his boots. *No corking this spigot. What did I just volunteer for... and where the fuck am I headed?*

His vision, obscure at best, had already begun to fade. Though he regarded himself a highly intelligent and educated man, his brain couldn't rationally process it. A fever dream. One so vivid, he was almost certain he was there. With crimson skies casting an eerie glow, a highly advanced civilization flourished. Towering over the landscape, a citadel of honey-comb-like structures that were sleek and rounded, painted in vibrant hues, stretching impossibly high. And inside, hundreds... no, thousands of the Antiquarian. Rows and rows of armed soldiers with long shiny spears stood in unison in front of a multi-arched temple. At its center, flanking two wide pillars, throned an ancient all-knowing being. One they called Zurik. Though there was something else. Something terrible had happened here. Something he'd already forgotten.

He couldn't grasp the meaning of it all, and the thought of it filled him with dread.

Suddenly, a strange pressure, unlike anything he'd felt before, churned in his belly. He tightened up, arms out, trying to maintain balance as an invisible force pulled him down, though he suspected he was, in fact, rising. He ambled to the corner wall near the Knight, gripping each side for added stability. As the craft began to move, plummeting his already impaired equilibrium, he searched for something, anything, to focus on, hoping the nausea that hit him would quickly subside. *The Templar Knight.* He studied this sad, metal man's dusty bones, envisioning crash landing on some distant land, wondering if that's how they (whoever *they* were) would eventually find him in the future. A relic.

Fuck no. He refused to go out that way. He stared down at his disheveled self, weak and bloodied. And, as the ship rocked, he glanced back toward the knight and did a double take.

7

Watching the first ship twist into the chartreuse haze and vanish into the night, Isaac noticed something. The ground outside his house... *trembled?* Clara quickly grabbed on to him for support, and he glanced down at her hand on his arm, realizing for the first time just how *small* her fingers were. His throat tightened. He would do everything in his power to be a better big brother and protector. A better man. Because he was all she had now.

The earth surrounding the pit cracked and fissured, separating at the seams; a bright white light poured through. Five widely separate points of earth rose several feet before falling away to reveal the star-shaped craft long buried underneath.

Clara and Isaac turned toward the house, scurrying into Nora's open arms. The narrow edge of one wing hooked under the outhouse. The wooden structure fell, crumbling to pieces. The air expelling underneath the ship created a robust, dust-laden whirlwind blowing back sack coats, blazers, and dresses. Clara raised a hand defensively against the incoming wind, dirt, and light.

White encompassed the perimeter, rivaling the moon and the green haze. The ship glowed so bright, it fully illuminated the Bennett property, the awestricken spectators beneath, and even much of the valley, exposing the silhouetted mountains many miles away. As it materialized from the earth, fully emerging, the Pecos rushed into its gap, filling the large, round void it left behind. All a stone's throw from where they stood. The ship rose straight up, slowly, for several hundred feet before angling and shifting diagonally, gaining a bit of speed. Isaac and Clara watched motionlessly, silently, as the ship's light dwindled, fading out of existence beyond the waning moon until only the tranquil hum of the ship continued to resonate across the valley.

8

Roswell regretted leaving the black box. The cumbersome weight, not to mention its physical shock to the little girl, prevented him from riding away with it. And now, to his dismay, he watched its spectacular departure from behind a tree at the opposite end of the Bennett property.

Feeling safe, he rounded the corner of the house and dismounted, joining the others. They all stood, spellbound, peering into the night sky, not one noticing his arrival.

"Can anyone explain to me what the hell happened here tonight," Foster asked dreamily, almost rhetorically, still staring up.

"Nothin," Roswell said simply. "Nothin happened here."

The rest of the group broke free from their bemused trance.

"Nothin!?" Foster clapped back. "I got sixteen dead men here, mayor. A number of other unidentified bodies, some of which look to be marshals, no less. And let us not completely disregard the fact we got an air ship with green flying, err, *things* which just raised the Devil in your backyard, then flew away into *outer space*!"

The group shot bewildered glances, as if the words actually *sounded* much crazier than the night appeared.

"Nothin happened here," Roswell repeated.

"I cannot go back to Texas with 'nothin,' Smith." Foster grew increasingly impatient. "Hell, there's green-yellow bodies all over the damn property! You think President Arthur ain't gonna catch wind of space creatures flyin around his country!?"

"Look, Lieutenant, I know this ain't your first rodeo. Nor is it mine. We know damn well how things work down in Washington. I'm tryin to develop this vast, unoccupied land in southeast New Mexico. Build out this town, which is in its infancy. My son, Vance, he started this town, made himself a post office, established himself a—a community!" Patience waning, he held up his hand, forming a letter C with his index finger and thumb. "We are *this* close to a charter! Now he's gone! I—I lost him tonight to those hideous *things*."

Foster's brows furrowed. "What exactly are you sayin, Smith?"

"What I'm sayin is this is clearly an isolated incident." He was getting somewhere with Foster, he realized. He let his tone rise to one of desperation, pleading. "And it's over now. No sense getting the public, the

Americans of these United States, in an unnecessary panic over nothin. Because nothin happened here… other than the capture and execution of notorious outlaw Joseph Griffin. Who shrewdly shot and killed most of your men."

Chisum, floored, interrupted. "You don't expect us to sell that horseshit, do ya, Smith?"

"And why not? He's one of *the* most wanted, and let's face it, egregious men left in the West, who's somehow managed to elude capture for two decades. As I hear it, he was sittin on an arsenal buried under his house. What's that tell ya?"

"Aw, hell, Smith. You're not gonna tarnish what's left of this man, this *family* man's name with lies and bullshit, are ya?"

"And what do you suppose it the alternative? You think anyone is goin to believe what happened here, John!? Let's face it. This town's full of misfits. Dregs of society who spilled in, all runnin away from some deplorable existence. Exposin this town is exposin them, and for Christ, I'm sure some of them don't want to be found."

"I don't know, Smith. It don't seem right."

"Course it don't. I thought you, of all people, would understand this from a business perspective. What do you think'll happen to all this land—*your* land, the hundreds of miles your cattle grazes on—once this gets out? How bout 'property of the United States government.' They'll be digging for air ships for decades." Roswell forced a chortle. "Hell, for all we know, they'll swiftly come in, take over this town in some covert operation, and keep it from the public, you know, like it never happened. Then silence us all." He raised a displaying arm to the yard of deceased extraterrestrial beings. "Besides, tryin to *explain* any of this shit to anyone, we'll all be carted off to the damn asylum! You know what they *do* to you in the asylum, don'tcha?"

Chisum's gaze drifted toward the spectacularly lighted valley.

Roswell, seeing the man's wheels turning, continued. "And just think: Roswell, New Mexico. Home and final restin place of notorious outlaw

Joseph Griffin. The people will come far and wide to take a peek. Hell, they just might settle here."

Aaron furrowed his brows, plainly disgusted by the conversation. "What about the bodies? They are all over."

"We burn the bodies. We burn the house. This never happened, you understand?"

"But you can't do this," Ms. Reynolds snapped.

God, he didn't have time for this nonsense. "The hell I can't! This is *my* town now, sweetheart."

"You bastard." Her eyes watered. "I know we didn't know Joe Griffin or whoever ya'll say he was, but Bill Potter was a kind man. A brave man."

He nearly rolled his eyes, unable to fathom what drastic actions he might have to take to make the townsfolk listen. Without them, there'd be no town; but they'd be foolish to cross him, especially with their sordid pasts.

"What is it you don't understand, huh? You think I don't know who *you* are, Reynolds, or your crooked banker husband? I'm tryin to protect y'all!" Roswell turned to the rest of the group. "I'm doin this for the sake of the future of this town, *this community*! Don't thank me now. You will."

Roswell glanced at Foster, knowing he, at least, understood the implications of what could happen to him and his men if he exposed what happened here.

Or hadn't.

Foster, visibly repulsed, turned to his men and waved his arm in a circle over his head. "Let's round em up, boys. Consider Colonial John Bennett's property, whatever it was, deconsecrated."

Ms. Reynolds leaned over and threw her face into her palms, blonde curls slumping over as she bawled. Aaron, standing nearby, put his arm around her, and she turned into his shoulder, trembling, almost wheezing.

Unable to stomach such histrionics, Roswell turned his attention to the scene before him.

Chisum pulled a chewed cigar from inside a disheveled blazer pocket and shoved it in his reticent face. His eyes drifted around John Bennet's chaotic property, taking in the ghastly sight before it completely vanished from existence.

The children stood motionless in the yard, continuing to stare up at the ship—a bright moving star, now farther than the moon. They watched it slowly dissipate into the atmosphere.

9

Finally done with its thorough inspection of the craft, the Antiquarian sat firmly in the captain's chair, strapped in under the five-point harness draping over the front of its torso, securing its waist, and leading down between its legs. A thin, clear headset emerged from the seat and wrapped the side of its head. The device covered its ear holes, crossed its mouth with a microphone, and completely connected in a form-fitting half oval.

The screen in front lit up as the Antiquarian tapped and swiped every button, punching in the coordinates for SH-2-275. The map zoomed out on the large, centralized screen as the planet pulled away, surpassing the other five in its path. Then the view expanded outward beyond the WL-9768 solar system, showing the solar system and its millions of star points. Finally, the screen narrowed in on a particular grouping of stars—which, the Antiquarian had discovered, the Earthlings dubbed the constellation of Monoceros. It zoomed into the eye of the "unicorn," exploding the magnificent, red, skull-shaped galaxy which filled the screen into fine, polychromatic detail.

According to craft's universal positioning system, home remained approximately fifteen hundred thirty-three parsecs away. Now that its comrades had repaired the hyper-drive, however, the Antiquarian would expect to arrive in twelve Earthling hours. Plenty fast enough for its captive to survive.

Mission complete.

Well, sort of. The Antiquarian figured this situation ended up with close to the most favorable outcome possible, considering that the beast locked in that cage had escaped. The female youngling held promise too, especially since she now possessed Knowledge. Knowledge beyond all comprehension of Earthling kind. She also commanded a certain aptitude the Antiquarian species strongly desired. Possibly too young, however, it had decided. The current captive proved the best option for its mission.

MISSION PARAMETERS:

    1. *Collect samples from this dying rock.*

    2. *Return with artifacts and a living specimen of higher intelligence, ideally one who possessed noble character, exhibiting the traits of a valiant warrior.*

    3. *Eradicate any and all probable threats.*

The Antiquarian didn't question the purpose or morality of these objectives. No. Its main function as a foot soldier was basic: follow orders. And it did just that. It had a feeling its superiors would be most pleased... if this Earthling survived the trip, that is.

The Antiquarian's lenses rolled back, its violet eyes narrowing in on the intricate backend software of the digital control panel. After some minor coding tweaks, it reprogramed the hyper-drive to activate once far enough outside this planet's orbit. Hopefully this antique vessel, with its stagnating parts lying dormant for centuries, would survive the jump and not crumble to pieces upon reentry.

The Antiquarian supposed it would soon find out.

10

The bayonet's rusted tip plunged effortlessly through the back of the seat and into the Antiquarian's neck, exiting the throat with enough force that the creature's vocal mechanism instantly severed. As the blade twisted, a surge of green fluid discharged around the weapon's narrow stem.

The Antiquarian writhed and twitched in unequivocal, albeit quiet, shock. Its arms flared out, only for a moment, before its head fell forward, lifeless, pinned to the seat. Potter, who'd stood perfectly still behind the chair for some time, sighed in relief. He'd slid the ever-sharp relic, one he'd hidden in his trousers before riding to the mill, perfectly into the damaged space between the creature's body armor and what he now assumed to be its helmet.

Potter walked around the chair, watching the dead creature. Soldier? Whatever the hell it was. Green fluid continued to ooze down its damaged, blood-soaked chest. Its flesh slowly faded from dark blue to a light gray, like cigar ash; its sinewy appearance pruned further, wrinkling and cracking as its life-force dissipated in a swift decomposition. The body armor hue, once in sync with the creature's skin tone, drained too, becoming translucent as glass. Disconnected. Its damage rippled visibly throughout, indeed quite extensive.

Potter tossed the strange, decomposed hand, which he'd found next to the Templar Knight, onto the corpse's lap.

The airship slightly jostled, reminding Potter that he stood not only on a moving vessel, but on an airborne one. He turned to the curved, U-shaped window. The glass returned an infinite ocean of darkness, heavily peppered with the white gleam of tiny stars, eons away. More than he'd ever seen or knew existed. A strange sensation overcame him as he walked over for a better look.

Earth spun below, off to the side. Dark Earth, mostly, except the eldritch, chartreuse haze. It twitched in the atmosphere, omnipresent, hovering thousands of miles across the continent. The lights moved and flowed, alive. Rich purples and reds issued from the green, mingling in an eloquent sky dance. Once one color moved, a shade more elegant than the last replaced it. What was *in* it?

The ship's destination remained a mystery to Potter. Somewhere into the wild blue, *or black*, yonder. Didn't matter. This ship, the dead pilots, the room full of artifacts, himself, none of it would arrive. He'd die before he let that happen... and, with any luck, he would do so soon. His luck had just about run out, but he'd hang on, just long enough, the hourglass grasping onto its last morsel of sand.

The dynamite he'd previously wired and set up now lay on the far end of the corridor. The fleet apparently had taken the explosives down in the limited time they spent tending to the craft's repairs before he arrived, leaving a mess of highly reactive material in a pile like children's toys. No concern to Potter, though. The dynamite was here, and that's all he could hope for. He brought it into the bridge and rewired it all, situating the explosives around himself.

Although he feared very little, he felt a sharp blade slowly twisting up into his guts. He would never see his children again. He would never see anyone again, at least, not on this plane of existence. He shuddered, remembering the purgatory Warren had described. Hard to believe he'd once worried over going to jail, where maybe he'd find some viable means of escape. Though technically, he supposed, he *had* escaped by way of leaving the planet. The thought brought a wry smile to his face.

Then the nausea struck him.

He sat in the chair closest to the window, removed his hat, and pulled the remaining half of the quirley from under the flap, lighting it with a last match struck by his thumbnail. He pulled back on the sweet smoke, filling his tired lungs and holding a moment before exhaling through slightly clogged nostrils. The spiked tobacco hit all the right nerves, and a relaxing warmth instantly washed over him. The pain in his face, his arm, and his leg began a sustained dissipation.

Magical.

The ship picked up an incremental amount of speed, nearly unperceivable to Potter, as it exited Earth's atmosphere.

Something in the distance sparkled brightly in his peripherals. He raised a trembling hand, glancing out through splayed fingers. On the curve of the horizon, beyond the thin, blue, hazy line of the atmosphere. Light. The morn unfolded with unhurried reverie, waking the Earth from a shadow of darkness. The vast blue ocean swam with ranks of small, puffy sheep's wool clouds, all under the ultimate, heart-stopping sunrise.

His planet, visible before him.

And my God, he'd never seen anything like it. A colossal Sundog; its ethereal glow nearly filled his entire view. The beaming yellow ball emerged, "rising" from behind the planet, surrounded by a golden round mist. A halo. From its center, the bright spot blazed, radiating a starburst of piercing light and casting an amber sheen over the Earth.

At the gut level, Potter finally accepted that he stood *in* space. And, staring over the mammoth sphere, he'd never felt so small. Even the Earth. He'd never realized the size, the finiteness, of his world until he looked out into the universe.

He took one final drag on the tail end of the quirley and, with the dwindling cherry glow, leaned over to light the fuse. It sparked and sizzled, beginning its trail of eradication back behind the Antiquarian's corpse. It would follow the slack to the door before running alongside the perimeter of the bridge and back to Potter.

He looked at his planet once more, now pulling out of reach, and sat back down, stretching out his legs and crossing them at the ankles. As the smoke sedated his weary body, his mind began to drift, lifetimes of thoughts flashing before his mind in the span of the few moments remaining to him.

His baby girl. He would never see her grow to be the strong, pioneering woman he always knew she would be. He'd never walk her down the aisle, giving her away to... some wealthy, swindling cattle rancher? A pretentious, stiff-necked Wells Fargo banker? He smiled. Who was he kidding? She was much smarter than that. He would've loved to see some grandchildren, though. Regardless... *That girl's gonna do big things.* The West had better heed his warning.

And his boy, his *man*. Isaac. With the way he excelled at the mill, Potter imagined his son becoming a prominent business owner, greasing the wheels for others to follow in his path. Wherever he wound up, Potter took pride in the man Isaac had already become.

And Nora. Oh, Nora. Never in a million years did he expect to find a soul so kind and loving, capable of helping him *feel* again, after Bessie. If only he had more time.

But Potter had no regrets. He glanced over, heavy-eyed, and watched the sizzling spark reach the bundled wicks, making its impartial way down seven tied branches and simultaneously entering each brown cylinder. It's not quite how he envisioned the end, *his* end, though going out with a bang seemed fitting.

Warren's voice echoed in his mind, reminding him that he'd be walking the earth in limbo for all eternity, destitute, while reliving the horrors of his vain existence. He shook his head. Prior to this evening's events, he surely didn't believe in such fantastical things. Now, though, he wondered. Maybe Bessie waited for him on the other side.

Doubtful.

Wherever you are, Warren, in the in-between... see ya in about fifteen seconds.

He shut his eyes; his mind blanked. He waited.

With the gentle hiss of an extinguishing match, the sizzling faded away.

Total, utter silence... like time stopped altogether.

Potter's eyes opened. Barely. He still sat in the chair. A minuscule whiff of smoke billowed from the dynamite bundle.

Duds.

Potter gently shook his head, flashing a wide, sardonic smile. Go fucking figure. *Now* he understood why the fleet had just left it.

His heart rate slowed, though the soothing sound intensified, gently thumping in his ear. Tired, so tired, and the uncertainty of his destination loomed. Not that the trip much mattered. He reckoned he'd be dead by the time he arrived.

He sat, fighting the weight of lead eyelids, staring out into the infinite, enchanting void of space.

II

*J*oseph Griffin, as you know from your history books, was gunned down in our home in a mythic firefight involving infamous bounty hunter Tynan Dunkin, along with two U.S. marshals and the entire Fort Hood Texan Army brigade. My father was portrayed as a villainous and ruthless monster in numerous publications, magazines, and in your motion pictures and the like. And such an image will most likely persist as time prevails, I'm sure.

Much of those days a blur to me now. Heck, I'd be lying if I didn't say just about all my past is. Most people, I think, have a sense of living a whole life, you know: start to finish, beginning to end, soup to nuts. My life is really just an accumulation of events. A series of incidents, haphazardly attached to one another in different points in time. Put them together in any order. Wouldn't make much sense or difference to me.

What I do remember about my father is that he was a loving husband, compassionate parent, and a brave, vigilant man. A man who never truly got over the death of our mother, the only woman who could make an honest man out of him. And as far as his vicious nature, I only bore witness to one of his violent acts. The time he shot three men dead. Right in front of my very eyes. Sadly, that day wasn't the first time I had seen another human being lose their life, but it was the first I saw death in such a savage and barbaric manner. Pa's violence was, however, in the service of another man. You'd call it self-defense, and in a court of law, today, they might say the same. In those days, though, it would have been blasphemous to kill three men, white men, to save a colored one. A man my father would, eventually and admittedly, call his "only friend in this cruel world."

Epilogue

Clara, in her favorite maroon and white polkadot tea dress, finished her interview in a cozy armchair in the back of Ivy's Books & Curiosities, surrounded by the hushed whispers of seventy patrons. Many comprised her late brother's closest friends and family along with The Roswell Press; behind them, CBS network affiliate KOB-TV out of Albuquerque wrapped their live broadcast and began breaking down set.

Her bestselling memoir *Misery Plaza,* published a month prior by Simon & Schuster, had quickly achieved remarkable commercial success. The publishing house had eagerly pursued the rights when rumors circulated that the daughter of the legendary outlaw was writing a book recounting her experiences as a U.S. Marshal. It was also their idea to have the official book launch in Roswell. At today's reading, the line for her signature stretched for three blocks, snaking its way down the sidewalk and past quiet storefronts. She smiled at each and every person that made their way up to her armchair, relieved to finally set the record straight. To discuss the true Griffin legacy left behind. Lord knew Isaac never spoke of such things.

Her last patron, a tall man in a black suit, stood with hands holding a fedora behind his back. Much like a young Shirley Temple, he wore a dirty blonde beret of springy curls wildly combed over the side of his head. A black patch concealed his left eye, the straps woven through wild locks. Most striking of all, he bore the bluest right eye, a rich turquoise, which reminded her of the gorgeous waters of Tamolitch Falls in the Willamette National Forest—the very place she'd apprehended Carlo

"Red Hands" Vitale, one of the most dangerous bootleggers of the 1920s.

"Howdy," he said, flashing a wide PR grin, his expressive Texan drawl immediately recognizable. "The one an' only Clarissa Griffin." He enunciated each word as if he had been well-informed about her fame, only now getting the long-awaited chance to make her acquaintance.

"Yes, that's me." She swept aside her cropped white hair, which spilled out from under her maroon pillbox fascinator beret as she glanced up to get a better look.

The patron's smile did not falter. In fact, it only seemed to grow, if that were at all possible.

"And you are?"

"Well, now, I've gone by a number of different names over time, ma'am," he said, replacing his fedora on his brow. "Haynes. Julian D. Haynes, esquire. Though people round here just call me Danny. I'm your brother Isaac's probate attorney and executor of his final will and testament."

She hesitated a moment, slightly bewildered. "I believe Mable said his estate was settled last year."

"Yes, well, uh, that is true. You see, Isaac wanted me to hand you this in person, explicitly, seeing how you weren't able to attend his service and all." Between two fingers held a small folded piece of paper. "I've been holdin on to this since."

Clara's hip ached, a physical reminder of the icy fall that had sidelined her for months and kept her from attending Isaac's funeral. She knew traveling halfway across country would only delay recovery. God, getting old sure wasn't easy.

He handed over a small piece of folded paper, and she opened a series of written numbers. She glanced up, eyes narrow.

Taking in her baffled expression, he pointed down at the paper. "Those are numbers."

"Well, I can see that. And what are they numbers to?"

"That there's the combination to your brother's safe. I'm told the location is in his home office, in the wall behind his desk. You are now the *third* person privy to that information." He winked. Isaac wanted, in the event of his untimely death—granted he pass *before* you—for you to procure its contents, which I have not been privy to."

"Untimely?" She placed the paper into a black purse. "He died from a long battle with cancer."

"Well, *I* personally believe *all* death is untimely, ma'am." He smiled. "Y'all have a lovely day now. He tipped his hat and turned to walk away.

"Mr. Haynes."

He stopped and glanced back.

"I'm curious. What exactly did he say to do with it if he didn't?"

"Ma'am?"

"Pass before me?"

"Since you *are* here, ma'am, I am not at liberty to say." He smiled politely and walked out the front door and into a black car slant parked in front.

Before Clara could give the strange encounter another thought, a local journalist appeared, asking after one of her high-profile cases. Despite her utter exhaustion, Clara answered all of his questions, delighted to discuss her work and family. Still, she was grateful when Ivy's owner finally waved him away. She had a long evening ahead at her sister-in-law's estate and wanted to make a stop in town before departing.

As she neared Ivy's front door, a shiny hardcover on the Staff Favorites shelf to her left caught her eye. The sight sent chills through her now heaving chest. She picked up the novel, studying the terrifying cover of an alien creature towering over a city. *The Battle of the Galaxy*, by H.P. Brooks.

Brooks... she knew that name. A face, a night, slowly trickled back.

She gently opened it. Originally published in 1898, she wondered how she'd yet to come across such a novel in fifty-one years. Perhaps she just hadn't paid it any mind. Illustrated versions were unlikely in previous editions, she supposed. She hesitated to turn another page, filled with disquiet, though some deep-seated curiosity prevented her from shelving the book.

She purchased it.

2

Isaac Joseph Griffin

1872 – 1948

Loving Husband, Father, Grandfather

Clara stood amongst the graves in the front section of the oldest and largest cemetery in Chaves County. Isaac's square tower headstone with Gothic arches loomed high on its marble pitch. He'd made an early decision to reserve his particular plot, located right next to one of the most popular tourist attractions in New Mexico and much of the South: the faded Gothic-ogee headstone of one Joseph Griffin. Their father.

Clara, the last alive to know an empty casket lay several feet below that marker, smiled.

The golden sun, still making its welcoming ascent above the Capitan Mountains, slowly began to warm the cool, crisp February morning air. A breeze shifting through the cemetery grounds stirred up fine clay sediment; specks of dust twinkled in the daylight. She buttoned her blue dress coat.

Following the book signing event, Clara briefly spoke with her sister-in-law, agreeing to meet Mable soon at the Griffin estate in North Roswell. First, though, she wanted to visit some old friends. Her great uncle John Bennett's stone stood two rows ahead, near the front, one of the town's earliest markers. And Coffey—*oh Coffey*. A name she hadn't regarded in many decades, a face obfuscated by time. One of the warmest, kindest men she'd ever known. Since 1903, he lay two rows behind.

A hazy vision of her father and Coffey sitting around the blazing firepit—barbequing, drinking, laughing—flashed in her mind. She could still hear the strums of his guitar while she and Isaac danced circles around the flames.

Vance Smith, Dave Mather, Gus Miller... they were all buried here, too. And Aaron Wilburn, who passed in 1935, lay to rest, from what Mable said, in a newer section of South Park.

Clara, unfortunately, didn't have time to wander quite so far today. She remained listless after yesterday's arduous flight to Albuquerque from Bradley International Airport, followed by a desolate, three-hour car ride in the back of a black Chrysler Imperial limousine. Upon her late-night arrival at the Griffin compound, a one-of-a-kind Victorian southern colonial structure made of adobe mud brick, she'd spoken briefly with Mable before retiring to the guest house alongside the main estate. Though she'd wished for time to settle in, get reacquainted with her sister-in-law, and catch up with nieces and nephews—and now *their* children—such a luxury had proved impossible with all the hullabaloo entailed in arranging a book tour.

Maybe, when the tour concluded, she could make time to be with the family she had left.

3

Clara sat kitty corner near a large bay window in a red velvet armchair, sipping coffee from fancy china and quietly overlooking the reception. Mable had hired professional caterers with a full bar, a stunning buffet spread, and a fully staffed, well-dressed crew. Maybe more appropriate for a wedding than a book launch, Clara thought. But her sister-in-law's efforts were clearly appreciated by the hundred or so guests shuffling through the large, open parlor and dining room. Heavens to Betsy, who even were all these people?

Clara took another deep sip of coffee, already on her second cup. She didn't drink—she never did—though she enjoyed watching the effect libation had on others. The guests, gleefully inebriated by one p.m., laughed and chatted amongst themselves. In the living room, people crowded around one of those television picture boxes, watching a variety show called *Hour Glass*. A stage theater, right in your own home. Every so often, she even noticed strangers staring over her way, gawking and whispering like she was some type of celebrity... *or* freak-show. The only living, immediate descendant of America's Most Wanted. With that kind of legacy, she could rival Katharine Hepburn or Judy Garland for attention.

Clara glanced around. Everyone at this reception seemed preoccupied. She stood, excused herself to no one in particular, and snuck off down a long hallway. The strange probate lawyer. That's all she could think about. The book. The piece of paper tucked under her beret. Her former profession didn't allow for coincidences, and she began to wonder if returning after all this time was a mistake.

Isaac's living-room size office stood in complete disarray, taking on the appearance of an enormous storage locker. A billiards table sat on one side, veiled under loose papers, folders, and random books. A leather sofa lay partially covered in cloth in the center of the room, over-stuffed bookshelves lined the back walls, and photographs of Griffin Woolen Mills filled any space between the tall, rectangular windows. Isaac and Aaron appeared timeless in most. She felt a surge of pride as she thought about their journey from a small textile mill to a leading manufacturer of fabric, providing material for designer suits as well as soldiers' uniforms in both World Wars. Though perhaps they were best known for their local and benevolent contributions. Most notably, they had established the New Mexico Military School, the first of its kind in 1894. She smiled at the youthful photo of them standing in front of it.

She reached the wide mahogany desk, neatly cluttered with thick manila folders, worn notebooks, and a couple novels. Items she figured Mable didn't know how to organize. Aside from the overall mess, everything appeared dust free—the benefits of an having an in-house housekeeping service, she guessed.

Clara looked up, and her mouth dropped. She was *home*. A painting, *her* painting, hung high against the wall behind the leather chair. Missouri Plaza at sunset. Just as she remembered it, though she hadn't seen the artwork in sixty-five years. A signature on the bottom right corner read, "Eleanor Reynolds, 1879." She walked around to touch it, whisking her fingers over the textured canvas as if she could feel the town living, breathing.

The town changed drastically after The Incident. Yet even devoid of carnage and destruction, Missouri Plaza, now Roswell, was never the same. While Isaac found a purpose, throwing himself into his work at the mill with Mr. Wilburn, Clara had floundered in a town brimming with emotional and devastating memories she couldn't speak of, hell, much less fathom. Ms. Nora didn't cope any better. Their new guardian gave birth to Clara's younger brother nine months after The Incident, but even Wesley Reynolds, a gift from God, wasn't enough to offset the depression which plagued her at the loss of her community and beloved Bill. Clara recalled overhearing Nora confiding in Aaron about her horrific nightmares of giant flying insects, which seemed to only subside when isolating in her store for days at a time. *Changing the town's name would never change its history.*

Sadly, Clara was the only person alive—as far as she knew, anyway—who'd remember Missouri Plaza. This fact was evident in both history books and public records. She had researched a case in New Mexico some years back and discovered that Roswell had been "established" in 1873. The shrewd man himself likely had his application back dated in hopes of erasing the old town from existence.

The painting shifted slightly at her touch. Carefully, she pulled back on the frame like a door, revealing the safe built flush into the wall. With the combination, she opened the little device easily.

A small note, open, sat front and center.

Our Secret Tunnel held some real treasure, didn't it?

She pulled out an item wrapped in beige wool. Quite heavy. She unfolded it to reveal a shiny blue LeMat revolver. Her father's prized pistol, deadliest handgun of the Old West. She assumed its sibling lay next to it, though the third wrapped item intrigued her. She squeezed the gun's diamond cut handle in her soft hand, glancing it over before re-wrapping it.

The faint aroma of gunpowder lingered as she reached for the next item. The gold pocket watch, a bit tarnished and scratched around the edges, still gleamed in spots as she dangled the chain along her forearm. She'd never seen the watch before, though it appeared quite old. Depressing the plunger, she popped the lid open, revealing the inscription DUNKIN etched behind. Suddenly, the watch's presence made sense. She knew where it had come from, *when* it had come from. And, just as she suspected, time had stopped—stopped on that very night at four thirty-five.

She sighed. *Time always prevails.*

With a few turns of the crown, the watch sprung to life. The seconds hand began its methodical journey, moving ever onwards.

The back of the safe held paper, neatly stacked. She pulled the piles out and flicked through them like a flip book, though the picture on these pages didn't move. "One thousand" was printed in each corner.

War bonds. Hundreds of war bonds. During the Second World War, Griffin Mills ceased producing textiles and instead produced ammunition. Isaac's noble contribution for the cause. She assumed he had been issued the bonds as some form of payment. She'd never asked nor accepted any offerings or handouts from her brother, though he tried like hell. *Looks like he finally got the last say.* She laughed and shook her head, touched by her sweet older brother. At seventy-four, she hadn't much need for such an amenity. Still, she knew of a place for a proper donation.

Finally, she pulled the last item. Not quite as heavy as the gun, albeit much smoother to the touch. She unfolded the cloth.

My God...

The azure crystal pieces. Pristine. She turned the chatoyant gems over in her hands, in awe of their beauty, their purity. A folded note, tucked in the cloth, fell from underneath. She picked it up.

Clara,

I've kept my promise. I've kept it from the Bad People. What you do with it now is up to you.

– Isaac

Clara hadn't been by the old Bennett property since that fateful night, but she vaguely recalled her brother mentioning they'd turned the land into a country club a few years back. Isaac, she imagined, must've hidden these items in that little basement ammunition cache this whole time, perhaps hoping they'd never be found, and retrieved them before the builders broke ground. She closed the safe, the painting, and placed the items in her black handbag, barely fitting the significant additional weight.

Someone pushed at the door, which cracked open with a creak. "Auntie Clara?"

She turned, startled, to Isaac's eldest daughter.

Lillian's head poked through the narrow opening, Montezuma Red lips smacking as she spoke. "Dessert is served, if you care for some pineapple upside down cake or, uh"—she snapped her matching red fingertips—"I believe it's pecan pie. Oh heavens, I'm not really sure."

"Oh, that sounds delightful, dear. Perhaps another splash of Arbuckles', if you have it."

"Of course." She looked at the space beyond Clara. "Whatcha doing? Can I help you with anything?"

Clara turned to the desk and grabbed the first thing she saw—*Textile Arts*. She held up the book. "You mind if I borrow this, dear?"

"Oh, uh, yes, of course."

Clara smiled wistfully, took one long-lasting look at Missouri Plaza, and walked out of the office behind Lillian.

4

Although winter brutally shuffled its bitter February air indiscriminately throughout Southern New England, this particular evening brought unseasonable warmth, the needle hovering around forty degrees. Clara, still adjusting to the temperature change from New Mexico, bundled herself inside her favorite black mountain sable fur coat and matching hat, which she'd received as an anniversary gift from her second husband in '31.

She'd taken the ten-a.m. flight back to Hartford, returning by cab in the early evening to her stately, two-story abode at the end of a desolate stretch of road behind downtown Norwich. Now, unpacked and bundled, Clara walked into her backyard as she did each evening to take in the gorgeous view of the Yantic and Thames River confluence surrounding the right edge of the property. The scene always brought back memories of her charming, adolescent years in the town next door, and this time of year, she could just about see The Triangle, where her father had grown up. The Jonathan Black Memorial Park and Otis Library stood in splendid view straight ahead, across the confluence. To her right, she could hear operatic scores of motion pictures echoing from the neon-lighted drive-in theater, just over the Thames. And to her left jutted Holly Hock Island, a narrow land mass home to Fort Hock. The brick military installation, abandoned some time ago, rested somberly in the middle of the Yantic inlet. She grinned. *By the week's end, the Fort Hock Authority will receive quite a generous, anonymous donation.* Maybe the money would revitalize the crumbling tourist landmark, or at the very least, the government could find a way to use the island for something good.

The tall, red maples lining much of Forest Street and the riverbank continued to expose their twisty, skeletal arms and venation of bare branches. Only the defiant Eastern white pine clung to its frozen fir. Despite the ashy, overcast skies, the view remained clear and perfect as she strode along the riverbank... except flashes of another, vaguer view superimposed itself atop her surroundings.

The eldritch vision had returned, though in snippets. Shadowy. Spellbinding. They made her incredibly uneasy. She almost wished Isaac hadn't dug up the crystals, or maybe found an alternate means of disposal.

Shiny towers and moving pictures across large panels.

She recalled seeing the television picture boxes in her brother's living room at the reception. Simply fascinating. How else could one describe seeing large picture screens miniaturized for personal enjoyment? And for six hundred dollars, you too could enjoy such luxury. Not Clara, though. Nothing on that television screen could ever compare to the life she'd led. Still, she figured, only a matter of time until the picture boxes popped up everywhere.

She considered her other visions—the technological progression through the natural lens of time—and wondered how much longer this fate, if that's what it truly was, could be. One hundred years? Two hundred? Things moved so quickly these days, maybe the future would arrive in just twenty.

Whatever fate had in store, however, the final visions would be long beyond her lifetime. She knew that, if nothing else.

The hourglass drains.

Clara took the six crystal pieces from her coat pocket and, with preternatural ease, completed the puzzle. She'd come to learn later in life that she was something of a savant, something her first husband had recognized, too. She couldn't have told you back then how to prepare his favorite dish, chicken à la king, always having to review the recipe. Nor could she say what time the Yantic River freight train howled past the two streets behind, always at the same time, twice daily. Solving puzzles, however, remained second nature. Ever since *that* night, the night she'd touched the electric sphere, she had developed this new, innate ability to see things, well, predict things, mostly, in a fantastical way. Though she could never quite explain her abilities, much less discuss them, they nonetheless made her keenly successful in her career, keeping her at least a half step ahead of her quarry. Her eye for patterns, for the future, served her well. And she always got her man or woman.

The tarnished side of that shining silver dollar was that her gifts played hell with her memories. Her mind wasn't quite what it used to be, she knew. Not much of a call for alarm, but she *had* noticed names and faces slipping, more so in recent years. She blanked on Isaac's children's names at the reception, and God forbid she recall her great nieces and nephews. Who could on a good day? Much of what she *did* remember about that night and the years to follow, she suppressed to the point that she'd just about forgotten—at least, until her return to New Mexico. The memories began with a slow trickle of flashing images, but by the time she'd departed, her whole history had just about returned.

The more these bizarre and twisty pieces of her past began to slide and lock, the less this paradoxical puzzle made sense. This thing in her hand proved the past *had* happened, at least, with she and this object now the last clandestine trinkets remaining from a bygone era. The Bad People *were* gone. This she believed true. And maybe, just maybe, some reason existed for why this crystal remained. The only thing she maintained with any level of certainty is that this device provided a daily, constant reminder of that one night in June 1884. The night of the rare, perigean strawberry moon. The night of The Carrington Event—a mystifying solar storm and aurora borealis. The night she and her brother *woke* the creature, which wreaked havoc and mayhem across their small-town life. Mostly, it reminded her of the night her father left aboard an alien space-craft disentombed from their backyard, disappearing into the oceanic void of that final frontier.

Standing before the river, she studied the iridescent crystal knot, roughly the size of a softball. Then she let it drop from her hands, splashing into the undulating waters.

5

Forest Street growled, gently shaking Clara's living room.

From her comfy recliner, she glanced out the front window. A large commercial vehicle, likely lost, swung stiffly around the cul-de-sac be-fore rip-roaring from whence it came. A nettlesome daily occurrence. Though, when she didn't leave her house—and sometimes she didn't for weeks on end—that sole, solemn noise reminded her she wasn't alone in this world. A tiny smile touched her lips at the thought. The daily mail, morning paper, and bi-weekly milk delivery proved that the world still spun on its axis, though she rarely glimpsed much of its machinations, including the deliveries' arrival.

She leaned gleefully back in her chair, a cup of Arbuckles' by her side and the H.P. Brooks novel in her lap. Curiosity overwhelmed her as she prepared to open his book. Her vision of him had deteriorated, but she recalled the kind young cavalryman having hung around Missouri Plaza for a week or so after The Incident to help clean up. Brooks proved chiefly valuable when it came to removing and disposing of the dead, some to the exact specifications of the mayor's orders: "incineration by all means necessary."

Seeking a fresh start, Clara, Nora, and Wes had packed up the schooner and made their way northeast a year after The Incident. The idea to find the Griffin family was mostly Nora's, though Clara's elated interest in meeting her relatives and Morgan Bennett's blessing helped facilitate the decision (he had arrived the previous October on his round-about route from Denver to Tucson with intentions of taking his grand-children with him, though a week with them and a pregnant Nora man-aged to change his mind; she provided the strong maternal presence they were missing, a quality Morgan valued highly). Clara's only reservation was leaving her big brother. She could see how much Isaac loved working at the mill; she couldn't ask him to go. He, too, understood that Clara and Ms. Nora couldn't stay in Roswell. Saying farewell broke Clara's heart, but she knew her brother would be safe and well taken care of with Mr. Wilburn, thanks to John Chisum's generous grant. They promised to write each other often.

Upon arriving in the gilded New England town of Norwich, Nora and company were welcomed with mild enthusiasm by the Griffin fam-ily. Joseph's parents had long since passed, and he, as the only living sibling remaining, left no other immediate family. The outlaw's unsavory legacy disparaged the Griffin family name in town as well as in the state of Connecticut, so much so that any extended family in The Triangle wanted nothing to do with him. The lack of welcome didn't discourage

Nora from settling down in the cozy neighboring town of Chesterville, which became her final resting place when a fatal case of the flu robbed her of life in 1902.

Clara lost track of her half-brother after he returned from fighting in the First World War. Before the turn of the century, she had already left Connecticut, devoting a significant amount of her life traveling with the U.S. Marshal Service, living in different cities across different states for periods ranging from six months to several years. Living out of a suitcase for so long made losing important mail, like a change of address, easy. It had been thirty years, and the question of his survival remained unanswered. Even her connections with the federal government turned up nothing.

Still, Clara had no regrets. Discovering her inability to conceive during her first marriage made the choice simple. *Work is life.* By the time she'd retired in '34, she'd just about seen the entire United States.

The road hummed once again, and her living room trembled. Glowering at the stupidity of drivers, Clara lifted the coffee cup to her mouth. The saucer continued its gentle rattle against the side table; the lamp shade quivered. Strange.

She peered out the window at the street between the pines. Not a single car, let alone a truck, in sight. While earthquakes were commonplace in her California and Oregon years, she only recalled one comparable event in southeastern Connecticut during the early forties, a three-point-five tremor on the Richter scale. This felt eerily similar.

The humming escalated to a bright whirring and, as her recliner began to vibrate, she stood to look out the window more fully. A shrill gasp fell from her mouth; the cup slipped from a trembling finger and thumb, crashing to the hardwood floor. Hot coffee splashed up her nylons and slippers. She felt nothing, only gaped up at a sight she hadn't witnessed in sixty-five long years.

The five-winged space craft hovered above the cul-de-sac, three points folding upward to begin its landing sequence. Inside, five pilot Antiquarian sat in their respective seats, communicating among one another through headgear. At the helm, Captain Joseph Griffin of the starship Monoceros, from the Phamotidyne District in the Rosette Nebula, sat strapped in, his arms fixed inside the cylindrical steering mechanism attached to the seat's armrest. His coordinates disclosed this location, a neighborhood he hadn't seen in decades.

Griffin couldn't believe an entire year had passed since he'd been gone. And what a year, too, with the final resolution of the decade-long, intergalactic conflict. The impressed Antiquarian had found a suitable specimen in him, accentuating his warrior spirit after reviving him from near death. Purpose beyond the grave.

The fatal chink in their armor, the inability to detect motionless adversaries, had plagued their species for eons, but all that changed with Griffin's arrival. There were no flies on *him*. He knew this fact now, forswearing the fallible hourglass, keeper of time and all its irrelevance. He tore hell for leather, absconding from the Pale Rider, cheek by jowl, leaving that hooded sonovabitch in a dust-plumed wake. Did he believe he was immortal? He reckoned not. No. He was just a survivor, a bad motherfucker who refused to die. That's all.

Stories of his prowess and legend would doubtless live on with the Antiquarian for centuries.

Who knew where the next adventure would've taken him, had the tracking prism not activated. Now, his sole inquiry was with the individual who triggered the device—at least, as far as the Antiquarian were concerned. Oblivious to the fact that their comrade had left the crystal behind, they sought to rescue whichever of their number had activated the signal. But Griffin knew. He knew in his heart, now filled with anticipation at the thought of reuniting with his baby girl, embracing her in his arms. Another chance to admire those captivating emerald eyes of hers. And Isaac, his brave young man. He wondered what accomplishments his boy had achieved with Wilburn. Griffin would surely have to visit. And, of course, a day hadn't gone by where he didn't think of Nora.

Griffin stood, put on his hat, and smiled.

He was home.

REVIEWS

Now that you have finished the book, (and I hope you enjoyed it!) I would love it if you could take a moment to share your thoughts by leaving a great review on Amazon. Reviews are critical to an author's success and even a few lines (or no lines at all, just stars) help propel the book into Amazon's tough marketing algorithms.

About the Author

J.J. Alo is a versatile force in the entertainment industry, known for his spellbinding work as a commercial actor, writer, and the acclaimed author behind the Southern New England Horror Anthology series.

With a macabre fascination, J.J. has spent years weaving award-winning horror screenplays and novels. His anthology series, teeming with deeply etched, complex characters and mesmerizing antiheroes, has become a sinister staple in horror literature, which ensnares readers and refuses to let go.

J.J. Alo's The Street Between the Pines has achieved the 2024 President's Book Award from the Florida Authors &Publishers Association and was a FINALIST in both the Chanticleer International Book Awards and the Killer Nashville Claymore Award Competition. Featured in the January 2024 issue of Kirkus Reviews magazine, the novel has received widespread critical acclaim from multiple editorial publications. Additionally, J.J. Alo's screenplay has garnered numerous accolades in the Best Horror/Thriller categories at prestigious competitions, including the Los Angeles Film and Script Festival, Fright Night Film Fest, and Zed Fest FilmFestival & Screenplay Competition.

Click the QR and Subscribe to J.J.'s Newsletter!